"SIT DOWN, GENTLEMEN. THIS IS GOING TO TAKE SOME TIME AND SOME PLANNING . . ."

"It's those two admirals you've heard about. A highly radical nationalistic cell from one of the Chinese destroyers went onshore at Maui two days ago and kidnapped the admirals and their whole families. They are demanding the release of all captives and reparations for the Chinese killed and ships sunk or damaged. If we don't agree to their demands, they will send us the head of one of the members of the admirals' families every four hours, starting with the youngest and working up. We already have the head of a little girl of five or six. I don't want to see another one. The deadline for hearing from us is twelve hundred hours.

"Commander, you have to take your men in and kill those sonsofbitches and rescue the admirals and their families before anyone else is murdered."

PL

BM

D1173405

SEAL TEAM SEVEN
TROPICAL TERROR

KEITH DOUGLASS

BERKLEY BOOKS, NEW YORK

Special thanks to Chet Cunningham for his contribution to this book.

SEAL TEAM SEVEN: TROPICAL TERROR

A Berkley Book / published by arrangement with
the author

PRINTING HISTORY
Berkley edition / November 2000

The Penguin Putnam Inc. World Wide Web site address is
http://www.penguinputnam.com

ISBN: 0-425-17740-8

BERKLEY®
Berkley Books are published by The Berkley Publishing Group,
a division of Penguin Putnam Inc.,
375 Hudson Street, New York, New York 10014.
BERKLEY and the ''B'' design
are trademarks belonging to Penguin Putnam Inc.

PRINTED IN THE UNITED STATES OF AMERICA

10 9 8 7 6 5 4 3 2 1

DEDICATION

This one is for
KATHLEEN,
who kept the home fires burning during
the wounded-wing times.

Thanks for saving our ship.

FOREWORD

On every book project there are always new developments and technology that beg to be included. Some of them are far-out and off-the-wall, but some are so intriguing and fascinating that they must be included.

Watch for two of them in this book. One is the slippery little machine the Army is trying out to be used as a genuine replacement for the World War II Jeep. The Humvee isn't in the same class. It's too big and too observable by the enemy for actual front-line action. This new little horse is called the "Flyer," has a diesel engine, four-wheel drive, and four-wheel disc brakes. It has a top speed of sixty mph, but has an extremely low profile, no top, mount for a .50-caliber machine gun, and is rugged. The driver sits in the single front seat, and two men in the rear seat. It has a high road clearance so it can work off-road. Price tag, about $100,000. It looked very good in testing when Marines put it through its paces recently at Camp Pendleton in California.

The other interesting development, which will soon work into civilian use, is the British Stealth Diving Suit. It's being used now by Britain's Ministry of Defense. It's the most technologically advanced underwater breathing apparatus yet developed. It's self-contained, no tell-tale bubbles. The heart of it is a computer-controlled oxygen and supplemental gas-delivery system to the closed breathing unit. This other gas often is nitrogen.

The unique part here is that the computer automatically controls the right mix of gases so the body can go up or down with total safety. Most current closed breathing systems are hard put to function at even fifty feet for any length of time.

Do you have any new weapons or systems that the SEALs might use? If so, drop me a line at my pickup box at: Keith Douglass, 8431 Beaver Lake Dr., San Diego, CA 92119.

Now, you have a good day.

—Keith Douglass
San Diego, CA

SEAL TEAM SEVEN

THIRD PLATOON*
CORONADO, CALIFORNIA

Commander Dean Masciarelli. 47, 5-11, 220 pounds. Annapolis. Commanding officer of SEAL Team Seven and its 230 men.

Master Chief Petty Officer Gordon MacKenzie. 47, 5-10, 180 pounds. Administrator and head enlisted man of all of SEAL Team Seven.

Lieutenant Commander Blake Murdock. 32, 6-2, 210 pounds. Platoon Leader, Third Platoon. Annapolis graduate. Six years in SEALs. Father important congressman from Virginia. Murdock recently promoted. Apartment in Coronado. Has a car and a motorcycle, loves to fish. Weapon: the new Alliant Bull Pup duo 5.56mm & 20mm explosive round. Alternate: H & K MP-5SD submachine gun.

ALPHA SQUAD

Willard "Will" Dobler. Boatswain's Mate Senior Chief. Top EM in platoon. Third in command. 37, 6-1, 180 pounds. Nineteen years service. Wife, Nancy; children, Helen, 14; Charles, 11. Sports nut. Knows dozens of major league baseball records. Competition pistol marksman. Weapon: Alliant Bull Pup duo 5.56mm & 20mm explosive round. Good with the men.

David "Jaybird" Sterling. Machinist Mate Second Class. Lead petty officer. 24, 5-10, 170 pounds. Quick mind, fine tactician. Single. Drinks too much sometimes. Crack shot with all arms. Helps plan attack operations. Weapon: H & K MP-5SD submachine gun.

*(Third Platoon assigned exclusively to the Central Intelligence Agency to perform any needed tasks on a covert basis anywhere in the world. All are top secret assignments. Goes around Navy chain of command. Direct orders from the CIA.)

Ron Holt. Radioman First Class. 22, 6-1, 170 pounds. Plays guitar, had a small band. Likes redheaded girls. Rabid baseball fan. Loves deep-sea fishing, is good at it. Platoon radio operator. Weapon: Alliant Bull Pup duo 5.56mm & 20mm explosive round.

Bill Bradford. Quartermaster First Class. 24, 6-2, 215 pounds. An artist in spare time. Paints oils. He sells his marine paintings. Single. Quiet. Reads a lot. Has two years of college. Squad sniper. Weapon: H & K PSG1 7.62 NATO sniper rifle or McMillan M-87R .50-caliber sniper rifle.

Joe "Ricochet" Lampedusa. Operations Specialist Third Class. 21, 5-11, 175 pounds. Good tracker, quick thinker. Had a year of college. Loves motorcycles. Wants a Hog. Pot smoker on the sly. Picks up plain girls. Platoon scout. Weapon: Colt M-4A1 with grenade launcher; alternate, Bull Pup duo 5.56mm & 20mm explosive round.

Kenneth Ching. Quartermaster's Mate First Class. Full-blooded Chinese. 25, 6-0, 180 pounds. Platoon translator. Speaks Mandarin Chinese, Japanese, Russian, and Spanish. Bicycling nut. Paid $1,200 for off-road bike. Is trying for Officer Candidate School. Weapon: Colt M-4A1 rifle with grenade launcher.

Harry "Horse" Ronson. Electrician's Mate Second Class. 24, 6-4, 240 pounds. Played football two years in college. Wants a ranch where he can raise horses. Good man in a brawl. Has broken his nose twice. Squad machine gunner. Weapon: H & K 21-E 7.62 NATO round machine gun.

BRAVO SQUAD

Lieutenant (j.g.) Ed DeWitt. Leader Bravo Squad. Second in command of the platoon. From Seattle. 30, 6-1, 175 pounds. Wiry. Has serious live-in woman, Milly. Annapolis graduate. A career man. Plays a good game of chess on traveling board.

Weapon: Alliant Bull Pup duo 5.56mm & 20mm explosive round. Alternate: H & K G-11 submachine gun.

George Canzoneri. Torpedoman's Mate First Class. 27, 5-11, 190 pounds. Married to Navy wife Phyllis. No kids. Nine years in Navy. Expert on explosives. Nicknamed "Petard" for almost hoisting himself one time. Top pick in platoon for explosive work. Weapon: Alliant Bull Pup duo 5.56mm & 20mm explosive round.

Miguel Fernandez. Gunner's Mate First Class. 26, 6-1, 180 pounds. Wife, Maria; daughter, Linda, 7, in Coronado. Spends his off time with them. Highly family-oriented. He has relatives in San Diego. Speaks Spanish, Portuguese. Squad sniper. Weapon: H & K PSG1 7.62 NATO sniper rifle.

Colt "Guns" Franklin. Yeoman Second Class. 24, 5-10, 175 pounds. A former gymnast. Powerful arms and shoulders. Expert mountain climber. Has a motorcycle, and does hang gliding. Speaks Farsi and Arabic. Weapon: Colt M-4A1 with grenade launcher.

Tran "Train" Khai. Torpedoman Second Class. 23, 6-1, 180 pounds. U.S. born Vietnamese. A whiz at languages and computers. Speaks Vietnamese, French, German, Spanish, and Arabic. Specialist in electronics. Understands the new 20mm Bull Pup weapon. Can repair the electronics in it. Plans on becoming an electronics engineer. Joined the Navy for $40,000 college funding. Entranced by SEALs. First hitch up in four months. Weapon: H & K G-11 with caseless rounds, 4.7mm submachine gun with fifty-round magazine.

Jack Mahanani. Hospital Corpsman First Class. 25, 6-4, 240 pounds. Platoon medic. Tahitian/Hawaiian. Expert swimmer. Bench-presses four hundred pounds. Once married, divorced. Top surfer. Wants the .50 sniper rifle. Weapon: Alliant Bull Pup duo 5.56 & 20mm explosive round. Alternate: Colt M-4A1 with grenade launcher.

Anthony "Tony" Ostercamp. Machinist Mate First Class. 24, 6-1, 210 pounds. Races stock cars in nearby El Cajon weekends. Top auto mechanic. Platoon driver. Weapon: H & K 21E 7.62 NATO round machine gun. Second radio operator.

Paul "Jeff" Jefferson. Engineman Second Class. Black man. 23, 6-1, 200 pounds. Expert in small arms. Can tear apart most weapons and reassemble them, repair, and innovate. A chess player to match Ed DeWitt. Weapon: Alliant Bull Pup duo 5.56mm & 20mm explosive round.

1

Oahu, Hawaii

Lieutenant Commander Blake Murdock squirmed deeper into the rain-forest foliage of the Koolau Mountains just off the Pali Highway overlooking Honolulu, and grinned. This was work? Here they were in the garden spot of the world. In a land where there were twenty shades of green and each one more vivid than the last. The trees and brush were tangled, beautiful, and always lush. Just beyond them he caught the sweep of the green of the valley far below that let him see all the way to the far side of Oahu.

He jerked his attention back to work as he saw a small tree shudder thirty yards in front of him. Somebody out there was damn good. He'd come up through the brush without any indication. Then he'd made one mistake. Murdock heard the chatter of a machine gun to the right. When the hell did they bring up that gun? Another deadly problem to worry about. He and the fifteen men of the Third Platoon of SEAL Team Seven were strung out along this upward slant of the Koolau Range in a thin defensive line.

He looked out and checked Honolulu in the distance, with Pearl Harbor just to the northwest. Hickam Air Force Base was down there right beside Pearl. Both famous as the targets of the Japanese surprise attack on Hawaii on December 7, 1941. As President Franklin Roosevelt had said, it was a day that would live in infamy.

Something moved to his left through the tropical growth of the Oahu rain forest. The brush tops wiggled again. Somebody or something worked through the area just below.

He lifted his rifle and aimed at the spot. It was less than thirty yards away. A helmet covered with greenery lifted out of the foliage for just a moment, then went down and out of sight. Yes, one of the attackers. Murdock waited. He'd been a Navy SEAL now for over six years. Patience had been trained into him.

More brush movement, then the man belonging to the helmet, with a camo-painted face, came up in a rush charging forward.

Murdock fired twice. Both rounds drilled into the chest of the rushing soldier and he went down on the ground, a clear kill. Murdock heard the rattle of weapons going off to his left. They were hitting hard over there again. He chanced a radio call.

"Alpha Squad, any casualties?" he said into the lip mike. It was the Motorola MX-300 radio for personal communications. A speaker in his left ear brought the sound through a wire down the back of his neck and through a slit in his shirt, and plugged into the Motorola transceiver secured to his combat harness. A filament mike perched just below his lip.

"Oh, hell, no casualty here," David "Jaybird" Sterling said. "They got some, though. Nailed me two. One KIA, the other looks like an arm wound. I'm A-okay. The line holds here."

Murdock had rolled twice just after he fired, and saw six rounds splatter where he had been. He came up behind a huge koa tree. The species of acacia soared over seventy feet above him and the trunk was more than three feet thick. He peered around the far side at the suspect area.

"No casualty here, Skipper. I snuffed one of the bastards and another one got away. He was moving in your direction." The voice belonged to Ron Holt, Radioman First Class and Murdock's radio operator.

The woods were quiet for a moment high on the ridge

line. Then the peace was spoiled by the faintly hollow sound of a machine gun spitting out rounds as it fired farther to the left.

"Trouble, Skip," Bill Bradford, Quartermaster First Class, said through the earplug. "Got six of the bastards moving up. One MG you heard and some idiot throwing hand grenades too damn far. Shit, there goes another one. I'm a dead duck if I stay here."

"Pull back to that pair of koa trees," Murdock said. "Can anybody give him cover?"

"Oh, yeah, cover's my middle name," Harry "Horse" Ronson, Electrician's Mate Second Class, said. At once his H & K 21-E 7.62 NATO round machine gun began spitting out five-round bursts of cover fire.

Murdock pushed forward two feet and parted some low branches on a young ohia tree. He could see down the narrow ridge the enemy had come up. There were at least forty attackers out there somewhere, with their job to overrun his smaller contingent of defenders who had not had time to dig in and presented a thin line of defense.

For a moment he stared beyond the ridge line to the sharp drop-off to the valley below. Several miles away he could see the soft morning fog burning off over Honolulu. What a marvelous place, Hawaii. If it wasn't for this current unpleasantness, this would be a true vacation. He grinned. Not really. He wouldn't have it any other way. This was what they kept training for year-round.

A flash caught his eye. It came from the area this side of Honolulu proper. Yes, the flash was near Pearl Harbor. He frowned. Another flash. Only then did the sound come through, the *karumph* of a massive explosion.

"What the hell?" Jaybird said on the net. "Those bombs I hear?"

Murdock had his binoculars up and trained on the area. Slowly he saw the pattern.

"It's Pearl," he said. "Somebody is bombing Pearl Harbor. No, not bombing, those are missiles. Shit! Look at that one hit. Not a nuke but a damn big payload. Who the hell could be attacking Pearl Harbor?"

"Missiles, that's a Roger," Lieutenant (j.g.) Ed DeWitt said on the radio. "I count four hits already, one secondary explosion. What the hell is going on?"

"By God, we're going to find out," Murdock said. He stood up and made a sign of time-out over his head. "Stop the clock, stop the exercise," Murdock bellowed. "This training exercise is over." Just then a red paint ball hit Murdock in the chest and he swore. "Hold fire, damnit. Can't you Brits understand English? The war games are over. We've got the real thing going on down there at Pearl." He turned and looked around.

"Holt, fire up the SATCOM," Murdock said. The SATCOM is officially the AN/PRC-117D portable radio. It makes direct connection with the Milstar satellite in a synchronous orbit 22,300 miles over the equator. It's fifteen inches high and three inches square and weighs fifteen pounds. It can be used to call any spot on earth.

Holt scrambled past some brush and dropped down beside Murdock. He had the small dish antenna folded out and aligned with the satellite, then turned on the set and looked at Murdock.

"What the hell," Ching said, running up. "Those really missiles hitting Pearl down there? Christ, who the hell is shooting at us?"

A British SAS trooper with heavy camouflage on his helmet and uniform stood up twenty yards away. He ran up to the others.

"Missiles? What the fuck you mean? Missiles, real ones going off down there in Pearl Harbor? Hard to believe."

"Believe it, Captain," Murdock said. "We're going to find out what the hell is happening."

"Voice?" Holt asked his skipper.

"Yes, on channel two."

The speaker made the three small beeps indicating that the dish antenna was properly aligned. Murdock took the handset and stared at Pearl Harbor, where two more missiles landed creating large explosions.

"CINCPAC, this is Commander Murdock. Respond. Over."

Nothing came over the air. Murdock repeated the message, but there was no answer. Two British SAS men stood from the brush in front and hurried up to the others.

"I say, what's happening down there?" Captain Haworth, leader of the Brits, asked.

"Trying to find out," Murdock said. "Looks like Pearl Harbor is getting plastered with some kind of medium-sized missiles." Murdock made one more transmission, but had no reply.

"Go to TAC Two," Murdock told Holt.

"What the fuck is happening?" Tony Ostercamp said on the Motorola. "The exercise over? You fuckers kidding about real live missiles on Pearl?"

"No kidding. Pearl is getting clobbered," Ed DeWitt said.

Murdock repeated the message into the mike and they waited.

A moment later the set responded.

"Commander Murdock. Heard your transmission to CINC-PAC. Not sure who the hell you are, but this is Air Force Eagle Six. We're airborne about five miles out on the leeward side of Oahu. I can't raise Hickam Field. You copy?"

"Eagle Six. Hickam might be off the air. Pearl Harbor next door has taken six or eight missile hits. Real ones. CINCPAC is off the air. There goes another missile into Pearl. We're on the Koolau Range about ten to twelve miles from the field. I can't raise CINCPAC."

"Yeah, Commander, your boss man in the Pacific. So where do we put down? We have six Air Force birds here without a lot of reserve in the tanks."

"You have an alternate field?"

"On Oahu? Only place they told us about was the Honolulu International, which also serves Hickam. Did the runways get hit?"

"We can't tell from here. I'd say the missile strike is over. But you can't land without some radio contact with the field. Suggest you make a call to Kaneohe Marine Corps Air Station. It's just across the ridge from Pearl flying northeast. About fifteen miles from Pearl. You can try radio contact with them on the emergency channel. They have a long runway there."

"That's a Roger, Commander Murdock. Thanks. We're out."

By that time all of the SEALs had gathered near the big tree, and about half of the Aussies and Brits.

Leftenant Anderson of the Australian Special Attack Forces shook his head. "Is something afoot we don't know about?"

"If CINCPAC is off the air, something damn big is happening," Murdock said. "They usually have security a mile deep down there and the communications room is like a tomb, it's so safe."

"Only not this time," Holt said. "How about giving Don Stroh a try?"

Murdock slapped Holt on the shoulder. "Good idea. Set it up and let's go."

Holt adjusted the settings on the radio and nodded. Murdock took the handset again.

"Commander Blake Murdock calling Don Stroh. Don Stroh, if you're there, get on the horn. We've got trouble in paradise. Somebody just shot eight or ten medium-sized missiles into Pearl Harbor. Come back."

There was no reply.

"It gets recorded and he gets beeped automatically when something comes in on his frequency," Holt said. "So he'll get it as soon as anyone can find him."

A British lieutenant came up with his men and asked what was going on.

"The training exercise is over," Murdock told them. "It's been good working with you SAS guys, but now it looks like we've got ourselves a real war going on down there. We've been attacked by missiles from someone. Seems like most of the communications are down. Time we get down there and see what's going on. We're about two miles from our base camp. Get your men down there fast and let's pack up. The trucks are another hour's hike out. Let's move, people."

After an hour, they stopped and tried the SATCOM again. The second time they had a response from Don Stroh.

"Yeah, Murdock. Good to know you're okay. We don't know what the hell is going on out there except that our reports show that someone has launched an attack against Oahu. Thinking here is it has to be China. Only one with any real problem with us in the Pacific who has the capability. When we can, we'll put you on TAD with CINCPAC. Keep us informed."

Murdock called Ed DeWitt over.

"Who was that commander who served as our liaison with CINCPAC the first day we arrived?"

"Somebody Johnson. Commander Johnson," Ed said. He watched his CO. "What the hell we going to do?"

"Maybe this Commander Johnson can tell us. We reported in at Pearl, right? What department was that?"

"He was from the Pearl Harbor Training Command, as I remember," Will Dobler, Senior Chief Boatswain's Mate, said. "He was grousing about it, wanting to get back to sea duty."

"Francis," Murdock said. "Commander Francis Johnson."

"Right," Ed said. "Only it was the CINCPAC Training Command."

"Try that on the radio," Murdock said. "Stow these paint guns and get out our usual weapons. We have live ammo, right?"

"Oh, yes," Senior Chief Dobler said. "The Brits wanted to see just how much gear and ammo we carried when we went into a mission."

"Pearl must be a mess after the attack, but CINCPAC is up on the hill five miles away," Murdock said, thinking out loud. "Why are they off the air? They told us to give them a call at CINCPAC whenever we needed anything."

"Hey, reminds me," DeWitt said. "Johnson gave me a phone number in case we got cut off by the CINCPAC of-ficialdom. Right here." He handed a small notebook to Murdock.

The commander looked at Holt, who made two settings on the SATCOM and looked up. "Ready for you to dial the cellular phone, Skipper."

Murdock hit the buttons and a few moments later the speaker came to life.

"Yes, yes. What do you want? All hell is still on the loose here. Who is this?"

"Commander Johnson, this is Lieutenant Commander Blake Murdock, with the SEALs. We were on the Koolau

Range when the missile hit. They were missiles, weren't they?"

"God, yes. But first, somehow they knocked out all of our radio communications. All we have are phones. Going mad. How fast can you get down here? The admiral wants you to do a small job for us. The faster the better. You have transport?"

"Right, we do. I'd say about an hour from here, depending on the traffic. Have the civilians panicked yet?"

"Not that we've heard about. All the damage is on-base. They were good, whoever the hell they were. Make it here in an hour and don't worry about stop signs and traffic lights. Blow your horn all the way. We need you here damn fast. Instead of Pearl, go right up to the Marine Corps' Camp Smith about five miles up the hill. The admiral has a job for you. A guide will be waiting for you at the gate. Move it, Commander."

Half the men were in the three trucks. Murdock bellowed that they were moving out. The rest loaded in less than two minutes. Murdock sat in the front seat of the lead six-by and told the driver the drill.

"Yes, sir, I can get there the fastest way. All you SEALs in this rig?" Murdock nodded. "Good, tell them to hold on."

The usually crowded Pali Highway was jammed by the time they got there. Horns honking, people yelling. The SEALs wound through traffic, on the shoulder, anywhere they could find room.

It wasn't panic traffic, but thousands of cars were on the move that usually wouldn't be. Some of the drivers were on the nervous edge, and there were six crashes that Murdock saw before they got to Highway 1 and Pearl City.

The driver knew where the Marine Camp was above Pearl City, and he drove right to the gate. It was blocked by two huge bulldozers.

Two Marines in helmets, combat gear, and weapons came forward and checked the truck.

"We've got orders to report to Commander Johnson at CINCPAC Training as fast as possible," Murdock told the SP.

The SP frowned. "You them SEAL guys? Told us you was coming."

"That's right, now move the machinery." They did.

The truck driver stopped just inside the gate. A guide waved him down. A major looked at the driver.

"You have the SEALs here, sailor?"

"Yes, sir."

"Is a Lieutenant Commander Murdock on board?"

"That's me, Major," Murdock said.

"Follow my rig." The major stepped into a Humvee and it roared away with the six-by right behind it.

Both vehicles stopped at an imposing building a short ways later. The major led Murdock, Lam, Senior Chief Dobler, and Ed DeWitt to a guarded door. The Marine guard saluted the major and opened the door. The SEALs wore their combat vests, cammies, and carried their weapons.

A commander just inside the door stared at them a moment. "Lieutenant Commander Blake Murdock?"

"Yes, sir. In response to Commander Johnson's message."

"Right. Glad you're here. You're going to talk to Admiral Birchard D. Bennington, and he's getting impatient waiting for you. This way."

"Can you tell us what happened to Pearl?"

"Half blown off the map. Missiles, but we're not sure who fired them. So far the brass thinks it's a Chinese attack."

The men went to an elevator and down two levels, through a concrete tunnel, and into a war room with huge maps on the wall, a dozen large video monitors, and a table in front with six men clustered around it. All were Navy captains and admirals.

A four-star admiral stood and stared at the four SEALs.

"Are you Lieutenant Commander Blake Murdock?"

"Yes, sir."

"About time. The CNO sends his regards. He has given me an assignment for you and your platoon."

The four SEALs had come stiffly to attention.

"At ease, men," the admiral said. "This is a rush job. You know we've been hit, Chinese we think. We also have lost most of our radio network. The key is the master communications center, Building Forty-two on Pearl. It was not damaged in the missile attack. Now it's locked down from the inside. Our best explanation is that some terrorists captured the facility at the exact time that the missiles hit. At any rate, they have complete control. They haven't sent us any messages, but right now they are seriously handicapping our situation. In short, we have only paste-up communications with the entire South Pacific. We've heard by phone that there has been an invasion on the windward coast at Kaneohe Bay. But we're not even sure of that."

The admiral looked at the four SEALs critically. "I see you have some of your combat gear. What you don't have we can supply here in quick time. Your assignment, straight from a man called Don Stroh and the President, sent through the CNO, is to capture the communications building and drive out the enemy there with as little damage to the equipment as possible. Do you have any questions?"

2

Pearl Harbor, Hawaii

Murdock looked at the four-star admiral, his face showing surprise.

"Sir, the communications building is like a fortress. I have fifteen men."

"And good ones, from what I'm told. The Chief of Naval Operations says you're the man for the job. Get it done as quickly as you can. We have a full-scale Chinese amphibious invasion in progress. We need our commo and we need it now."

"Yes, sir. I'll need equipment and arms."

"We don't want you simply blasting into the place and leaving it in rubble. We could do that. We want it to be on the air ten minutes after you liberate it. I understand you have a sound weapon that isn't destructive."

"We brought only four of the EAR weapons, sir, mostly for demonstration."

"Good, use them. Anything you want, Commander. And I mean anything: tanks, flamethowers, a company of Marine Rangers. Just ask. Commander Johnson is your liaison. Good luck."

"Aye, aye, sir," Murdock said. The four did about-faces

and walked out of the room. Commander Johnson was just outside.

"What's first, Commander?" Johnson asked.

"Recon and intel. I want a floor plan of the building. Base engineering should have it. Get about six men to help you run down things for us."

They walked down the tunnel to the elevator, then went up.

"Get one man to take my Senior Chief Dobler to ordnance with a truck to bring back ammo and weapons. We left some gear here two days ago. Find it and get it to our assembly area about two blocks from the target."

"I've got two Humvees and six men topside, Commander. We'll get in motion. Also, I've got a man who works in the commo building who can fill you in on some of the problems and the defenses."

At the six-by, Murdock told the men the assignment. He sent Senior Chief Dobler to ordnance. "Get all the exploding twenties they have, and regular 20mm rounds. Also we need TNAZ or C-5, whichever they have. Load up on 5.56 ammo. Anything else you think we might need. Some flashbangs would be good, a couple of dozen. Go. The Chinese are invading the other side of the island right now."

Murdock turned to meet a chief who came up with Johnson.

"Commander, this is Chief Natterby, a commo specialist who works in the center. He knows the layout."

"Welcome aboard, Chief. We've got work to do. You stay with me. We'll recon the place soon." He looked back at the liaison officer. "Johnson, if they have any Marine Recon or Rangers on-base, get me twenty of them combat-ready. I want them here as backup. Chief Natterby, we need a command post two blocks from the commo center. Tell Johnson where it should be so he can get the Marines there."

Murdock scowled for a moment, thinking. "Recon time. DeWitt, Jaybird, Natterby. On me in that first Humvee. Let's see what we have here to work against."

The Humvee had a driver. Natterby told him where to go. They edged up to the side of a building a few blocks later, and all climbed out.

Natterby had talked all the way over. The place was a fortress, but it had weak spots.

"What about a central air-conditioning system?" Jaybird asked. "Any way we could get to it?"

"The central air-conditioning has its only air intake on the rear of the building at ground level. There is no room-by-room control. Tough to shut off the air-con."

"Perfect spot for some tear-gas drills," Jaybird said.

Chief Natterby took a small cell phone from his pocket. "Sir, I can call ordnance and have them include tear-gas canisters with the other material your chief is picking up."

Murdock nodded.

"How many, sir?" asked Natterby.

"Fifty. No, make it eighty."

Now the men peered around the building at the communications center. It was a concrete block building, three stories high, with a 150-foot frontage on the street. Windows showed on the first two floors, but none on the third floor. The roof was a pincushion of antennas.

"Two doors in the rear," Natterby said. "One truck ramp. One door in front. It's electronic with a guard post outside. You need a thumbprint and retina check to get in normally. Right now the security post is empty. No easy access."

"What about the roof?" DeWitt asked.

"Never been up there. Must be access to service the antennas. Probably a weak spot."

"Any windowless area that extends all the way to the roof-line?" Murdock asked.

"Yes, sir. On the rear, our near side. Rope climb?"

Murdock nodded. "Okay, let's pick out our command post. Where should it be, Natterby? No more than two blocks from the target."

They picked out a vacant parking lot behind another big building. The six-by came moments later, and then the other Humvee. The platoon began working over gear. Natterby made four phone calls, then went to Murdock.

"I found the rest of your gear. I've arranged to have it brought here. Should arrive within a half hour."

"Good, check with ordnance and see if our truck there has

left yet. We can't do much until we get those canisters. That's going to be our opening move."

Joe Lampedusa came up and Murdock grabbed him. "Two blocks over is a three-storied building," Murdock said. "The commo center. I want you to do a recon all the way around it. Stay out of sight if possible. Look for any weak spots. Should be a rope-climb area back there without windows. Check it out. You have forty minutes. Leave your weapon here and your vest. Move it."

Ed DeWitt stood nearby, listening. Murdock waved him over. "Ed, take one man and check out the air-conditioning intake on the back of the place. See if we can get four men in there without being seen. We'll go with a hot firefight if we need to, to get to the intake. That will be a big factor here."

"Agree. I'll check it out now."

Ten minutes later the six-by came with the rest of the gear the SEALs had bought from the mainland, including the four EAR weapons. These are Enhanced Acoustical Rifles, and are non-lethal. They pump out a blast of sound waves that hit a target or go inside a room and bounce all around. A hit or near miss can put the target man down and unconscious for two to four hours. When the target wakes up, he is not damaged physically. The SEALs first used the weapon in the mission to Northern Japan.

Being non-lethal and non-destructive, the EARs would be important elements here.

Murdock assigned the EARs, two weapons to each squad. He had a mix of the H & K MP-5SD4 9mm submachine guns with suppressors, and the Bull Pups with the exploding rounds. When he was happy with the mix he called over Chief Natterby.

"Where are the sensitive areas, the transmitters, receivers, all the electronics equipment in the commo center?"

"Almost all of it is on the third floor. It's sealed up separately from the rest of the building for security and protection from an attack that would produce explosive fragments, shrapnel, accidental damage."

"First two floors administrative?"

"Yes, sir."

"How many friendlies do we have in the building? How many would normally be there on a working day like today?"

"Between a hundred ten to a hundred thirty. Usually there's a commander and a captain aboard."

"Now, how many terrorists would it take to capture and neutralize the communications center?"

"My guess would be at least ten, maybe fifteen. There are six separate master control centers. They would have to be shut down and locked down."

"Are there weapons in the building?"

"Not that I know of. Nobody wears weapons during working hours. The guards at night have side arms. Interior guards."

"There must be a weapons locker somewhere. You've never seen one or heard about one?"

"No, sir."

"So there's little chance for any armed resistance from inside. Let's hope that the tear gas and the EARs do their job and we don't have to use any of the 20mm."

Ed Dewitt came back with his report.

"The air intake is plainly marked, and we've got clear passage to it out of sight of anyone at the rear windows. No need to wait for darkness."

Five minutes later the two Humvees boiled into the parking lot with the weapons and ammo. DeWitt's squad grabbed the cases of tear-gas canisters. They came twenty to a carton and there were four cartons.

DeWitt talked to the Humvee driver, and took from his toolbox a heavy pair of side cutter pliers, a three-foot pry bar, a heavy hammer, and three screwdrivers.

Murdock looked at the tools.

"All we have to do is lift off a screen over the input pipe and we're in business," DeWitt said.

Murdock had scouted the area fronting the communications building. It was an administration office of some kind, with a two-foot-high rock wall in front of it next to the sidewalk. Plenty of cover for his riflemen.

"This is a radio net check," Murdock said on his lip mike. "Alpha Squad report."

He listened as six of his seven men reported. Kenneth Ching had not logged on.

"Jaybird, find Ching and get him wired," Murdock said.

Ed DeWitt checked his squad and counted all of them.

"Ed, it's your lead. Dump in at least forty of those canisters as fast as you can pop them. We've got another twenty rounds up here we can lob into the windows if we need to. We'll give it five minutes after you tell me the gas is on the way. Then if we have to, we'll use the EAR."

He looked around. All of the SEALs were there except Lam. "Bravo Squad men with the EAR, give them to Alpha. Your play, DeWitt."

DeWitt had parceled out the canisters to four of his squad. Each man had fifteen in a box. They moved out just as Lam came in from his recon.

"Place is wrapped up tight as a fourteen-year-old wannabe. Saw the section for climbing. Looks reasonable with no visual from the windows. Parking lot behind the building shows some activity. Like the rear door could be open from time to time. Might be good to watch it with three men for possible entry. That's about it, Cap."

"Lam, pick two men and cover the door. Take flashbangs and grenades, but use the fraggers judiciously. Could be over a hundred friendlies inside. Let us know on the Motorola if you get inside. Go."

Murdock looked at the rest of his squad. He carried his Bull Pup and an MP-5 over his back. He gave a case of twenty tear-gas canisters to Ronson and they moved out. They had no machine guns or long-range sniper rifles.

Murdock hesitated at the last cover before they would be in the open. He wanted the tear gas to get inside before he moved. He held up his hand and the men stopped.

Two minutes later he had word on his radio.

"Murdock, that's forty of the canisters into the intake pipe. Sucked the stuff away in an instant."

"Good. Hold there for another dose."

Murdock nodded at Jaybird, who led the way around the corner of the building. They walked down the sidewalk as if they belonged there, about ten feet apart. Then all at once they dropped behind the stone wall and had the entire 150-

foot frontage of the communications building covered.

Murdock edged up and looked over the top of the wall. No activity at the front door. The windows were all covered with blinds. He studied the windows again. They were a newer kind, not the old double-hung or casement. He figured they would extend up about six feet off the floor inside.

"Okay, we're in position if anyone runs out the front door gagging on the gas. The gas has been circulating through the air-conditioning system for . . . four minutes. We'll give it another three."

Somewhere ahead he heard a screeching as a window opened.

"Who spots that window?" Murdock asked.

"I've got it," Bradford said.

"Closest man to it with an EAR put a shot through that open window. Who has it?"

"Got the sucker," Ron Holt said. They heard the familiar whoosh of the enhanced beam of sound as it shot out, darted through the window, compressed, and thundered into an explosive-type sound with high-stress wavelengths.

"One EAR blast inside," Holt said.

They waited.

"We're inside," Lam said on the Motorola. "Took out two dudes in civvies and with non-military hardware. They are down and wasted. We're in some back rooms. Orders?"

"Can you smell any tear gas?" Murdock asked.

"Negative. In a small room—storage, incoming shipments, that sort of thing."

"Stay put for now. Capture anyone who comes in. See if you can look out the door without giving yourself away. Let me know if you smell the gas."

Another window opened along the front. Ching was closest with an EAR. He put a round through the opening.

They waited.

"The gas isn't doing it," Murdock said into the mike. "How many Bravo Squad at the trucks?"

Paul Jefferson, Engineman Second Class, came on the set. "Three of us, Cap," Jefferson said.

"Move out and meet DeWitt at the back door. Wait for him there."

"That's a Roger."

"Ed, dump the rest of your tear gas, then get to the back door unseen. Move in with Lam and begin to clear rooms. We'll be working the front side."

"You got it, Murdock. Dumping the stuff now. Take us about five to get out of here and through the buildings, then back to the other end of this one. Out."

"Sterling, Dobler. You both have C-5 and detonators?"

"Roger," they both said at once.

"We're going to do the rest of the twenty windows on the ground floor. I want one 5.56 round through the unopened windows. Followed closely by EAR rounds. Work out your territory. Start it now."

Two 5.56 rounds belched fire and broke the tops of two windows. Before the sound died, a dozen more rounds exploded at the block wall and shattered windows in the communications building. The EAR rounds followed shortly.

"Dobler, Jaybird, hit that front door. Better take extra C-5 with you and do the locking device, then the four hinges. Go."

JG Ed DeWitt crammed his long frame against the doorjamb and edged around it to check the hall just inside the first room at the rear door.

"Never seen anyone down there," Lam said.

"Let's try it," DeWitt said. "Keep those flashbangs handy. Remember, over a hundred friendlies in here." He led the way down the hallway, his Bull Pup set for two-shot bursts, his finger on the trigger.

They moved twenty feet to a cross hallway. DeWitt looked one way, and Lam the other way.

DeWitt swore. "I've got six coming this way. They have automatic rifles and are pushing half a dozen sailors in front of them. Hold your fire."

Down the hall the first two Chinese men fired between the sailors. The rounds whined down the corridor.

"What the hell should we do now?" Lam asked.

De Witt pulled back as another burst of automatic rifle fire tore off part of the corner of the hallway he had jolted back into.

"The fuckers mean business," Lam said. "They must know we're here. How can we fight them with a human shield of sailors out front?"

3

Communications Center
Pearl Harbor, Hawaii

Already DeWitt had jerked the safety pin from a flashbang grenade and flipped it around the wall down the corridor.

"Grenade," someone in the hallway bellowed.

"Cover up," DeWitt said into his lip mike. "Flashbang."

The SEALs had just time to cover their ears with hands and shut their eyes tightly when the series of jolting explosive sounds took place, followed by six super-brilliant flashes of light that penetrated their eyelids even though they were closed and around the corner from the grenade.

A second after the last flash, the SEALs pushed around the corner and opened their eyes. Six men writhed on the floor. One with a submachine gun leaned against the wall. DeWitt drilled him with two rounds of 5.56mm from his Bull Pup.

Another man staggered to his feet. He had on civilian clothes and held an M-16 rifle. Lam dropped him with a three-round burst from his MP-5. A blue-shirted sailor jumped on a third man who was groping for his weapon.

"We got them all," the second class said when he saw the

three SEALs come around the corner. "Need to tie this one up or waste him."

DeWitt tossed the sailor a plastic riot cuff, and watched as the man tied the terrorist's hands behind his back. Now DeWitt saw that the man was Chinese.

"How many more of them in here?" DeWitt asked.

A chief rolled over and got to his feet. He shook his head again and kept blinking. "Can't hear a damn thing yet, sir, but I'm damn glad to see you. They got us hog-tied upstairs. Must be twenty of them. All Chinese bragging about an invasion. They really land troops over on Kaneohe Bay?"

"What we hear." DeWitt looked at the rest of the sailors. "Men, we need two of you who know this place best. The rest of you get outside and well away from here. Who can help us go after these Chinks?"

The chief brightened. "I heard that. I can help. Me and Allison. The rest of you, out the back door. Move."

They rushed out. Lam put another riot cuff around the prisoner's ankles and the chief shook his head again.

"Damn those bastards are loud. First time I ever heard one. Okay. We're in the west wing. Nothing in here but admin. No Chinese at all. Most of them are upstairs. Two at the main door and one as a connecting-link man halfway up the stairs to the third."

"You have any casualties in the takeover?" DeWitt asked.

"Two dead, six wounded. Our CO, Captain Browder, thought they were joking. They shot him in the head. Couple of our guys had hideouts on their ankles. Killed one of the bastards before they ran out of ammo."

"How do we get to them?" DeWitt asked.

The chief waved them forward. "Oh, Lieutenant, I'm Master Chief Carpenter, top EM in this place. Got a spare weapon?"

DeWitt handed him a .25-caliber automatic from his right ankle. Carpenter chambered a round and waved them forward. They went the same way the Chinese had been going.

"Back stairs," Carpenter said. "Nothing much on the second floor but some offices. Head man is on the third with the vital transmitters, the one studio, all the electronics and readouts and screens so we know what the fuck we're doing.

This end we're going up holds records, transcriptions, the big humidity-and-temp-controlled storage room for all our mainframe tapes. Doubt if they'll have a man in there."

"So how close to the terrorists can we get?"

"They tell us they aren't terrorists, they are soldiers. Either way, we can get within maybe a hundred feet of them. I'd guess you don't want to blow up any of our equipment up here if we can help it?"

"Right. The admiral wants to be back on the air ten minutes after our takedown."

"Sounds like old Hairy Ass. That's what we call the admiral. He's got more body hair on him than Robin Williams, the comedian."

He held his finger to his lips now as Ed DeWitt and Lam and the whole Bravo Squad started up the wooden stairway. Not a board creaked. The second floor proved to be clear. Lam and Ostercamp checked it out. Then they worked on up the steps.

At the third floor they came to double doors. Master Chief Carpenter held up his hand and they all froze. He edged the door inward an inch and studied what he could see through the opening. He let it ease closed.

"Two of them, with weapons slung. You have any suppressed weapons?"

DeWitt took a look, then waved Colt Franklin up.

"Single shots. Silenced. Two of them, make sure."

Franklin nodded and edged the muzzle of his weapon through a two-inch opening between the door and the jamb. He waited a moment, then pulled the trigger, moved his sights, and fired again. He held up two fingers and then pointed his thumb down. Lam edged the door open and slipped through, followed by DeWitt and Carpenter and then the rest of the squad. Lam checked the two Chinese soldiers. Both were dead of heart shots. There was a partition ahead and another door. This section of the third floor was about twenty feet long, which left the main part beyond the wall ahead. They found the temperature-controlled area and dozens of racks of storage for tapes and supplies.

The area was clear of any more Chinese.

DeWitt waved his men forward toward a pair of doors in

the wall between them and the rest of the Chinese. They were spread out with four at one door and five at the other when a pair of Chinese in civilian clothes ran through the doors shouting something in Chinese, both with submachine guns up ready to fire.

Below in front of the communications building, the EAR rounds had produced exactly one Chinese man who jumped out a ground-floor window and kept rubbing his eyes as he ran right into Alpha Squad. He was quickly tied up and left behind the wall.

"Do the door," Murdock said in his mike, and Jaybird and Master Chief Dobler sprinted for the front door. There were no shots at the two SEALs. They applied the explosives, set the timers, and faded along the wall fifty feet, then held their hands over their ears. The explosions of almost a full pound of C-5 were enough to blow down a small building. In this case it blasted the double doors off their hinges and slammed them backward into the building.

The SEALs charged the opening, darted through it, and the acrid smell of the explosive, and into the main entryway of the communications building.

The two chunks of the big door lay against the wall twenty feet from where they usually perched. Someone cried out in pain near one of the doors. Murdock found a Chinese soldier with one leg blown off. He died a minute after Murdock found him. Jaybird found another dead Chinese. Then they took fire from someone on the stairway. The figure fired, then scurried on up the steps and out of sight on the second floor.

"Ronson, Bradford. Cover each other up the steps," Murdock told his lip mike.

A loudspeaker on the ground floor snapped on and a voice came out that spoke perfect English but had a bit of a Chinese accent.

"Yes, American force. We know you are inside the building. We have hostages here. If you do not vacate the building in two minutes, we will start shooting hostages. We are starting the timing now."

"Let's clear this floor," Murdock said. "Half of you each way."

Murdock's order was obeyed as two of the remaining SEALs went each way into the series of offices, hallways, and more cubicles and storage areas. Three minutes later they came back to the stairs.

All clear.

"Up the steps," Murdock said. He had heard on the radio earlier that DeWitt and his squad had penetrated the place and were moving past the second floor to the third, where the enemy had holed up with all of the vital broadcasting equipment and the hostages.

"On our way up the middle stairway," Murdock radioed.

"We're at the far end moving in," DeWitt replied. "You heard that about hostages? We have two of our EM who work here. The Chinese shot the captain in the head just after they took over. Don't plan on a quick surrender."

DeWitt sniffed. There was only a slight hint of tear gas in the air. Some damn efficient air filter had wiped the air clean before it exhausted it into the system. He checked his pockets.

"Let's go with flashbangs," he said quietly to the radio mike. "I want three men to throw two bangers into the main room. Get them as far inside as possible. Get them out and ready. Five seconds." He waited for a count to seven. "Throw them now."

He cracked the door and three men threw the non-lethal grenades into the other room, then let the doors close.

Inside the larger area, the flashbangs wouldn't be as effective, but they could easily put down and out of combat half the terrorists inside. When the last of the flashes blasted through the crack in the door, DeWitt and his men charged into the room.

It was one large area, with all sorts of communications gear. Three civilians with weapons tried to stand, but were cut down at once by 5.56mm rounds from the Bull Pups and the Colt Commandos. There were two aisles that led to the doors. Each had a group of partitioned offices with the walls seven feet high. DeWitt charged them, found two more Chinese civilians with guns and holding their heads. He kicked away weapons and had the men cuffed.

"I've got three over here," Jefferson said. "Hiding behind some expensive-looking hardware."

"Save the equipment," DeWitt said. "But don't get hurt. Maybe another flashbang beside them."

The room shook with the vibrations from the cracking explosions of the grenade. Then the strobes of intense light cut through the already bright room lights.

"Oh, yeah," Jefferson said. "Tony and me got the fuckers. Still holding their ears."

DeWitt heard Murdock bring Alpha Squad through the twin doors.

"What's the score?" Murdock asked on the radio.

"We've accounted for about twenty hostiles," DeWitt said. "Checking the rest of the area."

The Navy communications personnel began coming out from under desks. Two dozen had been locked in a storage room. The rest of them filtered back to their workstations.

A three-striper came boiling up and looked at Murdock. He held out his hand.

"Damn glad to see you and your men, Commander. They caught us with our pants down for damn sure. Won't ever happen again. This will be a personal-weapons station from now on." He paused. "Oh, I'm Commander Lethridge, operations officer."

"Lieutenant Commander Murdock here. The admiral said he wants the whole damn operation back in gear in ten minutes. Better call him right now and let him know you're on the way."

The commander shouted some orders, and the men and women sailors in the room settled into their assigned tasks, getting the communications system up and operating.

"Casualty report," Murdock told his lip mike. "Alpha Squad?"

The men chimed in one after the other in their line-of-march order. No one had even been scratched except for Lam. "Picked up a ricochet somewhere, Cap," Lam said on the net. "Figure it was in the hall and that first fire we took. Left arm, Band-Aid type."

"Jack, take a look," Murdock said.

Bravo Squad reported in with no injuries.

Commander Lethridge detailed some of his crew to haul the dead Chinese to the ground floor. He put the tied-up prisoners there as well.

The admiral telephoned his congratulations to Murdock, then went back to running his war.

Murdock took his platoon out of the building and gathered them in the parking lot in back of the commo building. The truck and two Humvees were there waiting for them. Murdock had Holt listening on the SATCOM for any news he could find. Several of the units were using SATCOMs as the only way to communicate with each other.

"Hey, Cap," Holt called. "The *Jefferson* heard about the invasion on Kaneohe Bay on the windward side and sent twenty F-18's over there. The pilots say they hit at the Chinese boats in the bay and some more coming in. The troops on the island were invisible. They had landed and moved inland through the civilian houses and into the country toward the hills of the Koolau ridges. No real targets on land, but they shot hell out of those landing craft."

"Keep up the eavesdropping, Holt. We need to know everything we can. Now, let's mount up and go back to the quarters we had before that training exercise this morning."

An hour later, they had their weapons cleaned and new loads of ammo in their combat vests when Murdock received a call. They had a new mission. Admiral Bennington was in full command again and was worried about the estimated two thousand men the Chinese had landed at Kaneohe Bay. They were somewhere in the green belt behind the highway and the town itself and the Koolau Range. Just where they were and what they were doing was a major concern.

The area was not densely populated, with fewer residents the closer you went to the mountains.

"Murdock, I want you and your team to go in there and find the enemy, then harass them. Cut any supply lines they may have, disrupt their communications, hit and run, night raids. Do anything you can do to keep them tied up and busy so they don't go pouring down the highway toward Kailua or try to get over to the highway heading for Honolulu. We can resupply you with arms and ammo and explosives by chopper out of Pearl or from the *Jefferson,* whichever is closer. I want you to be a damn loose cannon in there rattling around in their belly."

"Aye, aye, sir. We can go in with first dark if you have a Sea Knight chopper that can get us into the area."

"Commander Johnson is still your man. He can arrange it. You get my red-signature approval on anything asked for. Good luck."

"We'll stay in contact with you on the SATCOM for any change in orders." They hung up, and Murdock saw a Humvee pull up outside their barracks/operations center. Commander Johnson jumped out and ran for the operations center door.

He came in and wiped a bead of sweat off his forehead. "Hey, Commander Murdock. We've got our commo back again. The admiral says you need a chopper, a Sea Knight. I've put in the order with the air commander at Pearl. His aide said with the red-signature order he'll have one ready for combat in thirty minutes."

"Good, Johnson. Stick close to me. We're about to have a planning session like you probably haven't seen before."

Ten minutes later Murdock had DeWitt, Jaybird, Master Chief Dobler, and Lam sat around a table. All had pads and ballpoint pens.

"Now, you know our mission, so how do we best work it?" Murdock asked.

"No EAR rifles," Jaybird said. "We leave them here and use our twenties."

"Agreed," DeWitt said. "But we need the sniper rifles and the MGs."

"Amen to both of those," Murdock said. "I'm taking an MP-5 sub gun on my back. Anyone who wants to can have a second shooter."

"Hit and run, sounds like fun, but where do we stash our extra ammo?" Lam asked. "We'll be all over the place. We establish a cache of ammo and explosives that we can't carry?"

"Double ammo if we can pack it," Senior Chief Dobler said. "Yes, I'd agree, we need a stash somewhere. Maybe more than one."

They went at it for an hour and came out with their operations plan. Johnson was amazed.

"I've never seen an outfit work this way before," Johnson said. "Usually the officers work out the plan and the details. I like this way better. Everyone knows what's happening and you get input from your smartest EMs as well."

"You got the idea. You want to work the field with us?"

Johnson laughed. "Hey, I'm a desk guy. Last infantry-type shit I did was in boot camp. I don't even have my shots."

Murdock looked at his watch. It was 1630. "When does it get dark here?" Murdock asked.

Johnson frowned. "This time of year, about 1930, more or less."

"Be damn handy if we had a map of that area with the spot marked where the admiral thinks the Chinese are," Dobler said. "Then we can figure out where we drop in and set up our stash."

By 1800 they had a map.

The chopper was waiting on the pad at the runway.

Master Chief Dobler had the troops ready with fifty percent more ammo than normal. Six drag bags were loaded with ammo, grenades, explosives, and more ammo. They had an expanded first-aid kit as well as Mahanani's regular corpsman's gear.

Murdock checked everything. "Looks like we're about ready," he said. "Ed, you happy with your mix of weapons?"

"Right. We have the sniper and MG, five Bull Pups, and three MP-5 submachine guns as doubles."

"What's our mix on WP versus HE on the grenades?"

"Two HEs to one WP."

Murdock turned to Johnson. "How far is it to that chopper?"

"About a mile and a half."

"Have it set down in the parking lot behind this building within thirty minutes."

Johnson shook his head. "Can't do it, Commander. None of our choppers are cleared to land anywhere but at the regular designated areas."

Murdock grinned. "Commander, let's see just how good

that admiral's red signature is. Tell whoever you contact the level of the order and see what happens."

Johnson laughed. "Yeah, let's see. It should work like a charm. I don't get to play with that red sig often. In fact, never before."

Murdock got the right TAC frequency, and used the SAT-COM to talk directly with a recon plane over the Kaneohe invasion zone.

"The town itself was bypassed," the observer said. "They have some half-tracks, maybe six of them. Hard to hide their trails. They swung north of the town and moved about three miles from the coast in toward the mountains. Damn strange. They don't seem to be going anywhere. Just sitting there. Maybe waiting for orders. Maybe the Chinese command didn't think they would even get onshore."

Murdock told the observer his mission.

"Where do you suggest we sit down and set up our stash?"

"Not more than two miles from the beach. There's a little stream comes out in that area. Just to the south of their half-track trail."

Right on schedule, the Sea Knight, a CH-46 with the two big contra-rotating, three-blade main rotors, dropped in as requested. It kicked up a storm of dust even from the black-topped parking lot.

The Third Platoon of SEAL Team Seven moved on board, loaded on the drag bags at 1935, and lifted off two minutes later. Murdock showed the pilot on his map where he wanted to drop in.

"A recon plane reported that there should be no ground fire from that area," Murdock said. The kid flying the chopper looked barely old enough to be out of high school. Actually he was a JG with probably five years of duty.

"Bring you in at that point in about eighteen minutes, sir," the JG said. He wiped sweat off his forehead. "Sir, does this mean I'm getting combat pay?"

"Good guess, JG. Just be sure you live long enough to spend it. If we ask for a resupply, you'll probably be coming in to the same spot we land today. Memorize where it is."

They swept up and over the Naval base, then the town of Aiea. Beyond that it was green. This part of Oahu seemed

to be made up of three elements, housetops, blacktopped
streets and parking lots, and lush green foliage. Below, the
landscape began to rise as they headed for the north end of
the Koolau mountain range. The trees, shrubs, and grasses
below were intoxicatingly green. Murdock knew that if he
were down there they would even smell green.

They had planned to come in from the north, following
Highway 83 from the village of Kahaluu south. When about
two miles from Kaneohe they would swing inland and watch
for the half-track trail through the brush and trees. By this
time it was almost dark. Dusk came and went in a moment,
and the pilots used night-vision goggles to check the landscape below.

It was a harder target than in daylight, but after five
minutes of slow moving along the highway, the chopper pilot
spotted the smashed-down grass and small trees. He picked
out a cleared area nearby with a stark stone chimney standing
by itself, all that was left of a previous dwelling.

"We go in about a minute," Murdock told the troops. They
were up in marching order, ready to run out of the bird as
soon as the rear ramp dropped to the ground.

A light turned from red to green over the ramp and it
lowered. The SEALs charged out, established a point twenty
yards from the Sea Knight, then went back for the drag bags
filled with ammo, explosives, and grenades.

Four minutes after landing, the Sea Knight took off and
went back the way it had come to the north so it might escape
detection by the Chinese troops on the ground.

The SEALs divided the bags and put two in each location.
One by the chimney, the others by a struggling koa tree,
about sixty feet tall.

Murdock had the men spread out, and used the Motorola
to talk to them. "Recon said the main force of the Chinese
is to the left, tucked up against the first rise of the mountains.

"We sit here for half an hour and see if they send out a
patrol to investigate. If not, we move toward them or any
elements they may have strung out around their main force.
Remember, there are two thousand guns out there. We will
not get in an all-out firefight with that kind of odds. We

punch and run, shoot and haul ass. No heroics, nobody taking on a company or any of that shit. Everyone read me?"

He got a chorus of chirps on his earpiece.

"Good. Someplace along here the mountains come down closer to the ocean. Sometimes they hang back. This is one of those spots. In twenty-five minutes more we take a hike a mile due west and then start working south to find the bad guys."

Lam, the platoon's head scout and tracker, came on the net.

"Cap, we may not have to do much searching. Somebody is coming our way and not trying to be quiet. I'd guess there are six or seven of them, not more than fifty yards dead ahead."

4

North Shore, Hawaii

"We take them out," Murdock said. "Silenced weapons only. As soon as we positively ID them. On my MP-5."

They waited. Now the other men in the platoon could hear the soldiers coming. They sounded as if they were on a Sunday afternoon picnic. Only a few Chinese words came through.

"Can't make out the words, but they sound Mandarin," Ching said. "Want me to yell at them when they get in our sights?"

"Won't hurt," Murdock said. "Spread out in a line. Don't shoot each other."

They moved apart, but each SEAL could still see the man next to him in the moonlight. Another minute, then shadows came out of the gloom. Six men walked forward, two by two. When they were twenty yards away, Ching sang out with a question. In Mandarin he asked: "What are you men doing here?"

The six stopped, whispered among themselves, then lifted their rifles. Four MP-5's on three-round bursts hammered at them. The chuffing sound of the suppressors kept the noise down as five Chinese slammed to the ground. One tried to run. Three rounds hit him in the back and jolted him into a tree. He fell lifeless to the woodsy floor.

"Ching, check for survivors," Murdock said on the radio. The quartermaster ran forward, touched the men on the ground. He stopped at the third one. The talk was soft and in Mandarin. A minute later Ching worked the other bodies, then returned.

"Talked to one of them. They were on a patrol to see if there were any American troops back this way. He said the officers figured this must be a trap since it was so easy to land on the bay and work inland. Then he died."

"Leave them where they fell," Murdock said. "We'll push ahead a little faster. Might find the camp tonight and get in some more good deeds before daylight."

For an hour they moved ahead. Lam was out in front testing the waters, stopping and listening every hundred yards. He heard nothing unusual. He soon recognized a night bird and its short, repetitive call. He knew there were wild boar on the island, but they would most surely prowl for food during the day.

Fifteen minutes into the second hour of marching, Lam called to Murdock. He and DeWitt moved up to where Lam lay in some brush. They were still on the half-track's smashed-down trail. Lam was at the side on a small hill looking ahead and to the left.

"Campfire," Lam said. "Too big to be a cooking fire. Maybe an outpost?"

Murdock put his binoculars on the spot and studied it. DeWitt did the same thing.

The fire was 150 yards away, Murdock estimated. He could see men moving around the area, crossing in front of the fire.

"Can't get a count on the bodies," DeWitt said. "Too much brush. Bet you a buck the fire is against orders. How can an outpost do its job if it advertises with a fire? Might as well hire a band to play the hula."

Murdock and Lam moved out to get the vitals on the group. They worked ahead silently, sometimes walking, sometimes worming their way through the tangle of brush and vines. Voices and soft laughter came from the camp ahead. When they were forty feet away the two SEALs stopped, and each moved to a better position with an open field of fire.

The men in the firelight would be night-blind to anything outside that light. A large red star showed prominently on each man's uniform. They all had automatic rifles, one a submachine gun. Murdock counted nine men. Murdock had his MP-5 up. He knew that Lam carried the Bull Pup. They were going to have to get ordnance to build suppressors for the 5.56mm barrel.

The Chinese men were eating. One had just washed out a pair of socks, and held them on long sticks to the fire to dry.

"We take them?" Lam whispered into the mike.

"Yes. Let me see how I can do with the silenced rounds. At the first outcry, use your 5.56."

"That's a Roger."

Murdock zeroed in on the first Chinese, who lay to one side, evidently sleeping or trying to. The first round caught him in the chest and he moaned and rolled over, but didn't move again.

The second Chinese sat three feet from the dead man eating from a mess kit. No rice rolls? Murdock wondered. The Chinese Army was going soft. His round hit the soldier in the chest and spilled him backward. Somebody yelled something at the man and there was laughter.

Before Murdock got off a third round, one of the men cried out in alarm and lifted his rifle.

"Do it," Murdock said, switching his MP-5 selector to three-round. He chattered off three rounds at two men side by side, then moved his aim as he heard Lam's Bull Pup chunking off two rounds at a time.

One man fired his weapon back at them. He must have seen the muzzle flash on the Bull Pup. Another small problem. Murdock emptied one magazine, jammed in another one, and shot at anything that moved.

"Hold," Murdock said. They stopped shooting.

One man lifted up and began crawling out of the firelight. Murdock sent three rounds into him, and then all was quiet.

"Check them?" Lam asked.

"No. We made too much noise. Let's get the platoon and

haul ass out of here. The firing will bring somebody. Just
hope we don't run into a reinforced company."

They jogged back to the platoon, veering off the half-track
trail but paralleling it heading west. Lam kept twenty yards
ahead as the platoon moved out. A full moon crawled out of
the east and bathed the whole scene in a half light that
seemed too strong for the moon. It made trees cast shadows,
and was the kind of scene that could make a man mistake a
shadow for an enemy or perhaps a friend.

They kept working ahead.

Murdock heard it this time just before Lam used the radio.

"Yeah, Cap. My guess another moving patrol. Chinese
love them. Used them all the time in Korea, my dad told me.
Keep roaming around, trying to stir up something. They
don't try to be quiet. Must have heard my firing back there.
Looking for us."

"Coming close to us?" Murdock asked.

"Depends. Right now they're moving due east, which
would put them maybe five hundred yards away. On the
other hand, they could change directions at the whim of the
patrol leader and head right into our gullet."

"All stop," Murdock said. "Hunker down in place and
we'll see where they're going. If we need to bug out in a
rush, we head northeast. No radio talk except Lam. Out."

It was more than three minutes before Murdock heard the
night insects resume what must be their usual chatter. He
thought he heard a cricket, but he wasn't sure if Hawaii had
crickets. He remembered that almost every land animal and
many of the birds, plants, and trees on the island now had
been brought there by settlers and pioneers. He remembered
that the Polynesians had brought with them fleas, lice, and
flies.

The radio earpiece spoke.

"Oh, yeah, they changed directions. Can't see them, but
by the noise I'd guess it's at least a platoon, maybe forty
men. My guess is that they are now on the half-track roadway
and moving toward us. How far are we away from that
route?"

"My guess is about fifty yards," Murdock said. "Not

enough. They could have scouts out on both sides. Estimate their distance?"

"Six or seven hundred yards," Lam said.

"Everyone, we move silently as death a hundred yards to our right. Keep in visual with the man on each side of you. Let's go."

It took five minutes to make the silent move. Murdock was pleased with the operation. No noise. Everyone kept in sight except Lam, who would take care of himself. They bellied down in the mulch and leaves and grass, and could hear the enemy troops passing to their left. When the last jangle of equipment died out, the speaker in Murdock's ear came on.

"Cap, they're past. I got a closer look. Must have been about fifty troops. They had what I guess were automatic rifles and an MG or two. Maybe a reinforced platoon. Figure they were out hunting us or whoever made the noise with the firefight. Somebody might have radioed in at that last hit we made."

"Roger that, Lam. Let's get our men up to you and we'll try to backtrack them right into their soup kitchen. Any idea how far these troops came to get here?"

"They weren't dragging, no one lagging back. My guess is that they were fairly fresh, say not more than two miles into their hike."

"We're moving, SEALs. Let's find Lam and go after the home base. Jaybird, I want you in sight of the last man as our rear guard. What we don't want is them yahoos storming up on our tail end without our knowing it."

They hiked along the mashed-down half-track trail for almost an hour before Lam called a halt. DeWitt, Master Chief Dobler, and Murdock went up to where the scout stood looking down a slight grade at a camp. There were dozens of fires. Most of them small, as if serving as cooking fires for squads.

"Two thousand down there?" Dobler asked. "That's fifty platoons of forty men each. That many guns can do a lot of damage."

"Anyone see a pattern to the fires?" Murdock asked. "Like maybe they are in lines or squares to show where the units are set up. Would they have two-man tents or be roughing it?"

"I've heard that the Chinese Army doesn't believe in tents, except for its officers," Dobler said. "My dad said he never saw a Chinese tent in the Korean War."

"What kind of targets do we have?" DeWitt asked.

"Those half-tracks would be good ones," Lam said.

"Maybe we could spot a tent used for a CP," Murdock said. "Two thousand men. That would rank at least a major as the commander. He'd have a deluxe tent somewhere."

They watched the site. A few fires went out. Some new ones sprang up. The new ones were larger. Murdock looked at his watch and punched the light. It was almost 2100.

"We'll move down until we hit an outpost, go around it, and try to follow the tracks to the rigs. If no luck, we send out two patrols to find and blow two of the half-tracks. If no luck getting to the rigs, we pull back to a thousand yards and shell the place with 20mm exploding. Say we dump a hundred rounds in and around those fires, we should have a good body count in the morning."

DeWitt nodded. "Yes, I agree. Let's get it moving. Lam will stay out front."

Third Platoon was on the move again. Excitement had begun to creep into the men's actions and faces. This would be a real test of their abilities to get a job done. The half-tracks were the key. They moved quicker now, knowing where they were going and what they would be doing.

It took them an hour more to come up on the Chinese camp. It was huge, spread out along a valley with a small stream. When they were a mile from the camp, Lam slowed the pace watching for the first guards.

The first guard post had a fire going and rifles stacked like they were in their barracks. Lam led them around the outpost and another half mile before they came to the next guard post. This one was well manned and alert. The SEALs went around the outpost without a sound and followed the half-track's trail.

A quarter of a mile ahead they came to a stop. Lam told Murdock what he found.

"A perimeter defensive line, Cap. Looks like a sentry

about every twenty yards. I can take out two of them and we'll walk right through."

"Meet me," Murdock said. He took Jaybird and worked forward until they found Lam. He pointed out the nearest two guards.

"Each of you take out one silently. Then give us a double click on the Motorola and we'll come through."

Jaybird and Lam melted into the moonlit moderate growth of trees and brush. Jaybird had seen his target. He was just below a good-sized koa tree. Jaybird would come up behind the man.

The next fifty feet, Jaybird slithered along on hands and knees and belly, his MP-5 tied over his back. He spotted the big tree, then the Chinese soldier slumped under it. He had not dug in. Good. Jaybird went twenty yards behind the sentry, then began working silently toward him.

Jaybird was the best silent mover in the platoon. Sometimes he scouted when Lam was wounded. He inched his way toward the sentry, who he now saw had slid down the koa tree and sat leaning against it, his rifle in his lap. Jaybird pulled the fighting knife from his left-ankle scabbard and lay silently watching the man. Sleeping or just quiet? He didn't know.

Jaybird moved ahead another six feet. The soldier sat against the koa tree three feet ahead and to the left. In one fluid movement, Jaybird came upright and held the knife in his right hand. The blade had been sharpened on both sides of the point for slashing either direction. He held it waist high, stepped around the tree, and swiped the blade across the Chinese soldier's throat.

The only sound was a soft gurgle by the soldier before his head fell forward blocking the spray of blood from his left carotid artery. Jaybird held him against the tree for fifteen seconds, until he was unconscious, fast approaching death.

Jaybird eased away, leaving the soldier leaning against the tree. Then he looked to the left to see if he could spot the next Chinese soldier in the defensive line. He couldn't. Which meant that the enemy soldier couldn't see him either. He clicked his radio twice and waited.

A minute or two later he heard two clicks in his earpiece.

Lam had finished his task. The platoon would be coming. He lifted up, pulled the MP-5 subgun around from his back so he could use it if he had to, and made sure the silencer was in place. He had taken only three steps toward the center of the cleared zone when he spotted a Chinese officer walking quickly toward him. Another thirty feet and the man would start looking for the rifleman on the perimeter duty.

Jaybird froze where he was. He had to do something and do it damn fast or the whole operation could be blown right out of the water.

5

Near Koolau Mountains
Oahu, Hawaii

Jaybird still held the bloody knife in his right hand. As long as he didn't move, the officer wouldn't see him for a few more seconds. He kept coming closer. Now he was twenty-five feet away, then twenty. Jaybird pulled up the knife holding the blade above the blood.

Three seconds later the Chinese lieutenant looked directly at Jaybird and started to yell. The knife was already on its way. It spun once and the blade jolted through the officer's tailored shirt, driving through his rib cage, and piercing all the way through his heart. He stumbled, tried to grab the pistol at his side. Before he could get to it, his knees buckled and he fell forward on his face in the dead leaves and grass of the forest floor. He never moved again.

Jaybird retrieved his knife, wiped it clean on the officer's shirt, and hurried toward the center of the cleared section. He saw movement ahead and whipped up his MP-5, then saw it was Horse Ronson. He ran to Ronson and fell in behind him.

Lam worked back to the head of the column, and kept them moving for fifteen minutes more before he stopped.

Murdock and DeWitt went forward and checked it out.

"Six campfires dead ahead," Lam said. "I don't see the damn half-track anywhere."

"Figures," Murdock said. "A blocking force. Smart. Makes me wonder who's running this invasion. Why are they letting this outfit just sit here? It could be going over the mountain or do an end run along the coast for Honolulu."

Murdock stared at the six campfires. "So, we split up. DeWitt, you take your squad and Lam and go around the left side. Circle around looking for those half-tracks. Alpha Squad will do the same thing on this side. If you don't find a target by midnight, pull back eight hundred yards and fire sixty of the exploding twenties at tents or any target you can find. The range finder doesn't care if it's dark or not."

"Where we going to hole up for the daytime?" Lam asked.

"How about up the slope here a ways," Murdock said. "Gives us a good lookout and we can see what the Chinese are doing."

"How will we find you?" Lam asked.

Just follow the delightful aroma of the MREs." Murdock chuckled. "We'll be working the half-track search from this side. If we don't find anything we'll shoot our sixty rounds at midnight. Otherwise, blow the half-track, then shoot the sixty rounds. If one squad finds a rig before midnight, the other will jump in with the twenties at the same time. Let's do it."

The squads split, giving the blocking force plenty of room, and went around it. Jaybird worked the point for Alpha Squad, and they soon found a faint track that Jaybird said probably was one half-track instead of four or six on the same trail.

The track through the brush and trees made hiking much easier than it would have been crashing brush. They'd be doing plenty of that before this mission was over.

Ten minutes ahead they came to another campsite. This was the main one. Over fifty fires were still burning. The SEALs were close enough to see figures around the fires. They saw only a few tents, the size that the U.S. Army used to use for officers.

Jaybird shook his head. "No sign of the half-track. It turned in here, but nothing shows."

The camp was pasted against the side of the sudden rise of the Koolau mountain range.

"Maybe some altitude will give us a better idea where to look," Murdock said. "That first little ridge up there maybe three hundred feet."

It took them a half hour to climb up the slope, which was steeper and tougher than it looked. Once up, Murdock told the men to flake out for a while. He found a lookout spot, dug out his binoculars, and studied the moonlit camp below him. It stretched to the right for a quarter of a mile, maybe more.

Some background sound kept nudging at his consciousness. He listened closer and then had it. A small gas-powered generator motor. That would be for the major and his staff. But Murdock had no idea where it was. There were no electric lights burning anywhere that he could see.

Murdock made a note to get the generator when they could find it, then looked at the rest of the situation.

He tried the radio. DeWitt came in on the second try.

"Barely hear you, Cap. We've got a line on two of the half-tracks. One is almost on the edge of the camp, the other one fifty yards inside past about a hundred sleeping men."

"Do the first one with C-5 if you can, and target the second one with your twenties," Murdock said. "What's your timing?"

"We're set up now. I'd say Lam and Train Kahi will go in about fifteen minutes. Your twenties into the camp will help us on our getaway."

"Good, circle to the south. We're about a third of the way along the camp and on a cliff three hundred feet over the valley floor. When you get closer we'll give you some directions."

"That's a Roger. We're in motion here."

"Good luck."

Murdock spent the next ten minutes placing his weapons. Ronson still had his H & K 21-E machine gun. Bill Bradford had the sniper rifle. The rest of the squad had the twenties, and they all would fire into the camp as soon as they heard the first blast from Bravo Squad.

"As soon as we fire, we'll bug out and move at least two hundred yards up the ridge, so if they have any large counter-battery, it won't touch us," Murdock said.

A few minutes later the silence of the Hawaiian night burst open with a brilliant flash followed by a slow-moving crack of a dozen thunderclouds as the C-5 went off in the Chinese camp below.

"Let's do it," Murdock said into his radio mike. The machine gun chattered first. His shots fell short, and he raised his sights and kept firing five-round bursts. The range finder laser beams had done their work, and the first few rounds hit squarely in the middle of the rash of campfires below.

The airbursts tore into anything they could find, from sleeping bodies to supplies, weapons, and food. A large fire started that Jaybird said looked like a tent to him. Each of the five weapons fired twelve rounds. Then the sniper rifle and the MG closed down as well, and the men moved to the right more toward the center of the long thin camp. They found a new ledge off the ridge that would serve them well, and settled down.

They had heard firing from across the way, and it continued a short time after their own rounds had been used.

Murdock tried the Motorola again.

"Ed, you still there?"

"Fit and hearty and moving. Lam got the half-track, blew it to hell, and got out all right. We've taken a little return fire, but not much. So far no casualties."

"Bug out around the north end of the camp and get up against the hills. We'll get you into home port here somehow. Let us know if you hear or feel any kind of pursuit."

"Roger that. We're jogging. Out."

They waited. Half the fires in the camp below went out. Murdock figured that within ten minutes the rest of the fires would be snuffed and the camp would revert to just another shadow in the green Hawaiian hills.

He pulled Ron Holt up with the SATCOM, and they tried to remember what frequency the carrier *Jefferson* used. Holt tried three, and on the third one received a response.

The conversations were all encrypted and spat out, then turned back into the spoken word on the other end through the right encrypter machine.

"*Jefferson,* this is Murdock. Who am I speaking with?"

"Commander Hollingsworth. We've been told to watch for your signal. A party named Stroh has urgent need to contact you. He said if you call to ask you to get on TAC fourteen at Pearl. He said any time day or night. Any problems we can help you with?"

"Not at the moment. Thought I might have a target for you, but it's dark down there now. We'll call Stroh. Keep our gear safe. We'll be back to the ship eventually. Murdock out."

"TAC Fourteen? We don't have a Fourteen," Holt said.

"Is it on a dial?"

"Yeah."

"Dial in fourteen and see what happens."

"Okay, yeah, I did. The number is holding. I'll give it a try."

Murdock contacted Stroh on the third call.

"Murdock, glad I caught up with you. You're operational there now, I know, but a few dozen other items have come up. How is it going?"

The CIA man received a quick summary of activities from the SEAL. "Tomorrow morning we'll see what kind of damage we did and decide what else to do," Murdock said. "On the other hand, the Chinese may put out two hundred troops on a destroy mission and we'll be running for our lives. You at Pearl?"

"Yes, and with some news."

"Hold the news. Tell our liaison there that we may want that red-signature chopper back here for a pickup at any time. I want that bird on ten-minute call for us and nobody else."

"We can do that. Admiral Bennington is pleased with your work on the commo shack. I'll talk to Commander Johnson and keep the bird ready for you.

"Next, they found out an hour ago that there has been an invasion of Kauai. The admiral is putting together a task force to head out there. Recon planes estimate the forces there at something like fifteen hundred. Our other recon shows the Chinese stalled against the mountains inland from Kaneohe. Why the hell did they come onshore there and drive into the mountains?"

"Could have been a mistake. Probably their target was Kauai with the rest of the troops. I'd suggest you tell the admiral we think an air strike on these men would be advisable. Can't hurt any civilians. There aren't any out here now if there were in the first place. Some air strikes would keep them occupied and cut down the number you'll have to mop up with the Marines sooner or later."

"I'll tell him you suggest the air strike. It could come from the *Jefferson.* She's steaming closer to shore now off Maui. You have your Mugger along so you can give them precise coordinates?"

"Affirmative. What else?"

"They may want your guys to check the underwater approaches to Kauai. I know, I know. How much could the Chinese construct in twenty-four hours? Then there has been a concern about a pair of missing admirals who were vacationing on Maui with their families."

"Do you know how the Chinese slipped up on Hawaii even better than the Japs did fifty years ago?"

"It was a friendship tour of a Chinese strike force. Labeled as a goodwill gesture for all our differences in the past. State loved the idea. My boss hated it. He said just one miscue and the whole of Hawaii could go up in smoke. As I guess it is. So what should I tell the admiral?"

"About what? We're not done here yet. In the morning we'll take a look and see what's happening. A sunup missile and straffing attack would be good, before they have a chance to disperse."

"I'll tell the admiral."

"Tonight."

"It's a little after midnight, Murdock."

"Good, give him something to do. Tonight."

Lam brought Bravo Squad into the area and three radio directions later, the group hiked up to the rest of the platoon.

They had out two guards that night. Murdock took the first two-hour shift until 0200. He woke up Ronson and told him to get Ching up at 0400.

Murdock listened during his watch, but he didn't hear the Chinese moving out of their camp. It would be a complicated operation. Where could they move to?

Murdock was up with the sun. He hoped to see at least ten Navy fighters jolting across the Chinese camp below. Then he realized that he hadn't given Stroh the coordinates. No matter, the camp wouldn't be hard to find.

He went out on the edge of the ridge and looked down at the Chinese camp. He saw the burned-out tent first. Could have been a mess tent or for officers. Smoke came from what he guessed was the kitchen. With his field glasses he could spot the individual clusters of men. They must be in company groups. Fifty platoons of forty men each.

For a moment Murdock felt cold sweat on his neck. What if all two thousand of them turned and stormed up the hill on assault fire? He and his men wouldn't have a chance. Below him, he saw the camp slowly come to life. He wasn't sure how they cooked, but there was no central mess. Maybe each company had a cook. Just as he was about to wake up the rest of the platoon, two F-18's came slamming over the valley no more than twenty feet off the tops of the greenery. They made one sweep across the Chinese camp, then another the other way.

A chopper lifted up from behind some trees and a bullhorn blared out a message in Mandarin. Ching ran up beside Murdock and translated.

"Men of China. You have been led on a suicide mission. You are unsupported. Last night you took deadly fire. The warplanes that just departed will be back unless you fly a white flag and surrender at once. If you need medical help, a medical unit will be flown in within the hour to treat your wounded. Signify your acceptance of the surrender with white flags. Do it now."

To Murdock's surprise white flags were waved in every section of the small valley.

The chopper came closer to the edge of the camp.

"Very well. Now put your weapons in stacks in each of your units. Lay them down, unloaded, and form up in a column of fours."

As the Chinese did as instructed, four Sea Knight helicopters lifted from below some trees and swept into the camp. They landed in four spots well apart from each other, and twenty-five Marines in full combat gear poured out of each one.

The Marines settled the Chinese down in their formations. They inspected each man, then when satisfied, marched the Chinese out of the area in groups of two hundred.

The chopper with the bullhorn had been quiet while the Marines completed the surrender. Then the sound came on again.

"Commander Murdock. If you and your men are in the area, give us a green flare."

"Got it," Jaybird said, and fired a flare from his Colt Commando carbine.

"Good, Commander. You're wanted back at Pearl. If you and your men can work down to the camp here, we'll get you outbound on the first chopper. There is some urgency. It's a red-signed order."

"Let's move it," Murdock said into the Motorola. "We wouldn't want to keep Admiral Bennington waiting, now would we?"

They hiked down the hill and watched the last of the Chinese move out with their Marine escorts. The chopper with the bullhorn had landed, and now a Marine captain came over to meet Murdock.

"Commander, looks like your attack last night changed some minds down here. The hospital chopper is on the way. We have twenty-seven dead and over a hundred wounded. The minor wounds are marching out. There are still thirty that need attention here."

"Murdock grinned. "Captain, we do our best. Which chopper is ours? We have to make a stop at a burned-out house down the valley a ways. Have some goods and ammo to pick up from our stash."

They landed at Pearl about an hour later and Murdock, DeWitt, and Senior Chief Dobler were driven to the admiral's headquarters. The admiral looked like he hadn't slept all night. He hadn't.

"Is it Kauai, Admiral?" Murdock asked.

"No, no. The aircraft carrier *Jefferson* took care of that late last night and early this morning. No, we have a much tougher problem. Sit down, gentlemen. This is going to take some time, and some planning.

"It's those two admirals you've heard about. A highly radical nationalistic cell from one of the Chinese destroyers went onshore at Maui two days ago and kidnapped the admirals and their whole families. They are demanding the release of all captives and reparations for Chinese killed and ships sunk or damaged. If we don't agree to their demands, they will send us the head of one of the members of the admirals' families every four hours, starting with the youngest and working up. We already have the head of a little girl of five or six. I don't want to see another one. The deadline for hearing from us is twelve hundred hours.

"Commander, you have to take your men in and kill those sonsofbitches and rescue the admirals and their families before anyone else is murdered."

6

Pearl Harbor, Hawaii

Lieutenant Commander Blake Murdock watched the admiral closely, his mind already whirling with questions he was sure the Navy's head man in the Pacific wouldn't have answers for.

"What do we have to work with, Admiral?"

"Just two radio transmissions today and three phone calls yesterday. All were taped and we have copies of them for you. We know nothing about this splinter group of Chinese. We think they came from a Chinese destroyer and went ashore in a small boat. There could be only three or four or up to two dozen. We're flying blind here. All we have is a radio frequency, their call sign, and their say-so that they are on Maui. We know that's where our two men were vacationing with their families this week."

"You have radio triangulation equipment on-base?"

"I believe so. The chief will check at once."

A non-com left the room.

"We'll need that equipment and an open radio channel with you so you can contact the group frequently to help us find a location on them. There's a chance their transmitter isn't where the hostages are being held."

"Transport, Commander?"

"Two Sea Knights, to stay at the Maui airport at our disposal. Also, we'll need to pick up all of our gear here including the EAR weapons. My men need a change of uniforms, a good meal, and we'll be ready to go."

"Sleep, Commander?"

"We'll do that on the way to Maui."

Four more officers sat around the big table in the admiral's planning room.

"What about the radio?" Murdock asked. "We'll be using the SATCOM."

The admiral looked at one of the other officers, who spoke at once. "I can set up your transceiver to a clear channel. Take about five minutes. I'll go back to your quarters with you."

"Any restrictions on firing, sir?" Murdock asked.

"None. Remember, this is a civilian situation. Use your non-lethal when civilians or the hostages are involved. As for the Chinese, we want at least two of them alive to put on trial for the murder of little Patty."

"Right, sir. We better get moving. We'll work with Commander Johnson again for any equipment or resupply?"

"Correct."

Murdock, DeWitt, and Dobler all stood, did about-faces, and walked out of the room. Lieutenant Commander Johnson stood outside waiting for them.

"We have two combat-equipped Sea Knights standing by at the runway at Hickam. I've had all of your gear brought together at the equipment room at your quarters."

As they talked, the officer who'd spoken inside came out. He held out his hand.

"Commander Wilson. I'll recalibrate your SATCOM and make some radio checks for you. Oh, thanks for getting our commo center back in operation. We only found one bullet hole in a piece of equipment, and that we replaced quickly."

"Our job, Commander," Murdock said.

A Humvee pulled up, and Johnson motioned the men into it.

Two hours later, fed, with fresh cammies and restocked ammo pouches and equipment, the Third Platoon stepped out

of the Sea Knight chopper at the civilian airport near Kahului, Maui. Three white Ford extended vans met them on
the tarmac, and they drove away. A short time later, they
stopped on a vacant stretch of land overlooking the Pacific
Ocean.

A specialist had come along to set up the triangulation
equipment. He placed one receiver on the point of land, then
took the other two ten miles away north and south and set
them up. By 1600 they were ready.

Triangulation is a simple procedure whereby the three radio receivers will pick up a signal, each taking an accurate
compass reading on it. The three directions are plotted automatically on a computer and where the three cross, that
should be the place where the radio transmitter was operating. It does not always work. Sometimes there is distortion.
Sometimes the transmitter is in a car or van and can be moving during transmission, and then keep on going afterward
and be in an entirely new area.

This one had to work, Murdock told himself. They had
nothing else.

Ron Holt made a radio check with CINCPAC and told
them the trap was set. Ron changed his settings to pick up
the CINCPAC frequency they would use to contact the kid-
nappers.

"We wait," Murdock said.

Five minutes later the transmission went out. CINCPAC
had a question about the amount of payback money for Chinese Naval ships sunk during the operation.

A reply came from the Chinese, but it was in a burst such
as would come from a SATCOM-type radio. Lieutenant
Hamlin watched the readout on his computer.

"A burst. Without a computer and enhancement, we
wouldn't have a prayer. With it we can get a shot at it." The
reports came in from the other listening posts by radio signal,
and they were plotted on the computer and that overlaid on
a map of the area, which had been preprogrammed into the
computer.

Lieutenant Hamlin grinned. "Yes, we have a hit. It's in a
residential section of the small town of Keanae down the

coast about twelve miles. I've got it about fifty feet south of an intersection there. We might get lucky."

Two minutes later the van driver knew the location, and led the way with two of the vans loaded with SEALs. The lieutenant would try for another cross shot of any more transmissions.

They blasted down the coastal Highway 360 far above the speed limit, but they saw no traffic cops. It took them only ten minutes to hit the small town, then another five to find the right street. They parked a block away from the intersection, and saw a sprawling frame house halfway up the block. There were no other houses nearby.

"Could be it," Murdock told the troops. They had unloaded, but stayed behind the vans.

"DeWitt, take your squad through the block here and see how close you can get to the back door. Don't show yourself. We'll work the front from across the street." Bravo Squad moved out with Guns Franklin on the point.

Murdock looked at the two drivers. Both were young, clean-cut, and wore civilian clothes.

"Hey, drivers. You've just been promoted. You're both Mormons on a mission. All you have to do is walk down the street, go up to that house, and knock on the door. See if you can raise anyone. My bet is that nobody will answer. Then walk on toward the next house way up the block."

One of the drivers frowned. The other poked him in the shoulder. "Hey, you wanted in on some action. This is as close as we'll get. Let's do it."

They talked together for a minute, then both shrugged and took the walk.

The two white vans were out of sight of the house. Murdock and three of his men bellied through the grass up to a point where they could see the house and watch the drivers. Murdock wished that he could be with the drivers.

The two men walked a little self-consciously up the sidewalk to the house. It was in bad repair, but looked occupied. One of them knocked on the front door.

Nothing happened.

They waited and then the same man knocked again. They heard somebody yell from inside. A third knock brought a sudden jerking open of the door and a Chinese man with rumpled hair and in his twenties.

"Sleeping, for God's sakes," he said. "Can't you let a guy get some sleep? I work nights."

"Sorry, we're from the Church of Jesus Christ of Latter-day Saints and wondered if you have a home church."

"What the fuck are you saying? A church? Get the hell off my property. Come on, get off."

Just after the man said it, a radio spoke in another room in the house with the smooth voice of the CINCPAC operator.

The driver shrugged. "Hey, we're just trying to save your soul."

The Chinese man slammed the door hard in their faces. They lifted their brows and walked away, but instead of going the long way, they cut back toward where their vans were parked.

Murdock watched them with a frown. He had seen the door open and the short talk. Maybe they'd heard something that would help. He and the others wormed back out of sight, then ran to the vans.

Harley, the more talkative of the two drivers, gave Murdock a play-by-play account of the meet.

"You say you heard a radio voice that you swear was the same one you heard on our radio from CINCPAC?"

"Swear to God, the same voice."

Murdock looked at his watch. It was almost 1700. Be dark in two hours.

"We've got to move in before dark." He knew the other squad had heard his talk with Harley the driver.

"DeWitt, you copied that?"

"That's a Roger. We're about forty yards from the back door. No fences. Two rear windows have heavy drapes on them. Inside, they are blind to us unless they move the drapes."

"On my signal move up quietly, cover the rear windows and door." Murdock looked around. They were fifty yards from the house. Windows on the side were not draped.

"Windows in the front of the house, Harley. Were they covered or open?"

"Blinds drawn. That old kind that you pull down and roll up. Closed off tight."

"Lieutenant, any more transmissions from the house?"

The specialist looked up from his laptop computer. "One more that plotted about twenty feet from the first one."

"Alpha Squad, we're moving in. We have to get in front of the place first. Give us two minutes, DeWitt. Then we'll signal and both walk up to the place together."

It worked that way. Murdock heard nothing from inside the house. At the front door Bill Bradford lifted his size-thirteen boot and blasted the door open. It swung inside and Murdock was first through the open door, slanting right. Jaybird dove to the left.

"Clear," both SEALs said at the same time. They heard excited voices from another room. Murdock and Jaybird were on their feet looking through a connecting door.

They heard a crash that might have been the back door being kicked open. A handgun barked in one of the rooms. That sound was followed by a three-round burst from a submachine gun, and then another burst.

When the sound tapered off, the earpieces spoke.

"We have two prisoners and one KIA," Ed DeWitt said. "Are you inside, Alpha?"

"Inside and holding front two rooms. Move toward us carefully."

Just then a man stormed through the open door from the second room. Jaybird, standing near the door, heard him coming and clubbed him with the stock of his Bull Pup, swinging it like a baseball bat. The Chinese man went down in a heap of arms and legs. Jaybird promptly cuffed him with riot plastic strips.

Ed DeWitt peered through the door. "Clear up to here," he said.

"On the net. Everyone search this place. We need an address, a phone number, photos, anything that would tell us where the hostages might be. Move it."

They looked for half an hour, tearing the place apart. It had been unused for a long time and the recent occupants hadn't even messed up a coat of dust. It wasn't hard to see what had been moved and where such information might be.

"Not a fucking thing," Jaybird said. "We've been over this place with our fine-tooth a dozen times. No number on a scrap of paper. No note on a sleeping bag. Nothing."

"How many live ones do we have?" Murdock asked.

"Three and one KIA," DeWitt said.

"Separate them and interrogate," Murdock said. "Try in English, then let Ching go with his Mandarin."

As he said it they all heard a car driving up to the front door and stopping. The four men split to different sides of the front room and watched the door, which still hung open, with one hinge out of place.

"Hello, anyone home?" a voice asked from outside.

Jaybird jumped in front of the open door, his Bull Pup covering the visitor.

The young man wore a baseball cap and carried an "instant hot" pizza box.

"Hey, at least it's a different weapon this time. You owe me twelve dollars and forty-two cents."

Ten minutes later they finished talking with the delivery man. He knew nothing about the people in the house. Twice he had brought them pizza and cola. The first call was yesterday afternoon.

"That's twelve dollars and . . ."

Murdock waved him quiet. "We don't have any money. Hey, try the drivers of those two white vans a half block over. They look hungry."

The SEALs went back to the questioning. One of the men spoke English. He quickly admitted he was a U.S. citizen and had been sucked into this conspiracy. He did what they told him to do. He didn't even know that some Chinese had invaded two of the islands.

"No one has come to this house except the pizza guy," the Hawaiian-Chinese man said.

Murdock believed him.

The questioning with the Mandarin-talkers went slower. There was a minor language problem, but they could communicate. Ching quickly found the one in charge of the radio location. He refused even to give his name.

Ching hit him in the face with his big fist and knocked the tied man off the chair. He was put back on the chair and the same question asked. Ching hit him again, this time in his unprotected gut. The man turned pale. Then his eyes went wide and he vomited on the floor.

On a small radio that had been left precisely where it had been when they came in, Mandarin words were now heard. Ching picked up the transceiver and answered.

"Yes, we are here. There has been no report from the Americans."

"Where is Sung?"

"Taking a piss. Need any of us over there?"

"No. We're secure here. The plane is ready if we need it. Ask Chang if he thinks another body would infuriate the Americans and be counterproductive."

"Will do."

Ching put his hand over the microphone, and a moment later spoke into it. "Chang said the one kill should be enough. Any more would, as you say, be counterproductive."

"Keep in touch."

"We'll do that."

The set went silent.

Murdock had listened from the doorway. Ching translated the exchange. Then Murdock called for Holt, who had the radio out and was folding out the antenna as he ran into the room.

"CINCPAC, now."

Holt made the moves and gave Murdock the handset. He made one call and had a quick answer.

"CINCPAC, how many private landing strips on Maui big enough for a good-sized plane that are near or on the grounds of a large house or mansion?"

"One of my men is contacting the FAA here. We'll know in a few minutes. What progress?"

Murdock told the officer of their find and the dead end. "When we get a good lead, we'll let you know. Murdock out."

Holt moved the SATCOM to one side, leaving the antenna tuned on the satellite and the switches on to receive. He went to the table and stared at the radio the Chinese used.

"Look at that little thing," he said. "It isn't even Chinese. It's a low-priced walkie-talkie." He looked at the printed material on the sides and back and chuckled. "Damn, only a half-watt output. That means this shit-face radio can transmit not more than three or four miles at the most."

"Oh, yeah," Murdock yelped. "Holt, you wonderful motherfucker, don't you ever die. Get on the horn and ask CINCPAC for any airfields within four miles of this spot. Do it now. Let's suit up and get out of here. Didn't I see a cell phone in that van? Let's move. Leave these assholes here tied up. We'll phone the local cops to come pick them up and hold for the military."

They rushed back to the van, and Holt kept the SATCOM set up with the antenna positioned. It beeped again to confirm it was aligned right. He made the new transmission about a local airfield, and had back a quick response.

"A local tells us there is an airfield at an old Dole mansion about three miles out of town inland. The road is Dole Road. The place is huge with airfield, swimming pools, polo field, the works. Owned by a rich Chinese now, as I understand it from the local officer from that area."

"Could be the site of the hostages. We're moving. Be dark in another hour, just about right. SEALs work best in the dark. Out."

The vans were moving. The drivers knew the road and the mansion.

"Hell of a big place," Harley said. He'd been past it. As he remembered, it had a private road with a gate that was usually locked.

They drove up to the gate just after dusk with the patented flaming Hawaiian sunset behind them. The gate had two padlocks on it.

"Oh, yes, Mother," Miguel Fernandez said. "This one has an electrical keeper. If the gate is opened and the circuit is broken, it rings an alarm somewhere and we get company fast."

Murdock stared at the gate locks. The padlocks would come open with little trouble. The electric circuit was another matter. How in hell did they open the gate to get the vans through and not break the connection?

7

Countryside
Maui, Hawaii

Tran "Train" Khai went to the fence and looked at the locks and the electrical connection.

"No big problem, Commander. We still have that roll of commo wire?"

"Yeah, in back somewhere," Jaybird said.

"We cut off the locks, then do a splice on one end of the electrical and tie it in on the other end with the twenty feet of commo wire. The circuit won't be broken when we cut the present wiring, open the gate, and drive through holding the commo wire high overhead of the vans."

"Do it," Murdock said. "We'll take along two EARs this time. I want the two snipers to use them. Leave your regular weapon in the truck."

Horse Ronson brought up the long-handled bolt cutters, and took out the two padlocks in two quick snips. Train had the ends of forty feet of commo wire tied in with the ends of the electric cord. Then he cut the short electrical circuit and they pushed the gates open. The vans slipped under the commo wire, and they moved ahead down the lane.

Lam had come back from a quick recon.

"Cap, there are lights about a mile ahead. Looks like we're in the middle of a huge pineapple plantation. There are one hell of a lot of lights. Outside security, it looks like."

The vans had been driving with lights out. They kept moving until they could see the mansion's lights around a corner. Murdock called a halt and checked the area through his field glasses.

"It's a mansion, all right. Looks like they have put in a lot of security recently. A new chain-link fence for sure."

DeWitt came up from the second van. "Surprised they don't have a guard post out here on the road," DeWitt said.

"Let's dismount and form up," Murdock said to the mike. "Alpha Squad move out of the van." Murdock looked at the driver. "Can you handle a firearm?"

"Yes, sir."

Murdock gave him an automatic pistol. "Don't let anyone surprise you, and protect this rig and the gear inside. We'll be back."

"When?" the driver asked.

"Depends. A few hours, a few days. Take care."

They moved toward the lights in patrol formation. It was the same formation they had used since BUD/S training in Coronado, a large diamond for quick deployment and total security all the way around.

Three hundred yards from the wire, Lam stopped and gave the down signal, and they all went to ground. Lam came back to Murdock and shook his head.

"Looks damn secure, Cap. There is one gate in this side section of the chain link. Can't tell from here, but the fence looks like it could be electrified."

"What are they doing in there?" DeWitt asked. He had come up beside the other two.

"Waiting for their money and guarantees," Murdock said. "I can't see how this was part of the overall invasion plans. This one had lots of preplanning and cooperation with the owner of the mansion."

"So how do we get into this place?" Lam asked.

"Get Jaybird and Dobler up here," Murdock told Lam. "This one is going to take some planning work."

* * *

Inside the mansion at the pineapple plantation, Sing paced the elaborate living room. It was filled with hand-carved koa wood furniture, had silk prints on the walls, and fine carpets covering hardwood floors.

Sing wore the dress-blue uniform of a Chinese Naval commander. His lower jaw now slanted out as he stared at the monitors set up on one wall across from the large fireplace.

"Where is the night-vision camera? We are blind here without it. An enemy could now be slipping up on us and we would never know it until they killed us."

An older Chinese man dressed in a simple robe of pure silk sat in a recliner, puffing contentedly on a marijuana cigarette.

"Young man. Did I tell you that these marijuana joints, as you call them, do little for me? There is a pleasant feeling, but that's all. There is not the jolt of joy and wonder that the waterpipe can bring." He was in his seventies. He frowned and stared at his wife's second cousin from Beijing.

"You were asking about night vision. You have out your security guards. Surely that will be enough. There is little chance that the authorities will know you are on Maui, let alone find this retreat."

"Honored Grandfather. I have not stayed alive this long in the Chinese Navy by working on a 'little chance' basis. I deal in absolutes. I won this assignment over a dozen other highly qualified candidates. If all else fails in this invasion attempt, this part of the plan must succeed. It is vital to the prestige and face of China."

"From what you've told me, grandson, this is a fool's errand carried out by idiots. What were your commanders thinking? Strike at the center of power of the U.S. Navy at Pearl Harbor? Come with one aircraft carrier and only thirty planes and poorly trained pilots to compete with the U.S. Navy's crack carrier pilots? Someone is truly out of his head. Already I hear reports of one invasion force pasted against the mountains near Kaneohe on Oahu. What a stupid place to invade."

Sing surged across the space between himself and the older man and lifted his hand to slap his grandfather, but at the last moment stopped.

A siren went off. Sing turned and ran out of the room to a smaller one where more electronics and controls were set up. The old Chinese man walked over and looked into the room.

"Couldn't find us, could they?" said the lieutenant. "My sensors show a force of at least sixteen men is now approaching the north side of the plantation working through a pineapple field. Traitor! How did you tell the Navy where we were? How did you do it, old man? You have twenty seconds to tell me before I shoot you in the head."

Jiang Peng smiled. He had long ago confronted death and it held no terror for him. The young countryman was not a danger.

"Young man, I do not fear death. I am not afraid of you. The Americans are close, so now you have much work to do to move your captives to the secret places you have prepared. Don't worry about me. I did not notify the authorities. Why should I?

"Now, what defenses do you have and how much time to get done what you need to do?"

Sing hesitated. He shrugged and pushed the pistol back in his belt. Then he nodded.

"Yes, the men I have in front can handle a lot of problems. At best they have traced our radio signals. I thought I had the best technology. Somehow they defeated it. So I go from there.

"First the secret place. Yes." He turned and hurried through the room to a long attachment that had once been a part of an early pineapple operation. He kept going to another shed, then into a hidden door that led to an underground area. It had been constructed some years back for a special mushroom-growing operation that never proved out. Now Sing had turned it into a hiding place for the captives.

He checked with the three guards on the walled-off section. The gate was strong and triple-locked. The guards had submachine guns and plenty of magazines. He nodded at them and hurried back to the previous section. Now he pushed a switch on the wall, and a jagged section lifted from the side and pushed in front of the walled-off section. It had dirt and litter and broken equipment in front of it.

Yes. The deception was complete. No one could suspect there was any structure beyond this point. He hurried back to the house and checked with the guards by radio. He had guards posted fifty yards from the mansion on all sides. Eight men lay in wait for any possible attack.

He had left the destroyer with fifty men in three small boats. He'd lost three of the men in the surf landing in the night. Now there were four men lost at the main radio transmitter.

At least the old man had shown him about the secret underground area and the fake wall. Jiang had had it built early on when he was doing a bit of smuggling. Four times the authorities had searched his lands and buildings, but had found none of the hidden goods.

Back in the mansion Sing checked the monitors. He had intrusion alarms set off in one section. The intrusion alarms were the vibration type that gave the intruder no warning that he had been spotted. How many of them? Where would they attack? Would it be with rifle fire or machine guns? His men could stand off a good bit of firepower.

Quickly he called half his defense forces to the side of the building where the sensors had gone off. Then he scowled at the monitor displays. He could see sensors going off all around one side of the place. It was as if hundreds of men were moving in at every angle to the mansion. Impossible. Rabbits? Maybe. He hurried to the side door away from the main thrust of the intruders and checked his pickup. It was gassed and ready. It was a two-year-old four-wheel-drive rig that could move out of the area quickly and into the back country with a select group of protectors. That would be a last resort, and he was sure he could stand off the squad of men he figured were out there. The other sensors? Now he understood it. There could be one or two men making a recon jogging around the mansion. That would set off the other sensors. Yes.

He went back to the north section, where the threat was. He had five men there with submachine guns. Sing took the night-vision glasses from his top man and studied the area in front. At first he couldn't see anything move. Then he did. It looked to be no more than a squad or two of men moving

here. He invaded me. I am the victim here of a foreign attack. I'll want compensation from the Chinese government."

"You'll have to get in a long line for that one. If you don't mind, my men and I will check out the rest of your buildings."

"Please. That young Chinese sailor was not at all the kind of person I wish to have in my home. Thank you for driving him away."

"Oh, I don't think that he's too far away. We'll find him. Enjoy your smoke."

Murdock waved the rest of his SEALs through into more rooms. They found six bedrooms, three baths, two more large assembly rooms, and then at the back, a long refinished area that might have been part of the packing operation years ago. Now it was set up more like a playroom, with pool tables, Ping Pong, shuffleboard, and half a dozen dart boards.

They went through it quickly and came to the current packing sheds. Murdock met DeWitt coming back the other way.

"Nobody home, Cap. We've checked out the rest of the packing sheds. Found a barracks-like place with thirty sleeping bags in it and a whole shit-pot full of U.S. MREs. The foreign troops are getting desperate."

"So he had thirty men here. We captured five up front. Where are the rest of them?"

"I checked with Lam with his rear guard at the back," DeWitt said. "He said that no one had bugged out the back door. They're still here somewhere."

"Nooks and crannies wouldn't do it. There has to be a secret room or a tunnel out of here somewhere. Let's take this mansion apart until we find it. Won't do any good to talk to the old Chinese guy who owns the place. He's yelling for a payback for the damage to his windows."

They went through the house again, and then a third time. After they had checked the house the first time with no escape out the back, Lam and his two men came in to help on the search. They turned on every switch they could find until the house blazed with light.

Still they found nothing.

Murdock noticed it first. There had been a four-by-four

Ford pickup truck, a 350, the big one, parked alongside one of the packing sheds the first two times through. This time the pickup was gone.

Lam checked the tracks in the area. "Looks like eight or ten men pushed the rig down the slight slope all the way to the little road over there between the pineapples. Then they could start the engine and not be heard."

"So, we've got two problems," Murdock said. "We need to find the two fucking admirals and their families, but we can't let the kidnapper get away in his pickup." He stared into the night. "Guns Franklin," he said on the radio. "Leave your combat vest and weapon here and run back to the vans, and have them both drive up here as damn fast as you and they can get here. Go, now."

"Roger, Cap. I'm out-a-here."

"Hey, JG, I think I've found something," the radio chirped. "Down at the end of the packing shed. It looks like a door that leads down into some kind of underground tunnel or room or something."

"Hold right there," Murdock said. "We're coming down there to take a look."

8

Pineapple plantation
Maui, Hawaii

Murdock stared at what appeared to be a broken wall of some
sort that had been pushed back against the end of the packing
shed. There was a slight decline in the floor as it slanted
down some two feet. Lam hurried and held up his hand,
keeping the others back while he searched the dirt floor. He
went to his hands and knees and then stood grinning.

"Cap, there's been a lot of foot traffic back and forth
across this strip of dirt. I can make out more than a dozen
tracks, and several of them are women and children's shoes.
A lot more here than meets the eye."

"Where is this door?" Murdock asked.

Ostercamp looked up and shrugged. "Well, sir, it wasn't
exactly a door, but it looked like it could be. Over here."

He moved to a section of the broken wall that closed off
the end of the packing shed. He pushed on one section. "This
part looks loose, like it could move." Ostercamp kicked the
wall with the flat of his boot and it shook, then edged upward
six inches.

"Yes, it does move," Murdock said. "Kick that sucker
again."

Ostercamp jumped up and slammed both boots against the wall, then dropped to the ground. The wall section moved a few inches, then stopped for a moment before it lifted and swung back six feet to reveal a door in another wall.

"Easy and stand back," Murdock said. He moved up to the door and looked at the knob. The usual. He reached down and patted the metal knob. No electrical reaction. He turned the knob and pushed open the door with the muzzle of his Bull Pup. The door opened on oiled hinges. Inside they saw a set of steps leading down, and then a short tunnel to another door.

Murdock and the men hurried down the steps. Ed DeWitt tried the door. It was locked. He looked at Murdock, who nodded.

DeWitt used his Bull Pup and slammed two rounds into the door just in front of the doorknob where the lock would be. The sound of the shots in the enclosed tunnel blasted against the men's ears like a howitzer going off. The door shuddered a moment, then swung open inward.

Just inside the door they found two teenage boys, each armed with a three-foot-long wooden club. One of the boys dropped the club and ran forward.

"You guys Navy SEALs?" he asked.

"Yes," Murdock said. "I'd guess you're one of the hostages the Chinese have been holding. Are the two admirals here?"

"No, sir," the other boy said. "Half hour ago the Chinese commander came back, took my dad and Jake's dad, and hustled them out of here and locked the door. We don't know where they took them."

"Everyone else here okay?" DeWitt asked.

"Yes, sir," Jake said. "My mom is worried about Dad, but nobody else got shot or anything."

"We're sorry about Little Patty. That was terrible. Now, go get your families and bring them into the main house. The worst of this is over for you."

Murdock led the way out of the underground. He used his radio. "Franklin. Where the hell are you? We need one of the vans around to the side of the house pronto. Come back."

"Cap, we're almost there. Sprained my damn ankle on the run and that slowed me down. Be there in two."

"DeWitt. Assign two men to take care of the admirals' families. Then join First Squad with the rest of your men. We'll jam into the extended van and try to catch up with the Ford truck. Not many places he can run to out here."

The two vans came around the side of the house and slid to a stop. "Let's mount up that first van and ride. Everyone have TO&E ammo loads? Let's move."

Lam headed them out the right way, then jumped in the van. At the dirt track through the plantation, Lam stopped the rig and checked the dirt. He pointed to his right, which would lead back into the island more.

"Where can he be going?" Lam asked.

"Not the slightest," Murdock said. "Let's hope he doesn't have a chopper stashed up here somewhere. We don't know for sure how he got inland."

The dirt road continued for three miles, then left the pineapple field and struck out across undeveloped land. The driver swore.

"That pickup, was it lifted with four-wheel drive?" the driver asked.

Murdock scowled. "Yeah, it was lifted at least. Getting rough out there?"

Just then the van slowed and hit something. The front end dropped a foot and the rig came to a sudden stop.

"No way we can keep moving across this rough land," the driver said. "I didn't even see that ditch. We can't get out of it."

"Everyone out," Murdock barked. "Lam, get out front and track that bastard. We'll be right behind you."

The SEALs moved at a six-mile-an-hour pace as they jogged across the country. It became more rugged, and soon they could see spots where the four-wheel raised pickup had trouble getting through. One gully had three bumper marks on it where the pickup didn't quite make it across. The fourth time had been a winner.

"We should be gaining on them," Lam said. "This terrain is gonna stop them sooner or later."

It did, but it was a half hour later and the night sky was wide open and star-filled and the moon had waned a little from its fullness the night before. They found the pickup nosed down into a ditch it couldn't climb out of.

"Missed it in the darkness," Lam guessed. He went across the gully and used a pocket flash to figure out which way the walkers had headed. After two minutes of false starts he pointed almost due north.

"Looks like he's heading for the coast, Cap," Lam said. "What's he going to do, swim back to China?"

They kept moving. The trail was easier to follow now since the men were walking in a file and making a track with as many as twelve sets of footprints. Lam tried to jog again, but lost the trail when they turned toward a patch of trees. These were native koa and ohia trees in what looked like an area designed to produce firewood for stoves and fireplaces.

Murdock and Lam conferred. Then Lam headed out quickly and the SEALs waited. If the woods were clear, he'd give them a call on the Motorola.

Five minutes later he called and the SEALs jogged the half mile into the woods. Lam had been working to find where the Chinese men came out. It took him five minutes more before he stumbled on the discarded food can. It had Chinese characters on it. The trail led north again.

Murdock called up Franklin. "Take the driver and cut across country to the mansion. Fire up the other van and we'll try to connect on some roads up ahead. We're moving back into the more settled section of the place, and I'd guess the bastards will try to hijack a car or a truck. We need wheels over there. Go."

The crack of a rifle shot sent all the squad diving to the ground.

"Fucking thirty-ought-six," Jaybird said. "I've hunted with enough of them."

"Where from?" Murdock asked. They all stared ahead of their position just outside the patch of native woods.

"My bet is those eucalyptus over there to the right," Lam said.

"All mine," Murdock said. He lifted the Bull Pup and sent half a dozen rounds into the trees halfway up.

There was no response.

"Remember, we have two admirals with the bug-outs. We

don't want to endanger them. Spread out, ten yards, line of
skirmishers. We're running for those trees. Just a little over
a jog. Keep your weapons at the ready."

"My guess they're gone by now," DeWitt said as they
picked up the line and began to jog forward. Murdock moved
the line faster.

"Yeah, gone, but they know we're here. We'll have to be
careful. Hard telling what this sailor might do on unfamiliar
land in combat."

Murdock watched the trees as they came closer. The fast
jog ate up the landscape. They encountered no fire from the
trees. He didn't expect any. It had been a rear-guard action
to slow them down.

The eucalyptus were more than a hundred feet tall and
beautifully grotesque with their growth pattern of limbs. The
scent of the menthol nuts on the ground came through
sharply as they worked through the smaller trees to the far
edge of the woods.

Ahead they saw a farmhouse, complete with a barn, de-
tached garage, and what could only be an outhouse. The
buildings looked sixty or seventy years old and were badly
in need of repairs. Even through the dim light they could see
that any paint that had been used had long ago peeled and
fell away.

Murdock stared at the place.

"Abandoned," Lam suggested.

"Probably, but a good defensive setup. I wonder how
many weapons they have. The deer rifle could have come
from the mansion. They might have some handguns, but I'd
guess not much else. How far to the buildings?"

"Quarter of a mile, maybe another hundred," Lam said.
The buildings huddled in the moonlight. Even if they had
weapons inside, the darkness would cover the SEALs' attack.

"Let's move up," Murdock said to the lip mike. "No firing
unless I do. They probably are short on weapons. Move out."

The line of SEALs advanced at a walk. Murdock had been
listening for any sound coming from the buildings ahead.
There were none. If they were there, they had good disci-
pline. The two admirals were a long way from any field

exercises, but they would know enough to keep quiet and follow orders. One of the invaders must speak English.

They were halfway to the buildings when a pain-filled scream echoed across the flatness of the coastal plain.

The SEALs all hit the deck.

"What'n hell?" Ching whispered.

"Sounds like a bobcat in heat," Mahanani said on the net.

"No bobcats in Hawaii," Holt said.

"Sounded more like a cougar, about seven feet long and mean as hell," Ching added.

"What about a wild pig?" Canzoneri asked. "They do have feral pigs over here all over the place."

"Hey, I grew up on a farm," Bradford said. "No pig ever sounded that way."

"Moving out," Murdock said, closing the discussion.

The closer they came to the buildings, the more watchful they became. When they were twenty yards from the back of the barn, Murdock tapped his mike twice and the SEALs stopped and went to ground.

"Jaybird, on me," Murdock said. Jaybird moved out of line and worked ahead toward the barn with the commander. They parted in back and each went around one side.

Murdock checked the open door in the barn. It was high enough for a horse to walk in pulling a load. He sniffed. No animal odor. His NVGs came up and he scanned the place. A small stack of hay in one corner. A stall for a horse with a few recent droppings. Oil drips on the floor that might be from farm machinery or an older car. A pair of owls rocketed out of the place, their wings not the silent type. Could be the pueo owl the Hawaiians held to be a family-protecting spirit in their mythology.

"Nada," the earpiece whispered. Murdock met Jaybird in front of the barn. They looked at the run-down house thirty yards away. For just a second a white light blossomed through a window in the house, then snapped off.

"Hit it," Murdock barked, and the two men dove for the dirt and rolled away from each other.

The roar of the submachine gun caught them both by surprise as it raked the area where they had stood with a dozen rounds on full auto. They rolled farther apart. Murdock looked for some cover. The MG man worked his rounds toward Murdock's side. He spotted the old wooden watering trough, and dove for it just as hot lead kicked up dirt where he had been seconds before.

Murdock touched the lip mike. "Bradford. Get up here. Use the barn as cover for the house. Bring the EAR. When you get to the barn, come around the left side and put a jolt through the house window. Hope to hell you can find a window. I'm guessing it will blow the window out in front of it. Go, double time. It's getting hot up here."

"Backup?" DeWitt asked.

"Yeah, but keep cover from that sub gun in the house. Only response so far, but the bastard has NVGs for damn sure. Might be a one-man rear guard, but where the hell did they get a sub gun?"

"We're moving, Cap. Know the two aces might still be in the building. No deadly fire there. Will, spread out to both sides."

Murdock looked over where Jaybird had vanished. He couldn't make out the man in the dim light. "Jaybird, you five by five?"

There was no immediate answer. "Jaybird. Hey, buddy. Don't play possum on me. You see anything from that angle?"

Again there was no answer.

"Mahanani. Get to the right-hand side of the barn and wait. Might have some work for you."

"I heard. Leave him there, Cap. That NVG could get a lot of us killed out here tonight. We'll get Jaybird."

Less than two minutes later, Murdock heard the whoosh of the EAR weapon and the tingling in his ears. He clamped his hands over his ears just before glass shattered and a concussion and explosive force thundered through the small farmhouse like a freight train meeting a tornado head-on.

"Let's hit the house. Jack, check on Jaybird." Murdock came up from the water trough running. He held the Bull Pup in front of him and used the NVGs to find the door ten feet down from a blown-out window. He was closest and the first one there. The door had been blown entirely off its hinges and lay shattered ten feet from the house. Murdock stepped into the room with the NVGs and scanned it quickly.

A submachine gun lay on a counter pointed out the window that now held no glass. A man sprawled against the far wall, his head at a strange angle.

"Clear first room," Murdock said. He slanted toward an open door out of what he figured was the kitchen. The next room held only two old worn-out sofas and a chair. "Clear room two," he told the mike, and sprinted across it to another door. This one had two beds that had been neatly made up, a current calendar, and a copy of the Honolulu *Star-Bulletin* newspaper. Pizza boxes and remains of fried chicken take-outs littered one side of the room.

"Clear room three."

DeWitt charged into the room and kept going to the next door. He darted through the opening, his own NVGs working. Murdock sagged against the wall.

"Clear last two rooms," DeWitt said.

"Mahanani, was Jaybird hit?"

The earplug came on at once. "Yeah. Not good. Took a scalp graze that knocked him out. But there's a second wound in the lower belly. It's got to have hit some intestines. Peritonitis is a big problem here, Cap."

"Franklin, where the hell is that van?"

"Cap, we're down the road about two miles. We heard the sub gun and are moving that way. Jaybird is hit?"

"Floorboard that crate and get it up here. Make sure your driver knows where the best and closest emergency room is. You're backup for Jaybird into the operating room. Take no shit from nobody. Get it done. We're at an old farm with three buildings. Ronson, put up a green flare, now."

Lam had led the rest of the platoon through the complex and cleared it, and now he took out his three-cell flashlight and began searching the area. He found tire tracks at once.

"Tracks, Cap. Looks like at least two rigs. I'd say they are off-road or utility rigs. Lots of bootprints around the last set of tires."

"Estimated number?" Murdock asked.

"Can't tell. A lot of over-printing. Ten to thirty. Two utility vans could haul thirty men."

"Keep looking. DeWitt. Check the guy in the first room.

Looked like he had a broken neck. Solves the prisoner problem."

Murdock went outside to where the flashlight glowed. He came up to Lampedusa just as he bent and picked up something.

"Oh, shit, this is not good," Lam said.

"What is it?"

Lam held it out. "A thirty-round magazine, like they use on submachine guns and on some automatic rifles. Looks like the guys we're chasing have more than one automatic bang-bang."

9

**Old farm
Maui, Hawaii**

Commander Blake Murdock looked at the magazine. It carried 5.56mm rounds, which could be used in dozens of different international weapons. There was trouble ahead. So they'd snatched the two admirals. What were they going to do with them? Hold them hostage for some ridiculous prize was not reasonable. They must have a more practical plan.

"Holt, let's get on the air."

Ron Holt came up with the SATCOM radio, broke out the antenna, spread its little dish antenna, and aligned it with the right orbiting satellite. When the set beeped that it was in the right position, he gave the handset to Murdock. Only then did the commander look at his wristwatch. He punched the light button and saw that it was only a little after 2100.

He had a response from CINCPAC after the second transmission.

"Mr. Stroh is not here. He's on the phone with Washington. Admiral Bennington is anxious to hear about the two officers you're hunting."

Murdock brought the man up to date, and he said he'd relay the information to the admiral and to Stroh.

"Tell Stroh we may need some backup. The *Jefferson* could send us a pair of fully armed Sea Cobra gunships. Ask him to have the carrier put a pair on standby for us. Our Sea Knight choppers should be at the airport here for transport. We flushed out one bunch of armed Chinese, but the two admirals are still missing. We're moving out."

"That's a Roger on the aircraft, Commander. I'll get the signal off at once. Your red-signature order is still in effect."

"Good. We're out and gone."

The white van ground up to the front of the old house, and Murdock and Mahanani carried Jaybird to the van and laid him on the wide seat.

"Franklin, keep some pressure on that belly wound," the corpsman said. "Don't let it bleed. Keep him secure on the seat."

"Driver, you know where there's a hospital with an emergency room?" Murdock asked.

"Yeah, I been figuring the shortest way there. It's no more than six or eight miles from here. I'll get him there as fast as I can without wrecking this thing."

Murdock nodded. "Good. Franklin, you stay with him, keep his gear. Leave his weapon and vest and any explosives and ammo in the van. Move it."

Murdock watched the van roll out of the yard into the track of an old road and pick up speed.

"Now, ladies, we move into the interesting part of our demonstration. We find those bastards and kill them all. Let's move out. Lam, you're out in front as far as you can be and still see me. Go."

They moved through a field, past some dark houses, but Lam could tell that the trail did not divert to the houses. "The Chinese seemed to be in a hurry," Lam said.

Just over a small hill they came to what looked like an old manufacturing plant.

"Maybe used for pineapple processing," DeWitt said.

"Or sugarcane," Jefferson said. "Lots of cane back there a ways."

Murdock stared at the dark building a quarter of a mile away. He didn't like it. Too damn convenient. What did they have to gain going there? Murdock couldn't think of a thing

they could benefit from. Get the two admirals on board a
Chinese warship and they would have a bargaining chip. This
way?

DeWitt squatted beside Murdock. "What in hell they doing
out here with the top brass? How can they benefit?"

"What I've been trying to figure out." Murdock stopped.
"Let's move up on them. We need about fifty more yards.
Too damn far off here. We go now, troops."

The SEALs walked through a field that might have once
raised sugarcane. There was little cover. About forty yards
from the building they found what looked like an old irri-
gation ditch. Murdock put them in the grass-covered depression and watched the building again.

"See anything, anyone?" he asked the mike.

"Nada," somebody said.

Murdock waited for another two minutes, then frowned.

"Hear that? Lam?"

"Yeah, Cap. I've got it. Coming in from the beach. Some
kind of a chopper, but not the Sea Knight. Not big enough.
Coming this way fast."

They watched the sky to the west, but could see nothing.
Then the bird came almost directly over them.

"Four-place job," DeWitt said. "Yes. I can see the red and
yellow star over the red and yellow outlined bar of the Chinese Air Force."

"Take it down with twenties," Murdock thundered. He had
his own weapon up and sighted in with the laser. Three of
the Bull Pups fired at nearly the same time. One airburst
came just in front of the chopper. Two other rounds exploded
against the side and rear of the ship on contact. The engine
sputtered, then died. The rotors spun on automatic as the air
rushed passed them and the bird fell from three hundred feet
straight down. The small helicopter burst into flames when
it hit, and there could be no survivors.

"Move it fast," Murdock barked into the mike. "Fifty fast
yards to the left, go now. Go, go, go." They jumped up and
ran flat out for the fifty through what appeared to be a pasture. Moments after they left their previous position, it was
raked with more than a hundred rounds of machine-gun fire.

Murdock took another long look out front at the old packing plant. He had spotted at least three muzzle-flash areas. He had no idea how many weapons had fired at them.

DeWitt slid to the ground beside Murdock. "Now why in hell didn't they make a stand at the mansion? They had much better defenses over there."

"I'll ask them when we catch them. Lam says there can't be more than ten or twelve men left. They have the advantage because they know we won't open up on them as long as they have the two valuable admiral chips."

"The chopper," DeWitt said. "Coming in to take the admirals for a ride out to a Chinese destroyer?"

"Probably, then to their carrier. They have to have one out there somewhere. Why didn't the Navy see it? Maybe they did. Was it part of their goodwill visit as well, I wonder?"

"We have to take down that building or blow them out of there," DeWitt said.

"Great. How?"

"We'll use the old forty-five. I'll take Bravo Squad out to the far side and set up at a forty-five-degree angle to the target. You move up from here to a forty-five from this same side. We won't shoot up each other and we have a cross fire on the turkeys inside."

"We still can't blast away with the two chips inside."

"We can with the EAR weapons. We give them about three shots on each angle and wait and see what happens."

"Think it will work?" Murdock asked.

"One fucking way to find out."

"Then you and I go in on point and recon the place for survivors?" Murdock asked.

"You bet. Hell, you want to live forever?"

Murdock stared at the building again. Damn few windows. They would have to get shots through two of them. At least now they knew the sound blast would go through the average windowpane.

"Yeah, gung ho, let's do it," Murdock said. "Give me three clicks when you're set up and ready with the EAR."

Bravo Squad moved out two minutes later. They jogged like dark ghosts through the soft Hawaiian moonlight, past some trees and brush, and made it to the forty-five. Murdock moved his squad up to the right angle and called up Bradford, who carried the EAR weapon.

"Three shots through any two of those windows on the first floor. Only is one floor. Any questions?"

"We have that ten-second charge-up time between rounds, remember," Bradford said.

"Yeah. Get me three good ones. Then DeWitt and I are going in to check your handiwork. Make it damn good. I'm not ready to take ten or twelve NATO-sized rounds in my chest."

"No sweat."

Murdock grumbled. "You know that's exactly what Houdini said just before he tried that last escape trick that killed him?"

"Cap, who the hell is Houdini?"

Murdock snorted. Bradford didn't know. Figured. He settled down in the grass and made sure his Bull Pup was primed and ready. Then he waited for the three clicks on the Motorola.

They came a few breaths later. "Fire," Murdock said to Bradford. The big guy leveled in and checked for the red light, then pulled the trigger.

The swooshing sound came and Murdock tried to follow the blast of the highly compressed dart of ambient air. The window broke, and then inside there was a thumping sound, not nearly as heavy as the one at the mansion.

Another shot came from in front of them with the same results. It must be a wide-open area inside.

Ten seconds later both weapons fired again, then a third time.

"Moving out," Murdock said into the lip mike. "Just DeWitt and me. The rest of you stand backup." He came to his feet and sprinted the forty yards to the one door on this side of the structure. He saw DeWitt coming from his position. They had heard nothing from the building since the rounds from the Enhanced Audio Rifle went off inside. Nonlethal. They had to be non-lethal. No way he would say he'd killed two admirals.

DeWitt hit the wall next to the door. He nodded. Murdock turned the knob. The door opened inward. Ed kicked the door and dove through to the left. Murdock took the right, rolled once, and came up with the Bull Pup ready to blast.

Murdock coughed. The inside of the building was one huge dust cloud. He stifled the next cough and listened. He heard another cough to his left. He moved that way. DeWitt went the other direction. The man coughed again.

Could you cough when you were unconscious? He decided that a body could do that. He flipped down his NVGs and looked through the dust. Better. Another cough. He saw a man to his left. He lay on the floor, a submachine gun in his hands. Unconscious. Murdock tied riot cuffs on his hands and ankles and moved on. The dust settled more now, and he could see it was a large, open-beamed building with rows and rows of tables in it. Maybe a packing shed.

There were no lights.

"Found one out like a light," Murdock told the lip mike.

"I have one more over here."

"Where are the rest of them?"

Sing struggled through the darkness, glancing over his shoulder now and then at the packing plant that was supposed to be his salvation. He had radioed the chopper to come in. By this time he and the two American admirals should have been halfway to the coast in the helicopter heading for the deck of his destroyer.

He swore and stopped. It would take the Americans some time to clear the whole packing shed. He had left three men there to slow down the advance. It just might give him time to get into the town and fade into the Chinese community. That was one good part about being Chinese. There were ethnic Chinese in almost every nation in the world. With his good English, he would fit in perfectly. The seven men with him would have a harder time. It was better than being shot as invaders.

He had seven men, two automatic rifles, and the radio. He wondered if another Chinese destroyer would send in its helicopter on a dangerous mission to rescue him and his two prisoners. One might. He would try later when they were nearer to the coast. He had spent a week in this area and knew it well. He was four miles from the coast, and another mile or so to a safe house where he could settle down, get more American clothes, buy some identification, and become an American.

Where had it gone so wrong? The master plan had been a good one. Not even the admiral thought they could invade Hawaii and conquer it. Just a thrust to tell the world that China had reached the level of the other great powers. They had made a good start with the strike at Pearl Harbor with the missiles. Fired from over four hundred miles away from their best submarine. They carried only explosive warheads, but usually were fitted with nuclear warheads.

The two American admirals remained a problem. He had them tied together and hobbled so they could take only small steps. If he melted into the Chinese society, what did he do with the admirals? Should he kill them and hide the bodies? Would the Americans keep hunting him down if he did that? He was sure they would.

He nodded when his lieutenant came up.

"Sir, we have no word from the three men we left at the packing shed. I assume they were killed or captured."

Speaking was his second in command, who had been a strong leader during the mission.

"We head for the coast as fast as we can," Sing said. "A mile from here we will tie the two Americans and leave them unharmed. Then we get to the coast and have the submarine come into shore and pick us up. It is our only chance. Tell the men. We'll be working hard the next few hours, but it could mean our rescue."

He ordered the men to change into the civilian clothes they had brought in their packs. Every mile they would discard uniforms well off their trail. By the time they reached the beach settlement, they would be eight civilians on a hike. By then they would have hidden their weapons and be totally defenseless—but also that much harder to identify as Chinese invaders.

Sing stripped out of his commander's uniform and folded it carefully, then hid it under leaves and dirt well off the trail they were making through the countryside. It appeared to be a pasture on rocky ground. He had half his men put on their civilian clothes here. Then they left the admirals tied securely and jogged across the land toward the coast. By the time they came to the first row of houses and streetlights, they were seven civilians walking toward the coast. Sing was the only one who spoke English, so he was at the front of the group. They expected no trouble before they came to the sea. The radio with its powerful signal was stowed safely in the backpack one of the men wore. Now all they had to do was find the beach.

The Chinese officer led the men around a street blazing with lights. It was a business section. Two miles later they came over a green stretch of land and looked down at the Pacific Ocean. He smiled. It was like coming home. They jogged the last quarter mile, and huddled behind a small sand dune as the radioman took out the radio and began making his calls.

The plan was simple. They would call in the submarine, which would pinpoint their transmission location. It would come in to within a half mile of the shore. The men would swim out to meet the sub. The waterproof radio was also equipped with a sonar device to send a signal underwater to the sub for tracking. With no mixups, the last of the Chinese force sent to capture the two American admirals would be safely on board the submarine within two hours.

Murdock settled down next to the two admirals. Their mouths had been taped shut and arms and legs tied securely. Lam had spotted them twenty minutes ago, and had done a complete recon around them for a quarter of a mile. It was not a trap.

"How many Chinese are left?" Murdock asked.

The two-star admiral swallowed hard, then took another drink from Murdock's canteen and spat out the water.

"Damn mouth don't work good yet." He swallowed again. "How many? Seven or eight. Your men cut them down fast. I have no idea why they kidnapped us. Doubt if they knew either. Probably just some commander doing what he was told."

"You say they changed into civilian clothes?" DeWitt asked.

"Yes. I saw them all changing. They hid the uniforms. I saw two of them hide their automatic rifles as well."

"They'll hit town and pass as civilians," Murdock said.

"I want them caught, Commander, especially that snot-nosed one who speaks English."

"We're considering that, Admiral."

"I'm surprised you aren't charging ahead right now to catch them before they get into that little town out there. They shouldn't be hard to spot."

"Admiral, we're operating under strict orders from Admiral Bennington. Our job was to find and rescue you and your families. That we've done."

"Then, Commander, I'm ordering you to pursue and capture those damn chinks who kidnapped us."

"With all due respect, Admiral, this is a combat situation. We're at war with China. I am on a secret mission and in command of that mission. I report directly to the CNO in Washington, D.C., and the director of the CIA. As such, sir, and with all respect for your rank, I simply outrank you on this mission."

The admiral started to get red in the face, then relaxed and chuckled. "Yeah, Commander, you sure as hell do. I don't think I ever thanked you for rescuing our people back there at that mansion, and for finding us. Can we get the hell out of here now and back to our families?"

Murdock said they could. He called on the SATCOM for the Sea Knight chopper at the local airfield to come and get them. He had news about the two admirals' families as well.

"We'll have a chopper here in ten minutes, Admiral," Murdock said. "Your two families are now safely back in the resort where you were staying. We'll drop you off there on the way. We're all angry and sorry about your loss."

"Thank you, Commander Murdock. Thank you very much. You've done a fine job here. I'd like to write an addition to your after-action report."

"As you wish, Admiral."

Murdock called in their position and designated two men to put down red flares in the LZ. Holt came up to him.

"You called, Cap?"

"Yes, see if you can get on the phone system and find out

where Jaybird is. Some Maui hospital. Keep calling until you locate him and get a report on his condition."

"That's a Roger, sir." Holt sat down in the grass and began switching dials and talking. Soon he had the phone number of the Central Maui Memorial Hospital in Kahului. He talked to the emergency room. When he finished he found Murdock.

"The head nurse said that Jaybird took a serious gunshot wound and that he's being treated. He made it to the hospital in time and the peritonitis was minimal. He'll be there in recovery for at least a week, but he should heal completely."

"Good," Murdock said.

Five minutes later, Holt was back with a curious expression.

"Something cooking, Cap. Just had a call from some captain on board the carrier *Jefferson*. He said he had cleared it with Admiral Bennington, and Don Stroh. Our Sea Knight bird is to fly us directly to the carrier, which is about twenty miles off Maui. He says he has a highly classified and important mission for us. He said get our asses over there as fast as we can."

10

USS *Jefferson*
Off Maui, Hawaii

Commander Blake Murdock snapped to attention along with Senior Chief Will Dobler and Lieutenant (j.g.) DeWitt and First Class Petty Officer Kenneth Ching when the admiral came into the compartment. It was just off the admiral's quarters on the big aircraft carrier.

"At ease, gentlemen, be seated," Rear Admiral Matthew Magruder said as he slid into his chair behind the conference table. He stared for a moment at the four men, still in their stained and dirty combat cammies, sweat-streaked and with camo smudges on their faces. His own countenance was set in stone neutrality. That and his undertaker slate-gray eyes had landed him the call sign of "Tombstone" in his first F-14 squadron years ago. The name had stuck. Sometimes it was shortened to "Stoney," an even more apt description of his usual expression. Men who had flown with him for years swore that once or twice they remembered seeing him smile. Most of his people on his current watch doubted that.

"Thanks for coming right up from your chopper. We have a problem here that we need some help on." He hesitated.

"This one is a bit different than anything you've seen before."

"Different, sir?" Murdock asked.

"You men know about the Chinese invasion. They pulled their battle group into range of us by infiltrating operatives into our CINCPAC Fleet data correlation center headquarters at Pearl to falsify position and size reports on the Chinese battle group. Originally, it was to be a small contingent of Chinese warships on a goodwill mission.

"To brief you on the situation, we have an invasion of Kauai, with about five thousand troops ashore. They have little support, and we've eliminated most of their offshore resupply. We're presently assembling a force to counter that invasion.

"You know about the invasion on Oahu. It is stalled against the mountains and will be mopped up soon.

"We have CINCPAC headquarters back in our control thanks to you and your men. The Maui kidnapping is over.

"Our planes and ships are chasing the Chinese battle fleet across the Pacific. So far we have damaged them severely. The carrier, which we didn't even know they had, is limping along at half speed and will soon be sunk. We have cleared the skies of their planes and their fleet is scattered and running for its life.

"Now they spring a new demand. We've whipped them, and they won't give up. Through top-secret diplomatic channels they have given our State Department an ultimatum. They claim they have planted an activated nuclear bomb in the Pearl Harbor area."

"The bastards," Senior Chief Dobler said.

"True. They have given us a list of conditions we must meet or they will explode the bomb. They say it's in the one-hundred-megaton class which would destroy all of Honolulu and Pearl and half the island.

"Among other things, they demand that we surrender to Chinese forces on Hawaii, that we stop chasing their ships on the high seas, and that we deed the island of Kuai to China."

"Could they have smuggled a bomb into the base during all of the warfare activity and jitters?" Wade asked.

"Our security people at Pearl say it is highly likely that a bomb could have slipped through. Security was rather lax for two days right after the missile hit."

"Their demands are laughable," Wade said. "Except for the fact that they just might be crazy enough to plant a bomb on Pearl. Is there a chance that it's a bluff?"

"Our people in Washington and here don't think so," the admiral said. "This threat about the nuke is ultimate top secret. We don't want any word leaking. The fewer people that know about this threat the better. We don't want any panic in the streets of Pearl City or Honolulu.

"I understand that our diplomats have turned over a response from our top military directly to China that if there is a nuclear explosion on Hawaii, the U.S. will at once retaliate with nuclear weapons on their three nuclear production facilities, and the ten largest Chinese cities, plunging their nation into the Dark Ages."

"All we have to do is find the bomb and defuse it before they set it off," DeWitt said.

"Any idea where it could be on Pearl?" Wade asked. "Did it come in by ship, or is it in a suitcase? No, they don't have any weapon small enough yet for a suitcase."

"Wouldn't even need a ship," Ching said. "They could drive it right into Camp Catlin Naval Reservation adjacent to Pearl. Any delivery truck could haul a bomb in. Leave the truck or camouflage the bomb in a wooden box and drive away."

"They want us on the job to help find the bomb?" Wade asked.

"Right. CINCPAC has asked for you and the two top nuclear-deactivating men that I have to come to Pearl as quickly as possible. He thought you might have some additional equipment or gear here that you would need. He wants all of you on-site right now. We're attaching them to your platoon. You'll fly out of here as soon as we can get some clean cammies for you, a good meal, and another briefing."

"Sir, any machine we can use to sniff out this package?" DeWitt asked.

"Not unless the bomb is leaking radiation, which we hope it isn't."

"Do they still have those prisoners from the CINCPAC takeover?" Murdock asked.

"I'm sure they do."

"Might be a place to start. Questioning them. We must have something to start with. Anything. We can't fine-tooth-comb five or six hundred acres, hundreds of buildings, and all of the ships in Pearl."

"They lay out any kind of a schedule or deadline?" DeWitt asked.

The admiral scowled. "Damn them, they did. Tomorrow at noon we have to broadcast a message that we will receive a delegation from the Chinese battle group. Also, they say that all military operations against Chinese forces on land, sea, and air must cease immediately. That was about two hours ago."

"Have you shut down your chase?"

"Partially."

"What's the highest-ranking Chinese we captured at Pearl?"

"One of them claims he's a colonel in the Chinese Marines."

"I didn't know that China had any Marines."

"Over five thousand from what this colonel says." Admiral Magruder flipped a pencil onto his desk. "That's it. We have your Sea Knight serviced and ready to go."

"Let's go now," Murdock said. "No sense in keeping the Chinese waiting. We'll get a better feel of it when we get on-site."

"Good hunting," Admiral Magruder said.

"Oh, Admiral. Work out some way to stall them on that 1200 deadline tomorrow. Not a chance we can find the thing by then. Also, it's portable, so they may be moving the nuclear device around right under our noses."

"That's a Roger, Commander. I'll tell Admiral Bennington that you're on your way."

Hickam Field
Oahu, Hawaii

The fifteen SEALs and the two nuclear technicians deplaned at Hickam Field, next door to Pearl Harbor, looking much better. They had washed up as best they could, changed into clean cammies, and stowed their firepower.

A Humvee and Commander Johnson met them at the chopper. He explained the four planners were to report to CINCPAC GHQ at once. The rest of the platoon would be taken to the quarters on Pearl they had used before.

"Everyone is on this one, including a team from NEST that is flying in from Guam," Johnson said. "I think this whole bomb scare is a bluff, but it has to be checked out."

"How the hell do you inspect every square foot of land and building in Pearl in twelve hours?" DeWitt asked.

Ten minutes later, the same four SEALs who had talked with Admiral "Tombstone" Magruder on the carrier stood at attention in front of Vice Admiral Bennington.

"Be seated, men," the admiral said. There were six others in the room, half military, half in civilian clothes. "No need for introductions, we're all here to get a job done. So far we've decided on several courses of action. Every ship that has docked during the past week is in the process of a minute inspection of all spaces for any large heavy object that could be a somewhat crude Chinese nuclear device."

"What about Hickam?" Murdock asked. "Close counts in nuclear weapons and this device must be small enough to be hauled by a modest-sized truck. Security is not as high at Hickam as it is here."

The admiral nodded at a three-striper. "Get on it. Tell them we'll send search parties to help if they need us."

"Sir," Murdock said, and waited.

"Commander Murdock."

"Do we still have the POW Chinese Marine colonel?"

"Indeed. He's been in questioning for the past two hours. He tells us nothing and spouts Chinese propaganda he's been spoon-fed since he was in diapers."

"Sir, he looks like our only handle on the situation. He must know something. I'd like to put him one on one with one of my SEALs, Kenneth Ching, who is Chinese."

Admiral Bennington twirled a lead pencil in his fingers for a moment, then eased it down on the desk. His face, a bit long, now showed signs of strain. He rubbed his eyes with his left hand. "Yes, give it a try. Can't hurt."

Murdock nodded at Dobler and Ching, who left the room with Commander Johnson, their liaison.

"Anything more, Commander?" the admiral asked, looking at Murdock.

"Yes, sir. Anyone here from NEST?" He referred to the Nuclear Energy Search Team.

"I am, minding the local store," a civilian in light blue coveralls at the back of the room said. "Our five-man team is flying in from Guam."

"Do you have a local center here with equipment?"

"Yes, sir."

"You have leaded sheets and components to completely shield a leaking nuclear device?"

"Yes, sir. Bottle it up tight for as long as you want."

"Wouldn't that shielding work in reverse as well? Wouldn't it prevent any radio signals from penetrating the lead shielding?"

"Absolutely."

"Then I suggest that you have such material loaded on a truck and ready for deployment."

The admiral nodded. "So when we find the device, we cloak it in a lead blanket and no firing sequence of signals could get through to activate the bomb. Yes. Get on that, Casemore."

The civilian stood and hurried out of the room.

"Commander, to bring you up to date, a thorough and systematic search of all ships, aircraft buildings, and grounds is now under way. We have over three thousand officers and men scouring the base. It's been the opinion in this room that if they were clever enough to slip such a weapon on-base, they would have an ingenious method for concealing it. This whole threat may be a hoax, but it is the kind of problem that we must take seriously. The lives of more than a million people are riding on our decisions, our actions, and our ability to find the device."

DeWitt attracted the admiral's attention. He pointed at DeWitt.

"Sir, is there a holding area on-base for damaged or leaking nuclear devices?"

A voice came from the side. "I can answer that. Yes, we

do have such a facility. A week ago all but four devices were transshipped to another base where the items are being de-activated and disposed of. The four remaining items have been on-site for a little over two months, and we know that none was made by the Chinese. We believe we're clear in that area."

The phone on the desk buzzed three times. Admiral Bennington picked it up. He said hello and lifted his brows, then pushed a button on the phone and the speaker came on.

"Admiral Bennington, General Kerstan here. We're on your suggestion like a herd of wild grasshoppers at Hickam Field. Our people are furious about the Chinese attack and our losses. We won't let a stone get left in place over here hunting that damn bomb."

"Thanks, Kurt. I hope you get it. If you do, yell at us and we'll send over enough lead shielding to keep any detonation signal from getting to it."

The admiral hung up.

The talk went on for another hour. Murdock began to shift in his chair. The admiral stood up. Every man in the room shot to his feet.

"We're repeating ourselves, gentlemen. We'll meet here again at 1800 hours. Let's hope we have some news, or some new ideas, by then. That will be all."

The men filed out of the room.

Murdock and DeWitt stopped at the second of three desks outside the admiral's office, and asked where the Chinese colonel was being questioned.

The chief looked at them questioningly for a moment. "Oh, you just came from the admiral's office?"

"Yes."

"It's a restricted area. I'll get you badges and a guide. It's not far away."

Five minutes later they met Dobler in an underground facility with a one-way mirror showing another room. Ching sat on one side of a bare wooden table, and a small, crew-cut Chinese man sat across from him.

Dobler turned down the loudspeaker.

"Nothing so far," Dobler said. "They're speaking Mandarin, so I don't have a clue. My guess, just a warm-up chat."

Two video cameras recorded the scene from different angles.

Murdock turned on the speaker. Ching had switched to English.

"No, Zhang, you are the one who doesn't understand. The others were gentle with you; they were polite and civil. I am through with all three. From now on you will answer my questions truthfully, or you will die."

The Chinese colonel smiled. "It is easy for you to say, but you have no weapon. You are being recorded on videotape. I think you will not harm me."

"I am a U.S. Navy SEAL. A SEAL never is without a weapon." Ching reached to his left ankle and pulled up a .32-caliber automatic. The Chinese only smiled wider.

"I am not afraid of weapons."

"First I will shoot you in the shoulder, break the shoulder bones, and ruin the rotator cuff. It's more painful than you can imagine. I have the record in my outfit. Twenty-eight shots into a terrorist before he died. They said it was from bleeding to death.

"Now, let's start over from the beginning. Your name?"

"Colonel Zhang Ding-fa."

"You are a member of the Chinese Marines?"

"Yes, a full colonel."

"You and six men in your group came to Hawaii as tourists?"

"Yes. It was simple getting in."

"You know about the threat to set off a nuclear device in Pearl Harbor?"

"Only what you have told me."

"Untrue. You were one of the prime planners of this invasion. Your true rank is that of vice admiral, commander of the Chinese North Sea Fleet."

"That is not true."

"You were the only ranking Naval officer who spoke good enough English, so you were drafted for the role to infiltrate and subvert the communications center and downgrade the size of the 'goodwill' fleet coming to Hawaii."

"It worked, didn't it?"

"Then you are a vice admiral?"

"No."

Ching shot the Chinese officer in the right shoulder.

The roar of the gunshot in the small room was like a dozen bombs going off at once. Ching couldn't hear a thing. He watched Zhang. He had been thrown back against the chair by the force of the shot, but the force of the small round hadn't toppled the chair. He screeched in pain, but he couldn't hear himself.

"Two Navy SPs boiled into the viewing room outside the interrogation space.

"Heard a shot," one of them said.

"Sound effect," Murdock said. The SPs grunted, looked through the window at the men inside, and turned and left.

Gradually Ching sensed his hearing return. He waited until he could hear the prisoner moaning. He had slid the weapon back in his ankle holster soon after the shot.

Now he leaned toward Zhang. "Let's try that question again. You are a vice admiral, correct?"

Zhang nodded. "Yes."

"See how easy that was? Now we're making progress. You knew about bringing a live nuclear weapon onto Hawaiian soil when you came, right?"

"Yes, I knew." The prisoner gritted his teeth, evidently to stifle the pain between his words.

"Now, just where did those men who brought the nuclear device ashore hide it here on the Pearl Harbor Naval base?"

Ching watched him. Zhang looked up at Ching, started to say something. Then his eyes closed and he fell facedown on the table. Ching stared at the prisoner in surprise. Had he only fainted or was he dead?

11

Pearl Harbor, Hawaii

Murdock, DeWitt, and Dobler watched through the glass as Ching tried to bring the prisoner back to consciousness.

Then Murdock went inside. Ching looked at him.

"What the hell, Cap. Nothing else was working. We don't have time to play games."

"He's coming out of it," Murdock said.

Zhang shuddered. Then his hands moved and his shoulders hunched where he lay with his chest on the table. Ching had bandaged the Chinese man's shoulder and stopped the blood.

Zhang shook his head, then lifted it off his arms. Tears streamed out of his eyes. His face went white for a moment. Then his eyes half closed.

"You shot me!"

"I told you I would. The next one goes into your knee, so you'll never walk again. Like the sound of that?"

"No."

"So, back to the start. Where on our base has the nuclear weapon been hidden?"

"On the base. Weapon?" His face froze for a moment, then relaxed. "Yes, yes, I remember. Just don't shoot me again. I have a low tolerance for pain. No one knew before this. The weapon is a class-three bomb for aerial delivery. It is forty kilotons and is in a heavy wooden crate. The crate has been put into a truck and three men who are in sailor uniforms and are Caucasians. They move it from site to site on the base. They think it's a security test of the base. We told them it's a nuclear bomb. They think it's just an exercise."

"It's on the Pearl Harbor base?" Murdock asked.

The Chinese man looked up, seeing Murdock for the first time. "Ah. A commander. Shows more respect for my rank. Yes, a truck on Pearl Harbor itself. It was easy to come into the base with fake papers a week ago."

"What kind of a truck is it?"

"Navy truck we stole. It is outfitted with nuclear energy warning signs, and more signs indicating that this is a nuclear energy testing unit, sniffing out any radiation leakage on the base or from the ships or nuclear weapons."

"Good, Zhang. You're doing fine. You might live through the day after all. Now, just where is that truck?"

"I have no idea. No control."

"Where is it based?"

"This is an extra truck so it has no garage."

"How many of these trucks are on-base?"

"Twenty-five. Some in repair, most on duty watching for any leakage."

"Is the bomb fully armed, fused, and ready to explode?" Murdock asked.

"Absolutely. A threat is useless unless you can back it up." The prisoner shivered. "I need medical attention. I want a doctor."

Murdock left the room and found a phone in the observation area. He needed three tries to get the right office. It was the Radiation Search Facility. He dialed.

"No, sir, I'm sorry, all of our people are out looking for the nuclear device. I'm the only one here. I'm a civilian secretary."

"Do you have radio contact with your boss?"

"No sir, no radios left here. All in use in the field."

Murdock called Admiral Bennington's office. He got a captain and told him what they had found out from the prisoner.

"We think he's telling the truth. The man has a low pain threshold. He says there are twenty-five of these trucks. We need to find the right one."

The captain groaned. "I just authorized Commander Running to dispatch three of those rigs to Hickam and three more to the Camp Catlin Naval Reserve area. I'll see if I can get him back and have him pull all his units in for a quick check."

"Won't help much, Captain. The one we want won't have a radio and wouldn't come in anyway. It may be in hiding now."

On the far side of the Naval Reserve area, three men worked over a one-ton van-type truck. They had parked it in back of a grove of trees at the very bottom part of the camp near Highway H-1 and well out of sight of any prying eyes. They had taken compressed air bottles from inside the rig, attached them to hoses and nozzles, and quickly stripped off the Navy logos and Navy gray paint and all signs about nuclear energy. The triangle signs were removed, and what remained was a civilian truck in dull blue showing logos of a brewery.

They made one more inspection. Then two men went into the cab and the third into the back, and they drove through the military reservation to the back gate and had the guard check their papers. They were cleared to deliver beer to the non-com and the officers' clubs on this day and to use this gate.

The young Shore Patrolman on guard at the gate gave the papers a quick look and waved them through. He had been concentrating on the exercise underway to find a nuke bomb that had been planted somewhere in Pearl Harbor. There was always another test being run.

He turned his attention to three cars lined up at the barrier. It was a duty weekend coming up and the reservists were piling onto the base. It would be a busy time for him.

The three civilians in the truck used a cell phone and made contact the way they had been instructed.

"This is shit-kicking fun, outwitting the damn Navy," the tallest of the three said. His name was Charley Blount. He was driving and in charge of the truck and cargo and getting it to the right spot at the right time.

Charley checked his watch. Almost four in the afternoon. The rig was due near the front of the Ala Moana shopping center in downtown Honolulu at six P.M. sharp. The strange little man who had hired them had been precise. He had also been free with his money. He had given each of them five hundred dollars for the four days' work. It had been in advance, and was only a third of what they would earn when the job was done.

Charley drove at an even, legal speed. He'd been cautioned to obey every traffic law so he didn't get stopped by police. From the shopping center he would get instructions where to go. It was an exciting operation, and would help improve the security at the base. He wasn't sure just what being out here in the middle of Honolulu would prove, but it must fit in some way. The voice on the phone would have an explanation for the trip.

Back at the base, the twenty-five trucks used to test for radiation were slowly being ticked off by their commander. He had eighteen inspected and six more on their way in to the shop. He was sure none of his men or equipment had been compromised, and the best way to show it was to have an all-present-or-accounted-for report. If one of his trucks had been hijacked and used for the Chinese bomb, he might as well turn in his request for retirement tomorrow.

How in hell could the Chinese get a truck? How could they smuggle an active nuclear weapon into Hawaii and then get it on a truck? Questions he would probably never get answers for.

Two more trucks rolled into the big garage, and he went out to check them over himself. Both were set up strictly according to regs. No deviations, and certainly no place to put a one-ton crude nuclear weapon. The commander grinned. Only six more trucks to go.

Back at the SEALs' official quarters, it had been a half hour after their questioning of the Chinese prisoner. He had been sent by security to the hospital clinic, treated, and returned to a security cell. No questions had been asked about how the man had been shot.

Now Murdock told his fifteen men the update. He had ordered six vehicles, and put three men in three, two in the rest.

"The brass will look in the usual spots for a truck," he said. "We need to check out the long shots, where we would hide if we wanted to lose a truck. Work the boundary fences, the waterfront, anything or anywhere you can think of where you would want to hide a truck. Remember, this isn't a big rig, like a one-ton with a van body on back. Let's go."

Murdock and Dobler drove out in a new experimental rig called the Flyer. It looked a little like a World War II Jeep, but had only one seat for the driver in front and room for two men in back. In the center of it was a sturdy gun mount that would take a .50-caliber machine gun.

It had no top and had an extremely low profile for better use in combat and for hiding in shallow gullies, then popping up and slamming .50-caliber rounds into the enemy.

It also had a diesel engine that boomed the little crate along at sixty mph on an open road. It had full-time four-wheel drive and four disc brakes. The high road clearance meant it could drive over rough country and rubble and make it. Murdock had heard that the price on the skeletal little rig was a hundred thousand dollars. He hoped the price would come down if the military went for the little bouncer.

Murdock drove as they headed for the air base at Hickam Field and began their prowl. All the SEALs had on their Motorolas, and they would check out just how far they would reach.

Everywhere that Murdock drove he drew questions and admiring stares at the little Flyer. They prowled along the base fences, through an abandoned section, then past the Fort Kamehameha Military Reservation next door. Murdock stopped the Flyer and waved at some curious onlookers, then turned to Dobler.

"If you were hiding this truck, where would you put it?"

"Not out here in the open, for damn sure. I'd stash it in some trees or brush where nobody usually went. If there is any place like that on this reservation, or Hickam, or the Reserve area, or Pearl."

It was almost dark by the time they headed back. The radio call came through weak but readable.

"Commander Murdock, I think we have something. This is Lam and Bradford. We're on the south side of Camp Catlin, the Navy Reserve area. We've found what looks like stripped-off paint that shows nuclear danger signs. We even have three of the little triangular signs that warn of radiation. Looks like they used some kind of blasting power to peel the paint strips off the rig."

"Yeah, Lam. Get to a phone and call the admiral's office and report what you've found and where you are. We're on our way over there from Hickam."

By the time Murdock found his way off Hickam and to the south edge of Camp Catlin, there were three carloads of Shore Patrol and officers on the scene. A commander who looked like he was having a heart attack stood to one side.

"The bastards! They painted a truck to look like one of mine. I can see it all here. It must have cruised all over the bases, the way my other rigs do. Logos and everything. So they stripped off the paint. What does the truck look like now?"

"He probably went off-base," one of the captains said. He used a radio to ask the various gates if a one-ton truck had checked out that afternoon.

A NEST truck rolled up and six men came out in protective suits. They used sensors and began to scour the area, including the stripped-off paint and the ground where the truck must have parked.

The civilian Murdock had seen at the admiral's office flipped up a face mask and took off a head covering. He looked at a small meter and nodded.

"Yeah, I get a point-four reading. Which means there is a little bit of radiation leakage on the bomb. Not unusual. Not dangerous. A point-four is like about three hundred wristwatch dials glowing all at once."

Admiral Bennington stepped up. "So the truck with the bomb inside was parked here. You're sure?"

"Yes, sir."

The admiral turned to one of his aides. "Any reports from the gates? Most interested in the closest one."

"Yes, sir. I have a report from gate five that would be nearest to this spot. A beer truck went through about two hours ago. Looked like one of the trucks that normally services the clubs in this area."

The admiral headed for his car. At the door he pointed to Murdock. "SEALs follow me. They are off-base now. We can really use your talents for this one."

At the gate the same man who had checked the truck through was still on duty. He dug out the paper. The truck was not one that usually supplied the base. It was the New Wave Brewery. There was no such name in the phone book or with information.

Admiral Bennington leaned against his car and turned an unlit cigarette around and around with the fingers of one hand.

"We have a live, armed nuclear bomb out there in the city streets of Honolulu. It could be set off accidentally or on purpose at any time. How the hell do we find it?"

Three of his aides standing around simply shook their heads. The admiral looked over at the four SEALs.

"Murdock, you're the resident genius on this sort of chase. Just what the hell can we do next?"

"The civilian police have to be in on it now, sir. They might be able to find that beer truck. Honolulu PD and the State Police can throw out a lot of eyes watching and they can get on it in twenty seconds. They have a lot of units out there. Get the best hard description we can on that truck from the gate guard. Now we have to think about the entire island as the target area."

"The second I call the police, the newspapers and TV get the story. There could be a horrendous panic."

"Don't mention the Chinese or the bomb," Murdock said. "This truck could contain some highly secret material. That should be enough to get the cops moving and not create a panic."

The admiral talked quietly to another aide, who left for the admiral's car, where Murdock guessed there must be a radio or cell phone they could contact the police with.

Admiral Bennington looked up. "Now, what the hell can we do next?"

Nobody said a word. The admiral looked at the four SEALs.

"Murdock, you've been our answer man so far. Any more suggestions?"

"Yes, sir. If you haven't already, stall the noon deadline tomorrow with the Chinese about this situation."

"Working on that."

Murdock watched the NEST team trying to track the truck from where it parked. The men moved out ten feet, then reworked the ground with their sensors. They tried it again, then gave up.

The captain who had gone to the admiral's car pushed out of it and hurried over to the admiral. They talked a moment. Then Admiral Bennington turned to the two dozen men around him.

"You might as well know this up front. The State Department has just approved a request of the Chinese Navy. They have asked for safe passage for a Chinese cruiser and two destroyers to approach within a mile of Pearl and bring a cease-fire agreement. We don't know what it is. We have been ordered to stand down any aggressive action against the Chinese troops on or near Hawaii, on the sea or in the air. The State Department, speaking for the President and the National Security Council, has ordered us to stand down. We'll be notifying all of our commanders under fire of the order.

"We still have to find that damned truck. It isn't covered in any way by this order. Let's get on it, people."

12

Pearl Harbor, Hawaii

The admiral headed for gate number five, and Murdock and his men drove back to their quarters on Pearl. They turned their cars and trucks in at the motor pool. The big search on Pearl was over.

"Stand down," Lam said back in their quarters. "That mean all the shooting has stopped?"

"It's supposed to," DeWitt said. "Always hard to get the field units all to stop shooting at the same time."

"So where is the bomb being taken?" Ronson asked.

"Where would you take it?" Murdock asked.

"From that gate they could go north into Pearl City and up into the middle of the island. Or head for Honolulu and Waikiki Beach. Hell, I'd head for the beach."

"Hell, yes," Holt said. "Them bastards who smuggled in the bomb want to go for a midnight swim on the beach down there."

Murdock went to a phone. He'd been feeling downright naked ever since they turned in the vehicles. So if some cop did pick up a sighting on that beer truck, what could the SEALs do about it? Nothing.

"Admiral, thanks for taking my call. I have one more suggestion. How about my troops in a pair of Humvees with full arms and ammo ready to chase down that beer truck if the cops sight it anywhere? Be a hell of a lot better than to have the cops and their parabellums."

"You'd stay on-base?"

"Thinking about putting one rig in Honolulu and the other one in Pearl City. We could be ready in case they went south or north. We have one SATCOM. We'd need another one so both rigs would have them for coordination."

"Do it, but keep the weapons out of sight until you need them. We're supposed to stand down. I'll have a SATCOM sent over to the motor pool. We're on TAC Three at my HQ. Keep in touch there about your position."

"Thanks, Admiral. It would speed up things if one of your people could authorize the rigs from the motor pool."

"Done, SEAL, and good hunting."

An hour later they were rigged out and ready to go. In the bottom of the Humvee's open space there were two leaded blankets folded and ready for action, courtesy of the NEST contingent.

DeWitt took his pick of positions and chose to go north. Murdock took his squad south and worked the non-tourist streets near the Ala Moana Highway, which lanced through the heart of Honolulu. They had a generous supply of weapons, including the two EARs and all of their Bull Pups and MGs and sniper rifles.

It was just after midnight when the first report came in. Holt had the SATCOM tuned to the CINCPAC frequency and heard transmissions most of the night. No one had spotted the beer truck.

About 0030, he perked up and called to Murdock. He put the sound on the speaker.

"That's about it, Admiral. Unit 342 said he saw the beer truck and thought nothing about it. He had just come on duty and hadn't checked out all the standing orders. He's sure now it was the New Wave Brewery truck."

"His position and direction," the crisp military voice asked.

"He was on Kapiolani Boulevard and it looked like the truck was heading for the freeway."

"Thanks. Give a double alert for all your police units in that area and on the freeway to watch for the beer truck. A one-ton van with blue-and-red lettering and paint job."

Murdock told Ching to head for the freeway. It was in the center of town well north of the Ala Moana main drag. He made two turns and came out on the King Street on-ramp to the Lunalilo Freeway heading east.

"DeWitt, did you get that trans from CINCPAC?"

"We did. We're working on the best route from here to your position. If he comes west on the freeway, we might spot him. We will close the gap toward you, so keep us informed where this cat might be prowling. Set up a meet if you get any solid info about the truck. We're moving."

"That's a Roger, DeWitt."

All Alpha Squad watched for the truck. Ching hugged the right-hand lane at fifty miles an hour and let the traffic slice past him. They were on Hawaii Highway 1 for only a few minutes when the radio came on again.

"This is State Trooper Philbin. Saw your beer truck, it was in the slow lane on the other side, heading west. Not sure, but it probably was on the off-ramp to the Pali Highway Number 61. If so, he was heading north up the grade."

"Do it," Murdock growled. "Let's go north. The off-ramp is coming up."

Ching hit the cloverleaf off-ramp and nailed the Pali highway.

"If that was the rig and it came this way, he couldn't be more than a few miles ahead of us. Can you get any more speed out of this wreck?" Murdock asked.

With the load of the lead blanket and the SEALs, the Humvee was straining to keep up with traffic up the Pali Highway. They couldn't pass many cars, so Murdock wasn't sure they could catch the truck ahead of them.

He checked with DeWitt on the SATCOM. DeWitt had heard the transmissions and would turn north when he came to the Pali Highway. He figured he was still about six or seven miles from it. Murdock reported to CINCPAC that he and the other Humvee were heading up the Pali.

This all might be a wild-goose chase, but it was their wild goose and the only one in town right now.

At the first gas stop, they pulled in and Murdock talked to the attendant.

"Beer truck?" the redheaded kid asked. "Hail, no, bro, I ain't seen no beer truck up this way. Fact is, don't ever remember seeing one. I think they go around the mountain."

The second gas stop, and then the third, proved to have the same message. If there had been a one-ton-sized beer truck, the attendants hadn't seen it.

They took the turn toward Kaneohe on the other side of Pali, and Murdock began thinking. The beer truck guys might be heading for the Chinese troops over there. It was a chance.

Murdock talked to two more gas stations, and on the last one he hit gold.

"Beer truck? Yeah, never heard of that brand of beer. I asked the guy about it. He said he was sold out on this run, but he'd drop me off a free bottle next time he came through. Looked like the rig was still heavily loaded, but I didn't say nothing."

"Which way did they head when they left?"

"Guy asked me how to get to the Valley of the Temples, so I told him. On up the coast. Highway Number 83. Can't miss the signs to the left."

Murdock reported in to CINCPAC where he was and the first positive sighting of the beer truck and where it might be heading. Murdock grinned when he angled the Humvee back on the highway. "Oh, yeah, he's heading for the Chinese invasion force up here that we and the Marines captured. Wonder if he thinks they are still here, or if we didn't get all of them."

They drove.

It was less than half an hour later that Murdock recognized the valley where the chopper had dropped them off before. "These guys weren't looking for the Valley of the Temples, but the road this side of it," Murdock told Ching.

They pulled in a hundred yards and stopped. Murdock used the SATCOM and talked to DeWitt. He would be through Kaneohe in half an hour. Murdock decided to wait. He had the men check their equipment, reload their weapons, and get ready for some action.

DeWitt turned up in twenty minutes. He and Murdock

talked, and then they headed the two Humvees up the dirt road that led to the valley where they had found the Chinese invasion force before. It was a little spooky, Murdock admitted to himself. But if all the Chinese were gone from this area, why would they tell the truck driver to bring the bomb out here?

A half mile up the road Murdock had Ching pull over. Lam checked the dirt and gravel road. There was almost no development up toward the hills here. No reason for a black-topped road.

Lam came back with a big grin.

"Oh, yes, one set of fresh tire tracks. Soft place back there where I could make out the tire tread pattern. I'll know it if I see it again. They're moving up this road."

"Not far up here to the mountains," Murdock said. "Not too far to where we took on that battalion. We cleaned up on them and the Marines mopped them up and took away the POWs. Why is the bomb coming up this way?"

"Maybe we didn't get all the guys who came ashore," Lam said. "How about another battalion hiding in the trees and brush and laying still waiting for the Marines to go away?"

"Could have happened," Murdock admitted. "These guys are bringing the bomb up here for some reason. We better take it easy. Get Tran out there with you, Lam, and do point for us about a quarter of a mile ahead. Tell us if you run into anything that looks like a roadblock or an outpost."

They kept the Humvees in low gear with the lights off, and moved up the dirt road only by the light of the waning moon.

They had gone little over a half mile when Tran came out of the darkness and waved them down.

"Commander, we've found it. The beer truck is up ahead in a small clearing. Trouble is, there's at least fifty or sixty men around it in a perimeter defense. Lam says they're Chinese with weapons and dug in with good firing positions. He said no sign of any white men up there."

Murdock and DeWitt talked it over with Senior Chief Dobler.

"Twenties," DeWitt said.

"Damn right, but what's that going to do to the beer truck?" Murdock asked.

"Kill it probably," Dobler said. "Course we can always roll it down the hill. We're up here a ways on the slope."

"Going to blow all the tires if we do a job with the twenties," DeWitt said. "But if they're dug in, that's about the only way we can beat them."

"The EAR?" Murdock suggested.

"Won't be that effective in the open. We could nail about a third of them, but that leaves a lot of firepower up there."

"Will the twenties hurt the bomb?" Dobler asked.

"Not so you could notice," DeWitt said. "First the shrapnel has to get through the sides of the truck, then hit the wooden crate. Going to stop most of it."

"It must have an antenna on it somewhere if they plan to set it off by radio signal," Murdock said.

"Yeah, or maybe the keepers attach the antenna when they get the word to do so," Dobler said.

"Attach it and say hello to their ancestors." Murdock snorted.

He scratched his chin. "We leave the rigs here and move up on foot. We'll set up an arc and use the twenties. Then when we have them beat down, we'll fire six shots from the EAR and move in."

"Hoping the rest of the battalion doesn't rush down here and get in our way," DeWitt said.

"We worry about moving the rig after we get it," Dobler said. "We can always tow it with one of the Humvees."

Murdock called the men around and explained the situation and what they would do. There were no questions. The six men who usually used the Bull Pup twenties loaded up with ammo, and the rest checked their usual weapons.

Tran took them up to where Lam waited. He had pulled back to three hundred yards.

"Twenties?" he asked Murdock. The commander nodded. "How about I put two red flares in there for you to get your lasers on?"

Murdock said to do it when the troops were ready. He spread them out ten yards apart in a gentle arc around the near side of the target. He could make out part of the truck now with his NVGs. He spotted a few of the mounds of dirt.

"Go on the flares," Murdock said softly into his lip mike. Two reports came as the rifle flares were fired at the beer truck. One hit just behind it, and one twenty yards to the side. Both gave the Bull Pup's range finders and video cameras targets to laser on.

The men with the twenties began to fire only seconds after the flares hit. There was an immediate outcry and confusion in the line of Chinese troops around the truck. The SEALs could hear orders being shouted. Then more rounds exploded in deadly airbursts, and Murdock saw some of the dug-in men stumbling around with wounds. Others picked up and ran for the rear, away from the deadly shrapnel from the sky.

"Two more flares, white-parachute ones," Murdock ordered. The flares went up and burst over the scene, giving the other shooters targets in the sudden glare.

The firing sequence lasted only for three minutes. Murdock called a cease-fire. He could see no shots coming from the positions. One section right behind the beer truck could have suffered fewer casualties than the rest of the circle, but all had taken a deadly total.

"Two EAR rounds in the area," Murdock said. "One on the right side of the truck, the other on the left."

After a hurried radio talk, the two EAR shooters coordinated and fired.

When the whooshing turned into an ear-pounding roar, Murdock hit the lip mike.

"Let's move up in a line. No firing unless we get some shots from survivors. Moving out."

The SEALs swept forward. No shots came from the defenders. The SEALs used flashlights to check the bodies. Three shots were fired, dispatching wounded. There was no sign of the white men. Ching inspected the vehicle and told Murdock the bad news.

"The rig got hit hard. No way we can get the engine running. All the plug wires are shot to hell and half the other wiring. We've got four flat tires. The JG's suggestion about towing could work. We've got some chain in the Humvee."

"Go get the Hummer," Murdock said. "We'll stand guard in case some close-by friends of the family drop in. Make it fast. Some of them bugged out and will report down some line of vocal communication if no other way. I wonder how many of these troopers the Marines missed up here." Ching ran down the road.

Five minutes later Ching drove the Humvee into the small clearing and backed up to the nose of the beer truck. Murdock had checked the bomb in the wooden crate. First order was to take the lead-blanket shield out of the Humvee and drape it over the top and sides of the bomb. It was almost big enough.

By that time Ching had the tow cable fixed, and the men gathered around as he gunned the Humvee's 150-hp V8 diesel engine with the automatic transmission and eased up on the tow chain.

The chain strained. Then the beer truck inched forward. Lam sat in the driver's seat with one foot ready on the truck's brakes so it didn't slam into the Humvee. The men gave a whispered cheer as the Humvee moved down the road towing the beer truck behind it. The flat tires flapped and shuddered, but they weren't moving fast enough to throw the tires off the rims. It made easier going.

Soon the pair of rigs was up to nearly five miles an hour, and the straining Humvee diesel kept it moving in low gear. Murdock and Ronson took up a position as rear guard. DeWitt and Fernandez had the point.

It was too quiet. Murdock didn't like that. He left Ronson on the rear guard and jogged to the front of the column. The Humvee was straining over the more level ground, but still moving the bomb. They had to get it out where they could call in a chopper pickup. A pickup for the bomb. They stopped at the spot where the other Humvee sat. Quickly, the second lead blanket was added to the first one over the bomb crate and the parade continued.

They had traveled what Murdock figured was another mile, and he could almost smell the salt air, when DeWitt came boiling back from the front.

"Boss, we've got big troubles. I could hear them a mile

away. Didn't think they could be for real. When they came close enough, I made them with my NVGs. Must be a whole damn battalion out there in front of us in a blocking position right across the road. No way we can go cross-country with this beer truck."

"A battalion? How could they get in front of us? Where were they hiding when the Marines were here? Show me."

Five minutes later, Murdock was satisfied. The Chinese force straddled the road ahead and fanned out on both sides for at least a half mile. The troops were singing, shouting. He saw some cooking fires, even though it was not yet 0400. Murdock surveyed the landscape in the moonlight.

They were in what was left of the coastal plain. It couldn't be more than four or five miles to the ocean. The area was laced with networks of dirt tracks and roads.

"We set up the MGs and sniper rifles, and get out our Bull Pups and make a blast at their troops on the road and on each side." Murdock was instructing his men through the Motorola.

"We use the twenties and the EAR and everything we have. Hopefully, we can punch a hole through and blast out of here with the three rigs."

"At five miles an hour?" Lam asked on the net.

"Probably not, but it's worth a try. Let's get in a thick line across the road and take a shot at it."

Parachute flares walked down to the Chinese. They were five hundred yards ahead. The lasers targeted the Chinese in the light, and the deadly firepower of a full SEAL platoon lashed out at the enemy.

At once the SEALs took return fire, and dove into ditches and behind trees for protection. The lead Humvee took a dozen rounds, but the supplemental armor shed the lead and left little damage.

Murdock lifted up from the shallow ditch on the right-hand side and surveyed the situation. The Chinese had taken serious casualties from the twenties, but they still had enough men to throw out deadly counter-battery fire.

No chance to get through. Murdock scowled in the dark.

He hated leaving the bomb, but it was all he could do under the circumstances. They couldn't get the bomb through the Chinese force, that was clear. Now all he had to figure out was just what the hell they did next.

13

Windward side
Oahu, Hawaii

"Unhook the beer truck from the lead Hummer," Murdock barked. "We're bugging out into the fields to the north. We can outrun them in the rig and live to fight another day."

"What about the bomb?" DeWitt asked.

"We leave it here, for now. We'll be back. We'll contact CINCPAC for their suggestions. Maybe drop in two hundred Marines to secure the area and lift it out with a chopper. Let's choggie, ladies. Time we got the hell out of Dodge."

They dropped the tow chain and gave covering fire against the roadblock ahead as the two Humvees charged down a dirt track to the north and away from the Chinese.

Murdock went out a mile, then stopped, and Holt set up the SATCOM.

CINCPAC was excited.

"You found the bomb. You have it under control?"

Murdock explained the problem.

"We'll advise you. Get into a safe position and hold."

"Roger that," Murdock said, and started to turn off the mike. "Better leave it on receive," he said to Holt. "It might take them some time to figure out what to do."

"Right now the fucking Chinese have moved up the road and taken control of the beer truck and the bomb," DeWitt said, using his binoculars and his NVGs.

"Casualties?" Murdock asked over the Motorola.

"I'm not feeling what I'd call great."

Murdock recognized Ronson's voice. "Ronson, you hit?"

"Picked up a lead messenger in my chest. Not feeling at all chipper, Skipper."

Mahanani bailed out of the other Humvee and slid into Murdock's. He found Ronson sitting against the side of the rig. He laid the SEAL down and opened his vest and his shirt. His flashlight showed a round purple hole in Ronson's chest six inches below his left shoulder. When the corpsman felt around Ronson's back, his hand came out smeared with blood.

Mahanani put a bandage over the front entry wound, then eased Ronson over and checked his back under his shirt. An inch-wide gaping hole showed. He held the mini-flashlight in his mouth and put a gauze pad over the wound to stop bleeding, then treated it as best he could and bandaged it tightly.

"Ronson, buddy, you just lay there quiet. We're going to get you some help." He ran around the side to Murdock.

"Chest shot, Commander. He needs help right now. My suggestion we move easy-like a couple of miles away and get an evac chopper in here. Could be a lung or some big artery up in there. He could be bleeding internally. I don't like it. He's critical right now."

"Take a SATCOM and a driver and move this Humvee out near the highway. Stop and call CINCPAC. Tell them the problem and demand a chopper out here within thirty minutes. There's a Marine Corps Air Station not over ten miles away. They must have a hospital or clinic there. Go. Now. Go."

Franklin went along to keep Ronson from moving around. Mahanani drove. The rest of the squad bailed out of the Humvee. The rig moved toward the highway where Mahanani could see headlights. It was just after 0450. He stopped a mile from the road and used the SATCOM. He'd been told how to set up the antenna. CINCPAC came through on the first try.

"That's the story, CINCPAC. Could the Marines out here come get Ronson? He's critical right now with that chest shot."

"That's a Roger, SEALs. They will have an evacuation bird and medics in the air in five minutes. They say put out a flare, any color, for an LZ. You copy?"

"Copy, CINCPAC. No enemy fire this area. The patient is ready."

Mahanani drove closer to the highway, found a wide-open space, and parked. He took out three red flares from his vest and walked fifty yards away from the Humvee.

He looked toward the coast, and at once could hear a chopper. It was coming in fast and low. He pulled out the flares and held them ready. When he figured the bird was two hundred yards off, he popped the first flare, then a second one. The chopper came in fast, slowed, then settled to the ground between the flares. Mahanani ran to the helicopter.

Five minutes later Mahanani and Franklin watched the big chopper lift off. A doctor and a nurse on board were working on Ronson even before the liftoff. He was in good hands.

"Let's see if we can find the cap and check out where the action is," Mahanani said. They used the Motorola, and Murdock reported they were about a half mile north of where they had been before, watching the Chinese.

Murdock stared through his night-vision goggles and then his binoculars. He wasn't sure what went on in front of him. The Chinese had moved up and taken over the beer truck. They had no way to move it. Would they keep it there until daylight and then get one of their half-tracks back here? He had no idea where the rest of the Chinese troops were. He still thought the SEALs and Marines had captured all of them before.

Ten minutes after the radio call from Mahanani, the other Humvee steered into the area beside Murdock.

"The doc on the chopper said Ronson should make it. They'll stabilize him and keep him alive until they get him to the hospital. He said in fifteen minutes Ronson would be in an operating room."

"Good. Now what the hell are these fucking assholes going to do with their favorite nuclear bomb?" Murdock asked.

The SEALs quietly moved the Humvees into a slight depression where they would be out of sight of the Chinese troops. Some of the men caught quick naps. Murdock paced around the vehicle trying to come up with an answer. Why hadn't they found all the invading Chinese troops? Where had they hid? What would they do now? They had no way to transport the ton of crate and bomb.

It was a cool morning breeze that brought Murdock out of his nap where he leaned against the Humvee. The breeze was enhanced by a buzzing and then a whupping, and he scanned the sky looking for the chopper. Maybe the Marines were coming in with a thousand men to capture the bomb.

No, just one bird. It was low, so low that Murdock caught only quick looks at it as it came in from the sea. It circled and dropped down out of sight. Murdock swore. That was the spot where they had left the beer truck and the bomb. Almost any military chopper with a sling could carry a ton of goods. The helicopter could have come off any of the Chinese destroyers, which routinely carried one.

The rest of the platoon stirred and came alert. Lam sauntered up.

"What they doing with a chopper?" he asked.

"Moving the bomb, what else? Get Holt and the radio," Murdock snapped.

The radioman came up quickly, already setting up the dials and the antenna. The all-ready beep came, and Murdock took the handset.

"CINCPAC. This is Murdock. The Chinese have control of the bomb again. Now they have brought in a chopper. Don't know what they're up to. How close are the local Marines or maybe an F-14 from the *Jefferson?*"

"Carrier planes are all restricted. Marines can put an armed chopper up. Near the same area they picked up the wounded man."

"That's a Roger. Tell them to rush it or the bird and bomb might not still be here."

"Will do, Murdock."

Lam went forward to find out what the Chinese were doing. He had his Motorola hooked up.

Five minutes later the call came. "Damn, Skipper, they don't waste any time. They put slings on the whole damn beer truck. Couldn't get the bomb out of it, my take. The chopper has lifted off and now the sling is tightening. There it goes. You should be able to see it about now."

Murdock watched the whole beer truck lift slowly away from the green of Hawaii and move into the air. The trip would not be fast, as the helicopter seemed to be straining just a little to keep flying. It headed straight for the mountains, toward what looked to Murdock to be the most rugged section in sight.

There was no sign of the Marine chopper. Murdock talked to the lip mike. "Drivers, let's choggie. We're heading straight up the hill as far as these little donkeys will climb. Moving out."

Ed DeWitt came on the Motorola. "We going after the bomb?"

"How many defenders can they have around it up there?"

"Damn few. But what if they don't stop on top, but keep going over the summit and down the other side?"

"Then we contact CINCPAC for some tracking from that side of the mountains. Moving."

The Humvees were built for off-road work as well as blacktop, but there was a limit to how far up the slopes of the Koolau Mountains they could go. Ching got his rig over a ravine Murdock doubted that he could, and then the second Humvee made it, and they climbed another quarter of a mile before they came to a sharp gully that they could not beat.

"Hit the ground, we're walking," Murdock said. He had made a regular check behind them, but saw no sign of the Chinese forces that had captured the bomb from them. He had no idea where they had vanished to. They had to be hidden away somewhere in the immediate area. He'd let CINCPAC worry about that.

The undergrowth became thicker as they moved up the slopes. The higher they went, the more rain fell, and the more rain, the more trees and shrubs and grasses. They hiked up the ravines and ridges and more slopes and ridges. Now and then on a high spot, Murdock could see their objective. A slightly open spot in the rugged and green-covered spires where the chopper might have found room to land, or at least to hover while the sling was unhooked.

Lam kept to the point, and came back about ten minutes later.

"Something up ahead that looks like a small camp, maybe an outpost. I spotted four men. There's a fire and some lean-to shelters made from branches and poles."

"Sounds like a Boy Scout camp," Murdock said.

"No, sir, these were Chinese. I checked them with my glasses. They're all armed."

"We go through them or around them?" Murdock asked.

"No way to go around unless we want to slide down about fifty feet of sheer rock."

"So we go through them. Three or four rounds of twenties could do the trick."

"Sir, I'd go with the silent snipers. Won't warn anyone else on up the slope that we're coming. Must be other troops up there near the chopper."

"Agreed," Murdock said. Into the Motorola he called up Bradford and Fernandez. The rest of the platoon held its ground as the two snipers, Lam, and Murdock moved up to where they had good fields of fire. Murdock stayed just behind Bradford.

He hunkered down behind a giant koa tree and edged around it so he could see the campsite. It was only fifty yards ahead and he had perfect sight lines for firing.

Fernandez was twenty yards to the left, finding a shooting spot. The earpiece ticked three times and Bradford nodded. He sighted in on a Chinese soldier who had just stood up from behind the fire. He had a rice roll over his shoulder. Inside was enough cooked rice and other food to last him for a week.

Bradford fired and the Chinese soldier slammed backward out of sight.

Another Chinese soldier on the far side of the fire suddenly crumpled where he sat, sprawled on the green forest floor, and didn't move.

A third soldier leaped up and darted away from the shooters. One silent round caught him in the back and he slammed into a tree, slowly fell away, and sprawled on the ground. Murdock realized it was almost daylight. Fringes of dawn still shadowed some areas. The sun would be up soon.

"One more of them out there somewhere," Bradford said.

"Let's move up and find him," Murdock said. The four men moved like shadows from one tree to the next. If the Chinese soldier knew they were coming, he never heard them. He lifted up over a fallen log behind the fire and stared around, then dropped down.

Murdock clicked his mike twice and the four men stopped.

Bradford had seen the head come up and go back down. He aimed at the spot, just an inch over the top of the log, and held his sight and waited.

The head eased up again, then came higher so the man's eyes cleared the log. Bradford fired. The top of the man's head exploded into the green surroundings, turning some of the leaves a fall-like crimson and shades of pink and pale red.

The four moved up again. There were no other troops in the area. Lam took off up a hint of a trail toward the top and the chopper, while Murdock brought up the rest of the platoon. Lam came back and reported no evidence of any troops ahead for at least a half mile. The platoon moved on. The terrain became steeper and the men tied their weapons on their backs to use their hands to help them climb. It was fully light now.

Lam kept fifty yards ahead of them. He would double-click on the mike if he wanted them to stop.

Lam eyed the perpetual green of the lush windward side of Oahu. More rain here and more plants and flowers and trees. He could see the pinnacles maybe a half mile ahead now, but they were still high on the skyline. He wondered how the platoon would get up the last slants.

Lam carried a silenced Colt M-4A1 Commando set for three-round bursts. He parted a giant fern and looked ahead. Two Chinese soldiers saw him at the same time. He pivoted up the Commando and slammed six silent rounds at the two Chinese. They both jolted with the hot lead rounds, lost their weapons, and slid to the ground, dead before they came to a stop.

Lam dropped to a crouch hidden behind the fern. He waited. Had they been coming to reinforce the outpost? Maybe. He waited another minute, then double-clicked the mike and trotted back to where he found the platoon flat in the green of Hawaii. He told Murdock about the confrontation. They went back up for a look.

Murdock watched the bodies for five minutes. No one moved, no one came down the semblance of a trail.

"Let's take a look," he said. They moved up slowly, weapons covering the two men on the ground. A minute later Murdock saw that both Chinese were dead and that there seemed to be no alarm.

"Come on up," Murdock said to the radio. He held Lam until he saw the troops coming, then let him move out ahead on what by now had turned into a well-traveled and recent trail. The weeds and wild ferns had been trampled down, and some small trees even hacked off at ground level.

Lam move up cautiously. He could see a trail now that worked up the slope toward the pinnacles above. They were still a quarter of a mile and maybe six hundred feet above him. He had no idea how the trail could go up the sheer cliffs. They looked fifty feet high and went straight up.

He worked silently ahead through the emerald green of the Hawaiian forest. There were more kinds of trees than he had ever seen, and he knew that almost all of them had been brought to the islands by humans.

The woods thickened and the trail turned around a heavy stand of the native koa trees. He paused beside a large one and looked out. Ahead there was a level space that looked like a natural clearing. For a moment he didn't believe what he saw. Then when it registered and clicked into place, he shrank back so he was sure he was out of sight.

"Cap, you're gonna have to see this to believe it," Lam said softly to his lip mike. "Best get up here pronto."

14

Koolau Range
Oahu, Hawaii

Lieutenant Commander Blake Murdock stared through the screen of brush at the open place forty yards ahead.

"You're right, I don't believe my eyes," Murdock said. "Tell me about those four girls."

"You are seeing right, Cap. Those are four naked hula girls out there dancing up a fucking storm."

"Spread out on those green cloths on the ground. What's that?"

"True, Cap. Just what you think it is. All the goodies of a traditional Hawaiian luau. The pit for the pig is just behind them. You can still see steam and a little smoke coming from it. Looks like they have just opened up the imu, the fire pit, where the cooking is done."

"The four men. Chinese, I'd bet."

"Oh, you betcha, Commander. From their ages I'd say they are all officers. That same chopper could have brought them and the whole luau up here a few hours ago.

"Look over there at the imu. Looks like slabs of pork have been cooked after they wrapped them in ti and banana leaves. On the sides are the other goodies, the lau-lau. These bundles have in them chicken, fish, poi, sweet potatoes, and bananas."

Murdock looked at him in surprise. "How come you know so much about Hawaiian luaus?"

"My folks used to come here every summer. Got so we hated the luaus. We were teenagers then and wanted to swim and chase girls on the beach."

Murdock took out his binoculars and stared at neatly folded uniforms in back of the naked men. He spotted epaulets and some gold bars.

"Yeah, officers. The main body must be close by somewhere."

"We take them down with silenced shots?" Lam asked.

"No. I want information. We'll slip up and then confront them."

Lam nodded. He checked the area ahead. "We can move up through the brush to about thirty feet of them. Then burst out and cover them."

"Tie and gag them," Murdock said.

"Man, look at that end girl. She's got the biggest tits I've ever seen."

Murdock chuckled. "Maybe you haven't been getting out enough lately, Lam. Let's go get them." He grinned.

They worked ahead slowly, then charged out of the brush into the four officers' faces. Only one reached for a pistol. Lam kicked his hand away before he found it.

No words were necessary for the Chinese. The four girls stopped their hula and turned off the tape player.

"We won't hurt you," Lam said, watching the girls. All but one tried to cover themselves up with their hands. "How did they bring you up here?"

The one with the largest breasts, who was not covering them, laughed. "Oh, yeah. Brought us up in a helicopter. My first ride. They paid us good too. A thousand each for the day. They brought in the luau. Only one of them speaks English."

"Which one?" Murdock asked.

By then they had all four Chinese tied with the riot cuffs on ankles and wrists.

"The youngest one. We call him Well Hung." The girl laughed.

Murdock went up to the man indicated and hit him with a backhanded slap that knocked him over where he sat on the ground.

"You speak English," Murdock said.

"Yes. Some." The man sat up, scowling.

"Did the helicopter bring the bomb up here?"

"Yes, but you'll never find it."

"Is it up in the crags up there?"

"Perhaps."

Murdock slapped him again, toppling him the other way. Murdock saw that the girls were getting dressed. Good. He looked down at the Chinese officer.

"How many men do you have up here?"

The officer sat up with an effort. "Only half of a platoon. Twenty men. Bomb will go off up here and vaporize most of the island."

"Including you and the rest of your men."

"True. We are volunteers and know of our fate."

"Only, the bomb won't go off. We'll find it first, and you'll spend the rest of your life in a prison."

The Chinese man's face twisted a moment. Then he shook his head. "No, it can't happen. We have planned too well."

"Like your invasion down below? Invading this section of the island has absolutely no military benefit whatsoever."

Murdock looked at Lam. He was talking to one of the girls. "Lam, call up the troops. Keep them out of sight in the brush. We might as well put this luau food to good use."

The girls smiled, went to the pit, and began taking out the food and putting it on plates that the Chinese had provided.

"Looks like the package you can buy at some stores," Lam said. "Your own luau all put together with instructions, food, plates, and drinks."

"Good invading army technique for feeding the troops," Murdock said.

It was the best lunch stop the SEALs could remember. There was even cold beer, which Dobler rationed out one can per man. Murdock told the girls that he had to leave them there, but there would be a helicopter to come back and pick them up before dark.

Lam had eaten fast and worked on up the trail watching for any outposts. He came back a half hour later.

"Clear up for another six hundred yards, Cap. Then there's a detail of six or eight men at a log barricade. Looks like they have an MG and some other weapon set up there. The slant up to the pinnacles is no more than a hundred yards behind them."

"Any way we can bypass them?"

"None without dropping down five hundred feet into a gully and then climbing back up those damn slanted rock walls. They are set up on this little ridge top we've been working up for the last mile."

"So we take them out. We'll give the guys another ten minutes on the roast pork."

A short time later the food was all gone, except for the poi. Only Lam and Mahanani dug into the poi. There was plenty left.

Murdock put Bravo Squad in the lead as they moved up to the roadblock. Lam brought them to within two hundred yards of the Chinese. The SEALs worked slowly, cutting out clear fire lanes at the log barricade ahead.

Ed DeWitt checked his men. "Only six or eight of them up there. We do them with the twenties. Half of you on impact, the others on laser airbursts. Let's do it." He fired three rounds from his H & K G-11 sub gun. Then the heavier weapons fired.

DeWitt watched with satisfaction as the first two airbursts exploded directly over the log barricade in the tree branches, showering the men below it with shrapnel. He could see fifteen feet of the trail in back of the barricade before it faded into the trees. Two Chinese tried to run up the trail, but another airburst overhead blasted them into the ground and they didn't move.

The heavy machine gun pounded out six rounds, then went silent. A few rifle rounds came from the log barricade. Then even they stopped.

"Cease fire," DeWitt said into the Motorola. He watched and waited. A plaintive cry came from the barricade. It sounded again, then trailed off into silence.

"Take a look," Murdock said on the lip mike.

Ed DeWitt and Train Khai jolted away from the cover, darted twenty yards ahead, and then froze behind trees. No fire came from the logs. They worked the move and took cover twice more. Then they used assault fire and ran flat out for the barricade. No return fire sounded.

Moments later the earpiece spoke.

"All clear front," DeWitt said.

The SEALs moved up and occupied the roadblock. Lam had scouted the route ahead, and came back quickly to Murdock.

"Trouble ahead, Cap. There's a trail with switchbacks every twenty feet or so. About a sixty-degree slope. The whole fucking thing is without any cover and wide open to fire from the top, which is about sixty yards above. How the hell we get up there without getting slaughtered?"

"At the top, is it a cave or open on top?"

"Looks open to me. Oh, twenties?"

"You called it. Listen up, troops. Alpha Squad will take the hike. Bravo to give cover fire. We want all Bravo to have the Bull Pups. So trade off. We need eight shooters on this. Airbursts, so laser the top of the wall up there. Any questions?"

"When do we stop the cover fire, Cap?" Canzoneri asked.

"Depends on the situation and the terrain," Bradford cracked.

"Precisely," Murdock said. "We'll let you know the second we start to feel your hot shrapnel. We'll let you get in a dozen shots before we start up. Maybe you can blast them all to hell and we won't get any return fire. But don't count on it. Anything else?"

"The bloody bomb going to be up there?" Dobler asked.

"Tell you that in about a half hour," Murdock said. "Ed, get your men set up and fire when ready."

Murdock pointed to his men in the sequence he wanted them. He would be in front, Lam right behind him, then Holt, Bradford, Ching, and Dobler as Tail-end Charlie.

A minute later the first round fired and Murdock looked up at the rock pinnacle. The round exploded in the air just behind the front of the wall. He heard a scream from above. Then a half dozen more rounds hit, drowning out all other sounds. When the last of the dozen rounds exploded high on the pinnacle, Murdock waved his men forward and began moving up the switchbacks on the trail.

At once he saw why the trail took the sudden turns. It was nearly straight up but not quite. He soon looped his sub gun over his back so he could use his hands to help climb the slope. It became steeper as they moved upward. Now he could hear some shots coming from the top, but they gradually tapered off. He paused and looked behind him. One of his men sprawled on the ground. It was Dobler.

"DeWitt, check on Dobler. Get him back out of the line of fire. Looks like he's been hit."

"Two men on the way already," Murdock's earpiece told him. He surged upward again.

The big SEAL officer couldn't remember how many turns he had made on the switchbacks, but the top still looked a long way off. Then a chunk of shrapnel sang past his head and he used the lip mike.

"DeWitt, cease fire. That's a hold-it. Cease fire with the twenties. Use the five-five-sixes. Should help keep their heads down."

"That's a Roger."

Murdock surged upward. The top looked closer now. He couldn't make out any shots being fired from above, but there still could be. He made one more switchback and scanned the area ahead. He was only ten feet below the opening into the fortress. He swung down his sub gun, flicked off the safety, and charged up the last slope and darted into the opening.

"Cease fire fives," he heard in his earpiece. Then he was inside the top of the slope and the edge of the fortress. It wasn't that, only a four-foot wall and nothing behind it but another sharp incline up to a jagged peak twenty feet overhead.

He saw three bodies sprawled in the dust. One lifted up and tried to train his rifle on Murdock. A three-round blast from the H & K sub gun jolted the man into a quick reunion with his ancestors. Murdock ran to the far side, but saw nothing except a trail that continued around the side of the pinnacle. There was absolutely no place in this area where a helicopter could land or even drop off a nuclear weapon.

Behind him, three SEALs stormed into the position. Murdock used his radio. "Clear front. Three Chinks visiting their ancestors. No sign of the chopper or the bomb. Come on up."

Lam knelt down beside his leader. "Want me to check out the trail? Looks like it wraps around this point instead of going down."

Murdock waved him on his way.

"DeWitt, how is Dobler?"

"Took a graze on his forehead, knocked him out. That could have saved his life. He's still groggy, but in good enough shape to swear at me. He's just ahead of me moving up the hill."

"Good." Murdock looked around. "Holt?"

The radioman stepped up beside him. "Set up?"

"Right. We'll check in with CINCPAC. Get them on the wire."

A minute later Holt gave Murdock the handset.

"CINCPAC, this is Murdock. The Chinese took off with the bomb in a sling under a small chopper. Went up and over the cliffs here on the windward side. We're on top now, but don't see him yet. Working around some tall spires hunting. Will let you know what we find."

"Murdock, keep after him. The parley is still on, and we're doing almost nothing against the Chinese. I can break loose a chopper filled with Marines any time it will help. They're close by over there at Kaneohe Marine Air Station. Keep up the good work."

Lam came jogging back to where Murdock sat in the dust behind the overlook.

"Oh, yeah, found them. The chopper is about a quarter of a mile ahead. It's in a small open space between some tall rocks. My guess, about twenty troops in a perimeter defense around it. Some have cover, some don't."

Murdock jumped up. "Troops. I want Bradford with the fifty and all of the twenties on me now. Have sighted the chopper. Move, move, move."

Murdock was ten yards down the trail when Bradford and the others arrived. They jogged after him. They had eight of the 20mm weapons and the big fifty.

"We'll shoot the bastard down before he can take off again," Murdock told Lam. "He still hooked up to the bomb?"

"From what I saw. Either way it's a win."

They hiked for five minutes, and then Lam held up his hand. Murdock moved up six feet, and could see the chopper ahead. The bird's rotors were moving.

"He's getting ready to take off," Murdock said. "Rush it up here, men, and open fire."

Lam had up his twenty and got off a lasered shot before the others arrived. The round missed the laser mark or had the wrong one, and exploded well behind the chopper against an outcropping.

The bird lifted off and tightened the sling, and then it moved gradually into the air.

Only Lam was firing, the rest weren't up with them yet. His second shot missed as well, and he couldn't figure it out. Bradford dropped down, extended his bipod, and sighted in on the bird. He pulled the trigger on the big .50-caliber rifle.

"Motherfucker, what the hell?" Bradford slammed his palm against the weapon. "Jammed. It ain't jammed in six months."

The chopper rapidly moved away from them, just as Lam made his third shot, then vanished behind a pinnacle of solid rock and didn't show to them again.

"Holt, front and center," Murdock barked. The radioman ran up, dropped to the ground, and pulled out the dish antenna and positioned it until he heard the beep.

"CINCPAC is ready, Cap."

"CINCPAC, we lost the bomb. The chopper got away from us. Can you track it by AWAC? Need to know where it's going. Also want that Marine chopper to come get us so we can follow the other bird. Get them in the air, now."

"Murdock, I'll have to clear that with the admiral."

"CINCPAC, I have red signature pre-approval. Get that Marine chopper in here now and have him use this channel. I expect him here in not over ten minutes. Can you track that Chinese chopper?"

"Affirmative, on the track, it's in progress. Radioing the Marines now. How many men to transport?"

"Fourteen. Some prisoners and civilians, but you can come back and get them. We need that Marine chopper now."

"Stay on the air, Murdock. The Marines have had a chopper warmed up and on standby. Confirming now. Yes, the Marine bird is in the air. I'll put him on this channel so he can contact you. We have a good track on the Chinese chopper. It's currently heading toward the north end of Kaneohe Bay."

"This is Marine Chopper Charlie One looking for Murdock."

"Murdock here, Charlie One. We're on the pinnacles of the Koolau Range almost due east of your station. We'll give you red flares when we see you. Hit the range peaks and move north-south. We have an LZ near here we'll use red flares on. There is no enemy action in this area."

"Moving out, Murdock. Less than two minutes to your mountains. Red flares are best."

"We'll use them when we hear you, Charlie One."

Murdock stared back toward the Pacific Ocean. Kaneohe Bay. Why in hell would the chopper be taking the bomb back there? Had they given up on the bomb bluff? Just what the hell were those Chinese motherfuckers up to this time?

15

In Sea Knight chopper
Over Oahu, Hawaii

"I've got them coming in from the north," Lam said. He had the best ears in the platoon. They all looked to the north and soon could hear the bird, then see the ungainly Sea Knight helicopter with U.S. Marine Corps markings on it flitting along the peaks of the Koolau mountain range.

They had moved into an area three hundred yards from where the Chinese chopper had set down. Now there were no Chinese troops in the vicinity. Murdock had no idea where they had vanished.

Dobler threw out a red flare, and then another one hit the LZ. The big chopper circled once, let down slowly, then hit wheels-to-turf.

"Let's go get a ride," Murdock said into his Motorola, and the fourteen SEALs trotted toward the idling helicopter. The crew chief waved at them as they stepped into the aircraft. Then at once it lifted off and over the lowest of the ridges, and slanted down the windward side of Oahu toward the coast.

The lieutenant who flew the bird turned to Murdock.

"You Murdock?"

"Right."

"You pull a lot of weight around here. Rousted us out quicker than we've been done before. CINCPAC says they have a track on that Chinese chopper you were chasing."

"They know where it is now?" Murdock asked, half yelling so he could be heard.

"Yes, but far out of our area. They do tell me that it stopped somewhere around Kualoa Point. That's at the top of Kaneohe Bay, across from our base."

"It stopped?"

"Near as they can tell, but since it was over the bay it didn't set down. Paused there for a while, then moved on. Funny. When it continued, it was moving almost twice as fast as when it came up to the bay."

"Why?"

"They don't know. We don't know. I'm supposed to take you where you want to go. An honest-to-God red-signature order?"

"True. Not so common around here, I understand."

"I've only heard about one in the past two years."

The chopper circled once and Murdock looked over the area.

"They said right down there. Figured it was just off the point a ways, but they couldn't tell how far."

"They were sure it wasn't on the land?"

"Yes, sir, said it was over the water, at least a hundred yards from the closest landfall."

"Put us down on the point."

"Sir, that's not an authorized . . ." The pilot grinned. "Hell, I've got a red-signature order here. We're going down."

Murdock told the Marine pilot to stay on the ground until he gave him an order to take off.

The SEALs prowled around the point of land where the Pacific swells bathed it on three sides. Murdock shook his head. There was nothing they could do here.

"Back on board the bird," Murdock ordered in his radio. He went up front to talk to the pilot. "Take us back to your base. On the way I want you to get CINCPAC on the radio."

"CINCPAC? Damn, I've never talked to them before. Whatever you say, Commander."

Just before they took off, Murdock talked to the Pacific Fleet headquarters. The admiral was there.

"Murdock, hear we missed the bomb again. What happened?"

Murdock explained the sequence. "Admiral Bennington, right now we need all of our SEAL gear over here at the Marine air base. From there at Pearl. Especially our underwater gear. From reports by your people, the chopper paused over the bay here for a short time, then took off out to sea. Do your people know if he left the area at a much faster speed than he arrived?"

"I'll ask them. Your SEAL equipment will be on the way shortly by chopper. Everything in your quarters here. Anything else?"

"Not right now, Admiral, but maybe later. I have a hunch that chopper dropped the bomb in the bay here. All we have to do is find it."

"That question about speed. You're right. The chopper came in at a slow rate of speed. When it left the bay it headed out over twice as fast."

"Figures," Murdock said. "The bird had a heavy load. By dropping it here they could go a lot faster. Thanks, Admiral. Out."

Murdock went back and talked to Senior Chief Dobler.

"Damn sorry I acted like a wimp when I took that little scratch on my hard skull, Skipper. Usually I'm not so touchy."

"Chief, from what the corpsman says, you're damn lucky to be alive. Another quarter of an inch and you'd be in a body bag. Glad to have you with us. Now take it easy for a while. Could be a slight concussion up there and we don't want to aggravate it."

At the Marine Air Station on the peninsula extending out from Kaneohe Bay, there was a truck waiting for the SEALs. A Marine captain met the chopper and introduced himself to Murdock.

"Commander Murdock, I'm Captain Hassleman. I've been assigned as your liaison while you're on-base. Anything I can do for you, just ask. This rig will take us to your temporary quarters. I can arrange an open mess for your men whenever you say. Your equipment from Pearl should be here in about thirty minutes."

Murdock shook the man's hand after returning his salute.

"Captain Hassleman, glad to meet you. We'll need chow soon and some resupply on ammo. Mostly five-five-six and some fifty-caliber AP. What we really need is special twenty-mike laser rounds, but we'll have to go with what we have. Oh, ask that chopper we used to stand by. We'll be going back to the other side of the bay as soon as we get our underwater gear."

"Yes, sir. Soon as we get to a phone I'll do that."

"Why not hit the phone first, then take us to quarters? I like that pilot."

"Right away, Commander." The captain took off at a trot toward the nearest building. The SEALs crawled into the six-by and waited.

Murdock looked at his watch. It had been a busy morning, but he was surprised to see that it was almost 1500. Three hours of sun left if they were lucky.

By the time the captain came back, Murdock had been drumming his fingers on the truck's fender. They drove away to a faceless building half a mile across the base.

"Captain, we'd like to hold the truck here," Murdock told the Marine. "As soon as we get our underwater gear, we'll be going back to the point for a swim."

"Aye, aye, Commander."

The SEALs settled into the bunks. Then Dobler had them checking gear and ammo for resupply. He made a list. Murdock used the telephone and got the base clinic. They didn't have Chief Ronson on the station.

"We did some emergency stabilization and sent him by evac right to Tripler Army Medical Center above Pearl. They have the best facilities for chest wounds. We don't have any report on him. Sorry."

Captain Hassleman had ordered box lunches for the men, and brought in a thirty-cup urn of coffee. Their gear didn't arrive until twenty minutes after the coffee was gone.

"Full underwater gear," Murdock ordered. "We don't know what we might find out there. We're hunting that box with a bomb in it. At least we've seen it before. Captain, tell that pilot to warm up his rig. We'll be there in fifteen minutes."

They didn't put on their wet suits. The water temperature was over seventy, Murdock had heard. They put on clean cammies, their water boots and combat vests, and the Draegr rebreathers, and were ready.

It only took the chopper five minutes to find the spot off the point Murdock wanted.

"A hundred yards from the land," he told the pilot. "Come down to twenty feet and we'll bail out. Wait for us on the shore. Remember that red-sig order card you have."

The pilot grinned. "Indeed I do remember. Going down in my logbook for damn sure."

Murdock hit the water first, followed by his squad. Then DeWitt and his men jumped in. They surfaced and Murdock went over the general instructions again.

"Looking for that damn bomb. Not over a hundred feet here, and the water is clear. Let's see what we can do. We'll do a sweep out fifty yards on the surface just hoping. Then we go down to fifty feet and sweep back for a hundred yards. Let's do it."

The water was clear, but not a hundred feet clear. They could see down maybe thirty or thirty-five feet. At the fifty-yard mark they came heads-up and waved, then dove down to fifty feet and kept twenty feet apart as they stroked back the way they had come, watching below.

Again, it was too deep. Here and there a small hill showed and they could see the bottom. Nothing but sand. Almost no fish. They would be around the kelp plants and the masses of coral near the shore.

Murdock kicked down another twenty feet and felt a slight tingle in his body, but he ignored it. Now he could see the bottom most of the time. Sand. Here and there, what could have been a shell casing or part of an old car or an aircraft. Sea garbage. He checked his number of kicks and realized he had gone too far. He came up gradually.

The rest of the platoon waited for him on the surface. They swam back to shore where the Sea Knight perched on the side of the sand just off the highway. Six cars had stopped to stare at the bird, along with a city police cruiser. About twenty people milled around.

There was a small cry from some in the crowd as the SEALs came out of the water and dropped on the grassy place next to the roadway.

A young cop came over. "Who's in charge?"

Murdock waved at him.

"Any trouble here? Unusual for a chopper and a batch of frogmen to be out here on the point."

"True, Officer. Also unusual for China to invade Hawaii." He looked at the small crowd. "Have any of these people been here for, say, two or three hours?"

"Got me. Let's ask them."

Murdock walked over and waved at the crowd to quiet. When the people settled down, he asked them if anyone had been there for a while. One man nodded.

"Yeah, we were having a picnic down a ways when we saw this helicopter come in low from the land side and hover over the water. Had a sling on it with a small truck hanging under it. It dropped the damn thing in the water. That what you're hunting?"

"Yes," Murdock said. "About where did he drop it?"

"Close to where you guys jumped out of that chopper right over there. Maybe fifty yards off the point."

"Oh, hell, no," another voice piped up. A tall man with a red beard shook his head. "I been here all morning fishing. Not a damn bite. But I seen that chopper come in too. Must have been a Chinese kind, 'cause it didn't say U.S. Navy on it. It dropped the damn beer truck, sling and all, it was carrying, all right, but it had to be two hundred yards off the point and maybe half that far back toward the beach."

"No way," the first man said.

Murdock thanked them and started to leave.

"Are you frogmen?" a small boy shouted.

"Close enough," Murdock said. "Actually we're Navy SEALs. Thanks for your help."

Murdock went back to the chopper and had the pilot call in CINCPAC. The lieutenant seemed to love making the radio call. He gave Murdock the mike.

"CINCPAC, we're ninety-percent certain the Chinese

chopper dropped the beer truck and the bomb in the water here at Kaneohe Bay. How about a minesweeper with high-intensity metal detectors. They should be able to pinpoint the location of the device."

"The admiral is already working on that, Commander. Trouble is our top minesweeper detector-wise is in dry dock for a new drive shaft. The admiral has ordered the next-best ship to sail today at 1700."

"How far is the trip and how fast is the ship?"

"She's the *Chief*, MCM 14, a mine countermeasure vessel that can make thirteen knots."

Murdock frowned. "How far is the run around here? Fifty miles?"

"More like forty. Which means she'll be on station there in about three hours."

"Can she work after dark?"

The man on the other end of the radio laughed. "She doesn't care, night or day, just so she has a search grid."

"Be glad to give her that," Murdock said. "I'll be on the point. Have her send a boat to pick me up when she arrives."

"We'll do that, Commander. Good hunting."

Murdock stared at the mike for a minute, then handed it back to the lieutenant.

"Oh, there's one more pickup. There are four hula dancers and four naked Chinese officers on that same ridge where you picked me up. I promised the girls I'd get them off the place before dark. Talk with your station and have one of your birds go out and get them. They're at an open place with a good LZ. Let me know when the girls are safely back off the mountain and the four Chinese officers are in custody."

"You joking, Commander?"

"Not a chance. Just send the order and attach that red signature to it. I don't care much about the Chinese, but I want those girls down from there safe and happy before dark."

"Yes, sir," the lieutenant said, and picked up the mike. Murdock moved out to talk with his men. They had some decisions to make.

16

Kualoa Point
Oahu, Hawaii

Senior Chief Dobler, with a bandage on his forehead, asked the question first.

"Sir, we going to camp out here for the night?"

"Looks like it, Senior Chief. I bet you forgot your night-night teddy bear."

"Roger that, sir. And my sleeping bag. Can we put in an order for some more box lunches?"

"Sounds good, and some hot coffee. Get it from the Marines and tell them to send it over by launch. Cost Uncle less that way."

"I'm talking to the chopper pilot and using his radio," Dobler said.

Murdock sat on the grass and stared out at the bay. There was a bomb out there that could vaporize half of Oahu. Why had they put it in the water? It had twice the destructive force up on that pinnacle. Here the mountains would protect most of Honolulu. He shrugged. Maybe it was a hoax box after all. They could have put some hot material in the box so it would leak out just enough radioactive signals to make the thing seem real. Sure, but why? He still had the feeling that the bomb was real, a threat, and one they had to deactivate.

Lead blankets. He hadn't thought about them. He'd call NEST later on and have them bring out a pair. Or he could send the chopper up the mountain with two drivers to see if the Humvees were still functioning and drive them back. They each had a lead blanket. Or did the Chinese leave the lead on the bomb? No, they wouldn't. Maybe the Chinkos had left the lead blankets where they picked up the bomb.

He went to the chopper pilot and gave him instructions. It was still plenty light enough to find the two rigs.

"Ching and Fernandez, front and center on me," Murdock said into his lip mike. The two SEALs came up quickly.

"Yes, sir, Skipper?" Ching asked.

Murdock told them the assignment.

"Yeah, should be there unless the Chinese borrowed them," Fernandez said. "See you when we get back."

Murdock called the rest of the men around after the chopper took off, explaining where the two men went. Then he told them about the minesweeper coming around the coast from Pearl.

"It can work in the dark, right?" Lam asked.

"Better because the bay will be rid of any chop it might have had from the wind. You can sack out or play pocket pool or whatever. Senior chief has ordered some box lunches and coffee. We might have work to do early on after the sweeper gets here." The crowd of civilians had tired of watching nothing, and most of them had moved on. The cop came up and looked at Murdock.

"Commander, anything going to be happening here tonight that you'll need any police involvement for?"

"Not a thing, Officer. Be dark and we'll be on the bay. How do you like your 9mm pistol?"

"Okay. The Glock. Yeah. Gives us more firepower. I have two thirty-three-round magazines if things get hot. Hell of a lot better than the old five-shot revolvers."

"Ever jammed on you?"

"Never, and I've put all thirty-three through it in less than a minute. Gets warm, but never has jammed."

"Good. Officer, we'll be here most of the night, maybe all

night. Let your relief know about us so he won't be surprised. Thanks for your help."

"Yeah, Okay. Good luck with your hunt." The cop turned and walked away, looking like he wanted to talk some more.

Murdock checked his watch. Lots of time before dark, and almost two and a half hours before the minesweeper would arrive. Murdock kicked the turf. He hated this inaction. They had to do one more look, get deeper, they might find something. They would go out farther this time.

"Come on, you dildos with ears, let's get wet." The SEALs pulled on their rebreathers, fitted feet into fins, and walked backward into the warm Hawaiian water. There was only small wave action here.

"Let's take another look," Murdock said. "Search pattern, about five yards apart. We have enough light for a good look. Let's get down to at least sixty feet and level off. We're only looking for something on the bottom. That truck we saw sure as hell isn't going to motor away anywhere. Not much of a current or tide here, so it must have dropped straight down. Let's do it."

The SEALs went into the water, worked down to sixty feet, and began their sweep search straight out to the spot where the witnesses said the box got wet. Their Draegrs had been modified with a special gas mix so they could go down to sixty feet.

On the first pass they found nothing. Murdock signaled for them to do one more sweep, and they moved two hundred feet toward the shore, working slowly through the deep blue water. Murdock sent a signal to surface at the end of the two hundred feet. On top they pulled out their mouthpieces and talked.

"Might not be the right spot," Lam said. "The eyewitnesses could be wrong."

"Usually they are," Murdock said.

"How about moving back toward shore fifty yards more and try it again at seventy feet down," DeWitt said.

"Wish we could," Murdock said. "But not with these Draegrs. We'll do another run at fifty." They pushed the mouthpieces back in and duck-dived, heading down to fifty feet, each man keeping in touch with his buddies on both sides.

The long line of SEALs went to work again. They had only begun their next sweep through the clear waters off Oahu when something large and dark came at them head-on. The SEALs parted and watched the tiny submarine motor past them. Murdock saw it close up.

He signaled the men to the surface and they compared notes.

"Yeah, a two-man submarine," DeWitt said. "Looked like some of those the Italians designed. North Korea had a whole shit-pot full of them a few years ago, more than fifty."

"That sumbitch wasn't no more than fifteen, maybe twenty feet long," Murdock said. "Hell, we've got torpedoes almost that big."

"Where was it going and what is it doing here?" Dobler asked. "Was it Chinese? I didn't see any flag painted on it."

"Out of here," Murdock said, and began a strong crawl stroke toward the shore. Once there he stripped out of his Draegr and headed for the chopper. It wasn't back yet from the Hummer run. He yelled for Holt.

The radioman quickly set up the SATCOM and positioned the fold-out antenna. The beep came, showing the antenna was aligned correctly.

"Murdock to CINCPAC."

"Yes, Murdock. Any progress?"

"Ran into a strange little visitor. Looked like a North Korean two-man submarine. Did the Chinese buy some of them?"

"Our people know nothing about the Chinese having or using any two-man subs. What's it doing?"

"It's where we think the bomb dropped. If I had to guess, I'd say it's looking for the bomb just as we are."

"See any viewing ports in the sub?"

"No, sir."

"Then how could it be looking for the bomb? It can't have anything very sophisticated electronically on board. How long was the vessel?"

Murdock looked at his men, who had gathered around.

"Twenty feet," Mahanani said.

"Twenty-five," Ching suggested.

"Twenty, maybe twenty-five feet," Murdock told the handset.

"We have four antisub chaser choppers at the Marine base there. I'll get two of them in the air within five minutes. They can drop sonobuoys and pen him in. Which way was he headed?"

"Heading into the bay last thing we saw of him, but we don't know where he went after that."

"Stay out of the water, the choppers have lifted off. They are maybe five minutes from you. They will stay on this TAC frequency."

"That's a Roger, CINCPAC. We're out."

The SEALs watched the sky to the southwest, where the Marine base was situated. Seven minutes later they heard the birds coming. Two choppers in formation.

"Seahawks, the SH-60," Dobler said. "Prime antisub hunters. This should be fun to watch."

The choppers parted and the SEALs could see something dropping out of them.

"Sonobuoys," Dobler said. "They drop them in two lines and wait for one of the sensors to pick up a signal of the sub. Reads out on board."

The birds dropped another line of sonobuoys, and created a box about half a mile square.

The big choppers worked the area slowly, sometimes hovering at two hundred feet.

"If they get some readings on that sub, can they triangulate and pinpoint him?" Khaki asked.

Canzoneri, their Torpedoman's Mate First Class, snorted. "Hell, they can do better than that. They can tie down where that sucker is within fifteen feet."

"Yeah?" Jefferson asked. "So what do they do then?"

Canzoneri laughed. "Like shooting fish in a bucket in here. The Seahawk drops in a Mark 46 homing torpedo. It hits the water and looks for the mass of metal out front, tracks it, and boom, no more miniature sub."

Franklin looked worried. "So what happens to the nuke out there in the water? Does the blast set off the nuke?"

Canzoneri shrugged. "How'en hell would I know?"

Murdock saw nobody else was answering. "Most nuclear weapons are ultimately safe around explosions and jolts and bombs and earthquakes. They need a special fusing and that fuse has to be activated in a certain way. A strong explosion near nukes can shake up their insides so the firing mechanism might not work right. I've never heard of a nuke being set off anyway but by the established trigger and resulting procedure."

"Now that, Cap, keeps me happy," Tony Ostercamp said.

They watched the choppers again. They seemed to be concentrating on one section of the bay two miles from the shore.

"Something's cooking out there," DeWitt said. One of the choppers had moved in, then backed off and moved up again. They all cheered when they saw a longish object dropped from the chopper.

"That would be our old reliable Mark 46," Canzoneri said. "The party is almost over for that mini-sub."

An explosion came a few seconds later. The shock came through the ground, then a distant sound. Then the surface of the bay erupted in a twenty-foot geyser of boiling water.

Holt turned on the radio and tried two channels before he picked up the pilots.

"Bird Nest, this is Low Flyer One. We have made contact and it looks like a hit with a forty-six. Standing by for eval on the water surface."

"Roger that, Low Flyer One. Confirm, then return to base."

The water calmed and both helicopters flew over the spot, hovered, then worked a slow circle.

The SATCOM speaker came on again. "Bird Nest, we have confirmation. Lots of debris in the water, and an oil slick. Our sonobuoy readouts have lost the target. That's a kill."

"Return to base, Low Flyer One. Good shooting."

The two Seahawks turned and headed back southwest toward their field.

"By the book," DeWitt said, dropping onto the grass beside Murdock. "Now where is that minesweeper?"

"Not due for two hours?" Murdock said. "Be dark by that time."

Murdock stretched out on the grass of the small roadside park. "I'm catching some bunk time. You've got the con, JG. If the guys come back with the Humvees, have them park them and wait. I hope these search guys on the sweeper know what they're doing with their high-tech equipment."

DeWitt waved at his CO and checked the squads. Half of the men were sleeping. The others cleaned weapons or talked about the operation. It was getting dark fast then.

"Hey, JG, we gonna get any leave time over here?" Ron Holt asked. "I could spend a few days on the beach just watching them bikinis wiggling past."

"Sounds like a good idea, Holt. We'll wait and see how this mission turns out. We hope there'll be a Honolulu left to visit."

Less than a half hour later, their private chopper came back and settled down on the grass thirty yards from the SEALs. DeWitt talked to the pilot.

"Yeah, we found them. I waited to be sure that both of the rigs started and could drive. They should be back here in less than an hour."

DeWitt took a walk along the side of the bay. He wondered how Milly was getting along. If this settled down, he'd send an E-mail to their home computer. A sound caught his attention. Then he saw a boat powering toward them. It was a small-class patrol boat and came straight for the point, then turned a little toward the SEALs. Chow time.

The SEALs woke up for the food. The box lunches had double sandwiches, oranges, a turnover apple pie, and two cookies, and there was a thirty-cup-sized urn of coffee. The boat stayed until the coffee was drained, then pushed off heading back to the base. DeWitt kept four box lunches for the Humvee-driving SEALs.

Murdock ate his meal, then went back to sleep. He knew he'd better grab some snore time while he could. Hard telling what would happen next on this crazy mission.

He came awake when the Humvees boiled up on the road and shut down in the parking lot. Then an hour later, just at 2005, the minesweeper steamed into the bay and stopped two hundred yards offshore. By that time it was totally dark. Murdock used his flashlight and sent a Morse code word out. It was "Murdock."

A few minutes later they heard a small motor, and a gig came in to the point.

"Is Murdock here?" someone called from the boat as it grounded.

"Here and ready," Murdock said. He, Lam, and Dobler stepped into the gig and it powered back to the ship. The *Chief* turned out to be 224 feet long. The deck was crammed with machinery and equipment of all kinds. The SEALs went up a ladder and the gig was winched on board.

The ship's captain, Commander Lawson, met them at the rail.

"Glad to have you on board, Commander Murdock. You're welcome to observe everything we do. This is not a swift operation like the sonobuoy trick the choppers just worked."

"Understood. If we get in the way, boot our tails. You have any divers on board?"

"No, sir. I'd imagine that's where your men will come into play. What we do have is SLQ-37(V)3 magnetic/acoustic-influence sweep equipment. That's what should do the job. We can only sweep a relatively small section at a time and we move rather slowly, so we have time to evaluate any readings we get. Probably the best spot for you to view the process is at our readout screens. This way."

"Ever hunted a nuke before, Commander?"

"So far our record is perfect on that score, Commander Murdock. Which is to say, this is the first nuke that we've looked for."

In a map room, Murdock and the captain plotted out a search area. It came out a hundred yards due west of the land on the point, out six hundred yards, then a six-hundred-yard square including that one-hundred-yard point where the witnesses thought they saw the bomb dumped.

"Is that too large a search grid?" Murdock asked. "How long will it take to search that whole area?"

"Twelve to fourteen hours. If we don't run into too much garbage in the water."

"Could be too long," Murdock said. "We don't know for

sure if the Chinese have a method to detonate the bomb underwater without a surface antenna. Could you start at the most likely spot in the center and work outward from there?"

"That's the way we usually work, Commander. Settle back and enjoy the show."

They all watched the readout screen. Within fifteen minutes a small bell rang. They had picked up metal, but it turned out to be the rusting hulk of an old motor car. The machines whirled and the ship moved along slowly.

There was no camera on the search. It was all electronic with a readout. Any metal found had to be a certain size to register. Old tin cans did not show up.

A sailor came into the compartment with a message for the captain. He read it and handed it to Murdock.

It was from CINCPAC. "Negotiations with the Chinese have broken down. The Chinese now threaten to set off the bomb at 1200 tomorrow. Suggest all possible speed in the search." It was over the name of Admiral R.D. Bennington.

Commander Lawson shook his head. "Damn, there is no way we can make this equipment work any faster. Twelve hours, unless we get lucky on the sweet spot in the center."

Murdock scowled and took a deep breath. This was the part he hated. The whole damn world was about to be blasted into hell and there wasn't a fucking thing he could do about it.

17

Kaneohe Bay
Oahu, Hawaii

A half hour after the sweep by the big ship began, a sailor came to tell Murdock he was wanted in the radio room.

"CINCPAC is calling for you," the seaman said. "We don't get many messages from the top man in the Pacific."

Murdock took the handset and responded.

"Murdock here, sir."

"Yes. Good. Thought you would be on board the *Chief*. We've had some reaction from Admiral Magruder on the *Jefferson*. He's had some of his antisub choppers on a search pattern around the waters off Kaneohe Bay. Says there's a chance that the mini-sub was brought in by a regular Chinese sub latched to the deck. Then when they got into the shallow water of the bay, or near it, they sent the little guy in to look for the bomb."

"Yes, sounds like a good possibility."

"Now that the mini-sub is gone, the Chinese will have to use some other tactic. Chances are that the regular sub will come into the bay hunting the bomb, or it will send in divers or small boats. Magruder wanted you to be aware of this possibility and figured you might have some ideas."

"Yes, sir. Those sub-killing torpedoes are the best idea. Did the admiral say that they had any indications that there was a sub off the coast?"

"From their searches they have had some readings, but they fade out too fast. He says definitely there is at least one Chinese sub in this area, but they aren't sure exactly where."

"Sir, there's been some talk about the bomb threat as being a hoax. Any thinking on that?"

"We've worked it over a dozen times. The radiation we found where the bomb package had been could have been planted, or allowed to leak from some other radioactive material in that big box. Then, on the other hand, they have done a lot of work to plant the thing and move it. Feeling is here that we have to treat it as a real threat until somebody finds it and proves it's not a nuke."

"We'll go on that assumption, Admiral. Anything else?"

"Do what you can for us, Murdock. All we can ask."

"Do our best, Admiral Bennington."

They signed off and Murdock went back to the compartment where they had the readout.

"Nothing so far," the ship's captain told Murdock. "We're still working in what we call the hot zone. We could pick it up any minute if it's still there."

"Kind of hard to move that beer truck and the big box without some divers and a good tugboat," Murdock said. "Divers couldn't do it alone." They watched the readout.

A half hour later Murdock had a question. "Commander, if you needed to drop a package into the bay here and intended to come back for it, how would you do the job?"

"How? Equipment?"

"That and anything else that would help you locate the package."

"I don't know. A marker buoy would be good, but then anyone could find it. Maybe put a sonobuoy on it activated, then locate it with a line of sonobuoys."

"I thought they picked up signals for detecting subs. Could one sonobuoy find another one?"

"I don't know. I never tried it."

"How else could you mark a spot in the ocean and come back to it?"

"A radioactive leak?"

"It would get spread all over the place and not tell your Geiger counter where the leak came from."

Commander Lawson shook his head. "I think you have something there, Commander. Just what the clue is I don't know. If I wanted to drop something in the bay and come back for it, I'd mark it somehow, at least take its precise location with a mugger."

"So how was that Chinese mini-sub going to find the bomb?" Murdock asked.

Lam had been listening to the talk. "Skipper, what about those things they have built into airplanes that send out a signal when they go down? You know, that emergency radio signal that can be followed to find the crash site."

Murdock grinned. "A transponder. Yeah. It can work on radar, radio, or sonar. Most of them can start transmitting automatically in a crash, or they can be set to respond to an incoming signal, then send out a preprogrammed signal that can be tracked right back to the source."

"You suppose the Chinese slapped a transponder on that bomb before they dropped it in the drink?" Commander Lawson asked.

"It's a possibility. What can we lose by trying? Only what would it be on? Radio, radar, or sonar?"

"Sonar," Lam said.

Commander Lawson frowned. "My field," he said. "How do we know what power or frequency we would need to activate the transducer to respond to our signal?"

"We don't. But what about some common ones. Would the Chinese build their own or buy them from us through some third party? Let's assume they bought the transponders from some boat maker who put them into his pleasure crafts. What kind would that be and what power would it take to contact it?"

Commander Lawson nodded. "Let me get with an expert on sonar and we'll see what we can do. We do have an array that we can put in the water and tow to send out a narrow-band search signal, or we can send out a wide band search signal. Give me a half hour."

Murdock tried to remember all he could about sonar. The

term came from SOund NAvigation Ranging, SONAR. By
constant use it had dropped its acronym capitals and become
sonar. It is a method for locating and detecting objects sub-
merged in the water by means of echolocation.

It uses the transmission and reflection of pulse energy as
the basis of operation. But the detection ranges for both
military and civilian sonar go from one hundred meters to
one thousand meters. Wavelengths for acoustic signals go
from 0.5 centimeters to thirty centimeters. That corresponds
to frequencies of three hundred kilohertz and five kilohertz.

Right, but what frequency would the Chinese use? Murdock figured he would need that exact frequency to activate
a transponder on the bomb and get it to send out a signal
that they could home in on.

They could get the frequencies used on airliners. That
would be a standard that the Chinese might have picked up
on. No, that would be radio. Sonar, they needed sonar frequencies. Maybe the transponders used on big yachts in case
of trouble. Yes, that might be getting somewhere.

The same radioman came up and motioned to Murdock.

"Commander, you're needed in the radio shack again.
Right away."

"CINCPAC?"

"Yes, I think so, sir."

Murdock took the handset and reported in.

"Magruder tells me that they have had more indications of
that Chinese sub. Last contact was about five miles offshore
directly north of Kaneohe Bay. Evidence is that the sub is
moving your way."

"Admiral, we've been doing some brainstorming here and
have about decided that the bomb could have some kind of
a transponder on it. A sonar unit of some kind. Our thought
is that the Chinese left the bomb here with a response transponder, so they could walk down a beam and find it when
they wanted it, when it was safe to come and get it."

"Which would be at night."

"Exactly. Sub captains don't like a hundred feet of water
to crawl around in. The wide shelf here around the island is
about a hundred feet for a long way out. That's poison to a
sub."

"Unless they have another mini-sub on board that could tow the bomb out of there."

"Doubt it, Admiral."

"Me too."

"The Navy choppers going to try to follow the sub in and nail it here?"

"We don't know. This sub seems to have some tactic to become invisible. Working in and out of the thermal layer, I'd imagine. We'll keep you informed.

"Murdock, say the minesweeper finds the bomb, can you go down and get it? The sweeper doesn't have divers. Can you work down to, say, a hundred feet?"

"Not with any safety, Admiral. Our closed rebreathers are generally not good much below thirty feet for any length of time. We could program them with nitrox mixture of oxygen and nitrogen to work the Draegrs down to a hundred feet. But we don't have the goods with us. If we could get some regular open-system SCUBA outfits, our men can go down over a hundred feet to fasten cables on that truck if we find it."

"I'll see that four sets of gear are flown over there tonight. Keep us informed. Now, what about that damn Chinese sub?"

"Let's hope that the antisub guys can nail it before it gets to the bay. It could slip in during darkness and get the bomb, only I don't know how they would haul it out to deep water."

"We'll watch for them. Any late word on the sub?"

"No, but I'll let you know if it gets any closer."

"I'll get my men alerted," said the admiral. "If that sub comes in near the point, we might be able to spot it and trail it somehow."

"Good hunting," said Murdock.

He held the mike a moment, then gave it to the seaman and went to find the captain.

Ten minutes later the three SEALs were on shore talking to the rest of the men.

"So, that brings you guys up to date," Murdock said. "You know everything about it that I do. The commander is working on the transponder idea, trying to get the right frequency.

In the meantime we're on sub alert. Anybody remember how to disable a sub that's in operation?"

"Blow his fucking conning tower off," Jefferson said.

"Good idea, but we won't have that much C-5. How else?"

"If she's stopped you could blow off her propeller," Bradford said.

"But she's moving," Murdock prompted. He looked around. Nobody spoke up. "Okay, I don't know what the Navy calls them, but they are the exterior control panels that make the sub move up or down. Like a wing flap on a plane. If you jam these in one position with a charge, the sub is not able to control up or down direction and can't repair the damage without surfacing. It's a chance. If the periscope is up, you can always blow it off with a quarter-pound."

"So, we're going sub hunting?" Ostercamp asked.

"Just like deer hunting," Holt said. "Only a bigger target."

"When do we go for a swim?" someone asked.

"Not until we're pretty sure that the fish is going to motor into our pool," Dobler said. "Let's get some shut-eye so we'll be ready to go. The time is now 2213. Any questions?"

"They going to figure out the right megahertz to make that transponder talk, if there is one out there?" Mahanani asked.

"We damn well hope so," Murdock said. "Holt, let's play radio."

Murdock tried TAC Two, and caught the chopper pilots chasing the sub.

"Sunnyside One here. We've had two good strong contacts, then they fade out. He's working closer to shore and near as we can tell, we're still north and some west of that north point on Kaneohe Bay."

"That's a Roger, Sunnyside One. Keep at him."

Murdock triggered the send mike button. "Sunnyside One, this is Murdock on Kualoa Point. How far from us are you?"

"Murdock, yes. Estimate about three miles. He seems to be motoring your way at about eight knots. But he's doing a lot of thermal-layer work to confuse us."

"Hope you can nail him before he gets here, Sunnyside."

"Kind of what we had in mind. Watch for us. Sunnyside out."

Murdock looked around in the darkness at his men. "We'll

want to go out fully armed and with explosives and detonators. If some of you don't have them standard, share so every man has at least one charge. We don't know what we might meet out there tonight. I hope like hell we meet something."

The SEALs used small flashlights to check their equipment, then double-check a buddy. With that done, half of them crawled into the Humvees to get out of the soft breeze that had sprung up with sundown. Most of their cammies had dried out, but inside they were still damp. They were used to it. Better than walking around all day in a wet suit. Here the water was like a bathtub.

Murdock used the SATCOM and called the *Chief.* The radioman brought in the captain.

"Nothing so far on the scanners, Murdock. Been talking to some friends about that transponder idea. We've narrowed down the possible kilohertz bands to ten. It should be in that range. We're in the process of getting a towed array ready to put in the water. It will be a relatively narrow band, but we can do it at the same time we're working the sweep for the metal below. Once we get it functioning, we'll send on a band for fifteen seconds. If no response, we'll shift to the next band. Slow and painful, but it could produce results. Oh, you might have heard a chopper drop in on us a few minutes ago. We have a package for you with complete SCUBA gear and filled air tanks for four."

"Good. If we get lucky and find the bomb, the tanks are for deep dives to hook on some cables. I assume you can winch up the prize if we find it?"

"No trouble, Commander. Easy. First we find it. Hear that sub is still headed this way."

"True. We'll swim with it if it gets inside the bay."

They signed off and Murdock tried to relax. He had never tried to attack an active submarine before. Any charge big enough to do damage to the sub would also cause serious damage to any SEAL in the water close to it. The concussion would be devastating. But how could they signal the men to get their heads out of the water if one of them planted a bomb on the sub and pushed the timer? He had no idea.

Murdock frowned and looked to the west. He heard something. Then it came through, the *whup, whup* of a big heli-copter. That would be the sub-hunter choppers. Maybe the same kind they had seen before that killed the mini-sub. How many? Two? He kept listening. Lam came over and pointed to the west, and Murdock nodded.

"If they do come in, hope it's near the point up here," Lam said. "Make it a hell of a lot more convenient."

For ten minutes the sound of the helicopters faded in and out. Then it came stronger. The SATCOM, which Murdock had left set up to receive on TAC Two, came to life.

"Hey, Murdock. Looks like you're going to have com-pany. We can't get a good enough fix on this one to fire. We tried one shot but had no results. It's definitely heading into the shallows there around the point of the bay. Maybe a quarter of a mile or so south of you. Our cap says turn it over to you. Good luck. We're low on juice and going back to Home Base."

"Roger that, Sunnyside. You say they were maybe a quar-ter of a mile off the point when they enter the bay?"

"Just a guess. The sub was heading back toward us last hit. I'd figure no more than a quarter or maybe a half mile off the point southwest. You've got the con, Murdock."

Murdock closed down the set and yelled at his men. "On your feet, ladies, we're going for a swim, and we don't want to be late for the party."

18

Kaneohe Bay
Oahu, Hawaii

A quarter of a mile into the bay, the SEALs slowed their surface crawl and looked around. The *Chief* was on the far end of her grid pattern and turning for another sweep across the target area. Murdock had been wondering why the sub-chaser helicopters didn't come right into the bay. There was no thermal layer there for the Chinese to hide under. Be simple to pinpoint it and blow it out of the water with a homing torpedo.

Then he remembered the *Chief* motoring away through the same waters, and realized the torpedo might just as well home in on the minesweeper. One of them had to give way to the other, and the admiral must have decided to let the *Chief* have first crack at finding the bomb.

Murdock put into operation a new system. He had the fourteen SEALs ten yards apart and each one held onto a length of one-eighth-inch line. That way they could stay together and stay in communication with each other. If any of the men saw the sub working toward them, they would give two sharp pulls on the rope. The signal would be passed from one man to the next. Three sharp pulls meant to surface at once, the chance of a deadly concussion being imminent.

The SEALs formed a 140-yard screen across the bay. Murdock anchored one end and DeWitt the other. Murdock and the men had talked about the mission. Chances were the sub would stay near the surface to keep away from the deadly bottom.

"He'll just keep his conning tower under the water," Murdock said. "My guess. That means we'll stay at our fifteen feet and cruise. I hope that he knows that the bomb went into this northern section of the bay, so he'll come in here."

Now they prowled their turf and waited to see what happened. It could turn out to be a fool's mission. There was a good chance they would never see the Chinese sub. If they did find it, could they keep up with it? How fast would it move in quarters like this? Five knots? Seven? Could his men catch it and hold on somewhere and hope for a chance to plant some bombs on it? The whole bucket of questions kept churning around in Murdock's mind.

Every five minutes Murdock broke the surface and took a good look around. He didn't want the sub to surface and put out a diving party to go after the damn bomb. He'd been up three times now, and had not seen anything except the *Chief* working its business on the close-in grid around the suspect spot.

No submarine.

Good and bad.

The SEALs swam along at fifteen feet at half their usual speed. There was no rush. They worked out to what Murdock figured was three hundred yards from the suspected drop spot for the bomb. He gave three quick jerks on the line and surfaced. In quick succession the rest of the SEALs came up. He swam down the line, telling them it had been a test and had worked. Next time it would be for real. But that was only if they found the sub and planted some charges.

Murdock had DeWitt lead out the line heading back the way they had come. Murdock picked up his Tail-end Charlie rope and kept watching the water toward the sea. In the dark, visibility was no more than six feet. If they did come on the sub, it might be felt and heard in the water before they actually saw it.

Four times they made the run. Each time at the end they would surface, confer, bitch, and go back for another look. The fifth time, Murdock told them to stay on the surface with a nice steady sidestroke.

Twice they came close to the *Chief*, but they didn't get in its way. If it was still moving, that meant they hadn't found anything. If they did, the captain had said they would stop and work the area with all the power they had. So far it had been moving.

Lam had been in the line right behind Murdock. Now he swam up beside his commander. He had his face mask off and his wet suit hat thrown back off his head. He had one ear in the water and waved at Murdock. He came up and shouted at his chief.

"Something down there wasn't there before," Lam said. "I can hear some fucker down there just purring away."

Murdock pulled his cap off and poked his head underwater. He came up a minute later, grinning.

"Oh, yeah, but where?"

Lam pointed seaward. "Heard something last three or four minutes, Skip. Sure as hell is sounding louder. I think we got ourselves some undersea craft heading our way."

Murdock gave two sharp pulls on the rope, then three more. SEALs began popping to the surface.

"We hear something seaward," Murdock told the next man on the line. "Pass it along. We go down again when all have the word, and watch for this bastard, but we don't move unless somebody knows for sure which direction." Murdock pulled his cap back on and adjusted his mask. When he saw through the gloom of the waning moon the last man take the message, Murdock dropped under the surface and moved down to fifteen feet. He kept that depth and stared hard toward where the Pacific Ocean had to be. He couldn't see a damn thing but water. Now he couldn't hear what he had before. He slid his face mask down from his eyes, pulled the wet-suit cap off from his ears, and put his mask back on.

Now, at least he should be able to hear anything coming.

He soon heard something, but it was the steady diesel drone of the *Chief* far toward the shore. He blocked it out and tried to listen to anything from the other direction.

Nothing. He swam up to Lam, who also had his cap off. They both shook their heads and waited.

A moment later Murdock heard it. An engine. Then, slowly materializing almost directly in front of him, the ugly black snout of a submarine.

Chinese? He didn't know? He had studied the Chinese Naval forces a year ago, but he didn't remember much of it. He functioned on a garbage-can-type principle. Gather up everything you need on a topic, sort out the important stuff you must remember, and dump out the rest of it with the garbage.

He knew the Chinese had subs, five fleet and one that carried cruise missiles. Those would be the dangerous kind. The subs all had nuclear power, so they could roam worldwide. From somewhere he remembered a black conical nose on some of the Chinese subs.

He jerked the line twice. At once Lam saw the sub as well. It was thirty feet below them and moving at maybe five knots. Crawling along, worried about the bottom.

Lam looked at him and motioned toward the big black vessel. "Follow it?" he signed. Murdock nodded. There was no time to call down more of the SEALs. They could lose the sub in the dark waters. The side of the sub was under them. They swam down to it, felt the smooth surface of the metal as it slid past them. They needed somewhere to grab and hang on.

The conning tower came toward them. They swam faster and caught it as it went by, moved upward to where they could find fittings and a rail to hold on to. When Murdock saw that Lam had caught a good hold, he sorted his memory for subs. Most had two diving planes, one set fixed on or near the sail structure and one on the bow. He hoped on the sail. He began looking around, feeling. There were six pipes or antennas sticking up from the top of the sail. None of those. Lower. He slid down the front of the sail, letting the forward motion pin him to the metal. Halfway down he found a wide wing-like device. Looked like a stabilizer on an airplane. He'd seen them on subs before. Did they move? Yes. Hinged, with an effect on the level movement of the sub.

At last he found where the movable hinging area was. He packed a stick of TNAZ on each side of the sail on the hinging area, then signaled to Lam. They swam down from the sail to the deck and let the ship move under them as they made their way to the stern. There should be another set of diving planes back there.

The turbulence at the back of the sub made it harder and there was little to hold on to. At last they found a handhold and looked over the sleek end of the vessel.

The submarine slowed. It glided through the water, moving slower and slower, until it nearly stopped. Murdock and Lam swam to the extreme end and checked where there might be exterior diving planes. They found what could be them. Nothing else looked possible. Both men pasted one-quarter-pound sticks of TNAZ explosive on the planes and inserted the detonators. They set them for fifteen minutes with hand signals, then swam for the sail and the other set of explosives.

The sub began to move again and the swim was harder. Lam beat Murdock there, and grabbed him when he almost slanted past the sail.

Murdock went down the front of the sail to the diving plane, pushed a timer/detonator into the TNAZ, and set it for ten minutes. Then the two SEALs swam hard for the surface only thirty feet above them. They hit the surface and Murdock bellowed.

"SEALs, get on dry land. Keep your head above water. Explosives planted. Go, go, go." Far ahead he heard faint calls that they understood.

He and Lam began a fast crawl toward the point of land they could barely make out. They should have left the Hummer with parking lights on or a glow stick.

He heard some sounds in front of him, and decided it must be the rest of the platoon heading for shore.

The first explosion went off just as a small wave caught Murdock and propelled him toward the shore. The vibrations in the water made his legs tingle, and a shock wave hit him with a gentle nudge.

He stumbled ashore and found Lam and the other SEALs waiting for him.

"You found that fucker?" Bradford yelped.

"Did indeed. I heard one charge go off. Should be three more."

As he spoke they heard a low rumble, then a second and a third.

"Four out of four, Skipper," DeWitt said. "Did you get her in a vital spot?"

"Hope so. We worked the diving planes. Wasn't time to get any of the rest of you on the shoot or we'd have lost the sucker. Holt, get out that SATCOM, let's wake up some folks."

Five minutes later the plan was set. CINCPAC had ordered the minesweeper out of the bay and two miles offshore. The more experienced sub-hunters from the *Jefferson* were called in to find the Chinese sub.

"If you damaged her diving planes, she won't be able to surface or submerge any more than her ballast tanks will let her," the spokesman at CINCPAC said. "Good work. The antisub guys should have easy pickings if the boat is still in the bay."

The SEALs cleared their weapons of water, cleaned and oiled them as usual, and then some of the SEALs took off their wet cammies and let them dry. Murdock figured the nighttime temperature was near seventy degrees.

Ten minutes after the first call, two choppers came in from the north and east. They cruised the bay, then set up a picket fence of sonobuoys down the near end of the wide mouth of Kaneohe Bay. The other chopper laid out a line of sonobuoys at right angles to the first drop heading toward shore.

Holt had the SATCOM set for TAC Two, and they listened to the sub-hunters talking in their helicopters.

"So what can he do?" one voice asked. "He can only blow his tanks and surface so he can repair the diving planes. If that's what his problem is."

"Yeah, I'll give that bastard another problem if we find him. I have no contacts on my line."

"None here either. Let's move the box down the bay. He can maneuver left or right. My bet is he's moving down-bay to the slightly deeper water."

"In a hundred feet we could see him in the daylight, couldn't we?"

"Probably. Dropping a new line southeast continuing my line."

"I'll box that in on the end. Think he'll surface and try to get away in the night?"

"He can do maybe twelve knots surfaced. He'd do better to stay down and get about twenty-five."

"Hey, contact on number two and three. He's moving south. Range, four hundred yards. Dropping one Mark 46. It's in the wet."

"Home in on him, you motherfucker!"

"Yeah, go, go."

The SEALs gathered around the radio.

"Twenty-nine, thirty, thirty-one. You missed, Cowboy."

"It's circled around and taking another reading on all that metal mass. It won't miss. Oh, Lordy, look at that eruption of water and metal and Chinese body parts soaring into the air."

"Home Base, this is Birdgame Two. I have a kill. I repeat, I have a kill on one Chinese submarine."

"Very well, Birdgame Two. Stand by for continuing orders."

"Survivors?" the other chopper pilot asked.

"At fifty or sixty feet there should be dozens. Sub like that should carry seventy-five men. If it's one of their attack boats."

"Birdgame Two, drop flares over any wreckage spotted and watch for survivors. Fifty Marines from the air base there are on the way to pick up and control any survivors. How is your juice?"

"In the seventy-five-percent range, Home Base."

"Stand by."

Murdock had Holt switch the SATCOM to the CINCPAC channel. He got contact on the second call.

"Murdock, just heard about the Chinese sub. We're inserting the minesweeper again, but she tells me there will be junk and metal all over the place now, and that will make it a dozen times harder to find the device."

"Commander Lawson on the sweeper was hunting for the

right frequency on a transponder. Did he have any luck?"

"Didn't mention it. He'll be on station in a little over an hour. He'll call you on this channel when he's in position again."

"Thanks, CINCPAC. Will contact him then. Out."

Most of the SEALs went to sleep then, half in the Humvees, half out. The rescue operation went on most of the night with choppers showing lights and the Coast Guard and Marine boats picking Chinese sailors out of the bay. Last count Murdock heard was forty-five, some with serious injuries.

The *Chief* came back on-station and contacted Murdock on the SATCOM.

"Murdock, good work on that sub. Now, how do we find the damn bomb? I'm not at all optimistic about a quick find. We'll have dozens of chunks of metal all over this end of the bay."

"What about the right frequency for the transponder we think is on the bomb?"

"Not a lot of help. We have three that could work. We'll try them when we get some of this junk out of the way. The survivor guys are just about ready to wrap up. They'll be back with the daylight to pick bodies off the shore and out of the surf line."

"The Chinese know by now that they lost the sub. They'll be furious and might just shoot the bomb. The quicker we can find it the better."

"You can send out a signal to that transponder?"

"We have the gear. You want to come on board with three of your divers so you'll be ready if we get a contact?"

"Good idea. Can you send a boat?"

"If you don't want to swim out."

"Please send the damn boat."

Murdock rousted out the best swimmers and divers he had. Ed DeWitt would be one, Mahanani and Lam the other two. They stepped into the boat from the *Chief* at a little after 0400, and were met at the minesweeper with dry cammies, jackets, hot coffee, and sandwiches.

Commander Lawson took them into a room filled with electronics. "We do a lot of work from here. We have seven frequencies we want to try out. So far the first two did not produce any return. We're on number three now. We transmit for thirty seconds, and do that three times. If we hit it right, there should be an almost immediate response."

Fifteen minutes later they were on the next-to-last frequency. The technician triggered the transmission and sat back as he had done more than twenty times before.

"We have a response, sir," the chief said. "We have a continuous reply on that frequency. I can have direction for you in a few seconds." He worked some instruments in front of him. "Sir, that's at one hundred sixty degrees. You want sonar to give us a range?"

"Yes, Chief. That would be good."

"Range is two hundred and eighty yards."

Commander Lawson looked at Murdock. "Don't just sit there, SEAL. Go get into your diving gear and let's retrieve us a damn nuclear bomb."

19

Kaneohe Bay
Oahu, Hawaii

It took the four SEALs only three minutes to slip into the SCUBA gear, test the masks and airflow, and work down the ladder into the warm Hawaiian bay. They all had their wrist compasses, and moved out on the 160-degree heading. When they agreed they had covered the 280 yards, they stopped on the surface and treaded water as they talked.

"We all go down and find the box, then Mahanani comes back up. By that time the ship should be overhead, and they'll pass him a line or a cable and he'll bring one or two or three down to us. We hook them on, latch them up good and strong, and knock three times on the cable to start the lift. Everyone on the same page?"

They nodded in the dark, then duck-dived and began swimming down the one hundred feet to where the bomb should be.

It had been some time since Murdock had used a standard SCUBA outfit, and the heavy tank on his back seemed out of place and strange. But as he neared the bottom he forgot about it and concentrated on finding the bomb.

The bomb was not there. The bottom showed up darkly

sandy with a few scuttering fish, a rock or two, but no bomb. They moved straight ahead down the azimuth reading.

It loomed out of the dusky depths like a freight train gone wrong. It lay on one side, the same fake beer truck they had seen before. Inside would be the wooden box, with slats and holes and holding something dark and dangerous and deadly. They checked it out on all four sides. They gathered and nodded, gave the yes sign. It had to be the beer truck they had seen before.

If the Chinese had coordinated their attack better, surprise might have won for them. But the four Chinese frogmen came out of the gloom one at a time from the same direction, which meant finding the four SEALs there must have been a surprise for them as well as for the SEALs.

Murdock drew his KA-BAR fighting knife from the scabbard on his right leg, and charged the first knife-wielding Chinese. He saw the other SEALs pull out their knives and take up the hunt. The first Chinese may have been their best. He drove in, then darted the other way and made a wide swiping attack with his blade. It missed. That gave Murdock a chance to kick in hard and drive his knife at the Chinese man's exposed right side while the frogman's knife was high over his head.

Murdock felt the blade sink into flesh, but the victim twisted away. Not a killing thrust.

They parried, dove in, and then back. Murdock saw that it was a one-on-one fight times four. A SEAL could get hurt that way. He feinted one way, caught the Chinese frogman defending that way too far, and kicked hard through the water and sliced his heavy blade through the air hose right below the Chinese frogman's face. Air gushed out. The eyes of the man through the face mask were wide and filled with panic. Then he began to stroke upward toward the surface. Murdock caught his legs and held him down. Bubbles exploded out of the Chinese frogman's tank. His hands stabbed at Murdock's arms around his legs. Slowly his struggles eased, then stopped. He was dead.

Murdock turned just as one of the Chinese swam away from his fight with Lam to attack Murdock's unprotected back. Murdock swung his KA-BAR and saw blood from a slashed wrist stain the blue of the water. He followed up kicking the man in the stomach, then driving his blade into the man's chest. Murdock yanked the blade out with an effort, and saw the Chinese man go limp and drift away with the gentle current.

Remembering his near-fatal mistake, Murdock spun around now quickly to check for any attacker near him. He saw Mahanani grab his challenger from behind and drive his KA-BAR deeply into the man's chest, then let him go and watch him settle to the bottom.

Ed DeWitt swam toward the rest slowly. One hand held his air hose to his tank. A few bubbles seeped out around his hand.

He pointed upward and Murdock nodded. He pointed to Mahanani to go up, bring down the cables, and be sure that the JG made it to the top.

The two pushed off, working slowly toward the surface, hoping there wouldn't be any air-bubble trouble.

Murdock nodded. At only a hundred feet depth they shouldn't have any problem going up rather fast. The two SEALs left on the bottom pushed on to the beer truck. It lay partly on its side. It had only half the weight here it would on deck. They found that with a lot of shoving they could rock it, and then they heaved, and it tilted over and bounced on its flat tires, sitting upright. It was in a position now so that they could attach cables and hooks to four places on the frame, two in front, two in back. Murdock edged into the truck cab and looked in back. Yes, the same wooden crate was there. The bomb was still on board.

There was no sign of the sling that had brought it here. It could have come undone and floated away as the truck went straight to the bottom.

They waited. It wasn't long, but just staring at the device that could vaporize him and half of Oahu in a heartbeat left Murdock a little unsettled.

The damn lead blankets. He'd forgotten about them. Where were they? Yeah, on the point in the Humvee. Have to get them to the ship fast as soon as they got up. Or he could send Mahanani back up as soon as they got the cables down there and ask the captain to go get the blankets.

The Hawaiian came down then with a diver from the minesweeper. They each carried the end of two one-inch-thick cables. They were let out gently from on top so the men wouldn't be crushed by the weight of the heavy steel wire.

Murdock swam to Lam, and all four worked with the heavy cables to attach them to the frame. Hooks worked on the front. In back they had to loop the cable around the frame and secure the hook on the cable. Lam nodded. Murdock knew he had to go topside and have the lead blankets brought out to the minesweeper to cloak the bomb on board so no Chinese radio signal could set off the bomb. No way he could tell anyone else down here to go get the blankets.

He worked upward slowly. Then when he realized there were no bad effects on his bloodstream, he hurried and surfaced twenty yards from the boat. A crewman helped him up the ladder.

Commander Lawson was there waiting.

"It's the bomb, the same one you saw before?"

"Yes, and we need those two NEST lead blankets we have onshore. Can we get a boat and a crew to go get them so we have them here when the bomb hits your deck?"

"Oh, God, yes. I'd forgotten about that." He yelled at a chief, who lowered a twenty-foot boat over the side and took a crew of four and powered for shore.

Murdock went over by the winch where the cables were attached, and watched. DeWitt was there as well, showing no ill effects from the close encounter below. Soon a clanking came from the cables.

"The signal, sir, from below," said a sailor who sat on the winch seat in front of the controls.

"Ease her up gently three feet and see how she holds," Commander Lawson ordered.

It was done.

Twenty minutes later, the top of the beer truck broke the surface next to the minesweeper and the crew cheered. They hoisted it on the stern, and six men quickly opened the rear doors and covered the wooden crate with the two lead blankets from NEST.

"Better tell the admiral we have his bomb," Murdock said.

He slumped to the deck and let the tension and exhaustion drain out of him.

Commander Lawson came back a few minutes later and squatted beside Murdock.

"We'll put you and your men off at the point. The admiral told us to get up speed and start moving straight north away from the islands. He'll let me know when to stop. My guess is we'll go out far enough to get a chopper to lift it off and move it somewhere else. Just where, I'm not certain. The admiral wants it off the islands as far as possible. He said if we try to deactivate it the way we do our own, there could be some break-to-make circuits inside that would set it off."

"He could always fly it and a crew to Midway Island."

"Or one of the far-out northwestern Hawaiian islands. The chain stretches almost to Midway. I guess it's the end of the chain."

"How does he get it there fast?" Murdock asked.

"His problem as soon as he lifts it off my ship."

Ten minutes later, the SEALs had shucked out of the SCUBA gear and were back on the point of land at the top of Kaneohe Bay.

Senior Chief Dobler met them at the beach where the boat from the minesweeper had deposited them.

"We got the bomb, Senior Chief. Anything else cooking from Stroh or the admiral?"

"Nary a beep. Skipper, looks like time you had some quality sleep."

"What time is it?"

"Almost 0500. Sack time."

Murdock nodded, found some grass next to the Humvee, and slid down. He was sleeping before he could get his eyes closed.

Senior Chief Dobler watched the four divers find spots and go to sleep. He hadn't heard anything from the admiral, mostly because he told Holt to leave the SATCOM radio turned off. They deserved a little bunk time for a change. He wasn't sure when he had slept last, but he could get along with very little shut-eye.

He'd done this before with the other platoon. This was the second platoon he'd handled, and he figured it might be his last. He was coming up on thirty-eight years old. Dobler sighed and rubbed his left calf. An old injury. No, an old wound. A knife had gone in and all the way through. The bastard who cut him didn't live two minutes after that. A good trade-off.

When would he throw in the damn towel and call it a career with the SEALs? He had no notion just when. The first time he couldn't keep up with the platoon on a forced march, or couldn't lift his share of the burden on a mission, he would be out of the SEALs. Well, maybe not out of the SEALs, but for sure out of the platoons.

He could always get another spot in SEAL Team Seven. Lots of billets he could fill. He had in nineteen, only needed one more for retirement. Right now he had no idea of abandoning the ship on twenty. Maybe twenty-five or thirty. He hadn't promised his wife he'd quit at twenty. Some of his buddies had done that, and gotten in a whole shit-pot full of trouble. He grinned. Had to keep a strong hand at home just like with the platoon.

At 0800 Senior Chief Dobler roused the platoon and had Holt turn on the SATCOM to receive. It spoke at once. Murdock and the rest of the platoon had just come together to figure out what to do next.

"Lieutenant Commander Murdock, respond to CINCPAC. We've been trying to reach you. We have a problem. Contact us at once."

Holt passed the mike to Murdock.

"CINCPAC, this is Lieutenant Commander Murdock responding to your message."

The set spoke quickly.

"Good. Your position and situation, Commander."

Murdock told the speaker.

"Good. Use your transport to come to CINCPAC HQ at Pearl. The admiral has an assignment for you that we're two days late on already. Report in at the earliest possible time."

"Roger that, we're on our way."

DeWitt said what all of them were thinking. "The admiral has a project for us that we're two days late on already? What the fuck does he mean by that?"

20

The three SEALs stood stiffly at attention in front of Admiral Bennington's desk. He had just welcomed them on board.

"Stand at ease, men. This won't take long." The admiral rubbed his hand over his face. Murdock thought it showed a few more wrinkles and a drawn look it hadn't had before.

"When I said we were two days behind on a mission, what I meant is that something happened two days ago and we just found out about it this morning. The Hawaiian governor and four of his top aides and staff have been kidnapped by the invading forces. Quite simply, we want you to go and free them and bring them back all safe and sound."

"Kidnapped, sir?" Murdock asked.

"Strange set of circumstances. The day before the invasion, the governor and five of his people went on a reality retreat where they were going to test themselves and to do some hard planning for the year ahead. It's a primitive camp high up on Red Hill, the highest point on Maui. It's surrounded by a national forest reserve and a lot of woods and open spaces.

"The place is called Hardship Camp, and it's used by some

of our juvenile courts and church groups and by some big business firms for a total confrontation of personalities.

"There is no electricity, running water, or sanitary facilities whatsoever at the camp. The only access is a five-mile hike from the end of a horrendously crooked two-lane road leading up the north side.

"None of the campers were permitted to bring along cell phones, radios, laptop computers, any type of communication devices. They wanted to be isolated for four days so they could get some heavy work done."

"What about the operators of the camp?" Murdock said. "They must have some kind of communications."

"If they do, no one knows about it. Two ex-nuns run the place. They do a lot of meditating and prayer, and don't hold with modern conveniences."

"How do we know they're still there?" Ed DeWitt asked.

"The Chinese told us. They brayed it on their radio and in English so we all could get the message. The press picked it up. It's in tonight's papers and on the TV and radio. It's a huge story."

"How did the Chinese get in there?" Senior Chief Dobler asked.

"We assume by helicopter. In and out middle of the night."

"So they might have only twenty or thirty men there," Murdock said.

"A Lieutenant Hing of the Chinese Marines claims that he has a hundred men surrounding the top of the mountain. He says he can hold off a battalion of attackers."

"Realistically, how many men do you think he has?" DeWitt asked.

"My Marines say not more than fifty, maybe thirty-five. It's an easy spot to defend."

"So we go up and dig him out," Murdock said.

"My people suggested some kind of a silent approach and a surprise."

"I'd guess the mountain is forested," Murdock said. "Not a good spot for a parachute landing. That cuts down on the element of surprise."

"We could go in by small helicopters that wouldn't make

much sound," Dobler said. "Slip in on the off side of the mountain from the camp and work around to it."

"They'll have at least two layers of outpost security," DeWitt said.

"We go around or through them," Murdock said. "I like the idea of the smaller choppers at night. If there isn't an LZ up there we can rope down. I'd guess you'd want us to be up there tonight?"

"First dark if you can make it, Commander."

A commander at the side of the room came up and gave Murdock a letter.

"Show that wherever you need to and you'll have complete cooperation. This covers any supplies, services, or aircraft and vehicles you need."

"Thanks. Admiral, we better get moving. We have some planning and resupply to do. Can the choppers be at Hickam by 1800?"

"Should be no problem. Work that out with Commander Philder."

"Thank you, sir. We'll do our best."

"That's all we ask, Commander. That's a valuable package up on that mountain. Let's hope that there is no damage to any part of it."

"Yes, sir." Murdock said. The SEALs did about-faces and walked out the side door followed by Commander Philder.

They settled on one Sea Knight that was available at Hickam for use by the Navy. It took another two hours to check out the SEALs and work out resupply needs. They took extra ammo loads that would come in drag bags.

The retreat was on the south slope of Red Hill two miles from the end of the road, which came almost to the summit and dead-ended there. The roadway came up a rugged route from the north.

The SEALs checked out the maps in their quarters at Pearl.

"Looks like we can come in from the north and even in the Sea Knight we have a good chance they won't hear us on top," Dobler said. "We'll be about a mile down and land on the road. Quick on and off so we won't bother any midnight traffic."

"We take the twenties?" Holt asked.

"Two of the Bull Pups and two EARs," Murdock said. "Regular weapons as well. We don't know what we'll run into up there, or just where the hostages are kept."

"The description of the retreat brags that there aren't any permanent buildings, only a few tent floors and frames," DeWitt said.

Commander Philder came in and told them it was set with the Marine flyboys for transport. "The Sea Knight can do a hundred-and-fifty-four-mile-an-hour cruise speed, and the run over to Maui is only ninety-two miles. So you get there in little less than a half hour. The Sea Knights have plenty of range to return to base without refueling."

"When does it get dark?" Murdock asked.

"This time of year, about 1900 unless there's a rain squall. Then it's earlier. When do you want to leave Hickam?"

"Liftoff at 1830," Murdock said. The commander nodded and hurried outside.

The liftoff came on time, and it was still light enough that they could see most of Molokai as they slanted past it. Then some weather closed in and they missed Lanai. They came in on Maui on the southwest coast, and began climbing due west up to Red Hill. By the time they crossed into the Kula Forest Reserve, it was almost dark. The pilot had vectored them in slightly north of the peak so he could find the road from the north.

He nailed it, then followed it in the moonlight at a hundred feet over the wash of the ages-old spread of volcanic debris. They were at the very edge of the Haleakala National Park. It encompassed the huge caldron of the dormant Haleakala volcano.

It was almost dark now, but below they could see a wild variety of native trees, eucalyptus trees, and fields of cactus. The darkness closed in and the pilot dropped down lower. He came soon to a flat spot on the paved road, and set the chopper down on the blacktop. They could see no car lights either way.

"Pilot says we're a mile from the top, so all ashore," Murdock said as the wheels touched and the crewman let down the rear hatch. The SEALs moved out slowly, each with a drag bag filled with ammo and goods they might need for a stay of several days. They grouped well out of the rotor wash, and watched the bird button up and lift off, going back the way it had come.

"Welcome to Maui, ladies. Let's take a hike," Murdock said. They hiked up the road until they could see lights of the visitors' center. They went into the brush there and by-passed the center, then worked slightly downhill as they moved around the west side of the mountain. They had planned on avoiding the Skyline Trail, which wound around to a recreation area well below. The retreat was supposed to be two miles south from the summit on a small peak and with a flat place around it. Murdock figured the clients of the retreat walked in on the Skyline Trail.

As they moved through the darkness, the landscape changed. The towering eucalyptus trees gave way to brush and more rain-forest-type vegetation. Murdock had seen on one of the maps that this was a forest reserve. The wood and brush became thicker. Evidently this side of the island received more rainfall than the other side.

Murdock called a halt after a half hour. They had been scrambling along the side slope of the mountain, which made it tougher going. Each SEAL had his usual jungle cammies, floppy hat of the same design, and his weapons and ammo. The average load for this trip was from sixty to seventy pounds depending on the weapon and ammo. Four of the men carried two weapons, the Bull Pup or the EAR gun and their usual shooter. Add a forty-pound drag bag of ammo and supplies, and the men carried a load.

The break gave Murdock some time to think. He could lay out no plans for this mission. It was so blind he felt like he had a black cloth wrapped around his head. They would simply have to play it by ear and as the chips fell. The damn situation and terrain again.

He wondered what Ardith was doing this night in Washington, D.C.? Usually he didn't let thinking about her smash into his work on a mission. Somehow tonight was different. He missed her. God, how he missed her. She was special, more wonderful than any woman he had ever known, marvelous, a good friend, and a delicious and inventive lover. Oh, damn. He frowned. Had he said that last out loud? He looked around. Nobody paid any attention to him. They were recuperating for the next hike.

He checked his watch. Five minutes. Time enough. No, another five. This one was special. He didn't want to mess it up. If they were too tired they could stumble into an outpost. The damn Chinese would have guards out. He hadn't figured where they would be.

After ten minutes he lifted up. The others saw him and stood. There would be no talking the rest of the way. Murdock and Lam judged the distance. They were spread out ten yards apart, barely able to see each other, but it was safer that way in case of an ambush or a lucky hand grenade. Then only one man would go down, not four or five if they were close together.

Lam went out in front as the scout working through the trees and brush, staying at the same level on the mountain. From here it looked like they were about a thousand yards down from the top. Where they should be. Another mile and they would be in position. He wasn't sure if they should start up tonight or do some recon and find out what they were up against.

High on the slopes above them in the Hardship Camp, Governor Tom Itashi sat on the low wooden bunk built into the wooden sides of the tent foundation and frame. His hands were free, but a steel band tightly around his right ankle was locked to the side frame. Lieutenant Hing stared hard at him in the soft glow of one candle that had been waxed in place on the end of the bench.

"I ask you once more, Governor Itashi. How much time will it take your people to respond to our demands?"

"Lieutenant Hing, I have no idea. You ask for a helicopter and gold and a ship. I can offer you none of these. The U.S. Government and the Hawaiian State Government do not negotiate with terrorists for the lives of hostages. I've told you that a dozen times."

"You are not just a prisoner; you are the governor of Hawaii. An important man. They will not sacrifice you for their principles. In the end they will meet my demands."

"So, if you get the gold and the chopper and the ship, you

will vanish into the Pacific and be rich for the rest of your life?"

"Not true, Governor. I do everything for the great nation of China. I will take the gold to the ship and meet with the victorious Chinese Navy and be promoted to captain in the Marines."

"I am concerned about the welfare of my people. How are they? I haven't seen them since you captured us."

"They would be better if you cooperate. I have fed them once a day. Each has one blanket. None has been beaten, yet." Lieutenant Hing smiled. "Of course I could beat them one at a time while you watched, until you directed your people over the radio to bring the gold."

"Lieutenant Hing. That would not move me. I was a U.S. Marine. I have killed men with my bare hands. I have seen more death, torture, and wanton killing than you can even imagine. You're a child when it comes to persuasion, laughable."

Governor Itashi didn't see the blow coming. Lieutenant Hing slammed his fist into the governor's neck and toppled him sideways on the bench. Governor Itashi struggled to sit up. His jaw felt like it was broken. He moved it, then smiled. "Lieutenant, not bad for beginner. If you had some proper training and . . ."

He saw it coming this time, caught the fist on his arm, slanted it upward with his left, and counterpunched his right fist into Hing's belly. The man's eyes went wide and he staggered back, trying to recapture his breath. His face worked in fury. Then he stabbed his right hand at his waist and drew the pistol there. A 9mm probably, Itashi thought, as he saw the hand come up and the weapon fire.

The slug jolted into the governor's right thigh and felt like a white-hot iron rod had been drilled into him. He bellowed in pain, then cut it off. Had the round gone all the way through? He lifted his leg, but before he could feel underneath, the pistol slammed against the side of his head and dumped him sideways to the wooden bench again.

The governor sat up slower this time. "Did I tell you that I was a line-crosser in Vietnam? I did a lot of headhunting work. Most guys can do that job only a few months. I lasted for two years before I got shot up so bad they sent me home. When the chopper brought me out I had eight bullet holes in my hide. Yeah, eight. I should'a got a damn Purple Heart for each one."

Hing came up close to the governor, his nose an inch from the other man's face.

"You will use the radio and advise your people you have been shot and that they must obey my orders sent to them yesterday. The chopper has to be here no later than your time ten o'clock tomorrow morning, with the gold and the destination where we pick up the ship. You must do it, or all of you will die."

The governor ignored the man in his face. He reached under his right leg. There was no exit wound. The bullet had hit a bone or slanted upward or downward. It was still inside his leg. It had to come out of there within seventy-two hours or his life could be in danger.

"So, American politician, you think about your situation. I have a more pleasant task." He slapped Governor Itashi gently on the cheek and left the tent.

The lieutenant went down two tent frames and entered the fourth one. Two women were chained to the barren wooden bunks. Both sat watching the single candle that burned on a built-in table.

He saw fear growing on the women's faces.

"Was that a shot I heard?" the older one asked.

"Yes, the governor has one of my bullets in him. Now, which of you would like to volunteer for special duty?" He watched them closely. Neither said a word nor looked at him. The oldest one was about forty, he decided, but with a slim body she had taken good care of and with fine breasts. The younger one was chunky and not appealing.

He moved forward and unchained the older one. "Your name is Sara, as I remember." He took her by the hand. "Come, Sara, you have special duty tonight. I think you'll find it most interesting."

"No," the woman screamed. "I want to stay here."

He jerked the end of the chain locked around her left wrist. Sara screamed again. Lieutenant Hing snorted and yanked the chain, pulling her with him out the flap of the tent and toward his tent at the end of the line of six. Sara screamed all the way.

In the heavy growth less than five hundred yards below, Murdock and the rest of the SEALs heard the screams.

"The bastards must be doing the women," Dobler said. "Two on the staff up here are women, right?"

Murdock said he was right.

"Time we start moving up the hill," Murdock said into the Motorola. "We'll go in an assault line, ten yards between. They must be somewhere right above us. Let's move out, silently as all hell. I'd like to give these bastards a real SEAL surprise."

21

Red Hill
Maui, Hawaii

Murdock had been worried about the hostages ever since they took on this assignment. One of the women was forty-one years old, the other one twenty-six. The older one was the governor's chief administrative assistant, extremely competent and said by some to be the real brains behind the governor. She evidently was something of a triple threat. The short description of her he had read at Pearl said she was brilliant, pleasant, and a former Miss Hawaii who had a doctorate in government administration.

The other woman was reported to be smart as a computer and an expert in public relations, but as plain as a mud fence.

Murdock ran forward ten yards and stopped behind a tree trunk. He could hear nothing from above now. They must have protection out. But a 360-degree circle protection would be tough with the men spread thin. Still, the SEALs were getting so close. He would have had at least an outpost out this way.

Lam came on the Motorola. "Skipper, I don't understand this. Where the hell is the defense? It's a walk in the park right here. I must be no more than five hundred feet from the top of the ledge."

"Hang on. Won't bother me if we can walk right into the middle of them."

Five minutes later, they knew the problem. Murdock sat on the ground looking up. It was a sheer cliff with not a chance climbing it without a lot of pitons and ropes. No wonder the Chinese didn't need any security along here. It was natural protection.

Murdock used the radio softly. "Okay, we're stopped here. We move on around the side of the mountain until we find a way up. This rock wall can't last forever. Let's move out. Lam, get to the front of the column. Maintain the ten yards. Move it."

Sara Livingston stood in the middle of the tent and stared at her captor. "Lieutenant, I have no doubt why you brought me here. We are both intelligent adults. There is no reason that we should have to act like animals. I have been married twice. Usually I enjoy sex. Now, with your brutal start, I'm not sure that I would." She watched him closely for some indication of compassion. She found none.

"Lieutenant, I won't try to fight you off if sex is what you want. Is that why you brought me here?"

Lieutenant Hing smiled. "Of course. I spent four years in school at UCLA. I know all about American women and their fondness for wild sex. I'm glad that you are taking a reasonable approach to this situation. I find you most attractive."

Sara nodded and sat on the bunk, which had an air mattress on it and army blankets. She began to unbutton the white blouse that she wore under the warm ski jacket.

"What are you doing?" he asked.

"Undressing. I assume you want me to." She paused in the opening.

He smiled and then laughed softly. "Yes, but I want to do the unwrapping myself. Like on your Christmas."

Sara nodded and folded her hands in her lap. He sat down beside her.

"This will be much more pleasant for both of us," he said. His hands covered her breasts and fondled them through her blouse and bra. "Oh, yes. I had forgotten about you American women and your big tits. I love big breasts."

"You can call them tits, I don't mind."

As he undressed her, Sara let her mind drift away. She saw herself when she was thirteen and overwhelmingly interested in boys. She had found out something new about boys when one afternoon in the woods behind her parents' house, two boys undressed her. They were too frightened to do anything else. They both ejaculated and then ran away screeching in wonder and delight. She had smiled and put on her clothes.

He shook her gently. "Pretty Sara, you are not with me. You were far away. I like my women to be with me."

She saw that she was naked and so was he. He was just another man. Nothing she hadn't seen before. She sighed and nodded.

"What do you want me to do?" she asked.

He told her.

Afterward he said she might as well spend the night with him. The bed was softer and they had plenty of blankets. Sara nodded. It made little difference to her. Here she might be able to do some damage to the lieutenant, but she had seen nothing in the tent that she could use as a weapon. There was always the three-inch hat pin she used in her hair to keep part of the side in place. He might find that.

She looked around. He had been careful to keep his submachine gun and his knife on the far side away from the bed. She relaxed. This was just another small problem she had to help solve for the governor. The big problem was his wife. That one would take a lot of planning and work, but she would do it. The current first lady would be gone within a year. That had been the promise she made herself.

The lieutenant dressed and went outside to check on his troops. He told her not to dress; he would be back soon.

Now he came in shivering from the high-altitude chill, and flipped the blankets back and stared at her naked form.

"Again," he said.

She nodded. "Why not?" she whispered.

This time she thought about her first two marriages, her husbands. The first time when she was only twenty and Miss

Hawaii. Grand and glorious, a roller-coaster ride of ups and downs and loops and standing on your head wondering who you were and if people really liked you or only your title.

Then the year was over and she married in haste and not well. It lasted three months.

No, no. Don't think about old days. Today. How could she help Tom get out of this one? This jaunt was no surprise to anyone. Everyone had known where they were going for the week. The Chinese must have known as well. His gun. She had to get hold of his gun and kill him. She never blinked or wavered. As she had done all her life, she would do what was required to get the job done. She could do it. Now all that she needed was the opportunity.

From outside she heard gunfire rip into the softness of the Hawaiian night. Lieutenant Hing tensed for a moment, then leaped off the bed, ran naked toward the door of the tent, and looked out. He held the submachine gun in his right hand.

Quickly he pulled on his pants, scooped up a belt filled with magazines for the weapon, and ran outside.

Murdock fired again. "Where the hell them motherfuckers come from?" he bleated on the mike.

"Six of them up here from the look of the muzzle flashes," Lam said.

"I've got at least four on my end," DeWitt said.

"We've got a shit-pot full," Ron Holt chimed in.

For the past one hundred yards they had been moving around the slope of the mountain. They had been forced downward until they were at least a thousand feet below the camp. The terrain over them now looked to be one gentle slant up to the top. An ideal spot to attack, and just as perfect for the Chinese to set up a stiff defense.

"Use the twenties," Murdock said. "Laser on the flashes. It should work." As he spoke he brought up his Bull Pup and sighted in on the next series of flashes. Then he pulled the trigger. The weapon was new enough that the blast of the 20mm round caught him by surprise. The heavy weapon recoiled more then he remembered.

He sighted in on the next laser flash, but caught an airburst flash instead and triggered. By then there were six men firing the Bull Pups at the targets. He let each man fire four or five rounds, then called a cease-fire on the radio. One more flash came from above, then the night quieted.

"What the hell, we waste all them puppies?" Bill Bradford asked.

"At least we scared the shit out of them," Jefferson said.

"Any casualties?" Murdock asked on the net.

"My turn," a weak voice said.

"Doc, that you?" Murdock asked.

"Yeah. My lucky day. Caught one in the arm. When the fuck am I gonna learn to keep my damn head down."

"How bad, Doc?"

Jack Mahanani sighed. "Hell, not sure. Went through. A five-five-six maybe. Ostercamp, you near me?"

"Moving your way, Doc. Hang tough."

"Rest of us move forward," Murdock said. "We take it easy. If we get to some bodies up there, we grab their MGs and tote them. Never can tell."

They moved slowly, working up the hill through the darkness and the heavy growth for nearly fifty yards.

"Skip, I got Doc's arm bandaged up. Bleeding stopped. He's gung ho to keep coming with us. Your call."

"His call. Be glad to have him. Both of you get your tails up here with the troops."

Murdock stumbled over the first body a few minutes later. He put his back to the top of the hill and used his pencil flash. The Chinese trooper had shrapnel slashes on his head and torso. The twenty had nailed him.

They found five bodies. Two of them lay on weapons Murdock determined to be H & K 53's, a German submachine gun that fired a rifle cartridge in the 5.56 size. A beautiful little weapon. It had a curved twenty-five-round magazine. Murdock grabbed two full mags from the corpse and slung the 53 over his shoulder.

"Hold here until Doc and Ostercamp get here," Murdock said. "There are some good weapons here if you can find them H & K fifty-threes."

Murdock checked ahead. More trees and brush. He could barely see the top of the mountain against the rising moon.

"What next?" Lam asked on the net. "Now they know we're here with firepower."

"Lam, take a scouting walk to the left. Franklin, do the same on the right. Go out seventy-five yards or so and see if you can hear any more outposts."

Doc Mahanani and Ostercamp came up and the corpsman sat and leaned against a tree. Murdock knelt beside him.

"Hey, sawbones. Can you still pull a trigger?"

"Damn straight."

"What day is this?"

"Don't have the foggiest. I'm lucid. You kidding about a sub gun that shoots out a five-five-sixer?"

"No lie. You're lucid. We take five and wait to see that no outposts close in on us on our flanks."

Lam and Franklin both reported in that they'd neither found nor heard any outposts or Chinese activity.

"Come back, double time," Murdock said. "Then we're going to charge up this hill and overrun that outfit."

Above them at the camp, the four men prisoners were in the same tent. The Chinese had said it was for better security, only one tent to guard.

Karl Tucker was the governor's top money-raiser. He had the ideas and connections and could throw a thousand-dollar-a-plate dinner or a dog-on-a-stick picnic with equal panache. The governor knew his background, and had shown outward surprise at the way Tucker had acted when they were over-whelmed and captured. Two of the men had had to be knocked down and tied up. Tucker had dropped to the ground cowering when the armed Chinese ran toward him.

The governor had not spoken about it to Tucker. The man was brilliant. He must have something in mind.

Karl Tucker had been the smallest man in his company when he went through Marine Corps recruit training at San Diego. He stood no more than five-six with his boots on. His loose shirt concealed a muscular upper body that could power-lift more than three times his weight. He had excelled in hand-to-hand and other types of one-on-one combat exercises and training routines. He had applied to be in the

Marine Recon Force, but had missed passing the physical due to his height.

This night, he decided, was the right time. He had heard the gunfire outside, and could pick out the distinctive sound of the 20mm rounds exploding. He had no idea who had a twenty weapon up here, but it was time to help.

He was chained to the tent wall posts, as were the other men. There was no way to slip off the chain. The men had been stripped of all the items in their pockets, but Karl had saved a hairpin. He'd hidden it in his own hair.

Now he took it out and worked quickly on the locks on the chain around his wrist. He had it opened in less than thirty seconds. Only the governor was awake. They tended to go to sleep when it grew dark. Their tent had no candle.

Governor Itashi heard Karl moving. "Tucker, you all right?"

"Fine, Governor. Just waiting to make my move. Going to kill me a few Chinese, then try to hook up with that outfit attacking them. Must be some Marines out there."

"Be careful, Karl. We have big plans."

"I know, Governor. Semper fi."

It was the last sound Tucker made before he slipped out the tent's loose door and paused in the shadows checking out the area. He had tried to remember it from the first day. Six tents. No buildings. Where would the interior guards be? He waited. A shadow moved to his left, thirty feet away. For just a second a match flared, and Karl grinned. A sentry smoking. That was suicide. He moved that way. The guard would have no night vision after the flare of the match for at least a minute.

Karl hurried toward the sentry. Caught the smell of tobacco, then saw the glow of the cigarette. He moved up from the side, waiting until the man looked the other way.

When he turned, Karl hurtled at the sentry on silent feet, hit him with a shoulder block on the left side, and drove him off his feet to the ground. The sentry made only one gurgled sound before Karl's hands closed around his throat and cut off all sound and air. It took the man two minutes to die. Karl had felt a body go limp and dead before. He eased away, took the sentry's knife and his short, deadly weapon. Some

sort of submachine gun. Good. He found three full magazines
on the man, but nothing else of value. He looked at the end
tent. It would be the most obvious for the Chinese officer to
use. Then a squad of eight men jogged toward him. Karl
went flat on the ground next to the tree and held his breath.

The squad jogged on past in step and vanished into the
night to the west. He heard three more shots from the west.
That must be where the attack was taking place. He looked
at the end tent. At least two candles burned inside. With the
action outside, it was for sure that the lieutenant wouldn't
still be in his tent. There must be more guards around this
area.

He broke the camp into sections that he could see and
examined one square at a time. In the fifth unit at the east
end of the camp, he saw another guard. The man stood
against a tree, his weapon hung by a strap from his neck.
His hands were at his sides. He could be staring in all directions, or he could be sleeping. Karl moved through deep
shadows toward him. The last ten yards were across a
moonlight-bathed flat space.

Karl hesitated just inside the darkness. Was he trying to live
forever? Come on, semper fi. He made sure he had the safety
off and pointing down for full-automatic on the German-made
submachine gun. There was a round in the chamber. He put his
finger on the trigger and began a moderate walk toward the
guard.

At once the sentry came alert. He began to lift his weapon
slowly and shouted something in Chinese. Karl brought up
the sub gun and chattered off six rounds from his hip. He
saw the guard's body jolt backward, then turn slowly to
the right and dive into the dirt. The guard's finger closed
on the trigger in a death spasm and sprayed twenty rounds
into the trees.

Karl sprinted for the heavy timber and brush on the far
side of the camp. It was the side where he had heard the
firing. There must be some good guys down there. A dozen
rounds whispered through the air to one side of him. Then
he was safely into the brush.

More firing came from the right, to the west. He heard the
sound he figured had to be exploding 20mm rounds. How in

hell did they get a 20mm cannon up here? He began moving toward the sounds, again a Marine on dangerous duty, knowing that if he made the wrong move, both sides would try to blow his head off.

The sounds of firing from below the top and the camp came again, and he altered his direction and hurried. He wanted to get there before the fun was all over.

22

Below Red Hill Peak
Maui, Hawaii

Murdock stopped his SEALs fifty yards from what looked like the top of the mountain. In the darkness he could only estimate, but the distance felt right. Ed DeWitt came over and they worried it.

"We can't use the twenties anymore up here," DeWitt said. "We don't know where the hostages are. That damn shrapnel explodes out fifty to seventy-five yards on an airburst. That would go through a tent like leaves on a tree. Can't take the chance."

The fire from above had been murderous. They had machine guns overlapping, and could send down a killing barrage anytime they saw a target. Murdock had only one other casualty, that a heel shot off Ostercamp's boot.

"So how do we get up the damn hill?" Murdock asked.

"Wait until morning and establish our absolute limits on the use of the twenties. We might be able to use them on the machine guns after all."

"Long night ahead. Let's do some recon and try to pin down where the tents are." Murdock waved at his JG. "Have

Lam go take a gander. I'm going to check in with CINCPAC and see what else is going on."

DeWitt moved out to find Lam. Murdock used the Motorola to call up Ron Holt. They had to move to a new location where Holt could get a clear shot at the satellite. When the set beeped that the dish antenna was aligned properly, Holt gave the handset to Murdock.

"CINCPAC, this is Red Hill."

The speaker came on at once. Holt lunged forward to turn down the volume. "Yes, Red Hill. We read you."

"Have found the camp. Made contact with the hostage-takers, but have not located the tents and hostages yet. On hold until daylight and we can better assess."

"Thought you guys could do anything."

"Not against interlocked machine guns, sir."

"The other war fronts are winding down. Most of the little men are on the run, captured, or dead. We've been talking with a Lieutenant Hing about the captives. He knows we won't negotiate. He could be getting nervous and dangerous."

"He's already dangerous. Will report in tomorrow or with any new move here."

"That's a Roger, Red Hill. Out."

Murdock sat back and looked at the set. "Not one hell of a lot of help," he said to Holt.

"For damn sure, Skipper. We stuck here for a while?"

"Unless Lam can get us a hundred yards of separation between those machine guns and the tents." He used the Motorola. "Two on guard for each squad. The rest of you get some shut-eye. It could be a long night."

Karl Tucker bored into the rain forest–like growth and stopped after fifteen yards. He listened, looking behind, but no one chased him. There should be another guard down this way. He crept soundlessly back to the edge of the clearing and sectioned the area. Then he did his search again. One more guard, then he'd find the guys out there who were on his side.

He had to work harder to find the third guard. For ten minutes he searched the sectors. Karl was about to give up when he saw movement in a tree. Yes. This soldier wasn't smoking. He seemed to be alert. He sat in the low crotch of a tree. He was only six feet off the ground but had good sight lines.

The old Marine training took over and Karl worked through the brush to a spot where he had some good cover to move forward. The sentry had picked a spot at the very edge of the woods. This gave him an excellent view of his area, but also put him in more danger from the cover behind him.

After twenty minutes, Karl had worked his way soundlessly along the edge of the brushy woods to a spot fifteen feet from the Chinese sentry.

A sitting duck.

Karl knew he should simply shoot the guard and move on to find the Marines. There was no reason for stealth. Not after his shootout with the other guard. Karl grinned. He hadn't had a chance to play Marine for five years. The old urges were still there. He lifted the knife, an eight-inch blade with a well-balanced handle. He held the knife in one hand and crawled on hands and knees toward the sentry.

Karl froze as the Chinese soldier looked his way. He stared at the shadowed spot where Karl lay. Then his gaze moved on, covering his post and his assigned area. He was doing a good job, which made Karl's approach harder.

Karl surged forward ten feet when the guard looked the other way. Then he came up charging, the sub gun in his left hand, the knife in his right. He was six feet away from the sentry. The man turned back and saw Karl coming, but by then it was too late. The heavy knife drove into the Chinese man's chest and slammed him backward. Karl dove forward with the blade and landed hard on top of the sentry.

Karl kept up the pressure on the steel until the soldier gave one long sigh and his bowels discharged. Karl searched the dead guard quickly, took three filled magazines for the sub gun and pushed them inside his shirt, then slipped back into the brush and moved to his left, where he had heard the gunfire. Now all he had to do was find the Marines without getting his head blown off. He grinned. These were Marines. He'd have to be damn careful so he didn't get his hide full of 20mm cannon shrapnel. Karl grinned and began jogging forward.

Murdock took the patrol to the left. There had to be a better way to get up to the mesa than this slope. He worked beyond the fields of fire of the two machine guns, and found what he was afraid he would: another sheer cliff rising over a hundred feet almost straight up. None of his people were skilled at hard-rock climbing. That was why Hing had put his machine guns on the slope.

Murdock came back to his small HQ and looked at DeWitt.

"Nothing new, Skipper. No word from CINCPAC. A few rounds from the MG now and then to remind us they're still there."

"Lam back yet?"

DeWitt shook his head.

"If we don't have enough separation, we're in deep shit here, men." Murdock said. "No way we can go through those MGs. They could wipe us out with random fire and never know it."

"We've got to have enough space between them and the tents or we are in deep trouble," DeWitt said.

The machine guns cut in again, each weapon sending six bursts of six rounds across its field of fire. The SEALs jammed behind the largest trees available.

"I hate those fucking machine guns," Train Khai barked.

"Yeah, unless it's us who are firing them," Bradford countered.

The firing stopped. No SEALs returned any rounds.

"They won't know if we're still here or not this way," Murdock said. "Where in the hell is Lampedusa?"

"Right behind you, dead man," Lam said, stepping into the small cleared place from the brush. No one had heard him coming.

"So?"

"The MG on the left is plenty far from the tents, but I'm not positive about the one on the right. Too close to be safe."

Six of the SEALs had gathered around.

"We use the airbursts on the left one and contact detonation on the right one," Ching said. "The AP rounds should burrow through any sandbags they have and go off inside their little bunker."

"Sounds like a go to me," Bradford said. The others looked at Murdock.

"How about the forties?" Jefferson asked. "We can lay back two hundred yards and lob in a dozen or so, get ground bursts and not push out shrapnel more than thirty, forty yards."

"Small target," Canzoneri said. "We'd waste eighty percent of our rounds and might not get a direct hit."

"Let's go with the twenties," Murdock said. "Lam on the airbursts to the left. Get your laser on the muzzle flash, then on your own airbursts. Canzoneri with your twenty on Contact Detonation on the right-hand sucker. Disperse, find cover you can shoot around, and wait for the next machine-gun rounds. Six or eight rounds each should do the job."

Before they could move, a voice boomed at them from six feet away. "You guys sure as hell are funny-looking Marines."

The SEALs turned weapons on the sound.

"Hold your fire, I'm on your side. I'm Tucker, one of the former hostages up above. I used to be a Marine. Took out three of their guards and figured I'd come find better company."

"Come on in, Tucker," Murdock said. "We can use all the help we can get. Mostly for you to tell us the layout up there, how many men they have, and where those damned machine guns are."

Tucker came out of the gloom and grinned. "Damn glad to see some combat harness. Just who are you guys?"

Murdock explained.

"Heard how you shot up that outpost. The guy who escaped was screeching his head off about airbursts. True?"

"Damn straight," Murdock said. He explained the Bull Pup. "Now what do they have up there?"

"Came in with thirty men from two choppers that scurried back to sea. Off a destroyer, my guess. They should be down to twenty-two men now. A lieutenant in charge with two non-coms. Looked to be seasoned troops. All have rice rolls for chow. Most of them ate up what supplies we had brought. I don't know what they did with the two nuns who run the place."

"The machine guns?" Lam asked. "How far are the tents from the MGs directly above us?"

"Not over fifty yards if they're covering that gradual slope I saw the first two days we were here."

"Okay, same orders," Murdock said. "Let's get spread out and do in those MGs. When everyone is in place, check in with your squad." The SEALs moved.

"Airbursts with twenty-millimeters. Damn, wish we'd had that when I was in the Marines."

"When we're ready, I'll throw up a couple of .556 bursts to see if they will respond with the MGs," Murdock said. "Then we clobber them."

Murdock motioned for Tucker to find a tree. He slid behind a two-foot-thick pine tree someone had planted many years ago. Three minutes later word came in that all SEALs were in cover.

Murdock fired two three-round bursts from his MP-5. He aimed where he remembered the left-hand machine gun had fired from.

There was no immediate response. Then both MGs began to pound off rounds, most aimed at the spot where they had seen the muzzle flash. Canzoneri slammed six 20mm contact rounds into the right-hand MG nest. He heard the others firing, and saw the airbursts to the left. Then the last of the SEAL rounds exploded. Both MGs were silent.

"Did we nail them fuckers?" Mahanani asked on the net.

"You run up there and ask them if they're all dead," Fernandez directed.

A silence stretched out.

"Murdock?" DeWitt asked.

"Give it another ten minutes. Then I want DeWitt and Canzoneri to go up there with hand grenades and see what they can see. You take the right-hand side. Bradford and I will take the airburst bunch. In ten minutes from now. Mark."

"Skipper, I only have two frags," Bradford said.

"Work the squad. We should have six each. Bring me four when you're ready."

"Aye, aye, Skipper."

"I'll go up with you, Commander," Tucker said. "Then if it's clear, I can show you where the Chinese have set up their bivouac."

Murdock had decided to say no, but changed his mind. "Yeah, Tucker, you might come in handy. You say you killed three guards. How?"

"I had no weapon when I picked the lock on my chains, so I had to strangle the first guard. Dumb ass was smoking. Got this sub gun from the first guard, then the second one spotted me so I shot him. The third one I did silent with a Chinese knife. Not a bad weapon."

"You have ammo for the fifty-three."

"That what this is? Yeah, I have six mags."

"Good, you might need them."

Murdock gave them the marching orders at precisely 2304. Tucker fell in behind Bradford, and the three began working up the slope as quietly as possible. If there was even one man left alive on the MG, he would be ready to use it. By now the Chinese could have sent in a new squad to work the weapon. There was a chance that one of the airbursts had damaged the weapon itself so the machine gun wouldn't function. That was the best hope.

Murdock scowled. One way or another they would all know in about ten minutes.

Murdock scurried ten feet ahead and dropped behind a stout tree. He looked behind in the hazy moonlight and saw Tucker using proper techniques, working forward quietly and staying low. The guy must be for real.

Lam had led out. Murdock let him go halfway, then tapped him on the shoulder and worked his way past him. Four minutes later, the spot where they had seen the machine gun was no more than fifty feet ahead. Murdock stopped and listened. All he heard were some night birds far off, some buzzing insects, and the rustle of some small creature working through the forest floor searching for dinner.

A cough racked through the stillness.

Murdock turned toward the sound directly ahead of them in the area they thought had the machine gun. Survivors or a new crew? He checked the terrain again. They were still on the downslope, forty feet from the top. He could swing to the left and go up a steeper part, but would not be directly below the position. Then he remembered the hand grenades.

He had made no arrangements with DeWitt about when to use the bombs. The inference was whenever they got in position. He waved the other two men up. He passed a grenade to Tucker and indicated the target. Lam came up and shifted five yards to the side. They all pulled the safety pins on the bombs, looked at each other, and nodded. They all threw the grenades.

Murdock ducked with his head into the ground and counted off the four seconds. Never had it seemed to have taken so long for the explosions. Two came muffled. The third, evidently more in the open, detonated with a cracking roar.

He heard shrapnel singing through the three branches over his head. Somewhere to the west, a machine gun cut in with three six-round bursts. Before the last one finished, a grenade went off over there, then another, then two more.

Murdock looked for Tucker. He had left his former position and was crawling toward the machine gun. Murdock hurried after him. They went over the top of the short ledge together, and fell into a dug-out spot four feet deep. Murdock spotted the MG. It lay on its side in the bottom of the hole. A wooden crate had furnished it with a platform to fire over the lip of the ridge. One body sprawled on top of the weapon.

Lam came over the top and dropped to his feet. He nodded.

Tucker lifted up and stared to the west over the top of the bunker.

"This is the far east end of the clearing," he said. "The Chinese put a small tent bivouac under some trees about fifty yards back toward the tents."

"Murdock, clear on MG right." It was DeWitt.

"Clear on MG left. Hold your position. We may have the troops move up. Evaluating."

"They can't have more than twenty men left," Tucker said.

Murdock used the mike. "Whoever has those EAR rifles, get your asses up here. I want one in each of the old MG bunkers. Move your fat asses. We could get a counter at any

time and we can't use the twenties up here near the tents.
Move it now!"

Murdock didn't know who had the EARs, but they seemed
the best bet. Even the 5.56's could send a lot of danger at
the tents if the five men up here had to fire at oncoming
Chinese.

"Let me go take a look, Skip," Lam asked. "I'm sure none
of the little bastards are out this way. I won't make any
contact, just peek and snoop."

"Go. Radio me anything vital like you getting pinned
down. Take Tucker with you." Tucker grinned and nodded.
The two went over the side of the bunker on their bellies,
came to their hands and feet, and then ran soundlessly toward
a splotch of pine, cedar, and juniper on the left.

A pistol shot jolted through the bunker, and Murdock felt
the white-hot fury as a poker reamed into his left leg and
dug deep, burning all the way far into the flesh of his left
leg. He whirled and fired six rounds from the Bull Pup into
the body that had been draped over the MG on the bunker
floor. He must be tired. What the hell was he thinking? None
of them had made sure the body was dead. It was now. He
saw the pistol slip from the Chinese man's hand and a last
gush of air come from dead lungs.

"Skipper, you all right?" In his earpiece.

"Yeah, our Chinese friend wasn't quite dead. He is now."

"You hit?"

"Yeah, but not bad, just in the left leg. What are you finding?"

"Nothing yet." The words were whispers from the night.
"Tucker says the bivouac is just ahead."

There was silence for a few seconds. "Oh, shit, Skip. Here
they come, a damn assault line. Must be fifty of the little
bastards and they're heading straight for you."

23

Summit Red Hill
Maui, Hawaii

When the first firing broke out, Sara Livingston knew what it was. She grabbed the blankets, slid under the bunk on the floor, and pulled the blankets around her. The wooden sides of the tent frame would at least slow down any stray rounds. She'd seen enough shooting scenes to know what bullets could do. The tent top would not stop anything.

She huddled there for what she figured was an hour. Then the door jerked open and Lieutenant Hing stormed in. He was swearing in Chinese, she was sure. He rummaged around in a box that had been locked and pulled out another pistol. She watched him a moment, then cried and wiggled out from under the bed. She was still naked. She removed the three-inch hat pin from her hair and held it hidden in her hand.

"Who's shooting?" she asked. "Will they hurt any of us?"

He turned to look at her and some of the anger drained from his face.

"Wish I had time right now. You are so damn sexy. Just like those sophomore girls who wanted it all the time. Come here."

She walked to him, hips swaying, her breasts bouncing

and jiggling. He bent and kissed both breasts, then stepped back. He was about to say something when her right hand jolted out. She swung her hand straight at his heart. The hat pin stuck out between the knuckles of her closed fist like an ice pick.

Before he could cry or jump back, the hat pin lanced into his flesh, scraped off a rib, and plunged deeply into his heart. Surprise turned to shock and then to pain. He tried to grab his chest. Instead he caught her arm. He dropped to his knees, taking her with him. Then he shivered and shook his head. His other hand reached for her throat, but fell away. He let go of her wrist and dropped hard to one side.

Sara grabbed the pistol in the holster at his belt. Racked back the slide to make sure there was a round in the chamber. Then she shot the Chinese lieutenant four times in the chest. Sara watched him die with a hard smile on her face. The bastard got what he deserved. She just happened to be the one to pull the trigger. She stared at his dead body a moment more, then picked up the other pistol and held both of them. Sara had never killed anyone before. A shiver ran down her spine, but she lifted her chin and it went away. He should be dead. She wouldn't think about it anymore.

She picked up her clothes and dressed, then looked in the box to see if she could find the keys to the padlocks. Sara grabbed a ring with several keys on it.

She hurried to the tent door and looked outside. She still had one of the pistols in each hand. For a moment she saw nothing. Then her candle-lighted blindness receded and she saw two Chinese soldiers running to the east. There were no guards around the tents. Maybe they were fighting.

Sara slipped out of the tent and wished for shadows, but there were none. She walked toward the tent three down where she had been with Patricia. The candle still burned inside. Sara slipped in and found Patricia sleeping curled up in the blanket.

There were four keys on the ring. The third one opened the small padlock holding the metal strap around Patricia's wrist.

The woman came awake slowly, then reached out and hugged Sara.

"Oh, you're back. Sara, I was so frightened for you."

"That part is over. I have the keys, you're unlocked. Come on, let's get the men freed before any soldiers come back."

Patricia frowned. "But we're chained up." She lifted her arm to prove it, and when she saw it was free she shrieked in delight.

"How in the world . . ."

"Don't wonder, just hurry outside with me. Come on."

In the darkness of the men's tent they stumbled, and the governor came out of a troubled sleep.

"Who's there?" he asked.

"Just us chickens, Governor. I have the key to your padlock. You'll have to pick the right one. Let's get out of here."

"What about Lieutenant Hing?"

"Don't ask. We can talk later. Get your lock undone."

The others awoke. The governor got his cuff off and gave the key to Vince Yamamoto, who did the same. Harry Chung's lock needed a different key. Each of the two aides took one of the pistols.

"Where's Karl?" Chung asked.

"I heard him slip out about an hour or so ago," the governor said. "He opened the lock on his cuffs."

The five moved to the door and waited while the governor looked out.

"Looks clear. Where do we go?"

"Straight over there into the brush and trees, and then we hike for two hundred yards downhill so they can't find us," Chung said. They moved quickly across the thirty yards of cleared space to the nearest vegetation, and walked into it.

Once there, Sara told them what happened at the tent to the lieutenant.

The governor took one of the weapons, checked it for a load, and pushed on the safety. "Are you sure about the lieutenant?" he asked her softly so the others couldn't hear.

"He's dead. Now we should move farther from the camp."

They did.

Murdock could see some of the muzzle flashes blossoming in front of him. He had about ten seconds to decide. Did he cut and run and live to fight another day? Or did he use the twenty and see how much he could discourage the fifty Chinese troopers who were said to be storming toward his position?

There couldn't be fifty, but even twenty would be too many. Also, he didn't know where Lam and the Marine were. He might be firing right into them.

Something sounded beside him and he looked over at Ron Holt, who lifted the EAR weapon over the side of the bunker and fired at the muzzle flashes from the Chinese ahead of them.

Yes. That would help, might do the trick. Another of the familiar whooshing sounds came from the other machine-gun pit. Then Holt fired again. The gun flashes had been cut in half.

"Yes, Holt, do them again."

When the ten-second recharge turned the firing light red, Holt had his target and fired. Six more muzzle flashes ceased in front of them, and the gunners evidently went to ground.

The earpiece spoke to Murdock. "That old EAR job did the trick, Skipper. Looks like about a dozen of them left and they are moving back. Oh, yeah, now they're running."

"We used six shots. Any close to you guys?"

"No, we were well clear. Karl, the Marine, says looks like the Chinese bastards are heading for their bivouac. That could mean a hasty retreat."

"Stay with them. What about the hostages? You anywhere near the tents?"

"Another fifty yards. I can see lights in two of them. No, just one. Must be a candle. We'll check them out if we get that far."

"Roger that. Keep us up to date." Murdock nodded and whacked Holt on the shoulder.

"Nice shooting, radioman. I'd be Chinese stir-fry if you hadn't used that EAR. No way I could risk the twenties with Lam and Grant out in front. Tell the rest of the platoon to get their lazy asses up here. Nobody can push us off now. I'm going to do a little recon on my own." He stopped. "Right after I tie up this damn round through my leg." He used the kerchief he'd worn around his neck all day. When he had the blood stopped and the wrap tight, he moved.

Murdock lifted over the lip of the bunker and ran low and fast to the edge of the brush out thirty feet. Then he worked through it toward the west and where the hostages had to be.

A few minutes later he came on the Chinese bodies. They sprawled on the ground, all unconscious. Yes, he saw the argument that non-lethal weapons like the EAR could be used both ways. Knock them out and then execute them when you rolled over them. But not this time. There would be hours to take care of the silent ones later.

He moved toward the tents that he could see now. They showed only as a row of dark shadows in the dusky moonlight. All except one, where a flickering light stood out like a firefly at midnight. Now that he was closer, he watched for guards. There must be several around the captives.

"Skip, we might have some trouble over here."

It was Lam. "What and where?"

"We're near the Chinese bivouac. Looks like the soldiers are clearing out everything of value. My guess is that they're getting ready to make a permanent move."

"Which means we'd have all sorts of hell trying to find them in the heavily forested sections below."

"Right. Damn near impossible. I've got the twenty and Karl picked up another of the H & K 53's. Want us to nail all of them we can from here?"

"Impact on the twenties to keep them away from the tents?"

"Karl says we're more than seventy-five yards from the tent tops."

"I'm at the bodies. Where do I go from here to lend a hand?"

"We're about a hundred yards ahead of you and bear to the left around the side of the clearing. Can't miss us. I have my weapons free."

"Fire at will, sweetheart."

Murdock lifted up and ran hard forward as he spoke into the mike. "Holt, where the hell are the rest of the troops? We could use some more firepower up here."

"Jefferson and Ostercamp are here, Skip. We'll move up now at the firing. Rest of them are almost to the top."

"Move it, you three. Hang to the left of the clearing and do it in a sprint."

"We're gone, Skipper." The three SEALs lifted their weapons, charged in rounds, and ran flat out toward the men ahead of them.

Lam's first impact-round twenty hit a heavy tree trunk ten feet over the heads of the Chinese infantry. The splash of the shrapnel was deadly. It sliced open two soldiers nearby, put hot steel in four more, and killed three of them.

Karl opened up with the submachine gun firing the 5.56 rounds on full auto. He soon mastered the art of the six-round burst, and put the rest of the Chinese on the ground ducking behind trees and any other cover they could find.

Lam fired three more times with the twenty, the rounds exploding in the trees working almost like airbursts. Between rounds, four of the Chinese lifted up and raced into the brush on the near side of their small camp. They all carried weapons, and Lam heard harsh Chinese commands. Somebody in charge had rescued the few men he could from the shootout.

Karl emptied one magazine after the quartet, but missed them. He jammed in a fresh twenty-five-round supply, and watched through the murky night air to see if anyone else moved. One man rolled from one cover to a log. Karl moved his sights to the far end of the log, only twenty feet from the dense woods. He tracked halfway to the brush and waited.

His eyes almost closed, and then he snapped them open. Movement. Yes, there he went. Karl tracked the Chinese as he came away from the log in a sprint. Karl fired six rounds. Three of them spread to the left, the other three powered into the victim's side and back, killing him before he could roll into the ground cover less than five feet from the end of the log.

Murdock ran up and dove into the ground three feet from Lam, his Bull Pup ready to fire.

"Party is all over, but we lost four of them into the brush," Lam said.

"Man, you should have seen this guy blasting them Chinese with his twenty," Karl said. "I want one of them to play with."

"Let's check on the rest of the Chinese and make sure,"

Murdock said. He told Karl to stay and cover them. They darted ahead to the killing field. Three gunshots sounded as they made sure there were no wounded to care for. SEALs take no prisoners, and leave no wounded.

Murdock thought about that as he and Lam waved Karl forward and then ran for the tents. About time they checked in with the governor and his staff.

They were halfway across the open space when a 53 opened up on them from the shadows beyond the tents. Murdock took an immediate hit on the top of his right shoulder and went down. He rolled and tried to bring up his Bull Pup, but his right arm didn't work.

Lam dove to the ground and returned fire at the muzzle flash. He ripped twelve 5.56 rounds into the area, then emptied the magazine and jammed in another one. He picked up Murdock and dragged him out of the moonlight into the shadows.

"Bastard," Murdock exploded. "You nail him?"

"I think so, or I scared the shit out of him and he's running through the brush hoping to swim back to China. Let me look at that shoulder."

"Up high somewhere. My fucking arm doesn't work right. Does Mahanani still have the med kit?"

"Far as I know. Yeah, you caught a good one up there, Skipper. You stay put and I'll get Doc up here to paste you together."

He made the radio call. The medic had just hit the machine-gun pits, and swore he'd come right up and find Murdock.

Karl knelt down beside the commander. "You heading for the tents?" Karl asked. Murdock nodded, some of the pain in his shoulder burning like a seared finger on a barbecue.

"Hey, I'll back up Lam," Karl said. "The tents are just over there. That first one with the light is the one the lieutenant in charge used."

"Go," Murdock said.

They went in spurts of ten yards at a time, but drew no more enemy fire. They edged up to the platform and the screen door slowly. Then, when both were in position, Karl pulled open the screen door and Lam surged inside the tent frame.

"Clear first tent," he said in the mike. Karl stepped inside and swore.

"Look at that bastard. Got himself a few shots in his chest. Wonder if Sara did it." He told Lam about the officer dragging Sara out of the next tent as she screamed up a battle cry.

"So who is leading their troops?" Lam asked.

"There were two sergeants. One of them must have taken over. Let's check the other tents."

They took the candle with them after blowing it out. They lit it in the next tent, which was empty. Karl motioned them down to the next-to-last tent.

"The women were in here. Patricia Combs should be here."

Nobody was in the tent. The padlocks had been unlocked. They checked the men's tent and found the same thing, along with a ring of keys on the floor.

Lam used the net. "Skipper, the two women and three men hostages are gone. A lieutenant in charge is dead of chest wounds. Looks like the hostages might have escaped. What the hell can we do now?"

Before he finished talking, the snarl of the 53 submachine gun sounded down the clearing to the right. Lam and Karl ran that way, their weapons up and with fingers on the triggers.

24

Red Hill
Maui, Hawaii

Vince Yamamoto, Governor Itashi's press secretary and a former Army sergeant, led the hostages into the woodlands. They stopped about five hundred yards down the hill in a clump of cedar trees.

"Governor, I suggest we stay here for the rest of the night. Then I'll slip back up to the camp and see if I can find out what's going on. The Chinese there came under attack by someone. Maybe Marines or Army troops. They should be able to rout them now that the Chinese have lost their commander."

"Sounds good, Vince. Tell the others. We'll try to stay warm as best we can. This ten-thousand-foot altitude seems a lot colder out here in the open. Is there any way we can have a fire?"

Harry Chung, the governor's executive assistant, heard them talking and stepped up with a small cigarette lighter. "Our Chinese friends missed this in my shirt pocket when they searched us that first day," he said. "I'll find some firewood and shield the flames from the top so no one will be able to see it."

Ten minutes later Chung had a small fire going, and they took turns at warming themselves. He made the fire larger gradually, until they could use three sides of it for warmth.

They didn't talk about the Chinese. Sara had told them that she had surprised Lieutenant Hing and stabbed him with her hat pin, then grabbed his pistol and shot him. After that, the subject was closed. Chung had cleaned and bandaged the governor's leg wound. It would need medical attention soon.

The governor warmed his hands over the fire. They hadn't taken time to grab the jackets they had brought to the camp. Most of them were in shirts and blouses.

"Hey, people," the governor said. "We'll be all right now. Harry's fire has saved the day. This was supposed to be a rugged, challenging experience. I didn't plan on it being this tough. In the morning, Vince will slip back up the hill and find out what's going on. If the Marines landed and have whipped the Chinese, we'll chopper out of here within two hours.

"Hey, it's a little after one A.M., which means we have only half the night to go. We can do this standing on our heads."

The others murmured their agreement. Sara shivered. She wanted to run to the governor and hug him until he gave up and kissed her. She had been wanting him for so long. They had touched, and twice he had given her shoulder hugs for a job well done.

Each time she had been so thrilled she couldn't talk. All of her tough professionalism had melted into sticky goo in twenty seconds. She looked at him and saw he had been watching her. She moved around the fire and wedged in beside him.

"Can I share some of your fire?"

"We have plenty. Help yourself."

As she edged in, her hip touched his and neither of them moved. No one noticed it in the firelight. Sara felt a surge of emotion she had difficulty holding in. She looked up at him, and he was watching her.

"Yes, Sara, stay close," he whispered so no one else could hear. His smile deepened. He went on in the whisper. "We're all so proud of you. We know it must have been tremendously difficult . . . with the gun. I'm so proud of you I could kiss you."

She wanted to whisper right back to him something witty like: "I'll take a rain check," or maybe: "Hey, kiss me once and kiss me twice and kiss me once again," like the song. She only pressed her hip harder against his and nodded, her eyes brimming with tears of wonder and joy. Why couldn't he tell she was in love with him? Watching him now and feeling the wonder of the fire's heat, she thought that maybe he did but he didn't want any Clintonesque problems. Oh, damn.

"Governor, I'll take a rain check on that kiss until after we're rescued and I'm warm enough to enjoy it." She had whispered it up at him so only he could hear.

Surprise flooded his face, and then his marvelous grin came. Oh, but how she loved that grin. "A deal," he whispered back. Then he put both hands out to the warmth of the fire.

Somewhere above they heard rifle and other small-arms fire.

"Machine guns," Vince said. "Somebody up there is getting the hell shot out of them."

"Let's hope it's our side doing the shooting," the governor said.

Murdock grimaced through the pain. Hell of a time to get hit. Almost had the bastards nailed to the wall. He heard the firing and tried to track it to the left. The escaped Chinese might have circled around and hit them.

Mahanani slid to the ground beside Murdock.

"Shoulder, I hear?"

Murdock nodded.

"Not the best, Skipper. Can you raise your arm?"

"Yeah, some."

"How high?"

"Got it almost to my shoulder once."

The machine guns rattled again. Mahanani dropped down on top of Murdock as the slugs went zinging over their heads. He got up and pulled Murdock by the left arm farther into the shadows of some brush.

"DeWitt, where are you?" Murdock asked his lip mike.

"At the Chinese bodies. Have them all tied up. Heard the automatic fire. We'll come up in the brush fringe on the north. How is the shoulder?"

"Not good. You've got the con. The attackers might be the two we flushed into the brush before."

"We'll get them. You take it easy."

Lam and Karl ran past where Murdock and Mahanani lay, then dove into the edge of the brush. All firing had stopped.

"Lam, can you find me?" DeWitt asked.

"We're on the north side brush, forty yards from the tents. The bodies are about sixty yards east of us."

"Hang there, we're moving up," DeWitt said.

Five minutes later the SEALs had joined up.

"Some Chinkos over on the right fired again," Lam said. "The hostages are out of the tent, so no worry on the twenties. I'd suggest a few rounds into that area, JG."

DeWitt nodded in the pale moonlight. "Give us a twenty burst to sight in on," the JG said.

Lam sent one round into the trees where he figured the Chinese might be.

At once he took small-arms fire from fifty feet farther to the right. Six SEAL weapons opened up on the new firing point. Four twenty rounds burst in the trees and brush, and the other weapons riddled the area with two hundred rounds.

"Hold fire," DeWitt bellowed.

"I'll check them out," Lam said.

"No," DeWitt countered. "You've been on point too much tonight. Canzoneri and Train, work up there but stay out of our sight lines. See what you can find. We'll cover you if they fire."

Canzoneri and Train vanished into the brush and worked forward.

"Mahanani, how is our leader?" DeWitt asked on the Motorola.

"Took a serious hit on the top front of his shoulder. Might have broken some bones or at least cut up some tendons and muscle. He won't be shooting much the rest of the night."

"Get him in a safe place."

"Chrissakes, I can talk, JG. Just a little shoulder ding.

Yeah, we're moving over into the woods out of sight at least.
I'm kicking the sawbones back to you. He stopped the bleeding and bandaged my damn arm so I can barely move it. I
think he wants to be a veterinarian."

"We're checking out the last fight," DeWitt said. "Might
have nailed those last four who got away."

"Why would they come back?"

"Honor, to save face. Where else can they go? Damn long
swim back home."

Lam came on the net. "Skipper, we hear movement. We're
maybe twenty yards from the site and we hear one, maybe
two men taking off through the brush."

"Go after them. Use the twenty whenever you get a shot.
Nail the last of the bastards and let's get off this damn mountain."

"We're moving, Skip."

"Thanks for giving me the con," DeWitt said.

"Yeah, sorry. Old habits."

"We're almost to the last firefight site," DeWitt said.
"Right, the airbursts and tree bursts slaughtered two of them.
One is a sergeant. So we have two EM out there running."

Murdock and Mahanani found a spot ten feet inside the
brush line behind a huge pine tree. It offered Murdock a
sweeping view of about half the cleared area including the
tents.

"You hang tough here, Skip. Gave you one shot of morphine, which should keep you at least civil through your
pain."

"Get out of here, Mahanani, and earn your pay."

Ahead of them a hundred yards, Canzoneri stopped behind
a large tree and listened. He could hear feet crashing brush
ahead of him. The woods here were green, but with plenty
of dry sticks and brush to make noise. He motioned to Train
close behind him, and they moved ahead as quietly as possible in the forest.

Every twenty yards, Canzoneri stopped and listened. The
third time they stopped he heard nothing ahead. He waited
and checked the time on his lighted dial watch. Three
minutes later the motion ahead began again. He'd outwaited
the Chinese.

Canzoneri moved quietly, listening for each step made
ahead of him. He figured the enemy couldn't be more than
twenty yards in front. The woods thinned here on a rocky
stretch. Canzoneri and Trail stayed behind solid trees and
watched ahead.

Canzoneri spotted one of the Chinese rushing from one
tree to the next. Just like hunting season on the pond. He
sighted in with the 5.56 on the spot and waited. A moment
later the man moved again. Canzoneri tracked him and fired
four rounds. Three of the four jolted into the running man's
back and he crunched into the rocks and brush, dead in a
heartbeat.

The other Chinese must not have moved, or if he did they
never heard him. They waited, then moved ahead.

Five minutes later Train found the first body. They took
his 53 submachine gun and searched for the second man. If
it had been light there was a chance they could have tracked
him in the soft ground under the trees. Now it was impossible. They reported in, and DeWitt told them to return to
the camp.

Chun knew he had been lucky up to now. He had been spared
in the first barrage of instant death from the sky and escaped
with his sergeant. But then the non-com had made them come
back and attack the Army troops again. He had spoken out
against the idea, and had been knocked down for his trouble.

Now his last friend had died almost in front of him. If he
wasn't careful, he would be dead as well. Slowly he laid
down his submachine gun, and took off his web belt and
combat harness with all of his fighting gear on. He kept only
the rice roll over his shoulder. It was half gone, but he could
live off it for another week.

So silently that not even an owl could hear him, Chun
began to work his way away from the two soldiers hunting
him. He had seen them twice. Now he would vanish.

He had plans. When he had volunteered for this mission
six months ago, they had said they wanted men who knew
English or could learn. He'd said he could learn. At the last
test, he had proven not quite good enough with English to
be an interpreter and a spy to land ahead of the invasion.

But he knew his English was better than many of the Chinese immigrants who had landed in this country. He knew that he could pass as an American with a Chinese background. In some town called Pearl City he had a distant cousin he had written to in English and received letters back from. All he had to do now was escape the men hunting him and make his way to Pearl City somewhere on this Hawaiian island.

Chun rested a moment, then worked his way down the mountain. He found a ravine, slid into it, and moved faster then, sure that he was well away from the hunters. He would go as far as he could during the night, then evaluate his situation. He needed to find a house where he could steal some civilian clothes. That was first on his list.

Next came some American money. That would be essential if he didn't want to walk all the way to Pearl City.

He would walk all night, making good progress. Any ravine would have a small stream where he could get water. The water would be on its path to the coast. At the coast he could find people and watch for a secluded household where he could get clothes and perhaps money as well.

He had no idea how far it was to the beach. He had seen the maps the lieutenant had. They showed there was a wide stretch of forested land, then a stretch of grazing land about the same size that went all the way to the surf. He remembered the lieutenant saying to the sergeants that they would fight their way the ten miles to the beach if they had to. So it was only ten miles.

Ten miles. Five years ago he had run marathons. Ten miles was nothing. He would be at the beach before daylight. What time was it? He had no watch. He could tell the time by the stars in his youth, but not now. He renewed his efforts, hit a fairly easy slope, and began a gentle run. It felt good. Yes, he would get to the beach before daylight, find a house and get clothes, and then be on his way to Pearl City. First he'd have to find out just where it was located. Would there be a bus moving along a coast highway? He would have to wait and see.

Chun felt a wave of excitement. His cousin had told him that he should come to America. Now he had. He must make the best of it. He must reach his cousin. Chinese relatives helped each other. He would be taken in like family. Yes. All he had to do was get to the coast and find new clothes.

Ed Dewitt had established a small command post in dense growth with solid pine trees twenty feet off the clearing and a hundred yards from the tents. It was near the center of the cleared camp area.

Canzoneri and Train had come back, and now he had all of his men together. Murdock sat to one side against a tree. He said he didn't want any more medication, but Mahanani gave him another ampoule of morphine anyway. Now Murdock couldn't even lift his arm.

DeWitt had the men gathered around. "We stay under cover until daylight. I want each of you to set up in a defensive position so you can cover a portion of the cleared area. At dawn we'll decide what to do. There could still be some Chinese stragglers around.

"Ostercamp, you go back and baby-sit our prisoners. Some of them could be waking up pretty soon. Make sure they don't make any noise or get away. Go.

"The rest of you find your spots and settle in. No sleeping. We'll do a net check every fifteen minutes. Right now it is zero-two-twelve. Holt, hang with the commander and me. Let's move it."

Ed talked to Murdock. "One of the Chinese got away. There may be a few more hiding out waiting for dawn. We'll wait with them. Any suggestions?"

"You're doing fine, JG. Hate this fucking shoulder. Is it busted all to hell?"

"Can't tell, Skipper. We'll let the medics in the big Army medical center above Pearl work that out. I figure we should keep CINCPAC up to date on our progress. Holt, fire it up and get CINCPAC."

Holt had to move out from under the trees to get a good sighting on the satellite, then motioned to DeWitt.

"CINCPAC, Red Hill calling."

"Go ahead, Red Hill."

"Progress report. We have taken the top of the hill where the camp is. The hostages are not in the tents. We believe they may have escaped into the brush. All opposition here has been eliminated for now. We're holding to morning to see if we can flush out any more Chinese. Commander Murdock has a serious shoulder wound. We'll need a chopper to fly us out of here early in the morning if all goes right. Could you send a Sea Knight to the Maui airport for a quick pickup?"

"Red Hill, copy. Will relay this to the admiral and contact you. Bird on Maui seems good idea. Do you have any prisoners?"

"Yes, CINCPAC. We have twelve Chinese with no wounds. Make that two choppers for the evac."

"Roger that. Who is this speaking?"

"Lieutenant (j.g.) DeWitt, sir. Second in command."

"Thank you. Expect a reply within two hours."

When DeWitt went back under the trees to his small CP, he found Murdock sleeping. He touched his forehead. DeWitt scowled.

"Hey, Doc, Murdock is burning up with a fever. Get up here and see what the hell is wrong with him and what you can do about it."

25

Red Hill
Maui, Hawaii

Murdock woke up as soon as Mahanani started to check him.

"Hey, Skipper, you're flaking out on me? Where did this temperature come from? You have a fever?"

"Hell, you're the corpsman."

"You allergic to morphine?"

"Never have been before."

The big Hawaiian/Tahitian scowled. "Might have developed it. I'll hit you with some ibuprofen, that might do it. Just don't put any pressure on the shoulder. I better put your arm in a sling to be sure you don't forget and use it."

He rigged a sling from a big square of cloth and tied it around Murdock's neck. "Now, just chill out the rest of the night, Skip. We'll get some medics working on you first thing in the morning."

"Yeah, right. Get back to your post." Murdock frowned. What the hell, he felt like he was sloughing off. He should at least have a spot in the perimeter. Hell, what was going on? He knew he should be doing something. Ed. Ed DeWitt had the con. Yeah. Relax. Good old Ed would do the job.

Yeah, try and relax. Tired. So fucking tired. Yeah. Maybe he could grab a little nap about now. Maybe.

When DeWitt checked Murdock ten minutes later he was sleeping. Good. He needed it. His shoulder was more than just a flesh wound. DeWitt didn't want to think what might happen in the future with a bad shoulder wound. He couldn't worry about that. He had the here and now.

"Net check. Alpha Squad first." DeWitt listened as the five remaining members of the group checked in. Then his Bravo Squad all reported in. Good. Now they waited.

It would be a long night. DeWitt made sure there was a round in the chamber of his weapon, and settled down to scan the open places in front of him. He had done it fifty times already. He'd do it two hundred more times before daylight. Part of the job.

By 0416 there had been no response from CINCPAC. He stirred Ron Holt out of his nest and had him ring up the commander of the Pacific.

"Red Hill calling CINCPAC."

He had to make the call three times before he had any response.

"Yes, Red Hill. Go ahead."

"No response from you on request for two Sea Knights to be flown to the Maui airport for quick evac of our wounded, prisoners and hostages. Any report?"

"Yes, Red Hill. We've been busy tonight. The admiral approved the birds and they should be in position at Kahului airport by now. You can check on TAC Two. They will return everyone to Hickam. Keep us posted. Have you found the governor yet?"

"Negative on the governor. Expect to find him with daylight in about two hours."

"Roger that. CINCPAC out."

DeWitt decided to wait on trying to contact the choppers. Time enough for that when they needed them. Another hour until any kind of light at all. How did they try to find the hostages? Stand on the cliff and yell? Might be a thought. Maybe the hostages would find them. That was a better idea. He hoped that they had escaped and hadn't been unchained, led out somewhere, and assassinated.

He sent Holt back to his position and began another sweep of the zone in front where he could see. Nothing. Nothing again. All night he had been waiting for something to show up. Now he was just as pleased that nothing had developed. Had they taken out all of the Chinese? Shortly after daylight they should know.

It was still an hour until daylight when Chun found the first house. He wasn't sure if it had something to do with the cattle range he had been crossing for the past five miles. It sat on a rise a mile from the beach. He could see the surf through the predawn twilight.

The house had a garage and two barns. It stood at the end of a dirt road. Two old trucks were parked at one side. Neither looked as if it could run. On the far side a pole corral waited for occupants with the gate open. There were no lights on in the house.

He checked for any kind of an outside clothesline. Nothing. The house would be a large risk. Still, he had to get out of his Chinese Army uniform. At the lower elevation it was warmer, and he had taken off his Army blouse and discarded it, shivering in his round-necked white undershirt.

Chun lay beside a tree for ten minutes watching the house. Nothing moved. No sounds came. Evidently there was no dog, or it would have smelled and heard him by now. By nature he was not a violent man. But this was something he had to do. His very life depended on it.

His mind made up, he sprinted across the open area to the side door of the house. He tried the knob. Unlocked. Gently he pushed the door inward. In the deeper darkness he could see little. He waited for his eyes to adjust. Gradually he made out shadows and forms. It was a food kitchen with table and chairs. No one was there. He looked around for clothes, but there were none.

Chun heard someone coming. He ducked low against the wall. The room blazed with light as a hand turned a switch just inside a door across the room. Blinded by the light, Chun remained motionless. He opened his eyes a little at a time, then closed them. It was a man who had come into the room.

He went to cupboards and took out food and turned on a gas flame under a pot of water.

For tea, or coffee. Chun lifted up and charged the man with only his hands as weapons.

"What the hell? Who are you?" the man blurted out. But he didn't have time to avoid the rush of the Chinese soldier. Chun hit the rancher in the side with his shoulder, slammed him against the cupboards, then pushed him to the floor.

"Give up and I won't hurt you," Chun said, his English precisely correct.

"Who the hell are you?"

Chun dropped hard on top of the man and pinned him to the floor. One of the rancher's arms had fallen behind him and now he lay on it. Chun's hands circled the man's throat. He applied enough pressure to cut off the air to the man's lungs. He knew how long to hold it. This had been part of his hand-to-hand–combat training. When the man's eyes bulged and he went limp, Chun pulled his hands away. Yes, the man was about his own size. He would strip off the clothes and vanish before anyone else in the household awoke.

An hour later, Chun walked along the Coast Highway 31 on his way to Kaupo. Signs along the way told how many units it was to the town. Since this was America, it must mean miles. As he walked, he examined the billfold that had been in the rancher's pocket. He had been trained in American money. He counted 148 dollars and some change.

A car came up fast behind him. He remembered about hitchhiking and pushed out his thumb. The car slashed past him and vanished around a curve. The identification in the billfold might be a handicap if anyone were looking for him. He threw away all of the cards with the man's name on them, kept the billfold and money, and continued walking.

A half hour later, a farm truck slowed as it came near him, and stopped when he held out his thumb. Chun ran toward the rig and peered in the window.

"Can you take me into town?" he asked the gray-bearded man who drove the rig.

"Sure can, boy. You must be new around here. Don't remember seeing you before."

"Yes, just arrived. Taking the grand tour before I go to work in my cousin's store."

"Chinese, right?" the man said.

"Yes."

"Always have admired how you people take care of your own. I mean, you get jobs for each other, help start businesses that need opening. Damn fine job. Us haoles never quite got it together so we could do that. Where you come from?"

He thought fast. Should he say China or San Francisco? "Yes, I come from China after long wait."

"Your English is good. Your cousin here on Maui?"

"Oh, no. He is in Pearl City."

"Yep, been there a time or two. On Oahu up above the big Navy base there. Cost a few bucks to fly over there, but you know that since you must have flown over here. You sure travel light."

"Oh, left suitcase in locker at airport."

The rig came to a stop. They had entered a small town with a lot of people up and on the streets already. It couldn't be a half hour after sunrise.

"This is where I turn off. Going to see my new grandson. You have a good life there now, young man. You do that."

Chun stepped down from the old truck and waved. Yes, he would. He certainly would have a good life. Now, all he had to do was take a bus to the airport. He could find that easily. He was going to Oahu and to Pearl City, where he did have a cousin.

Murdock could not remember feeling so miserable. He blinked open his eyes. It was almost light. Not really, but not dark either. In the misty changeover before the light had completely gobbled up the shards of darkness. He moved where he lay on the ground, and a stab of white-hot pain seared through his right shoulder.

What the hell?

Oh, yeah. Some bastard had shot him. He blinked back the pain and looked around. He was in the fringes of the brush near some good-sized pine trees. Ten feet across the forest floor he saw DeWitt looking out at the clearing.

"See anybody out there yet?" Murdock asked.

DeWitt came up with a start and turned and looked at Murdock. He stood and walked over to his unit commander.

"Hey, thought you were going into Daffy Duck land. Glad you're back. We're almost ready to start a sweep and see who we missed last night, if anybody."

"If we missed any chinks last night they must be halfway to Guam by now. Wouldn't you be?"

"Sure, but we have to make the sweep. Then if it's cleared and safe, we'll get in gear to find the hostages."

"Right. Be with you in a shake." He forgot and pushed with his right hand to sit up, and screeched in surprise and pain.

"Oh, damn."

"You stay put, CO. I have enough men for this. You take it easy on that shoulder. Mahanani tells me it could be a bad one. So just sit and stay."

"Like a good dog?"

"Whatever it takes. I'll be back in about thirty. Follow us on your Motorola."

DeWitt called the troops up and they worked the brush on the side of the clearing all the way around. In the thickest part of the brush and woods near the far end of the clearing, they found a well-worn trail that led away from the clearing. DeWitt and Ostercamp followed it. Fifty yards along on a small rise, they found a cabin that had been camouflaged so well they didn't see it until they were within ten yards of it.

"The nuns who run the place?" DeWitt asked.

He called out, but had no response. Ostercamp opened the door slowly and DeWitt darted inside.

"Goddamn," he bellowed.

Ostercamp charged through the door and stopped in a second. The two nuns in their simple habits sat at a plain wooden table they had probably made themselves. Food on the table and clean plates and silverware indicated they had not yet started their meal. Both had multiple bullet wounds in their chests.

"Bastards," Ostercamp said.

"Leave them just the way they are," DeWitt said. "We'll let the civilian authorities take care of this part."

They finished the sweep of the rest of the camp and the brush twenty yards deep on all sides in an hour. Their twelve Chinese prisoners were yelling and calling to them. Ching talked to them in Mandarin and told them that they were not going to be shot. They were POWs and would get taken care of soon.

DeWitt used the SATCOM and raised the Sea Knights on TAC Two.

"Yes, Red Hill, we know the area. Give us an LZ and we can be there in a half hour. A red flare would be nice."

"You have a doctor with you?"

"Negative on the sawbones."

"Roger that. We'll see you soon."

The last hour before sunrise, Governor Itashi couldn't sleep. He paced back and forth in their small campsite under the tall trees and tried to think it through. They had heard nothing through the night. No more shooting, thank God. He stared upward. Before long, Vince would be working his way up through the brush to see what had happened at the campsite above.

He shook his head. It had been a nightmare. From what he knew about Sara, she must have been raped by the Chinese officer. That could have been the only way she could have surprised him enough to stab him, then shoot him. She was a remarkable woman. Just remarkable. So intelligent, so smart, so practical. He didn't know what he would do without her on his staff.

As he thought about it, Sara stirred, then sat up. She saw him, and stood at once and walked over to him. She motioned to him, and they walked a dozen feet away from the camp and out of sight of the others.

"Tom, I just want to say how well you're holding up. I think this trauma is about over for all of us."

He caught her hands. "I admire you for what you must have done up there so you could rescue us. I'll never forget it. You must have some reward."

She looked up, her eyes twinkling in a soft smile. "As I remember, I have a rain check for a kiss."

"Oh, yes, at least one." He bent and kissed her lips tentatively. Then again with more seriousness. Her arms came around his neck and they kissed again, both of them breathing heavily. She pulled away. Her smile was broader now, as if some landmark had been reached.

They went back to the small clearing and the governor roused Vince.

"Hey, time to play spy," Governor Itashi said.

Vince came up wide awake. "Damn, already light. I wanted to go up there a half hour ago. So, I go now but with a lot more care. I don't want either side to shoot me full of holes."

"Take it easy. Don't get hurt." The governor gave him the pistol. "If it's all right for us to come up there, fire three quick shots."

"I can do that."

Vince took one more look at them, then pushed the pistol into his belt and worked through the brush up the hill.

It took him only ten minutes to scramble to within twenty feet of the clearing above. The camp looked deserted. Then he saw three soldiers of some kind come out of the brush on the far side and head toward the center. They were definitely not Chinese. He waited a moment longer. Four more men in cammies and floppy hats showed, and went into the same brushy area across from him. Some kind of a gathering place.

Vince wasn't sure what to do. He'd never been in the Army. He wasn't sure how the gunmen would react if he suddenly appeared. A call. Yeah. Might work. He waited until he saw another of the armed men, and called out in a loud baritone.

"Help. We need help over here."

The military man said something into a lip mike near his mouth and ran toward where he had heard the sound.

Vince waited. The soldier came and waved his weapon at the area. "Who said that? Where are you?"

"Who are you?" Vince called. "You don't look Chinese."

As he said it twelve more men surged from the brush across the way and ran toward him.

"We're American Navy SEALs," the armed man said.

Vince frowned. Navy? Sure looked like Army. "You hunting somebody?"

"The governor and his staff. You part of it?"

A civilian ran up and came near the edge of the brush. It was Karl Tucker. Vince recognized him.

"Vince Yamamoto, is that you, you son of a bitch?"

"Oh, yeah, Karl, I'm coming out. Tell your friends not to shoot me."

Vince and Tucker talked a minute, and then Vince fired the pistol three times.

"We're going down and help them come up," Karl called to the SEALs. Then they rushed down the slope.

A half hour later, the governor and his staff were all back in the tents, trying to unwind. The first Sea Knight had landed and taken Murdock and half the SEALs and the twelve Chinese prisoners off the mountain, heading for Hickam air base on Oahu.

The governor said he wanted to be the last one off the mountain. He had gone to look at the nuns, and he'd wept as he saw what had happened to them.

"I'd been afraid of that. They never appeared after the Chinese came in their helicopters. How can we notify the Maui authorities?"

DeWitt did it on the SATCOM. CINCPAC said they would put through a radio call to the civilian lawmen in the area.

DeWitt ushered the last of the SEALs and the governor and his staff into the second Sea Knight.

"It's not the first-class flights you're used to, but at least no one is going to be shooting at you," Dewitt said.

The governor smiled. "We're overjoyed to be going home, even if it is one day early. We thank the Navy SEALs for rescuing us."

DeWitt shook his head. "We only helped, Governor. Whoever had the key that let you get free of those chains is the person who should be thanked for your rescue. If you had been in those tents when we attacked, it would have been much harder for us. You have a hero in your midst. I hope that person gets the proper recognition."

The governor nodded. "She will, at least a medal of some kind. Yes, I guarantee to you all that she will be recognized and honored."

26

Hickam Field
Oahu, Hawaii

The Sea Knight settled down in a restricted area of Hickam
Field. There a limousine met the governor and his party and
hurried them toward the nearest hospital where the governor's leg would be treated. The news conference would come
later. Ed held his squad on the bird until the limo was well
away. Then they walked off and headed the other way. An
Air Force bus hurried·up and a first lieutenant stepped out.

"Sorry we missed you at the chopper. We're to take you
where you want to go."

When Ed DeWitt stepped out, the two saluted. "We need
to get to our quarters over on Pearl. Possible?"

"Absolutely." The Air Force officer stared at the EAR rifle
and shook his head. "That's the strangest-looking weapon
I've ever seen. What does it do?"

"Strange things, Lieutenant, that we can't talk about."

"Yes, sir. I understand."

Twenty minutes later the SEALs unloaded in front of their
temporary quarters at Pearl Harbor. DeWitt called the base
hospital and found out that Murdock was there and at the
moment in surgery. He had kept the bus waiting while he

made the call, and the driver took him and Mahanani to the hospital. The doctors treated both sides of the bullet wound in the corpsman's left arm, and told him to come back in three days for a change of the dressing.

They were still working on Murdock in surgery. DeWitt tried to find out how bad the hit was, but nobody from the ER had come out and the other doctors in that area didn't know.

He and Mahanani sat and waited for the surgeons to finish their work. A really serious wound could knock Murdock right out of the SEALs' field work. That wasn't the way any SEAL wanted to end his career. Ed got up and paced, then sat down and tried to read a magazine. It was a year-old *Time*.

After another hour a doctor came out of the OR and pulled down his mask. He looked at the two men with dirty uniforms.

"You the SEALs waiting for the commander?"

"Yes, sir," DeWitt said, jumping up. Mahanani was right beside him.

"The commander has taken a serious wound to the shoulder. The bullet cut a notch out of the tendon that goes over the top of the shoulder and controls your ability to lift your arm over your head.

"We did an MRI on it, then went in and stitched the tendon back together again. Similar to a rotator cuff surgery, but not so extreme or serious.

"With proper physical therapy, the commander should be back to ninety-five percent within two months. That means a serious, planned program of physical therapy and lots of rest."

"Oh, yeah, that's good news, Doctor," Mahanani said. "We appreciate your help."

"He should be in recovery and out of the general anesthesia in about a half hour. We also cleaned the bullet wound in his left leg and rebandaged it. I'll have a corpsman show you where he'll be."

Murdock looked angry when they saw him in recovery. He had an IV in his left arm, a bandage on his right shoulder, and he was clean.

"They almost gave me a fu . . ." He looked around. There were two other patients in the large recovery area. "Tried to give me a bath. I told them I didn't hurt there."

He sobered. "They didn't tell me a damn thing. How is the wing? Is it as bad as they said in the chopper?"

"Doubt it," DeWitt said. "One doctor told us you should get back ninety-five percent of your strength in the arm. That's not bad."

Murdock looked over at his SIC. "Ninety-five? Hell, I can whip all of you guys together one-handed if I get back ninety-five. Now, where is the platoon? What's going on? You guys just get back? What's happening?"

"Impatience, thy resounding name is Murdock," DeWitt said. Mahanani looked up at him with a frown.

Murdock snorted.

"You can't even quote it right. So? So? What's up?"

"Nothing. Just dropped off the men at the quarters and came over here. Expect to do an after-action on this one if I have time. Expect a call from CINCPAC and get our part here wrapped up. We have twenty-five-percent casualties. I'm requesting we get pulled off the front lines. At least no more missions."

"Heard before I went into the OR that the war was about over. Just a little bit of mop-up. Casualty rate around here has gone way down lately."

A nurse came in and waved them outside.

"Looks like the boss is ejecting us, little buddy. We'll see you as soon as they turn you loose. Probably tomorrow. Get some sleep. About what I'm going to do."

When they returned to the SEALs' quarters there was a message. It said DeWitt should see the CINCPAC as soon as possible. Not even time to shower. DeWitt took Senior Chief Dobler with him. A Navy sedan had been standing by to transport them up the hill to see the admiral.

The four-star wasn't smiling when the two SEALs walked into his office and froze at attention.

"All right, relax, sit down," the admiral said. "It isn't your fault. But you're going to have to help us dig out of this new mess."

"What mess?" DeWitt wanted to ask, but he didn't.

Admiral Bennington pushed up from his chair and walked around the office. He stared out a window for a moment, then came back and sat down. "That used to help. Not this time. All of my Marines are tied up on the other side of the island chasing down stray Chinese soldiers.

"We don't have any Delta Forces here, and so I'm going to have to ask you SEALs to do one more small favor for Uncle Sam."

"That's what we're here for, Admiral," DeWitt said.

"Yes, well. Let's hope you feel that way when you hear what we want you to do." The admiral pointed to a captain, who lowered a large-scale map. DeWitt saw that it was a section of Honolulu.

"The problem, SEALs, is that there is a group of fanatic Chinese who have taken over the Bishop Museum and are threatening to burn and tear and slash everything inside if we do not allow them safe passage out of the city and to one of their remaining Naval vessels.

"Hawaiian cultural groups and the hundreds of thousands of friends of the Bishop Museum are pressuring the city to give in to the fanatic terrorists and let them go. We in the military don't function that way. We want you and your men to move in and take out the enemy there with no damage whatsoever to the museum building or the employees or the artifacts."

"Oh, boy." DeWitt shook his head. "The admiral isn't joking about this, are you?"

"Not even a little bit. You may know that the Bishop Museum is the continuing research and display center for the histories, sciences, and cultures of all of the Pacific people. It's a shrine to many. We have to be sure it stays that way."

"How, Admiral Bennington? We specialize in slash and burn, shoot and scoot."

"You have the EAR weapons."

"True, but they could shatter pottery and china, might rip apart tightly framed artwork. I'm not sure how much we could rely on them inside a building like that."

"You'll have to find out. I understand that Commander Murdock will recover nearly full use of his right arm. We're pleased about that. That cuts your platoon down to thirteen men, which I've found in combat is often a lucky number."

"When, Admiral?"

"I'll have transport for you at your quarters at 2300. We hope you can go into the building through a seldom-used side door by 2400. Take any weapons you think you might need. The fanatics inside are expendable, the art treasures are not. You better get some sleep and some chow and get ready to move out."

"Thank you, sir," DeWitt said. Both SEALs did perfect about-faces and walked out of the office.

"It can't be done," Dobler exploded as soon as they were outside. "I've been in the Bishop a dozen times. It's crammed with all sorts of precious stuff."

"Zero damage was our orders. From a practical standpoint, we'll do the job with as little damage as possible. It's the only way we can win on this one. We'll take both our EARs. Wish we had four more. Where are the others?"

"In San Diego."

"Damn."

Outside, they found a big sedan. It had the admiral's plates on, but they were covered. A blanket had been draped in the backseat where the SEALs would sit. The Marine sergeant driver grinned at them.

"Hey, usually I don't get such high-flying VIPs in such dirty uniforms to drive around. Welcome to the best ride in the South Pacific."

"Shut up and drive," Dobler said. "We got problems to figure out."

By the time they arrived at the front of their quarters, they had decided on a few things. They would take all of the flashbang grenades they could find, and the EAR guns and their sub guns and carbines. The heavy stuff would stay outside. They'd all have night-vision goggles.

Half of the SEALs had showered, eaten, and flaked out on their bunks. Dobler rounded up the rest of them from the PX, and DeWitt got them down to business. He explained their mission and the men groaned.

"Why do we get all of these don't-touch-the-goods kind of assignments?" Lam asked. "It could ruin our tough-guy image."

"What else can we use inside there?" Dobler asked.

"What about Honolulu PD's SWAT Team's shotguns with stun balls," Guns Franklin asked. "They'll put a man down but won't wound him. Some have strings and beads on them that inflict a lot of non-lethal pain."

DeWitt looked around and saw heads nod. "Franklin, call our liaison, that Commander Johnson we were working with. See if he can get six of those shotguns and, say, fifty rounds. Go."

"How we going to do this, JG?" Dobler asked.

"First we need some sketches of the place, what is where and where the Chinese might be holed up. Then we move inside and hunt them down."

"Sounds easy, JG. We have a bunch of non-lethal so all they have to do is shoot us with their damn lethal bullets," Fernandez said.

DeWitt looked around. "Okay, so it won't be a walk in the park. We might get lucky. We'll try the EAR first and see if it causes any damage. If it doesn't or it's minimal, we'll have nineteen shots left. Hey, make sure both weapons are on full charge. Ostercamp, check out both of those EARs now."

The JG looked around. "Train. Get over to communications and find a fax number you can use. Then call up the Bishop Museum Association here in town and have them fax you half a dozen drawings of the layout of the museum. Also have them send brochures about the museum. Get that done as fast as you can. Urge them to reply by return phone call."

Train nodded and hurried out of the room.

Dobler and DeWitt decided that they had done all they could before the actual assault on the museum. DeWitt left Dobler in charge of the troops, and he went back to the base hospital, where he had been told that David Sterling and Harry Ronson were recovering from their wounds received earlier in the Hawaiian mission.

DeWitt found the men both in the same four-man room in beds next to each other. DeWitt had talked to the floor nurse before he saw the men. She had been brisk, frank, and unemotional.

"The gut-shot one is still in trouble. We're not sure what

else we can do for him. The bullet is out, but there was more
damage to the intestines than we had at first thought. He
needs another operation to do some repair work down there.
There is no danger of peritonitis, but his condition could
change at any time. We watch him closely.

"The chest-shot man is in better shape. The slug missed
all vital organs, but caught a good-sized vein so there was
considerable interior bleeding by the time we repaired the
vein. Most of that problem has been taken care of. I'd say
he has another week here with us before we can release him
to Balboa in San Diego."

DeWitt had thanked her and found his two men.

"Well, the damn war must be over. Look who dragged his
JG heels in here to check up on us," Jaybird croaked. "We
didn't do it, JG."

"That's the problem, Jaybird. You were supposed to do it.
How the hell are you?"

"Ready to blow out of this dump. Haven't had an MRE
since I signed in here. I'm getting sloppy homesick."

"Tough life. What about you, Ronson? Miss the slow-
paced life of a SEAL on special duty?"

"Damn right, JG. When am I getting out of here? I keep
telling them I can outrun any of them and do ten times the
push-ups any of them can do. They won't even challenge
me."

"I'll challenge you, hotshot," DeWitt said. "You'll get out
when the white coats tell you to leave. Oh, you don't know,
but the skipper is down on the fourth floor. He got a shoulder
shot up."

"Bad, JG?"

"Not good, but the docs said he should get most of the
strength back in the shoulder and arm. So he can hang with
us."

"Damn glad of that," Jaybird said. "Hey, how are those
twenties working?"

"Best weapon we have. They pay their way." He watched
the two normally active SEALs, who were now laid up and
helpless. "Hey, they feeding you guys enough?"

"Oh, yeah," Jaybird said.

"If I get to eat half of the kid's chow, I can make out," Ronson said.

The JG nodded and slapped his cammy hat on the bed rail. "Good, 'cause I need to bug out of here. We've got a walk in the park coming up tonight at 2300. You guys take care."

"What is it?" Jaybird asked. "Where you going?"

"Like I said. A walk in the park. Tell you later. Now be good in here so when you get out we can all be bad."

"Oh, yeah, hoooooo-ha!" both SEALs said in unison.

Back in the SEAL quarters a half hour later, DeWitt worked over the mission and what they could do. They could use some of those nets that shotguns shot out, trapping a victim, but he knew there weren't any of them around.

He and Dobler went over everything again. The men would take the two EARs and the sub guns and the Colt M-4Al Commandos. The Honolulu Police SWAT team ferried over four shotguns and forty rounds of the special string balls. They didn't ask any questions. Just took a signed receipt and left.

Commander Johnson was back with them with his red-signature letter. He arranged early chow for them, steak dinner with baked potatoes, three vegetables, and ice cream sundaes for dessert. DeWitt put everyone down for three hours' sleep. Then they were up at 2200 checking and double-checking their gear. They carried less than usual, so they checked it all three times. Everyone wore the personal radio communication device. The small Navy bus had been waiting outside for them since 2100. There was one driver who didn't want to be late on a project authorized by the admiral.

DeWitt touched his lip mike. "Okay, you cowboys, let's get out of here and go see what kind of fun we can have over at the Bishop Museum."

27

Bishop Museum
Honolulu, Hawaii

Lieutenant (j.g.) DeWitt went over everything he knew about the Bishop Museum. It was almost a shrine. It was the Pacific Basin's foremost museum of anthropology and natural history. It consisted of more than a dozen buildings, one of the latest the new Planetarium near the entrance.

. "That's where the parley has been taking place, at the new entrance building," DeWitt said. "From what the negotiators gather, most of the Chinese are in that first building and the Planetarium. We might not have to go too far into the museum buildings to dig them out."

"But we don't go in the front door?" Dobler asked.

"The people who know the place say there is a little-used gate at the rear parking lot in back of Pauahi Hall. If we can't bust open the gate, we can climb the chain-link fence there and get on the grounds. The buildings are not connected. It's more like a campus with grass and flowers and a series of buildings. Some of them were made before 1900.

"We have printouts from the museum's Web site showing us the buildings and the layout of the grounds. I'll pass them around. Memorize which buildings are where. Especially the top rank, Pauahi, Paki, and Hawaiian Halls. What looks like grass is around most of them, and some concrete sidewalks.

"We'll try coming over or through the fence, past the three halls, and get to the Hall of Discovery, which is part of or right next to the new Planetarium."

"Won't they have guards out?" someone asked.

"They might," Dobler said. "But we are told there are no more than a dozen Chinese inside. That's a guess, and they might be off by five or ten. The Chinese slipped in with the regular folks, then took off civilian clothes to show their Army uniforms and closed down the place. Turned off the lights and ordered everyone out, including the staff and workers.

"There could be some of the staff still inside, so we have to be doubly careful." He looked around at the group. "How many of you have been to the Bishop before?"

Four men raised their hands.

"I've been there three or four times," DeWitt said. "It's always different. We won't know what it's like this time until we get inside. They were still building the new Planetarium the last time I was there. Remember, we keep it as non-lethal and non-destructive as possible."

Dobler chimed in. "On this one we fire our deadly weapons only to save our own or someone else's life. That's our orders until we go weapons-free. Any questions?"

"We get those bolt cutters?" Holt asked.

"We did," Ching said. "Twenty-four-inchers and heavy little bastards. But it's guaranteed."

"We get off the bus at the north end of the rear parking lot and work down toward the gate near Pauahi Hall," said DeWitt. "First, we're watching for Chinese guards or lookouts. If we don't see any, we go in the easiest way. Just another mission. Let's get this one done without anybody getting hurt. Keep your damn heads down if they start to shoot. Relax. We should be there in about twenty minutes."

For twenty minutes Ed DeWitt thought about Milly back in Coronado. She was a saint. She had to be to put up with him and this crazy SEAL Team life. When he made it back home this time, he was going to carve out more time for her.

A drive up the coast or maybe down into Baja California. Milly loved Mexico.

Slowly DeWitt realized he was homesick for his lady. It hadn't been that long. They had been on the carrier for a month on a wait-and-see that had never happened. Then the training on Oahu and the damned Chinese invasion. Yes, home was sounding better and better.

Milly. He could see her dark eyes, her mischievous smile, the quick sure way she worked out a computer problem for him on his laptop. He wondered if he'd have time to do some shopping for her before they left the islands. He hoped so. He had in mind buying for her some . . .

"JG, we're here. Parking lot back side."

DeWitt came out of the reverie in a flash. "Dobler, you have what's left of the first squad. Take them off and find some cover along the bushes. Be right behind you. We'll do a commo check as soon as we're all off. Go."

DeWitt surveyed the buildings and the fence as he stepped down from the bus. About as he remembered it. Lots of plants, the imposing stone buildings mixed in with the newer, more modern kinds. Twelve, maybe thirteen structures in the complex. Everyone checked in on the net. He had a dozen men. Thirteen counting him. They were minus some important cogs in their machinery.

"Move it down the fence line," he said on the Motorola. "Work slowly. Watch inside for any sign of Chinese."

Five minutes later they were at the gate in the chain-link fence. A short chain and two padlocks secured it. Ching worked the bolt cutters and left them beside the gate as he swung it open. The squad went through the gate and to the rear wall of Pauahi Hall without making any contact with the Chinese.

DeWitt and Lam took the point as they worked north around the hall, and then past Paki Hall and toward Hawaiian Hall, which was just across from the Planetarium.

Bill Bradford carried one of the EAR guns and walked just in back of DeWitt. Ostercamp had the other EAR weapon back in the Bravo Squad. All of the SEALs carried the police-type thin plastic riot cuffs that they could use to tie up a prisoner securely and quickly.

Ahead, Lam went flat against the wall and slowly slid down to the ground.

"DeWitt, two Chinese just came around the side of the hall here," Lam whispered into his lip mike. "Both have rifles and are in green fatigues. You should be able to see them in about five seconds."

"Take them out, Bradford," DeWitt said.

Bradford stepped away from the wall, lifted the heavy EAR weapon, and aimed it at the end of the wall and waited. Two green-clad men came around the corner. He fired.

The now-familiar sound of the whooshing jet of concentrated sound jolted from the EAR and unleashed its enhanced sound power on the two Chinese soldiers, who fell in midstride not knowing what had hit them and struck them down quietly. Canzoneri and Fernandez ran up and carried the inert bodies into the tropical plantings along the north fence across from Paki Hall. Both Chinese were disarmed and bound with the riot cuffs on wrists and ankles.

Lam and DeWitt looked around the corner of Hawaiian Hall and saw ahead the Hall of Discovery. It evidently was attached to the new Planetarium. The Chinese might have come from a door that was marked Employees Only.

"Lam, Ostercamp with the EAR, check out the door," DeWitt said on his radio. "If it's open wait for two-man backup, then try inside."

Lam darted across the open space to the door. Ostercamp came from the rear of the squad and joined him at the door. Lam turned the knob and pulled it out an inch. He nodded.

DeWitt and Train Khai surged across the space to Discovery and waited against the wall. Lam saw them arrive, edged the door open a foot, and slid inside. Ostercamp went in right behind him, with Khai catching the door for himself and DeWitt.

At first Lam could see nothing. He flipped down his NVGs and looked again. The soft green glow in the darkness showed it was a stockroom. He moved forward to a door across the way. The others came closely behind him.

"I'll try the next door," Lam said.

DeWitt picked it up on his Motorola. Suddenly it all felt wrong. "Hold it on the door," DeWitt snapped. He rushed across the room and glared at the door. There was no indication what was on the other side. He had his NVGs on as well. He took the knob and turned it slowly until it stopped, then eased the door back a half inch, then more, until a sliver of bright yellow light slanted through the crack. He pushed up the NVGs and shut his eyes for a few seconds. Then he opened them and looked at the light before he edged the panel back another two inches.

DeWitt stood on the latch side of the door against the wall. He leaned over to look through the slot. Six angry, hot lead slugs slammed into the panel door and splintered through into the room. They missed the SEALs.

"Ostercamp, one round," he whispered into the radio. Ostercamp moved forward, knelt next to the wall, and pushed the muzzle of the EAR through the door opening, angled it upward, and fired.

The whooshing sound came louder here, and the sound of the enhanced audio in the next room seemed more like a grenade going off than they had heard before.

As soon as the round echoed around the next room, DeWitt jerked the door open and rushed inside, followed by his three SEALs. It was a display room. He saw one large sign that said this was an exhibit of the Royal Treasures of the Hawaiian Royal Monarchy. In the middle of the room was a richly decorated carriage. He saw two men on the floor, one holding his ears. Both were unconscious. The four SEALs searched the room quickly. Only the two men were there.

Ed took a special look at the displays. The rig in the center was the Queen's Royal Carriage recently restored. There were dozens of other early Hawaiian artifacts and paintings, three busts of kings and queens, and items of everyday life that had belonged to the monarchs. He examined them carefully. None had been damaged. Good. They could use the EAR again.

Two doors led out of the display area. He was about to open one of them when he saw the knob turn. He leaped aside. Two Chinese soldiers backed into the room. They carried a long cardboard box that two more soldiers held at the other end.

"Hooooo-ha!" DeWitt bellowed. The four soldiers saw the SEALs for the first time, all four pointing automatic weapons at them. They dropped the box. One, who had officer insignia on his shoulders, went for his belted pistol. DeWitt shot him with his sub gun on single-shot. The round hit the Chinese officer in the chest and he stumbled backward, hit the wall, and slumped to the floor.

The three soldiers lifted their hands. The SEALs cuffed them and put them against the far wall behind part of the display. DeWitt checked the officer. Dead. He dragged him behind the display.

Lam pointed to the second door. DeWitt nodded. Lam opened it cautiously. When he could see out, he waved over DeWitt, who looked.

It was a lobby with entrance, ticket booth, and doors on the far side about forty feet across the open area. High on a wall over the entrance were the words: THE NEW PLANETARIUM. So they were almost there. They had eliminated eight Chinese so far. What the hell did the SEALs do next? Charge across the open space and go into the Planetarium? Not smart.

Watch and wait? Maybe.

"Skipper, we've got trouble back here."

It was Dobler on the net. "What?"

"Four Chinks with weapons. Some kind of extended-stock automatic carbines. Moving along Hawaiian Hall directly at us. We're just around the corner."

"Use the EAR now," DeWitt commanded.

He could send back some help. No, Dobler had more men now than *he* did. Should be nine of them back there somewhere. He listened for the EAR shot, but knew he couldn't hear it inside. His attention came back to the front and the entrance to the empty Planetarium. Ordinarily, there would be four or five hundred people milling around inside. Was the inside the Chinese HQ? How many Chinese were here?

As he thought, the door across the way opened and four civilians in museum uniforms came out, followed by two soldiers with weapons at the ready. They marched them across the lobby to a set of doors that led out toward what

DeWitt remembered as the new entrance building. He let them go.

Outside at the corner of Hawaiian Hall, Dobler nodded and Bradford fired the EAR round. This time they heard the enhanced audio explosion/concussion where it went off less than twenty yards from them. Both SEALs ducked back around the corner as soon as the shot was fired.

Dobler felt his floppy hat twirled around on his head as the concussion caused a gush of air. When he looked around again, he saw all four soldiers down on the narrow sidewalk. They all looked unconscious.

Dobler looked around. No bushes there. Not enough vegetation to hide the bodies.

He waved up Jefferson and Franklin. "Go up there and grab those weapons and leave the Chinese where they lay. Then get back here pronto. Skipper, four more Chinks down and out. We can't hide this bunch. All else under control."

"Good, Dobler. Send me up two more men. Keep the EAR there. Going to try to clear the Planetarium."

"Roger that. Ching, Jefferson. Go through that door up there marked Employees Only. The skipper needs you inside."

He watched as the two men ran down the sidewalk, opened the door into the building, and vanished.

Inside, DeWitt had sent Train Khai back to the other room to bring in the new shooters. He watched the outside. No more movement. There must be more of them across the way where the two soldiers had led out the civilians. Were they just clearing out the last of the workers, or were those four hostages?

Ching and Jefferson arrived. He had six men now, including himself. It would have to do. He caught their attention. "We're going to charge across the open lobby out there to the double doors, which I guess lead inside the Planetarium. Must be some more Chinese in there. We send Lam in first, then the EAR and we support. No live rounds unless absolutely necessary. Let's go."

Lam led the way and beat the others to the door. He tried the pulls and found the doors unlocked. He opened one a crack, but could see nothing inside. He pulled it open all the

way and rushed inside, followed by Ostercamp and his EAR.
The other four SEALs charged in behind them.

Inside, there was a hallway that opened on five or six
stairways that evidently led up to the sharply canted seats.
They saw no one Lam and Ostercamp hurried to the end of
the hallway and looked up the stairs.

"Nada, Skipper."

Then the SEALs heard loud voices speaking Chinese,
coming from the central stairs. They faded into the other
stairs to be out of sight and watched.

"No EAR," DeWitt whispered into the mike. "One round
in here would knock out friend and foe for from four to six
hours. Single shot only."

The voices increased, and soon six Chinese soldiers came
out from the stairs into the hall. When all were in the open,
DeWitt fired one round into the wall, and all the SEALs
leaped out of their cover and trained their weapons on the
Chinese.

"Ching, tell them," DeWitt said into his mike.

Ching rattled off some Mandarin. One of the men reached
for a belted pistol. Lam saw the move and fired one round
from his Colt Carbine, hitting the man in the shoulder and
dropping him to the ground.

"Put your hands high," Ching ordered. The remaining men
did. Lam had rushed up to kick away the wounded man's
weapon. Now he worked with the others, who closed in on
the five standees, taking away weapons and cuffing them,
hands and feet. The SEALs left them in the hall and fanned
out to go up the steps all at once and check the elegant,
impressive Planetarium with its huge ceiling screens and dozens of projectors and special lean-back seating.

"Could be fifty of them hiding in here," Lam said into his
mike.

"We might never find them," DeWitt said.

"Let me sing out and see if I can raise anyone," Ching
said.

"Go," DeWitt said.

Ching made three quick calls in Mandarin, then three
more, but there was no response.

"Let's call the game in here," DeWitt said. As they started
back to the front of the Planetarium the radio sounded.

"Skipper, we just missed something. We're deployed along
the front of Hawaiian Hall here. Thirty seconds ago we saw
about fifteen Chinese rush away from that entrance pavilion,
Jabulka, and storm into the foyer that leads into this Hawaiian Hall. I think they're inside now."

"Keep your powder dry, Dobler. We're done in here and
on the way out. We will have a confrontation with those kind
Orientals shortly. Right now I want you to move up until
you can see that door into the building and hold. We'll be
across that grassy area toward the entrance building. Don't
let any more go in or out. Use the EAR out there in the open
if you need to."

DeWitt turned to his men. "Let's try those other doors over
there and get out of here. We have friends waiting for us
over in the Hawaiian Hall."

28

Hawaiian Hall
Bishop Museum
Honolulu, Hawaii

"Mr. DeWitt, the Chinese have just barricaded the front doors to Hawaiian Hall and a couple of others by the looks," Senior Chief Dobler said on the radio. "Not sure what they are trying to do. We need another door. Any ideas?"

"Seems to me I remember an open court around back," DeWitt said. "Take your men around there and try it. You might beat them to it. We'll check out the front and then the side."

From the front of the Jabulka building, he looked at the closest big structure. It was Hawaiian Hall, and it appeared that two other buildings were attached. Maybe the far one would be productive. No sense trying the front door since the Chinese were watching it and had it barricaded. He took his men quickly down the sidewalk, across part of the Great Lawn, and around the far end of the building.

He spotted two doors. One that looked like it was for deliveries or for moving large exhibits. Another man-sized door was nearby. They tried the door. Locked. Minimum damage. He lifted his sub gun and fired three rounds into the lock mechanism near the handle. The door shook a moment, then swung outward two inches.

Lam jerked it open and darted inside. DeWitt went in right behind him. The room was large, with lights on and various displays and artifacts spread out on two rows of tables. A workroom.

They saw a door at the far end of the space twenty feet away, and rushed toward it. All six of the team were inside by then. DeWitt tried the door. Unlocked. He motioned for Ostercamp to come up with his EAR gun. Slowly DeWitt turned the knob and inched the door back so he could see out a slit. Nothing. He pulled it more, careful to stay on the wall side of the door handle. Inside he could see exhibits. He wasn't sure what they were, but they looked like artifacts from the days of the kingdom. Busts of kings, brilliant robes, seashell displays.

DeWitt could see no Chinese soldiers. He opened the door all the way, staying against the wall. No rifle fire. He looked out, then rushed into the display area and crouched behind a wood carving of one of the kings. Nothing happened.

"Come," he said into the Motorola. Lam was there quickly. DeWitt pointed toward an open archway that showed twenty feet ahead. They worked around the displays of ordinary items used in the earliest days of the islands.

Lam leaned around the side of a six-foot-wide archway and looked into the next room. More exhibits. These were all wooden products, bowls, bows, all sorts of carved artifacts. A huge koa tree was featured, with charts showing the many things the early Hawaiians made from the wood of the koa tree.

"JG, we have trouble," Dobler said on the Motorola.

"What kind?" DeWitt asked.

"Found this back door, but it's locked."

"Three rounds into the lock and you should be inside. We're in the far left end of the place."

"Yeah, just realized this end of it is three stories tall. If we try to flush them, they could go all over."

"Try not to do that. Let me know when you're inside."

DeWitt led his men through the next room and then came to an open area. Ahead he could see a reception desk with a small lobby and four Chinese soldiers evidently talking something over.

Ostercamp rolled into position beside DeWitt and fired one round from the zapper EAR gun. They saw the four men freeze in place for a second, then topple over and crash into each other and the floor.

"Move up," DeWitt said into the lip mike, and his men rushed forward and took over the small area just inside the main entrance. Two rifle shots exploded in the closed area and sounded like rockets. The SEALs scattered for cover, and Train used the Motorola to say he saw two Chinese troopers at the back end of the main floor exhibit. He thought one of them had fired the shots.

"We're inside," Dobler said on the radio.

"We're using the EAR on the first floor," DeWitt said.

"There are some back stairs this side," Dobler reported. "We can take over the second floor and see if any of them got up that way."

"Go."

DeWitt checked in front of him into the main floor display devoted to Ancient Hawaii. Overhead he saw the open area three floors tall where a giant whale hung. It was nearly as long as the building. In one terrible second he saw a Chinese soldier lift up from behind a display fifteen feet away and aim his rifle directly at him. The SEAL brought up his submachine gun and splattered six rounds into the invader before he got off a shot.

DeWitt ran through the displays to where he had seen the Chinese man. He lay across an ancient canoe, three bullet holes in his upper chest.

"Five down, ten to go," DeWitt said into the mike. "Let's dig them out."

As he said it he heard the whooshing sound of the EAR gun go off. It seemed different this time, and then he realized he might be well in advance of where it was fired. The enhanced audio made a smaller sound when it hit.

DeWitt felt something pound him in the belly, then drive him to his knees. He dropped his machine gun, but grabbed it at once. He tried to stand, but his balance wasn't working. He began to crawl back the way he had run only a minute ago. He crawled and crawled and came around a display, and found two SEALs with hands over their ears.

They saw him and ran to him, getting him onto his feet and walking him back toward the main entrance. He was aware that everything was silent, and that confused him. He saw lips moving but heard nothing. Then traces of sound slipped past the barrier.

He could walk again by himself. He shook his head and rubbed his ears, and more sounds came in. A moment later he could hear the men around him.

"JG, you okay?" Someone said it again. He turned and saw Ostercamp. "You okay, JG? We found you crawling back. I had just blasted three of the little devils. Afraid you were too close up there and caught some of it. We decided not to use the EAR anymore inside here. We have eight of them down and tied now, JG."

DeWitt tried to swallow. He couldn't. He nodded at Ostercamp. He tried to swallow again. This time he made it.

He tried his voice. "Good. Good." It was scratchy, but they understood him. "Let's sweep this floor. Side to side. We still have at least seven bogies in here somewhere. We still have six men?"

"That's a Roger," Lam said. "When I saw you coming back I counted. All accounted for."

"Let's do it, people."

They worked from exhibit to exhibit, all from the earliest days of the Hawaiian people when there were dozens of gods and sacred spots and the kings and queens ruled. Twenty minutes later they came to the far wall and worked behind the exhibits, but found no more Chinese.

DeWitt used the radio. "Dobler, you doing any good up there?"

"Found two who gave up. Still looking for five more. There's the third floor."

"Moving up there," DeWitt said. They went up the stairs, put up in 1899 with the main building.

"Found one more hiding on the second," Dobler said on the net. "Should leave four we know about."

At the top of the stairs, Lam caught DeWitt's shoulder.

"JG, you stay here. Let us do the sweep. You took quite a jolt back there."

DeWitt shook his head, but when he did it, he saw two of Lam, two of everything. He sat down with his back against the wall, and waved the men forward.

Lam pointed the other men down aisles. These exhibits showed the diverse cultures that make up the current Hawaii. The SEALs went past a thatched early Hawaiian house and a finely worked red and yellow cape made of feathers. The Chinese, Japanese, and Filipinos were all represented.

Lam came around a corner of a display and found a Chinese lying on the floor with his rifle pointed at him. The rifle fired. The bullet missed. Lam's weapon jolted down and snapped off three shots, drilling the Chinese from chin to chest. He died in an instant. Lam heard firing two aisles over. He charged that way.

Train stood over two soldiers, both gasping out their last breaths. Train's Colt M-4A1 still covered the two. When they died, he kicked them both and then dropped to his knees, his hand on his left shoulder coming away bloody.

"Three more down and out," Lam said on the net. "We have one wounded. Train caught one in the shoulder. I don't know how bad."

"Clear floor two," Dobler said on the net.

"Clear floor three," Lam said. He hurried back to talk to DeWitt. He grinned when he saw the JG. He was standing up, walking around in a small circle. He grabbed Lam.

"How bad is Train?"

"Not sure. Quite a bit of blood. We'll let Doc look at him."

"I'm back to normal, Lam. Thanks for the work up here. Let's get the troops on the ground and compare notes."

On the ground floor, they continued on out the back door of Hawaiian Hall and flaked out on the grass. After a five-minute talk they decided that none of the invaders could have left the building. When the first EAR round went off, Dobler and his squad had had the rear entrance blocked. The Chinese must have all gone upstairs and been caught or killed.

"Hang tough here," DeWitt said. "Lam and I will go out front and see if we can find somebody to talk to. They're going to need a coroner and some ambulances and a police unit to do a clean sweep of the whole inside of the museum campus. We'll be back."

They found two police cars with radios and six museum officials at the front entrance eager to come inside. DeWitt explained to them what they'd done.

"There is some incidental damage, but nothing major. It could have been a lot worse. Two doors had their locks shot off and one or two exhibits got nicked by flying bullets."

The museum director gripped DeWitt's hands. "We thank you and all the ancient Hawaiian gods for your good work here. We're sorry to hear there are casualties, but it was not our war in the first place."

One of the cops waved his small notebook. "I'll need some statements from you about any deaths."

DeWitt smiled. "This is a military operation, Officer. It's out of your jurisdiction. You can talk with Admiral Bennington out at Pearl if you want any statements. Now, I have a wounded man I need to get to the hospital."

DeWitt and Lam turned, their submachine guns slung over their shoulders, and walked away from the gaping civilians at the front entrance.

The bus had stayed where DeWitt told the driver to hold. The SEALs loaded on and soon were on their way back to Pearl.

Train's wound just below the shoulder through the fleshy part of the arm, miss the bone. It would heal in a month or so.

When they arrived at Pearl Harbor, DeWitt let the men off at their quarters, then took Train with him to the hospital. The corpsman looked Train over, treated his shoulder, and released him. Then the two went and visited Murdock. His shoulder was giving him fits and he had given the nurses a bad time. The doctor said he could be transferred to Balboa Naval Hospital in San Diego in a day or two.

Both Ronson and Jaybird Sterling were recovering and out of danger. Both could be transferred to Balboa after a final check.

Back in their quarters at Pearl, DeWitt reported to the men on the medical cases. Then he took a call from CINCPAC.

"Yes, sir, we cleared up the problem. Suffered one casualty but his wound is not serious." He listened for a minute.

"We figured there were about thirty-five of them. We killed or captured thirty-three, and figured we had them all. The thirty-five was an estimate."

He listened again.

"Yes, sir. We're functioning at a forty-percent casualty rate, sir, and request that we be returned to our home base at Coronado within the next week."

DeWitt smiled. "Yes, sir. Thank you, sir. It's been a pleasure. We'll coordinate with Commander Johnson. Thank you again, Admiral Bennington."

DeWitt put his feet up on the training table and grinned. So, they were to be cleared for return within a week. The war was over for all but a few mop-ups. The Chinese Navy had suffered tremendous losses, and it might be ten years before it recovered.

All that and there still would be time to do some shopping in Honolulu for Milly. He grinned and went to tell the men the good news. All of them were at special chow or sleeping. Yeah, he could tell them in the morning. Ed DeWitt grinned all the way to his quarters. It was going to be a great week ahead.

29

NAVSPECWARGRUP-ONE
Coronado, California

At the SEAL Team Seven headquarters and SEAL BUD/S training command, just south of Hotel Del Coronado on the Pacific Ocean, Lieutenant (j.g.) Ed DeWitt sat in the commander's chair at Third Platoon's HQ and reviewed the past week. They had been pulled out of Hawaii and the co-op training with the British and Aussies and sent home to recuperate. He still had three men in the hospital and two more recovering from gunshot wounds.

Jaybird was at Balboa Hospital with the other two. He was still in the worst shape. They had done a second operation to repair damage to his large intestine. He had been responding well, but had a relapse and been critical for a day or two. Now he was doing better, and the doctors said he should be fit to return to duty, but not for at least three months.

Harry Ronson was doing better. He would be discharged in another week. His chest shot had missed his lung. Took out an artery that had been patched up. He would be on Navy light duty for a month, then available for return to active duty with his SEAL unit.

Commander Murdock waited at Balboa for the day he

could be released. The doctors there had checked the surgery and pronounced it sound. The MRI showed that the tendon repair had been correct and would heal in time.

"They got me on this damn pulley thing that I know is tearing my arm apart," Murdock brayed. "They say I have to use this for one minute every hour I'm awake. Ripping me into small pieces. I have to try to get my hand as high over my head as I can. Told them I can get it all the way up. Had to prove it to them. They said, good, now keep getting it up there sixteen times a day for a minute each rotation. That's about forty damn times up and down.

"I'm supposed to be out of here in two more days. Hell, in civilian hospitals they do this same operation, only tougher, as an outpatient procedure."

The two doctors talked with DeWitt outside. "The commander is going to need physical therapy in another four weeks. He's a SEAL, right? He won't be back to lifting those logs or swimming twenty miles for at least three months. He'll think he can. If he gets too active, he can tear the tendon apart again and we'll have to start all over."

"Understood, sir. We'll baby him. Well, we'll try. The commander has a mind of his own."

"Might be, but right now his body belongs to us."

"I'll remind him of that, Doctor."

DeWitt had been placed in temporary command of the Third Platoon. Which didn't mean a lot. He did wrangle seven days of liberty for the men. Most of them scattered all over the country. He had laid out a three-day trip for himself. Milly had wanted to go north again, up into the wine country. They would leave tomorrow.

Master Chief Gordon MacKenzie had helped him over the rough spots the first few days. DeWitt had done the after-action report and filed copies with Admiral Bennington in Pearl and with his own CO here on base. Master Chief MacKenzie had hovered over DeWitt for three days until DeWitt told him to get back to his own office.

DeWitt had planned the usual fish fry for the first evening after all the troops were home from liberty and when at least Murdock and Ronson would be out of Balboa. His specialty was grill-fried salmon. But that was next week.

He closed up and drove home to his apartment, where Milly waited for him. She had taken the week off from her computer work.

"This week I'm forgetting about computer problems and networking and all that," she had told him the first day he came home. "I'm devoting this week to you and saying a quick little prayer of thanks for your safe return. Sometimes I think I'm like one of those women in New England harbors who paced the skywalk on top of their houses where they could look out to sea. They walked every evening until sundown hoping they could spot the incoming sails of their husbands' ships."

"Glad you saw my sails coming in this time," he'd said.

Now he watched her from the bed as she undressed. Damn, what a woman. She knew exactly what excited him. A slow striptease was one of them. It had been a long, tough day and he thought he might be too tired. But he wasn't. Then she revived him an hour later, and again at three in the morning. He swore she had set an alarm clock.

"Not true," Milly said. "I couldn't sleep. I just lay there watching you. Then when I couldn't stand it any longer, I woke you up. I hope you didn't mind."

He grinned and kissed her again.

The next morning they began their drive up the coast. They used her two-year-old Mercury Grand Marquis. It was a much better road car than his little Ford. He loved to drive it. They wound up the coast, then through Oakland to get around San Francisco and into the wine country. Napa, Sonoma, and Mendocino. They never got past Napa.

The small bed-and-breakfast was right near a winery. "Brothers Wines, since 1842." He doubted the heritage date, but the wines were pleasant and they bought several bottles to take with them.

"At least this time I know where you were," Milly said. "The Chinese invasion of Hawaii. They were idiots to think they could wade ashore on the foremost bastion of U.S. Naval power in the whole Pacific."

"Did I say I was in Hawaii?"

She laughed. "You didn't have to. You brought me that matching Hawaiian shirt and the flowered muumuu. I know

I'm not a rocket scientist or a brain surgeon, but even I could figure that one out."

She sobered. They lay in bed in another bed-and-breakfast, watching the countryside out the window. It was two hours before dusk and they hadn't dressed since their last love-making.

"Hey, sailor. You've been a SEAL for three years now, right?"

"Three years, and almost a half."

"Good. Just wanted to remind you that anytime you've had enough of getting shot at and stabbed and blown apart, I'll be willing to take in your shattered body and help you move out of SEAL fieldwork." He started to say something, and she shushed him.

"No, wait a minute. Everytime you go out there and put your life on the line for your country, I keep thinking and hoping that this will be the last time. So, nobody was killed on this mission. Great. One sailor in a couple of hundred thousand a year gets killed in the regular Navy. The SEAL death and injury rate is the highest in the Navy. I don't have to ask anyone to know that. How many of your men have died in the platoon since you became the second in command?"

He frowned. "Not sure. Maybe eight or ten in the last three years. A hell of a lot too many."

"One of those ten could have been you. Or might be you on the next two or three missions. We're playing the odds here. Usually your men don't get killed because they foul up or do something wrong. They are just in the wrong place at the wrong time when that bullet slams through. . . ." She stopped. Tears flowed down her cheeks. She grabbed him and held him so tightly, she almost cut off his breath.

When her head came up where he could see it, he kissed her tears away, then kissed her eyes and rolled over on top of her.

"Oh, damn," Milly said. "I did it again. I promised myself that I wouldn't do it this time. When Maria Fernandez and Nancy Dobler and I had our weekly gab session at the restaurant, we promised ourselves that we wouldn't talk about our men getting out of the SEALs. That's a great support group we have. We're good friends now."

"I'm glad. How is Maria doing?"

"She's better. She usually calls me once a week at night when you guys are gone. We talked almost two hours the last time. I think it helped."

"She likes you."

"I like her. Oh, did I tell you that Ardith Manchester called me two days before you came home? She said you were scheduled to return. Not sure how she knew. I phoned the other two girls. It's great to have her on our side."

"She's on both sides. She probably knows more state secrets and hush-hush things than anyone in Washington."

"She'll be here as soon as Murdock gets out of Balboa."

"I bet she will. They ever going to get married?"

She kissed him and grinned. "Are *we* ever going to get married?"

He watched her. She was serious. "I didn't know that you were all that interested in . . ."

Her look stopped him. "Maybe not a year ago," she said. "Now I am. I'm tired of being thought of as a fallen woman."

"Who would even think that these days?"

"Lots of women. My mother's friends in Boston are the case in point. They don't think the sixties ever existed. They think that marriage is the only way to have sex."

"We sure proved them wrong on that point."

She didn't laugh. Still serious.

"Hey, it takes three days to get married," he said. "We only have one day left on our trip."

"So go AWOL." She sighed and shook her head. "Forget that last crack. I'm getting bitchy. That time of the millennium. Hey, right now it's your call. I'm ready, willing, and able to tie the knot at any time or place you pick. How is that for a proposal?"

"Best one I've ever had."

She hit him on the shoulder. "Nobody has ever asked you to marry her. You would have told me."

"Mary Beth, an Atlanta girl with fine Southern charm and upbringing who was fantastic in bed." He stopped. "Strike that last statement."

"Better than me?" Milly asked.

He laughed. "I can't answer that question on grounds that it could tend to get me in really, really big trouble." She pushed him off her and got up on her hands and knees.

"Come over here, lover. I've been reading my *Joy of Sex, Book Three.* Have I got some surprises for you. Now don't beg, you asked for it with that crack about Mary Beth. Just be good, do what I tell you to do, and take your punishment."

He did.

Somehow they missed dinner. Then it was midnight and they tried for some takeout, but nobody delivered that late in the small Napa Valley town.

A week after the SEALs returned from Hawaii, Murdock was released from the Balboa Naval Hospital in San Diego, with a visit scheduled for five days later to take out the stitches on his shoulder. He had his right arm in a cloth sling with a strap around his neck, and hated it.

"Nothing like a sling on my right arm to increase and magnify my command presence with the men," he fumed to Master Chief MacKenzie as he stepped over the quarterdeck that Thursday morning.

"Looks quite chipper to me, Commander. Haven't seen one of those around here for two or three years."

"Lieutenant MacCarthy had to wear one after a shoulder wound. You remember it. You teased him until he nearly called you up on charges."

"Always a bit testy, that MacCarthy. Glad you're back with us, lad. Been a bit quiet around here. Will you be needing any new men?"

"No. I have two wounded who should be back on partial duty in two to three weeks. You tell Don Stroh to blow it out his ass if he has any thoughts of an assignment for us in the next three months."

"But, Commander, if the President asks for your platoon . . ."

"Tell the President to blow it out his Presidential ass." Murdock waved and continued on to the Third Platoon headquarters office. He was first one on duty that morning, and glad. He could see what Ed DeWitt had done to keep the platoon together.

Four new file folders lay on his desk, each with a neatly designated title. The first was messages. He flipped through them quickly. Some glad-you're-back types, and then one in the master chief's individualistic uphill handwriting.

It was dated that morning from Washington, D.C. "Phone call from D.C., woman's voice, left no message. Will call again." That would be Ardith Jane Manchester. He leaned back and smiled. He had been thinking of her every day. She had known through her spy system and her own private operators that he'd come home and been in the hospital. Fact is, he had called her the third day and they'd talked for an hour. Now she must know he was out. He thought of calling her, but instead decided she was already on a plane and would be there that afternoon.

With that good thought he tore through the rest of the files, pushing two aside for later study, including one on a new British-developed Stealth Diving Suit. The British Ministry of Defense had taken delivery of thirty of the new devices. They looked long and bulky, with exposed tubing and fully enclosed face mask.

The material in the file said the new system had a computer-controlled mixture of oxygen and other gases in its delivery system. The computer automatically adjusted the mix of the gases to provide for the most rapid descent or ascent and decompression that the diver's body could tolerate.

It was fully enclosed without bubbles. A unit like that would have let them dive to 150 feet with the enclosed system. They could have used three or four of them in Hawaii to go get that live nuclear bomb. He marked it for action. He wanted to order at least six of the suits from the Divex Company of Scotland.

He checked the roster. Jaybird was the critical one. He was still at Balboa. The doctors said they didn't know how long it would take for his intestine to heal enough for strenuous duty. Ronson was released yesterday, should report in today. Light duty for him for at least a month.

Then there was the CO of this outfit. How long would it

be before he could do the rope climb? That was the big one. His shoulder hurt, but not enough to use the pain medication they gave him. They said it was addictive and he shouldn't use it for more than a week. No problem there. His arm hurt only when he moved it in certain ways or tried to lift his hand upward halfway to his shoulder.

He had full use of his fingers, wrists, and elbow. But none of them would help him run the OC in his usual good time. He swore softly, and answered the phone.

"Good work out there in Lotus Land," Don Stroh said.

"At least nobody refused to come pull us out of harm's way this time. Stroh, you never did see us in Hawaii."

"We had a whole damn war to fight."

"A short one."

"True. How is the shoulder?"

"Great. Want to arm wrestle?"

"Not by long distance. Just wanted to check in. We know your group had itself shot up some. Nothing looks imminent back here right now."

"If it does, go for another platoon. Ours won't be ready for combat action for three months."

"A lot might happen in three months, Murdock."

"Call another fireman. Our fire extinguishers need refilling."

"I'll keep that in mind."

A buzzer sounded on Murdock's desk.

Murdock grinned. Saved by the bell. "Hey, just got a summons to the boss's office. I'll get back to you . . . in about three months." He hung up and waited three beats. When he picked up the phone, Stroh was gone. He dialed the quarter-deck.

"Murdock here. You buzzed."

"Yes, sir, you have a call on line two. I'll put it through."

"Hello?"

"Oh, good, Murdock. I was wondering about lunch at your place. I'm putting together a fancy tomato, bacon, and lettuce sandwich I think you'll like."

"Ardith, how in hell?"

"Connections. I phoned earlier from the plane. Can you

struggle and get away early today, like about now? I bet you have some leave time coming."

"Aye, aye, ma'am. I'm on my way. What kind of a sandwich was that again?" It was a private joke.

"You'll have to wait and see. Now hurry home."

30

Apartment 141-B
Coronado, California

Murdock eased into his parking slot at the apartment complex less than a mile from the quarterdeck and let a small groan slip out. He had tried to shift the car into park with his right hand the way he always did.

The knifing pain in his shoulder stopped him. He reached through the steering wheel with his left hand, shifted into park, and put on the safety club. With an effort he held it in place with his right hand and spread it apart with his left. So damn much trouble. He eased out of the car, closed the door with his left hand, and zapped the locks on with the button on his key ring, again with his left hand. Too damn much trouble.

He looked up and saw Ardith waiting for him on the small balcony/porch in front of his second-floor unit. It wasn't large. He was there only a third of the time. He ran up the steps, and pulled her inside and kissed her thoroughly.

"Oh, my, now that's what I call a welcome to California," she said.

"That's only a fraction of the welcome you're going to get."

"Good. Right here?"

He led her into the bedroom and opened the buttons of he
pure white blouse.

"What about your shoulder? I don't want to hurt you."

"We'll figure out a way that won't hurt."

They did.

Later, they went back to the living room and stared at the
small blaze she'd built in the fireplace.

"I'm interested. How did you know when I was released?"

"Would you believe I guessed?" She let her long blond
hair swing outward around her face, then fall until it nearly
covered her bare breasts.

"No. Not a chance."

"So I called a friend out here and asked him to call me
when you hit the bricks. He did."

"Navy, he'd have to be Navy, and a medical man. Which
one?"

"Your surgeon. He's a lieutenant commander. I promised
him that I'd take a quick look at the promotion list to see if
he made commander. He did. I told him. He called me. I
flew."

They made love again, then watched the fire, and then
simply looked at each other. Their desire grew and multiplied
until he laughed softly and lay on the rug on his back.

"This way it can't hurt my shoulder at all."

She moved on top of him and positioned herself, then
thrust forward and down. Her passion made her face even
more beautiful. "Lover Blake. At the moment your shoulder
is not the part of you I'm most interested in."

At 2330 they called for Chinese food. Three restaurants
didn't deliver that late. They settled for two small pizzas
topped with sausage, pineapple, and ham.

"Did you sign yourself out for a seven-day liberty?"

"Can't until tomorrow when DeWitt comes back. Did I
tell you what a great job he did in Hawaii after I had my
small problem?"

Ardith touched his shoulder tenderly. "You call this a
small problem? If it doesn't heal right it could knock you
off the SEAL field teams roster. Doesn't that bother you?"

He wiped his left hand slowly over his face. A long sigh

me from Murdock and he kissed her cheek. "Yes, it bothers
. It bothers me more than anything has in the past five
ars. It scares the hell out of me."

She wrapped her arms around him and pulled his head
wn to cushion on her breasts. "Have you thought about
ying?"

He looked up at her and frowned. "Woman, there ain't no
ch thing as crying in the SEALs. You know that."

"I won't tell."

"Better not. I cry when one of my men dies. That's the
ne for crying. That's off-line, off the record, not available
r comment. This isn't something I cry about. I worry. I
onder. I wish like hell it never happened."

"Tell me about it."

"Nothing to tell. We had most of them captured or dead
top of the mountain at a rustic-challenge type of camp.
ree of us headed across an open space aiming for the tents
ere we figured the Chinese held the hostages. It was dark
d I felt fairly secure. Then some slant-eyed little fucking
stard blasted away from the shadows and cut me down. I
ed to bring up my weapon, but my right arm didn't work
ht. I never saw the Chink shit-eater who shot me."

"That's a good start. What would it mean if you couldn't
ay in the Third Platoon?"

"Cut my heart out. It's more now than just the SEALs.
s this connection with the CIA and the CNO, the top man
the whole damn Navy, and that phone call that comes
metimes from the President himself saying, 'Good job,
EALs.' It's a surge of marvelous feeling that puts my best
imax to shame. It's a high that cocaine can't touch. It's a
sh like no man has ever felt before.

"Knowing that we're out there on the cutting edge of
merican policy and enforcement and the covert jobs we go
. It's knowing all those state secrets nobody else knows
out, and the jobs that we do and never get credit for, and
e say, 'So what? Who gives a damn? We were there. We
d it. We made a huge difference in the history of the United
ates and of the whole damn world.' "

He sat up and stared at her. "What the hell am I doing?
ve never put how I felt about this outfit into words before.

Am I too damn late? Is it all over but the medics pinnin;
red badge on my fitness file?"

She bent forward and kissed his lips so tenderly that
barely felt it. It was the brush of a butterfly's wings.

"This is good, talking it out. Hey, my gut feeling is t
your shoulder is going to heal just fine. The doctor I tall
with said that an injury like yours is similar to a rotator-c
problem. Only, here your tendon was not torn apart. Wh
means it has an even better chance of getting back to 1
use, and full-charge-ahead SEAL work."

He put his left hand on her flat naked belly. "Womar
hope to hell that your gut feeling is right. I don't even ha
those kinds of feelings yet. Maybe after a month. I have t
damn sling for another two weeks."

"Which must mean that you don't want your men to
you with the sling. Are you afraid that would help erode yo
command presence?"

"Could do some of that."

"How many of the men currently in your platoon ha
been wounded in your missions?"

"Hell, most of them. Ed has. Maybe only two out of
sixteen haven't been shot up here and there. Hey, I ne
thought of that." He shook his head and took another lo
breath. "Okay, maybe the sling isn't such a big deal."

"Then Ed will take the men on their training runs a
conditioning swims and other training, right?"

"He'll damn well have to. I can't."

"It's hard to accept, isn't it?"

"What, smart lady from Washington, D.C.?"

"The fact that you're wounded, probably worse than y
ever have been before."

"I think I understand that part of it after almost two wee
of pain."

"You understand the fact of it, but do you accept the
ality of it?"

"Hey, I'm no shrink. I just do the job."

"Good. Right now your job, your only job, is to get t
shoulder well so you can stay with the platoon."

"Only job?"

"Absolutely, your only job. Otherwise you're pushing

ncil somewhere in the non-field swamp that makes up the
st of the SEAL Team Seven."

"I'll be damned, woman. How can you be so beautiful and
smart at the same time?"

"I've been hanging out with a bunch of rowdy SEALs.
aat's my only defense."

"Sounds reasonable to me."

They were still talking when the sun came up. Ardith sat
 and stretched.

"Suppose it's time we got to sleep?"

"Probably. Maybe just one small nap."

They slept until noon.

Over a bacon and eggs and flapjack breakfast, Murdock
lled Master Chief MacKenzie. Before he could get in a
ord, the master chief was off.

"Commander, sir. Do you realize that you have almost
ree months of leave built up? You haven't been taking your
irty days and it's a shame."

"Then why don't your write me up for two weeks, Master
hief. Do the paperwork and sign it for me starting as of
day. Tell DeWitt he has the con until I get back. Make it
edical leave or whatever you want. I'll see you in two
eeks."

"Yes, lad. That's fine. My compliments to that nice lady
rdith Manchester. Oh, one small item. The JG asked me to
ll you that he's having the traditional fish fry tonight at his
artment recreation area. All SEALs of the Third are re-
ired to attend, except Jaybird. Any SEAL is entitled to
ing one lady friend—wife or mistress, it doesn't matter. He
as hoping that you could make it, sir."

Murdock grinned. Tradition? Since when. "Master Chief,
u tell the JG that Ardith and I will be delighted to attend.
ll bring an extra can of lighter fluid just to be sure he can
t the charcoal started."

"I'll tell him that, Commander. Oh, one more small matter.
ommander Masciarelli wants to see you. I told him you
ere on leave for a week or maybe two. He said some unkind
ords and hung up without saying gud'ay."

"A shame, Master Chief. Looks like I'll have to stop by
d see the commander when I return."

"Sounds about right."

"See you tonight for fish?"

"Afraid not. My stomach, you know. I gave my regrets the JG."

"Thanks, Gordon."

"You bet, Commander. See you when you get back."

31

2214 Wake Island Place
Coronado, California

The party was well under way when Murdock and Ardith arrived at 1830. The recreation area of DeWitt's apartment complex was near the back, with three stationary barbecues and six picnic tables and benches solidly bolted to the concrete slabs.

Ed and Milly met them at the gate and ushered them in. Everyone was in mufti and looking comfortable. Ed and Milly wore their matching Hawaiian flowered aloha shirts.

"About time you got here, Skipper," Ed said. "Now we can put on the fish before the guys get too bombed to eat."

The salmon fillets went on the grill and DeWitt, Ching, and Mahanani wielded the spatulas, vying to see who could turn out the best cooked salmon. Maria Fernandez hurried over and grabbed Ardith and Milly, and they walked to a table where Nancy Dobler sat. Soon the four women were in a gab session.

Murdock grabbed a cold beer from a cooler and watched his men. He wasn't used to drinking left-handed, but he got by. There was no way he could lift the can up to his mouth with his right hand.

Two or three of the men had brought bimbos with them
He had no idea where the SEALs had grabbed up the women
on such short notice. A half hour after he arrived, Murdock
saw Lampedusa and a slinky little brunette make their way
out of the recreation area and head for DeWitt's apartment
Boys would be boys.

Tony Ostercamp and Bill Bradford got into an argument
that Senior Chief Dobler had to settle. They all grinned
tipped their beers, and went to yell at the three cooks.

"Get your plates off the first table," DeWitt called. "This
salmon takes about three minutes on each side, so it's almost
done."

The men lined up at the barbecues, and then moved back
giving the ladies the first run at the salmon.

Before they could start serving, somebody bellowed from
near the gate.

"Hold the chow, you Boy Scouts. Let the real SEAL show
up and take charge." An orderly complete with white cap
and uniform powered a wheelchair over the ground toward
the grills.

"Jaybird, you roustabout," Ching yelled. "What the hell
you doing out of the pigpen?" Then they all ran to where his
wheelchair had hit rough ground. They picked it up and car
ried it the last fifty feet to the tables.

"Easy, easy, I'm a surgical case here," Jaybird brayed a
them.

"I've got some surgery you can do on me," Franklin
yelped.

"How the hell you get out of the hospital?" Murdock
asked.

"Got my keeper here, Charlie, and he's so dry he needs
about a dozen beers. Get him some, guys. Charlie has my
liberty chit and I've got to be back in that bed by midnight
Sort of."

"Yeah, but who authorized it?" DeWitt asked.

"Authorized it myself. Wrote up the order, made the rank
a bit confused, and pushed it through. Nobody gave a damn
Just so I don't get busted up none."

"On this salmon you might," Jefferson barked, and they
all laughed.

They moved back to the grills and everyone was served. The meal had side dishes of baked potatoes, three kinds of steaming vegetables, hot rolls, and tea, coffee, or beer.

Another argument broke out, and DeWitt stepped in to calm down Jefferson and Ron Holt.

"Come on, you guys," DeWitt said. "No fighting at least until you're half drunk. Then you'll have an excuse."

It would not have been a fair fight. They shook hands, then raced for the grills for seconds on salmon.

Murdock and Ardith sat at a table across from Nancy and Senior Chief Dobler. The women talked kids for ten minutes. Then they stood and walked over by the swings, talking all the way. Murdock went to the grill for more salmon.

Three SEALs began singing a loud and bawdy song. Their women for the night giggled, then laughed, trying to join in. Beer flowed and flowed. When the food was gone, DeWitt brought out wrapped ice-cream bars and handed them out.

Murdock stopped DeWitt. "Hey, when did this barbecue get to be a tradition?"

"Few months back after you and Stroh went fishing. Don't you remember?"

"Sure, but we never caught any salmon."

"Try harder next time," DeWitt said, and tossed Murdock two more cold beers.

Murdock noticed more of the single SEALs make trips to the apartment with their girls of the night. There were more songs and bawdy stories. Then Jaybird had the idea.

"Hey, guys. Let's go down to MacB's and see what the babes look like."

"What good could you do them?" Jefferson asked, and they all howled in delight.

"More good than you could ever figure. Who's with me? Anybody got a van I could roll into?"

Ardith had been enjoying talking with the other SEAL women. Now she came back to where Murdock stood near the grills.

"You can't let Jaybird go," she said.

Murdock took her elbow and walked out of the lights into the darkness.

"I can't stop him. He's over twenty-one and a SEAL."

"But isn't that a rowdy bar with lots of fights?"

"True, favorite hangout of the guys. They can take care of themselves and watch out for Jaybird. Let's help Ed and Milly clean up this place."

The SEALs hurried out the gate, and piled into half a dozen cars and roared away. Jaybird's keeper/orderly didn't object. He was so drunk he had passed out once already. They would leave him in the car.

It was less than five minutes to the waterfront-type bar where the SEALs liked to hang out and where they had certain privileges.

Twelve half-drunk SEALs and four party-dressed women charged into MacB's ten minutes later and took over the place. There were fifteen men and two women there at the time. Eight of the white-sided-haircut young men were drinking together.

Tran Khai bumped into one of the white-sides as he eased into a stool at the bar. Train was the first SEAL to get drunk at every outing. The military-haircut man turned and growled. Mahanani loomed over the white-side a second later.

"Hey, my little buddy here is in his cups. He didn't mean any harm. What say?"

"Who the hell you think you are, sad ass?"

"We're SEALs and we're celebrating. Who the hell do you think you are, grab ass?"

"We're Marines, and we think all SEALs are chicken-fuckers."

Suddenly the place was quiet. The Marine's words had rung out sharp and clear in the bar.

Then the Marine threw half a glass of beer in Mahanani's face. It took only a microsecond for the big Hawaiian/Tahitian to react. His right fist came out and sank four inches into the Marine's surprised gut. Then his left looped upward, found the Marine's chin just as he started to bend over to relieve his gut pain. The Halls of Montezuma man arched backward and fell on a table where three civilians sat. The table lost a leg and crashed to the floor with the dazed Marine on top of it.

"What the fuck?" another Marine shrilled.

Four more Marines rushed up, and the civilians from the smashed table jumped away from it, and then headed for Mahanani and Train.

For a moment it looked like seven on two. Then three more SEALs spotted the trouble and waded in. Fists flew, bodies dropped and jumped up. It turned into a free-for-all with all the SEALs except Jaybird in the center of the battle with the eight Marines and five or six civilians who chose the wrong side.

Lampedusa found himself facing a snarling Marine who was almost as drunk as he was. They swung, missed, and swung again, and both hit. Lam came sober in a rush, and jabbed the Marine twice with his left, then swung from the bleachers with his right fist and tagged the corporal on the side of the jaw. The Marine jolted back a step, stood there as his eyes glazed, then dropped to his knees and fell flat on his face on the barroom floor.

Canzoneri dragged a civilian off Ostercamp and jabbed a hard right fist into his face, then threw two left jabs and lifted his right knee hard into the civilian's crotch. The man's eyes went wide. He tried to scream, but only a gargled belch came out as he grabbed his crotch with both hands and staggered toward the wall, clearly out of action.

Bill Bradford told himself to stay out of the fight. He was drunk and when he tried to fight when he was drunk, he always took a drubbing. Then it was too late. Two Marines rushed him. He lifted one foot and caught one of them in the belly, driving him into the wall. The other one came through, clubbing him in the shoulder, but then unable to get out of the way of Bradford's right fist, which slammed into the Marine's nose, bringing a spout of blood. Somebody grabbed Bradford from behind, and he jolted his head backward, crashing his skull into the head of the man behind him.

The man bellowed in pain and released Bradford, who spun around and jolted a hard left jab into the civilian's right eye, and then a looping right that hit him on the side of the head and spilled him into a chair next to the wall.

One by one the Marines went down and didn't get up. Another table and a chair crashed into bits and pieces.

Behind the bar, Mac himself blew on his police whistle

until he turned blue, and then gave up. He grabbed the old .45 from the cash drawer, racked in a round, and fired into the wall behind him in a spot where he knew the wall and insulation would corral the bullet. The weapon going off in the bar had no effect on the series of small battles still going on.

He saw the last of the SEALs leave the girls and charge into the battle. Even the guy in the wheelchair tried to swing at a guy. Mac gave up and called the Shore Patrol. Then he called an old friend, Master Chief Gordon MacKenzie.

By the time the Shore Patrol arrived with six armed men and two patrol wagons, some semblance of order had been restored. Mac had bellowed that he'd called the Shore Patrol, and that had cooled off most of the battles. Mahanani had kept punishing the Marine who'd started the whole ruckus, but then Master Chief MacKenzie had come into the bar and scowled at the SEALs.

Five minutes later, a chief petty officer led the Shore Patrol into the bar and looked around. He spotted Master Chief MacKenzie and waved at his men to relax. MacKenzie sat at the bar with a beer. He pointed to a foaming, cold beer in front of an empty stool beside him. The chief walked up and stood looking at MacKenzie.

"Some mess your boys are in here, I'd say, MacKenzie."

"True, Chief Billbray, but they didn't start the ruckus. Marines did it. Ask Mac. He saw it all."

"I'll do that." He pushed down the bar and talked to the owner of the business, then came back, sat on the stool, and sipped at the brew.

"That one big Marine with the black eye and not much of a nose left started it," the Shore Patrol chief said.

They both sipped at the beer. Nobody said a word in the bar. One Marine groaned, and another one kicked him to quiet down.

"Chief to chief on this one, Billbray?"

"The Shore Patrol chief had another swallow of beer, wiped his mouth, and looked at MacKenzie.

"It's been a while. Your boys have been on their best behavior lately. You get new guidelines, or has the Mormon Church taken over the SEALs' training and operation?"

"Something like that." MacKenzie waved at Mac, who came sliding down the bar with a wet cloth in one hand.

"Aye?"

"How much for damages, Mac? And lost business, incidentals, and pain and suffering?"

The saloon owner grinned. "Them two tables wasn't much count anyway. Cost me maybe forty bucks to replace them. Actually, business is up tonight. Pain and suffering usually goes at about two million, but I'm easy. Another forty should keep me happy."

MacKenzie took five twenty-dollar bills from his wallet and pushed them across the bar. "That and a tip for good service." MacKenzie made a curt motion to the SEALs, and they straightened chairs, picked up a broken glass, and began to move toward the door.

"Oh, Mac. You should start to cultivate the Shore Patrol when they're off duty," MacKenzie said. "Fine group of lads. Be a favor to me if you could set up a round of beers for these SP lads next time they come in."

MacB's brows went up. Then he chuckled. "Sure, and I'd be glad to do just that."

"Chief Billbray, I'd say that I owe you a favor, chief to chief. Yes, I'm in your debt. These are good lads I've got. This platoon just came back from the fighting in Hawaii. Nasty bit out there. I hope you understand."

Chief Billbray drained the glass and wiped his mouth. "Looks like that one Marine will need some medical attention. The emergency room at the hospital here might do the job. Let my men help him along his way."

The two chiefs shook hands, and the SEALs drifted out the front door. They forgot Jaybird, who sat in his wheelchair.

Master Chief MacKenzie wheeled him out just as Mahanani came looking for him.

"Sailor, you best get this lad back to Balboa before somebody reports him AWOL," the chief said. "Hurry on now. I've missed enough sleep already."

"Yes, Master Chief, right away."

It took MacKenzie three calls to finally find Murdock at JG DeWitt's home. They talked for five minutes, and then the master chief hung up. There was a small smile on his face as he headed home.

Murdock came away from the phone. Everyone had left the party, and Milly and Ardith were finishing up doing the dishes and putting away the leftovers.

"I'm going to be eating salmon for a week," DeWitt said. He looked at Murdock. "What did the master chief want?"

"MacB's turned out to be a bad idea. Big fight with eight Marines and some civilians. Shore Patrol showed up and Mac called MacKenzie. They worked it out with the Shore Patrol chief. Your boys will have some split lips and black eyes come working hours tomorrow."

"Figures. Where you guys going on your vacation?"

"Flagstaff, Arizona. Supposed to be high and cool and interesting."

"I'll be working. Won't be like the wine country, but I'll make it."

"Check on Jaybird. Let's hope he doesn't get in trouble over that little trip he took tonight. Work it out."

The women came in, and they settled on the soft cushions.

"Show him," Ardith said. She watched Milly. "Go ahead, show him. It won't change things, but let him see it."

Milly went over to Murdock and held out her left hand. One finger held a solitaire diamond.

"An engagement ring," Ardith said. "I just couldn't resist the chance to let you see it."

Murdock stood and gave Milly a kiss on the cheek. "Couldn't happen to a nicer couple. When?"

Milly looked at DeWitt. "We decided sometime in the spring. I'll take a month off and we'll go up to Seattle for the honeymoon."

The next day in Flagstaff, neither of them mentioned the engagement. Ardith had a satisfied little smile most of the time, and Murdock put up with it. They had a lot of talking to do before they even came close to getting engaged.

He flexed his elbow and moved it until his shoulder hurt, then put his right arm deeper into the sling. It was going to be an interesting two weeks. As they toured the small town, e kept thinking about his life and Ardith and where he was heading. He couldn't be sure of anything yet, not until his shoulder healed and he had the muscles and tendons trained again to the finely honed excellence that being a SEAL required. If he could do it.

What would happen if he couldn't meet his own set of standards for physical ability? He refused to think about it. Instead he wondered who would jump up to challenge the U.S. next? What small country would try for something extra in international relations? Who would shoot down a U.S. airliner, or try to capture one of our ships and hold it for ransom? There were so many ways that terrorists could affect the world.

He wanted to be there, to be back on the cutting edge. He flexed his right shoulder and winced. No pain medication, but no fun either. Now he had just one job, as Ardith had pointed out to him. He had to get his shoulder back to pre-bullet proficiency. He had to get it healed and trained and strengthened so he could be a SEAL again.

The only question he had now was, could he do it? Could he stay in the SEALs as commander of Third Platoon with special commitment to the CIA, the CNO, and the President?

Only the next three months could give him that answer.

SEAL TALK

MILITARY GLOSSARY

Aalvin: Small U.S. two-man submarine.

Admin: Short for administration.

Aegis: Advanced Naval air defense radar system.

AH-1W Super Cobra: Has M179 undernose turret with 20mm Gatling gun.

AK-47: 7.63-round Russian Kalashnikov automatic rifle. Most widely used assault rifle in the world.

AK-74: New, improved version of the Kalashnikov. Fires the 5.45mm round. Has 30-round magazine. Rate of fire 600 rounds per minute. Many slight variations made for many different nations.

AN/PRC-117D: Radio, also called SATCOM. Works with Milstar satellite in 22,300-mile equatorial orbit for instant worldwide radio, voice, or video communications. Size 15 inches high, 3 inches wide, 3 inches deep. Weighs 1. pounds. Microphone and voice output. Has encrypter, capable of burst transmissions of less than a second.

AN/PUS-7: Night-Vision Goggles. Weighs 1.5 pounds.

ANVIS-6: Night-Vision Goggles on air crewmen's helmets.

APC: Armored Personnel Carrier.

ASROC: Nuclear-tipped antisubmarine rocket torpedoe launched by Navy ships.

Assault Vest: Combat vest with full loadouts of ammo, gear.

ASW: Anti-Submarine Warfare.

Attack Board: Molded plastic with two handgrips with bubble compass on it. Also depth gauge and Cyalume chemical lights with twist knob to regulate amount of light. Used for underwater guidance on long swim.

Aurora: Air Force recon plane. Can circle at 90,000 feet. Can't be seen or heard from ground. Used for thermal imaging.

AWACS: Airborne Warning And Control System. Radar units in high-flying aircraft to scan for planes at any altitude out 200 miles. Controls air-to-air engagements with enemy forces. Planes have a mass of communication and electronic equipment.

Balaclavas: Headgear worn by some SEALs.

Bent Spear: Less serious nuclear violation of safety.

BKA, Bundeskriminant: Germany's federal investigation unit.

Black Talon: Lethal hollow-point ammunition made by Winchester. Outlawed some places.

Blivet: A collapsible fuel container. SEALs sometimes use it.

BLU-43B: Antipersonnel mine used by SEALs.

BLU-96: A fuel-air explosive bomb. It disperses a fuel oil into the air, then explodes the cloud. Many times more powerful than conventional bombs because it doesn't carry its own chemical oxidizers.

BMP-1: Soviet armored fighting vehicle (AFV), low, boxy, crew of 3 and 8 combat troops. Has tracks and a 73mm cannon. Also an AT-3 Sagger antitank missile and coaxial machine gun.

Body Armor: Far too heavy for SEAL use in the water.

Bogey: Pilots' word for an unidentified aircraft.

Boghammar Boat: Long, narrow, low dagger boat; high-speed patrol craft. Swedish make. Iran had 40 of them in 1993.

Boomer: A nuclear-powered missile submarine.

Bought It: A man has been killed. Also "bought the farm."

Bow Cat: The bow catapult on a carrier to launch jets.

Broken Arrow: Any accident with nuclear weapons, or any incident of nuclear material lost, shot down, crashed, stolen, hijacked.

Browning 9mm High Power: A Belgium 9mm pistol, 13 rounds in magazine. First made 1935.

Buddy Line: 6 feet long, ties 2 SEALs together in the water for control and help if needed.

BUD/S: Coronado, California, nickname for SEAL training facility for six months' course.

Bull Pup. Still in testing; new soldier's rifle. SEALs have a dozen of them for regular use. Army gets them in 2005. Has a 5.56 kinetic round, 30-shot clip. Also 20mm high-explosive round and 5-shot magazine. Twenties can be fused for proximity airbursts with use of video camera laser range finder, and laser targeting. Fuses by number of turns the round needs to reach laser spot. Max range 1200 yards. Twenty round can also detonate on contact and has delay fuse. Weapon weighs 14 pounds. SEALs love it. Can in effect "shoot around corners" with the airburst feature.

BUPERS: BUreau of PERSonnel.

C-2A Greyhound: 2-engine turboprop cargo plane that lands on carriers. Also called COD, Carrier Onboard Delivery. Two pilots and engineer. Rear fuselage loading ramp. Cruise speed 300 mph, range 1,000 miles. Will hold 39 combat troops. Lands on CVN carriers at sea.

C-4: Plastic explosive. A claylike explosive that can be molded and shaped. It will burn. Fairly stable.

C-6 Plastique: Plastic explosive. Developed from C-4 and C-5. Is often used in bombs with radio detonator or digital timer.

C-9 Nightingale: Douglas DC-9 fitted as a medical evacuation transport plane.

C-130 Hercules: Air Force transporter for long haul. 4 engines.

C-141 Starlifter: Airlift transport for cargo, paratroops evac for long distances. Top speed 566 mph. Range with payload 2,935 miles. Ceiling 41,600 feet.

Caltrops: Small four-pointed spikes used to flatten tires. Used in the Crusades to disable horses.

Camel Back: Used with drinking tube for 70 ounces of water attached to vest.

Cammies: Working camouflaged wear for SEALs. Two different patterns and colors. Jungle and desert.

Cannon Fodder: Old term for soldiers in line of fire destined to die in the grand scheme of warfare.

Capped: Killed, shot, or otherwise snuffed.

CAR-15: The Colt M-4Al. Sliding-stock carbine with grenade launcher under barrel. Knight sound-suppressor. Can have AN/PAQ-4 laser aiming light under the carrying handle. .223 round. 20- or 30-round magazine. Rate of fire: 700 to 1,000 rounds per minute.

Cascade Radiation: U-235 triggers secondary radiation in other dense materials.

Cast Off: Leave a dock, port, land. Get lost. Navy: long, then short signal of horn, whistle, or light.

Castle Keep: The main tower in any castle.

Caving Ladder: Roll-up ladder that can be let down to climb.

CH-46E: Sea Knight chopper. Twin rotors, transport. Can carry 25 combat troops. Has a crew of 3. Cruise speed 154 mph. Range 420 miles.

CH-53D Sea Stallion: Big Chopper. Not used much anymore.

Chaff: A small cloud of thin pieces of metal, such as tinsel, that can be picked up by enemy radar and that can attract a radar-guided missile away from the plane to hit the chaff.

Charlie-Mike: Code words for continue the mission.

Chief to Chief: Bad conduct by EM handled by chiefs so no record shows or is passed up the chain of command.

Chocolate Mountains: Land training center for SEALs near these mountains in the California desert.

Christians In Action: SEAL talk for not-always-friendly CIA.

CIA: Central Intelligence Agency.

CIC: Combat Information Center. The place on a ship where communications and control areas are situated to open and control combat fire.

CINC: Commander IN Chief.

CINCLANT: Navy Commander IN Chief, atLANTtic.

CINCPAC: Commander-IN-Chief, PACific.

Class of 1978: Not a single man finished BUD/S training in this class. All-time record.

Claymore: An antipersonnel mine carried by SEALs on many of their missions.

Cluster Bombs: A canister bomb that explodes and spreads small bomblets over a great area. Used against parked aircraft, massed troops, and unarmored vehicles.

CNO: Chief of Naval Operations.

CO-2 Poisoning: During deep dives. Abort dive at once and surface.

COD: Carrier On Board Delivery plane.

Cold Pack Rations: Food carried by SEALs to use if needed.

Combat Harness: American Body Armor nylon-mesh special-operations vest. 6 2-magazine pouches for drum fed belts, other pouches for other weapons, waterproof pouch for Motorola.

CONUS: The Continental United States.

Corfams: Dress shoes for SEALs.

Covert Action Staff: A CIA group that handles all covert action by the SEALs.

CQB: Close Quarters Battle house. Training facility near Nyland in the desert training area. Also called the Kill House.

CQB: Close Quarters Battle. A fight that's up close, hand to-hand, whites-of-his-eyes, blood all over you.

CRRC Bundle: Roll it off plane, sub, boat. The assault boat for 8 SEALs. Also the IBS, Inflatable Boat Small.

Cutting Charge: Lead-sheathed explosive. Triangular strip of high-velocity explosive sheathed in metal. Point of the triangle focuses a shaped-charge effect. Cuts a pencil-line wide hole to slice a steel girder in half.

CVN: A U.S. aircraft carrier with nuclear power. Largest that we have in fleet.

CYA: Cover Your Ass, protect yourself from friendlies or officers above you and JAG people.

Damfino: Damned if I know. SEAL talk.

DDS: Dry Dock Shelter. A clamshell unit on subs to deliver SEALs and SDVs to a mission.

DEFCON: DEFense CONdition. How serious is the threat?

Delta Forces: Army special forces, much like SEALs.

Desert Cammies: Three-color, desert tan and pale green with streaks of pink. For use on land.

DIA: Defense Intelligence Agency.

Dilos Class Patrol Boat: Greek, 29 feet long, 75 tons displacement.

Dirty Shirt Mess: Officers can eat there in flying suits on board a carrier.

DNS: Doppler Navigation System.

Draegr LAR V: Rebreather that SEALs use. No bubbles.

DREC: Digitally Reconnoiterable Electronic Component. Top-secret computer chip from NSA that lets it decipher any U.S. military electronic code.

E-2C Hawkeye: Navy, carrier-based, Airborne Early Warning craft for long-range early warning and threat-assessment and fighter-direction. Has a 24-foot saucer-like rotodome over the wing. Crew 5, max speed 326 knots, ceiling 30,800 feet, radius 175 nautical miles with 4 hours on station.

E-3A Skywarrior: Old electronic intelligence craft. Replaced by the newer ES-3A.

E-4B NEACP: Called Kneecap. National Emergency Airborne Command Post. A greatly modified Boeing 747 used as a communications base for the President of the United States and other high-ranking officials in an emergency and in wartime.

E & E: SEAL talk for escape and evasion.

EA-6B Prowler: Navy plane with electronic countermeasures. Crew of 4, max speed 566 knots, ceiling 41,200 feet, range with max load 955 nautical miles.

EAR: Enhanced Acoustic Rifle. Fires not bullets, but a high-impact blast of sound that puts the target down and unconscious for up to six hours. Leaves him with almost no aftereffects. Used as a non-lethal weapon. The sound blast will bounce around inside a building, vehicle, or ship and knock out anyone who is within range. Ten shots before the weapon must be electrically charged. Range: about 200 yards.

Easy: The only easy day was yesterday. SEAL talk.

ELINT: Electronic INTelligence. Often from satellite in orbit, picture-taker, or other electronic communications.

EOD: Navy experts in nuclear material and radioactivity who do Explosive Ordnance Disposal.

Equatorial Satellite Pointing Guide: To aim antenna for radio to pick up satellite signals.

ES-3A: Electronic Intelligence (ELINT) intercept craft. The platform for the battle group Passive Horizon Extension System. Stays up for long patrol periods, has comprehensive set of sensors, lands and takes off from a carrier. Has 63 antennas.

ETA: Estimated Time of Arrival.

Executive Order 12333: By President Reagan authorizing Special Warfare units such as the SEALs.

Exfil: Exfiltrate, to get out of an area.

F/A-18 Hornet: Carrier-based interceptor that can change from air-to-air to air-to-ground attack mode while in flight.

Fitrep: Fitness Report.

Flashbang Grenade: Non-lethal grenade that gives off a series of piercing explosive sounds and a series of brilliant strobe-type lights to disable an enemy.

Flotation Bag: To hold equipment, ammo, gear on a wet operation.

Fort Fumble: SEALs' name for the Pentagon.

Forty-mm Rifle Grenade: The M576 multipurpose round, contains 20 large lead balls. SEALs use on Colt M-4A1.

Four-Striper: A Navy captain.

Fox Three: In air warfare, a code phrase showing that a Navy F-14 has launched a Phoenix air-to-air missile.

FUBAR: SEAL talk. Fucked Up Beyond All Repair.

Full Helmet Masks: For high-altitude jumps. Oxygen in mask.

G-3: German-made assault rifle.

Gloves: SEALs wear sage-green, fire-resistant Nomex flight gloves.

GMT: Greenwich Mean Time. Where it's all measured from.

GPS: Global Positioning System. A program with satellites around Earth to pinpoint precisely aircraft, ships, vehicles, and ground troops. Position information is to a plus or minus ten feet. Also can give speed of a plane or ship to one quarter of a mile per hour.

GPSL: A radio antenna with floating wire that pops to the surface. Antenna picks up positioning from the closest 4 global positioning satellites and gives an exact position within 10 feet.

Green Tape: Green sticky ordnance tape that has a hundred uses for a SEAL.

GSG-9: Flashbang grenade developed by Germans. A cardboard tube filled with 5 separate charges timed to burst in rapid succession. Blinding and giving concussion to enemy, leaving targets stunned, easy to kill or capture. Usually non-lethal.

GSG9: Grenzschutzgruppe Nine. Germany's best special warfare unit, counterterrorist group.

Gulfstream II (VCII): Large executive jet used by services for transport of small groups quickly. Crew of 3 and 18 passengers. Cruises at 581 mph. Maximum range 4,275 miles.

H & K 21A1: Machine gun with 7.62 NATO round. Replaces the older, more fragile M-60 E3. Fires 900 rounds per minute. Range 1,100 meters. All types of NATO rounds, ball, incendiary, tracer.

H & K G-11: Automatic rifle, new type. 4.7mm caseless ammunition. 50-round magazine. The bullet is in a sleeve of solid propellant with a special thin plastic coating around it. Fires 600 rounds per minute. Single-shot, three-round burst, or fully automatic.

H & K MP-5SD: 9mm submachine gun with integral silenced barrel, single-shot, three-shot, or fully automatic. Rate 800 rds/min.

H & K P9S: Heckler & Koch's 9mm Parabellum double-action semiauto pistol with 9-round magazine.

H & K PSG1: 7.62 NATO round. High-precision, bolt-action, sniping rifle. 5- to 20-round magazine. Roller lock delayed blowback breech system. Fully adjustable stock. 6×42 telescopic sights. Sound suppressor.

HAHO: High Altitude jump, High Opening. From 30,000 feet, open chute for glide up to 15 miles to ground. Up to 75 minutes in glide. To enter enemy territory or enemy position unheard.

Half-Track: Military vehicle with tracked rear drive and wheels in front, usually armed and armored.

HALO: High Altitude jump, Low Opening. From 30,000 feet. Free fall in 2 minutes to 2,000 feet and open chute. Little forward movement. Get to ground quickly, silently.

Hamburgers: Often called sliders on a Navy carrier.

Handie-Talkie: Small, handheld personal radio. Short range.

HELO: SEAL talk for helicopter.

Herky Bird: C-130 Hercules transport. Most-flown military transport in the world. For cargo or passengers, paratroops, aerial refueling, search and rescue, communications, and as a gunship. Has flown from a Navy carrier deck without use of catapult. Four turboprop engines, max speed 325 knots, range at max payload 2,356 miles.

Hezbollah: Lebanese Shiite Moslem militia. Party of God.

HMMWU: The Humvee, U.S. light utility truck, replaced the honored Jeep. Multipurpose wheeled vehicle, 4×4, automatic transmission, power steering. Engine: Detroit Diesel 150-hp diesel V-8 air-cooled. Top speed 65 mph. Range 300 miles.

Hotels: SEAL talk for hostages.

Humint: Human Intelligence. Acquired on the ground; a person as opposed to satellite or photo recon.

Hydra-Shock: Lethal hollow-point ammunition made by Federal Cartridge Company. Outlawed in some areas.

Hypothermia: Danger to SEALs. A drop in body temperature that can be fatal.

IBS: Inflatable Boat Small. 12×6 feet. Carries 8 men and 1,000 pounds of weapons and gear. Hard to sink. Quiet motor. Used for silent beach, bay, lake landings.

IR Beacon: Infrared beacon. For silent nighttime signaling.

IR Goggles: "Sees" heat instead of light.

Islamic Jihad: Arab holy war.

Isothermal layer: A colder layer of ocean water that deflects sonar rays. Submarines can hide below it, but then are also blind to what's going on above them since their sonar will not penetrate the layer.

IV Pack: Intravenous fluid that you can drink if out of water.

JAG: Judge Advocate General. The Navy's legal investigating arm that is independent of any Navy command.

JNA: Yugoslav National Army.

JP-4: Normal military jet fuel.

JSOC: Joint Special Operations Command.

JSOCCOMCENT: Joint Special Operations Command Center in the Pentagon.

KA-BAR: SEALs' combat, fighting knife.

KATN: Kick Ass and Take Names. SEAL talk, get the mission in gear.

KH-11: Spy satellite, takes pictures of ground, IR photos, etc.

KIA: Killed In Action.

KISS: Keep It Simple, Stupid. SEAL talk for streamlined operations.

Klick: A kilometer of distance. Often used as a mile. From Vietnam era, but still widely used in military.

Krytrons: Complicated, intricate timers used in making nuclear explosive detonators.

KV-57: Encoder for messages, scrambles.

LT: Short for lieutenant in SEAL talk.

Laser Pistol: The SIW pinpoint of ruby light emitted on any pistol for aiming. Usually a silenced weapon.

Left Behind: In 30 years SEALs have seldom left behind a dead comrade, never a wounded one. Never been taken prisoner.

Let's Get the Hell out of Dodge: SEAL talk for leaving a place, bugging out, hauling ass.

Liaison: Close-connection, cooperating person from one unit or service to another. Military liaison.

Light Sticks: Chemical units that make light after twisting to release chemicals that phosphoresce.

Loot & Shoot: SEAL talk for getting into action on a mission.

LZ: Landing Zone.

M1-8: Russian Chopper.

M1A1 M-14: Match rifle upgraded for SEAL snipers.

M-3 Submachine gun: WWII grease gun, .45-caliber. Cheap. Introduced in 1942.

M-16: Automatic U.S. rifle. 5.56 round. Magazine 20 or 30, rate of fire 700 to 950 rds/min. Can attach M203 40mm grenade launcher under barrel.

M-18 Claymore: Antipersonnel mine. A slab of C-4 with 200 small ball bearings. Set off electrically or by trip wire. Can be positioned and aimed. Sprays out a cloud of balls. Kill zone 50 meters.

M60 Machine Gun: Can use 100-round ammo box snapped onto the gun's receiver. Not used much now by SEALs.

M-60E3: Lightweight handheld machine gun. Not used now by the SEALs.

M61A1: The usual 20mm cannon used on many American fighter planes.

M61(j): Machine Pistol. Yugoslav make.

M662: A red flare for signaling.

M-86: Pursuit Deterrent Munitions. Various types of mines, grenades, trip-wire explosives, and other devices in antipersonnel use.

M-203: A 40mm grenade launcher fitted under an M-16 or the M-4A1 Commando. Can fire a variety of grenade types up to 200 yards.

MagSafe: Lethal ammunition that fragments in human body and does not exit. Favored by some police units to cut down on second kill from regular ammunition exiting a body.

Make a Peek: A quick look, usually out of the water, to check your position or tactical situation.

Mark 23 Mod O: Special operations offensive handgun system. Double-action, 12-round magazine. Ambidextrous safety and mag-release catches. Knight screw-on suppressor. Snap-on laser for sighting. .45-caliber. Weighs 4 pounds loaded. 9.5 inches long; with silencer, 16.5 inches long.

Mark II Knife: Navy-issue combat knife.

Mark VIII SDV: Swimmer Delivery Vehicle. A bus, SEAL

talk. 21 feet long, beam and draft 4 feet, 6 knots for 6 hours.

Master-at-Arms: Military police commander on board a ship.

MAVRIC Lance: A nuclear alert for stolen nukes or radioactive goods.

MC-130 Combat Talon: A specially equipped Hercules for covert missions in enemy or unfriendly territory.

McMillan M87R: Bolt-action sniper rifle. .50-caliber. 53 inches long. Bipod, fixed 5- or 10-round magazine. Bulbous muzzle brake on end of barrel. Deadly up to a mile. All types .50-caliber ammo.

MGS: Modified Grooming Standards. So SEALs don't all look like military, to enable them to do undercover work in mufti.

MH-53J: Chopper, updated CH053 from Nam days. 200 mph, called the Pave Low III.

MH-60K Black Hawk: Navy chopper. Forward infrared system for low-level night flight. Radar for terra follow/avoidance. Crew of 3, takes 12 troops. Top speed 225 mph. Ceiling 4,000 feet. Range radius 230 miles. Arms: 2 12.7mm machine guns.

MIDEASTFOR: Middle East Force.

MiG: Russian-built fighter, many versions, used in many nations around the world.

Mike Boat: Liberty boat off a large ship.

Mike-Mike: Short for mm, millimeter, as 9 mike-mike.

Milstar: Communications satellite for pickup and bouncing from SATCOM and other radio transmitters. Used by SEALs.

Minigun: In choppers. Can fire 2,000 rounds per minute. Gatling gun-type.

Mitrajez M80: Machine gun from Yugoslavia.

MI-15: British domestic intelligence agency.

MI-16: British foreign intelligence and espionage.

Mocha: Food energy bar SEALs carry in vest pockets.

Mossberg: Pump-action, pistol-grip, 5-round magazine. SEALs use it for close-in work.

Motorola Radio: Personal radio, short range, lip mike, earpiece, belt pack.

MRE: Meals Ready to Eat. Field rations used by most of U.S. Armed Forces and the SEALs as well. Long-lasting.

MSPF: Maritime Special Purpose Force.

Mugger: MUGR, Miniature Underwater Global locator device. Sends up antenna for pickup on positioning satellites. Works under water or above. Gives location within 10 feet.

Mujahideen: A soldier of Allah in Muslim nations.

NAVAIR: NAVy AIR command.

NAVSPECWAR GRUP-ONE: Naval Special Warfare Group One Based on Calmoloi Cal. SEALs are in this command.

NAVSPECWARGRUP-TWO: Naval Special Warfare Group Two based at Norfolk.

NCIS: Naval Criminal Investigative Service. A civilian operation not reporting to any Navy authority to make it more responsible and responsive. Replaces the old NIS, Naval Investigation Service, that did report to the closest admiral.

NEST: Nuclear Energy Search Team. Non-military unit that reports at once to any spill, problem, or Broken Arrow to determine the extent of the radiation problem.

NEWBIE: A new man, officer, or commander of an established military unit.

NKSF: North Korean Special Forces.

NLA: Iranian National Liberation Army. About 4,500 men in South Iraq, helped by Iraq for possible use against Iran.

Nomex: The type of material used for flight suits and hoods.

NPIC: National Photographic Interpretation Center in D.C.

NRO: National Reconnaissance Office. To run and coordinate satellite development and operations for the intelligence community.

NSA: National Security Agency.

NSC: National Security Council. Meets in Situation Room, support facility in the Executive Office Building in D.C. Main security group in the nation.

NSVHURAWN: Iranian Marines.

NUCFLASH: An alert for any nuclear problem.

NVG One Eye: Litton single-eyepiece Night Vision Goggles. Prevents NVG blindness in both eyes if a flare goes off. Scope shows green-tinted field at night.

NVGs: Night Vision Goggles. One eye or two. Give good night vision in the dark with a greenish view.

OAS: Obstacle Avoidance Sonar. Used on many low-flying attack aircraft.

OIC: Officer In Charge.

Oil Tanker: One is: 885 feet long, 140 feet beam, 121,000 tons, 13 cargo tanks that hold 35.8 million gallons of fuel, oil, or gas. 24 in the crew. This is a regular-sized tanker. Not a supertanker.

OOD: Officer Of the Deck.

Orion P-3: Navy's long-range patrol and antisub aircraft. Some adapted to ELINT roles. Crew of 10. Max speed loaded 473 mph. Ceiling 28,300 feet. Arms: internal weapons bay and 10 external weapons stations for a mix of torpedoes, mines, rockets, and bombs.

Passive Sonar: Listening for engine noise of a ship or sub. It doesn't give away the hunter's presence as an active sonar would.

Pave Low III: A Navy chopper.

PBR: Patrol Boat River. U.S. has many shapes, sizes, and with various types of armament.

PC-170: Patrol Coastal-Class 170-foot SEAL delivery vehicle. Powered by 4 3,350 hp diesel engines, beam of 25 feet and draft of 7.8 feet. Top speed 35 knots, range 2,000 nautical miles. Fixed swimmer platform on stern. Crew of 4 officers and 24 EM, carries 8 SEALs.

Plank Owners: Original men in the start-up of a new military unit.

Polycarbonate material: Bullet-proof glass.

PRF: People's Revolutionary Front. Fictional group in *NUCFLASH,* a SEAL Team Seven book.

Prowl & Growl: SEAL talk for moving into a combat mission.

Quitting Bell: In BUD/S training. Ring it and you quit the SEAL unit. Helmets of men who quit the class are lined up below the bell in Coronado. (Recently they have stopped ringing the bell. Dropouts simply place their helmet below the bell and go.)

RAF: Red Army Faction. A once-powerful German terrorist group, not so active now.

Remington 200: Sniper Rifle. Not used by SEALs now.

Remington 700: Sniper rifle with Starlight Scope. Can extend night vision to 400 meters.

RIB: Rigid Inflatable Boat. 3 sizes, one 10 meters, 40 knots.

Ring Knocker: An Annapolis graduate with the ring.

RIO: Radar Intercept Officer. The officer who sits in the backseat of an F-14 Tomcat off a carrier. The job: find enemy targets in the air and on the sea.

Roger That: A yes, an affirmative, a go answer to a command or statement.

RPG: Rocket Propelled Grenade. Quick and easy, shoulder-fired. Favorite weapon of terrorists, insurgents.

SAS: British Special Air Service. Commandos. Special warfare men. Best that Britain has. Works with SEALs.

SATCOM: Satellite-based communications system for instant contact with anyone anywhere in the world. SEALs rely on it.

SAW: Squad's Automatic Weapon. Usually a machine gun or automatic rifle.

SBS: Special Boat Squadron. On-site Navy unit that transports SEALs to many of their missions. Located across the street from the SEALs' Coronado, California, headquarters.

SD3: Sound-suppression system on the H & K MP5 weapon.

SDV: Swimmer Delivery Vehicle. SEALs use a variety of them.

Seahawk SH-60: Navy chopper for ASW and SAR. Top speed 180 knots, ceiling 13,800 feet, range 503 miles, arms: 2 Mark 46 torpedoes.

SEAL Headgear: Boonie hat, wool balaclava, green scarf, watch cap, bandanna roll.

Second in Command: Also 2IC for short in SEAL talk.

SERE: Survival, Evasion, Resistance, and Escape training.

Shipped for Six: Enlisted for six more years in the Navy.

Shit City: Coronado SEALs' name for Norfolk.

Show Colors: In combat put U.S. flag or other identification on back for easy identification by friendly air or ground units.

Sierra Charlie: SEAL talk for everything on schedule.

Simunition: Canadian product for training that uses paint balls instead of lead for bullets.

Sixteen-Man Platoon: Basic SEAL combat force. Up from 14 men a few years ago.

Sked: SEAL talk for schedule.

Sonobuoy: Small underwater device that detects sounds and transmits them by radio to plane or ship.

Space Blanket: Green foil blanket to keep troops warm. Vacuum-packed and folded to a cigarette-sized package.

Sprayers and Prayers: Not the SEAL way. These men spray bullets all over the place hoping for hits. SEALs do more aimed firing for sure kills.

SS-19: Russian ICBM missile.

STABO: Use harness and lines under chopper to get down to the ground.

STAR: Surface To Air Recovery operation.

Starflash Round: Shotgun round that shoots out sparkling fireballs that ricochet wildly around a room, confusing and terrifying the occupants. Non-lethal.

Stasi: Old-time East German secret police.

Stick: British terminology: 2 4-man SAS teams. 8 men.

Stokes: A kind of Navy stretcher. Open coffin shaped of wire mesh and white canvas for emergency patient transport.

STOL: Short TakeOff and Landing. Aircraft with high-lift wings and vectored-thrust engines to produced extremely short takeoffs and landings.

Sub Gun: Submachine gun, often the suppressed H & K MP5.

Suits: Civilians, usually government officials wearing suits.

Sweat: The more SEALs sweat in peacetime, the less they bleed in war.

Sykes-Fairbairn: A commando fighting knife.

Syrette: Small syringe for field administration often filled with morphine. Can be self-administered.

Tango: SEAL talk for a terrorist.

TDY: Temporary duty assigned outside of normal job designation.

Terr: Another term for terrorist. Shorthand SEAL talk.

Tetrahedral reflectors: Show up on multi-mode radar like tiny suns.

Thermal Imager: Device to detect warmth, as a human body, at night or through light cover.

Thermal Tape: ID for night-vision-goggle user to see. Used on friendlies.

TNAZ: Trinittroaze Tidine. Explosive to replace C-4. 15% stronger than C-4 and 20% lighter.

TO&E: Table showing organization and equipment of a military unit.

Top SEAL Tribute: "You sweet motherfucker, don't you never die!"

Trailing Array: A group of antennas for sonar pickup trailed out of a submarine.

Train: For contact in smoke, no light, fog, etc. Men directly behind each other. Right hand on weapon, left hand on shoulder of man ahead. Squeeze shoulder to signal.

Trident: SEALs' emblem. An eagle with talons clutching a Revolutionary War pistol, and Neptune's trident superimposed on the Navy's traditional anchor.

TRW: A camera's digital record that is sent by SATCOM.

TT33: Tokarev, a Russian pistol.

UAZ: A Soviet 1-ton truck.

UBA Mark XV: Underwater life support with computer to regulate the rebreather's gas mixture.

UGS: Unmanned Ground Sensors. Can be used to explode booby traps and claymore mines.

UNODIR: Unless otherwise directed. The unit will start the operation unless they are told not to.

VBSS: Orders to "visit, board, search, and seize."

Wadi: A gully or ravine, usually in a desert.

White Shirt: Man responsible for safety on carrier deck as he leads around civilians and personnel unfamiliar with the flight deck.

WIA: Wounded In Action.

Zodiac: Also called an IBS, Inflatable Boat Small. 15 by feet, weighs 265 pounds. The "rubber duck" can carry fully equipped SEALs. Can do 18 knots with a range of 65 nautical miles.

ulu: Means Greenwich Mean Time, GMT. Used in all formal military communications.